T0277961

RETURN to SENDER

RETURN to SENDER

LAUREN DRAPER

HARPER TEEN
An Imprint of HarperCollins Publishers

HarperTeen is an imprint of HarperCollins Publishers.

Return to Sender
Copyright © 2024 by Lauren Draper
All rights reserved. Printed in the United States of America.

Library of Congress Control Number: 2023944532
ISBN 978-0-06-334036-7

Typography by Catherine Lee
24 25 26 27 28 LBC 5 4 3 2 1

First Edition

For my sister, Holly.
And for all the wild girls with big hearts and impossible dreams.

1

I want to be very clear that I was not *technically* arrested.

Good old Detective Richard Sawyer just really enjoys hauling me down to the station.

And I mean, sure, I *was* trespassing. But that's a stupid law. It's not even a proper law—like, *Don't murder people.* That's a good law. Don't embezzle money. Don't litter. Fine. Whatever. Those all make sense.

But *don't cross Dwight's junkyard to take the shortcut home?* That's just stupid. No one was even *there.* No one would have even noticed, except in the three years I've been gone, Dwight went and got himself some guard dogs that chased me up a six-foot wire fence. And then my pants got stuck.

It was not my most dignified moment: waiting to be rescued, two drooling German shepherds below, my favorite blue jeans slowly ripping in the butt, my backpack spewing snacks and clean undies, plus the few meager possessions I managed to pack with me on the train.

Someone must have heard me yelling and called the police. The rookie cop who answered the call probably would have just let me go—she was laughing too much to even issue a ticket. But somebody must have snitched, because just as I was arranging my backpack so no one could see my butt through the tear, a flood of red and blue lights flashed across the junkyard and the detective's car rolled in.

Anyway.

The Warwick Police Station is really just a room in the Town Hall with a reception area, a handful of desks, and one single jail cell. The whole place is very dignified: plush blue carpets, gold doorknobs, antique tables holding proper china teacups, and a shiny state-of-the-art coffee machine. There's also a waiting area with some leather chesterfield lounges, where people sit while officers fill out reports for things like lost wallets, parking tickets, jaywalking. Nothing exciting. There's never been a murder here, no assaults, no missing kids. Well. One. Doesn't really count, though—it was twenty years ago. His poster is still on the wall, yellowed and illegible.

Because Detective Dick is kind of a jerk, he steers me away from the comfy old couches and makes me wait in the cell while they "consider arrangements." Which is a total joke, because I can hear him on the phone to Dwight right now, and the office is quiet enough that I can hear Dwight yelling that *they shouldn't have woken him up at this damn indecent hour, and anyway, she didn't take anything this time, did she?*

I bristle with annoyance. *This time?* I never—

Oh. The old Jeep. Whoops.

I sigh, leaning back against the wall. Barbara hobbles over, passing me a cup of tea through the bars.

"You want a cookie, doll?"

I shake my head, stirring in the sugar cubes she's given me. "Have you called my nan?"

She *tut-tuts*. Barbara has been here since I can remember. She's about a thousand years old, and she's spawned so many grandchildren that her family probably makes up half the town population. She's also got a soft spot for delinquents.

"She's not answering. Might have the ringer off; it's late."

I shrug. "She didn't know I was coming."

Barbara *tut-tuts* again. "You shouldn't be walking home in the dark."

"I'd be home by now if they'd just let me go," I grumble. Which is mean, because Barbara is only trying to be nice. She doesn't know my family has shipped me off. Again.

Barbara shucks her cardigan and passes it to me. There's little poodles knitted into it, their tails made of bushy pom-poms. It hangs nearly to my knees, so I'm all covered—and warm.

"Thanks," I say, forcing a smile. "Is he gonna let me out soon?"

She snorts, glancing over at Richard. "I already called someone to come get you. He's just in a mood today. Possums again, in the roof." She swings the cell door open. It wasn't even locked. "Why don't you sneak on out? Your ride will be here in a minute. Tell your nan I said hello."

I grab my backpack, edging away to the rear exit. "Wait," I whisper, half hidden behind the watercooler. "Who'd you call?"

Barbara frowns, about to answer, but then I hear the sound of a phone receiver being slammed down and she trots over to the front desk, ready to intervene.

As far as accomplices go, Barb's pretty great. I sprint to the exit, rushing out into the cool night.

Cold air hits me all at once, and just for a moment, I pause at the top of the station stairs, peering down at Warwick. There's a fog over the town; it's covered the valley like a blanket, edges frayed and thinning where the light fades. From here, it looks like a scene from an old black-and-white movie. Little houses, all lined in a row. The Rydal Woods to the south, train station to the north.

And not a whole lot else.

I can see the red slate roof of the post office from here, sitting proudly on Barney's Hill. The windows are dark—Nan must be sleeping already. I sigh, dropping now-useless headphones over my shoulders. Guess it's the long way home this time.

I pause halfway down the stairs, hesitating under the yellow glow of a streetlight. There's an echo in the dark, an engine idling on the curb. I don't think it's my ride—bless Barbara for trying, but I don't really have any friends left. None that would pick me up from the police station, at least.

And then I see it.

The red Jeep, front window down, one arm tapping a sharp rhythm on the metal, shirtsleeve rolled to the elbow.

"Oh, *fu*—"

He sees me before I can turn around. The smile is too sweet, hiding a well-mannered hatred—all straight white teeth and dazzling blue eyes.

"Well, if it isn't the McKellon Felon," he says. "Nice sweater."

I don't answer.

He rolls his too-pretty eyes. "Get in, Brodie."

4

"What, so you can drive me into the woods and dump my body? No *thank you*."

I turn onto the footpath, walking stubbornly beside the car as he eases his foot off the brake. "Barbara called me."

"I didn't ask her to."

"Figured."

"Go away, Levi."

"Get in the car, Brodie."

I continue stomping my way up Compton Road, cursing my too-thin shoes and dead phone battery. I resolve not to speak to him. He can follow me home in silence, watching the little poodle pom-poms bounce in the dark. Serves him right, for all those years ago.

Then the first raindrop hits.

I keep walking. He keeps pace, the car rolling forward at a crawl. More raindrops. I scoop wet hair out of my eyes, determined not to look at him, even though I think he just laughed a little. Then there's a crack of lightning so bright it lights up the street like daylight. A thunderclap rolls in a few seconds later, so loud I can feel the rumble in my chest.

I sigh. He pops the door open.

And that's how Levi Sawyer ends up driving me home.

Even though he hates me now.

Guess being a jerk runs in the family.

The Warwick post office is a gray-and-green-painted brick building; three stories high, leaning slightly to the left, with Gothic arched windows and a wrought-iron balcony that you can shinny up if you are particularly desperate to get inside. Notably, there's also a flaking blue sign out front, the paint curling from hot summer days and blustery winter nights. In the right light, you can still see the original stencil: THE DEAD LETTER OFFICE.

You're not really supposed to call it that anymore. Officially, it's the Warwick Mail Redistribution Center, but that's . . . a lot of syllables. And not nearly as entertaining.

I love it here. It's a strange old house, with forgotten nooks and crannies, and even if it gets drafty in the wintertime, I never minded. Because this house is *home*—not the cramped apartment Dad bought in the city, not the boarding school I got kicked out of, and definitely not the university we toured last year.

I managed to shinny up the balcony last night, feet scrambling for purchase, cursing my lack of upper-body strength, until I heaved myself over the edge. The windows were unlocked, like they always are, though the hinges were sticky and groaned when forced open.

The house was dark inside, but it didn't matter. I've never needed light to find my way through these halls. The carpet pressed under my shoes like a weary sigh, breathing *Welcome back*. Nan always says this place is alive. Actually, she says it's haunted and "alive with spirits," but that's basically the same thing.

The gas heater in my old bedroom spluttered to life as I dressed in too-small pajamas, and I barely managed to plug in my phone before I collapsed on the bed and fell asleep.

Hours later, I wake up with sunlight streaming through the curtains I forgot to close, and Nan perched on the end of my mattress; a heavy book balanced on one knee, ginger cat on the other.

I crack one eyelid open and smile.

"Good morning," she says, adjusting her glasses so they sit straight on her nose. "What did you dream about?"

My eyes are crusty, my mouth feels like something died in it, and I slept so deeply I'm not sure if I dreamed at all. I sit up, grimacing at the memory of Levi Sawyer's stupid face as he drove away. "Snakes," I mumble.

She doesn't even need to open the book. "That's a good one. Forgiveness?"

I snort. "Definitely not."

"Hmm, betrayal then. Watch yourself." She leans over and kisses my nose. "You should have woken me."

"Sorry, it was late."

"You can always wake me up," she says, rising. Mabel, the geriatric old cat that *just won't die*, leaps from her lap. Nan opens her arms and I fold myself into her hug. She smells like the powder she puts in her hair, and I nearly cry with exhaustion. "Doesn't matter," she says, hands rubbing a soothing circle on my back. "I'm just glad you're here."

My heart cracks open a small fraction. "I missed you."

She pats my cheeks, clucking as she finds them thinner than the last time I came to visit. "How long are you staying?"

"Uh . . ."

She cocks an eyebrow. "Does your father know you're here?"

"Yeah. He . . . he's gone again. Contract work, interstate."

"And school?"

"Would you believe me if I said 'spontaneous combustion'?"

Nan glances up at the ceiling, looking for divine intervention. "Lord help me. Pancakes or eggs?"

"Really? That's it?" No lecture? No questions? Unless Dad called her already . . . though I don't see how he would have had the time between packing his bags and driving to the airport, not even bothering to clear out the fridge or drop me at the station.

Nan holds my cheeks in her hands for a long moment. "You can always come home," she says. "Always." Her face has more wrinkles than I remember. Her hair is a salt-and-pepper coif, more salt now than it used to be. I haven't seen her since two Christmases ago, when Dad shipped me to Rowley and the airfares got too expensive to keep coming back.

I swallow against the lump in my throat, squeezing her hands. "I know."

"Good. Eggs then? Mabel likes eggs, don't you, old girl?"

"Sure," I answer, following her down the hall. She makes me sit at the breakfast bench while she chats happily about the things I've missed. There's not a whole lot, as it turns out. The school got a new library. The museum got an old painting. The town council had a meeting about the lake, and now there's a supervised swim hole. Some kid drowned in it, forever ago. Nan says something bad is going to happen again—she sees it in her cards. Nan is a very, um, *spiritual* person. She reads tarot and consults her dream book and talks to the ghosts in the attic. She says they linger until their letters are claimed. Unfinished business, she says.

I don't actually believe in ghosts. Well. Much. The occasional phantom footstep when the house is empty does make me wonder.

But I'm also pretty sure Nan had a really good time in the seventies, and I've resolved to never, *ever* ask about it.

I wait until I've politely scarfed the eggs she makes, watching as Mabel mews at my feet. Nan got her just before I was born. As such, Mabel is considered my senior, and commands a certain level of respect. I scruff her ears, and her rummy eyes look at me petulantly until I give her a toast crust. (Can she eat toast? Does she have enough teeth left? If I kill her, Mabel *would* haunt me forever.)

I watch her carefully, to make sure she doesn't choke, while Nan washes the iron skillet.

"You can head downstairs, if you like," she says. "I know you want to."

I grin and slide off the barstool, racing down the corridor to the bottom floor. It's split into two sides: the "regular" post office, with letters, postcards, envelopes, overpriced kids' toys at the counter alongside online orders waiting to be picked up.

And then there's the Dead Letter Office.

Sorry, Mail Redistribution Center.

There's a pretty strict law that says you can't claim someone else's mail—mostly so you can't, you know, steal someone's identity or their new flat-screen TV. But the Dead Letter Office is where unclaimed, undeliverable mail goes, usually because the intended recipient has kicked the metaphorical bucket.

It was a popular thing after the war, mostly, given all the soldiers who never made it home. Women were deemed more trustworthy with private affairs, so Nan found herself in charge of the Warwick center. Most big cities share one huge warehouse now, and you have to drive out for ages to visit. But Warwick clung on to this strange old custom, so we have our very own. There's less and less mail these days—mostly because technology has improved so much and not many letters get sent anymore—but every so often, someone will come in and collect their grandparents' mail, or old Christmas cards, or little gifts that are still perfectly wrapped. Usually people cry, for the moments that were unfairly snatched away. Birthday cards for a birthday that never happened. Baby photos that were never seen.

But sometimes they laugh. All those envelopes hold a little piece of life inside. Handwritten words that someone cared enough to write down. A thought or a joke or a lover's words, captured forever, declared with pride.

I love it in here.

Nan left this room exactly like it was when it first opened: dark wooden shelves, gold key-locked drawers, green-leather reading chairs. It's warm and dusty and cozy. The kind of place where you'd want to cherish last moments.

My fingertips drift over some new arrivals: letters rescued and waiting to be returned. There's a custom stamp on one envelope, and I wonder who will collect it and whether they'll smile. Not much else, though: a postcard from the beach, a parcel with Christmas tape. Small moments, a few words—but they mean so much to the people who collect them. Waiting in their cubbies, ready to be claimed.

Except for one.

I hear the soft pad of her slippers behind me as I turn and ask the question that's been on my mind since I first stepped off the train last night. "No one claimed them yet?"

"Poppet, I would have called the moment it happened. They're still there—though for what it's worth, I still think it's none of your damn business."

She drifts toward the register, stabbing a few buttons and muttering about receipt paper, while I edge toward the only box that's never been claimed: *Item 130: First name: August. Surname: Undeclared.*

Still here. Still ours, for now.

I guess you'd call them love letters. But not really. There's no sordid descriptions or crude euphemisms. They're more intimate than that, filled with hopes and dreams and desires, secrets whispered between best friends at midnight. There are at least three writers, a boy and two girls, but I think they're all using fake names. Maybe that's why we've never been able to find their families; I searched town registries, microfiched the old library newspapers, trawled the internet, and even tried to convince Barbara to use the police database. Nothing. I don't even know what *year* I'm looking in, because they never wrote them down—only the day and month, or not at all.

I snatch up an envelope at random, and it's like dipping into a story halfway.

Dear Winnie,

Do you think I could build a house in the woods? I'd make it so tall you could see all the way across the lake—all the way across the world, in a room made of glass. Would you come with me? You can pick any room you want, and it'll be all

11

yours. You can fill it with books and paintings, and we'll live
there forever, until the townsfolk forget we're even people, and
they'll think a couple ghosts built it all.

August

I flip through the other letters, trying to sort them roughly into
order. The date stamps are mostly still visible, though there are a
few that are totally illegible, plus a handful that aren't stamped
at all.

There are so many they barely fit into one cubby. Nan says
she doesn't remember receiving them, though that's not especially
unusual. There were a lot of dead letters back then. All I know is,
they've been here as long as I can remember. Nobody has ever asked
about them.

There's one from the third writer that must have been hand-
delivered, because there's nothing but a first name on the envelope.

You can't take her, August. I love her too, she's my best
friend. Sometimes I think she was made for both of us—a
heart pieced together of you and me, and we were always
meant to be three of us. But if that's true, then one of us was
always going to lose.
And it feels like I'm losing.

June

I wonder where they all went. Three friends, suddenly just . . .
gone. Did August and Winnie run away together? Did they leave
June behind? Why did June feel so compelled to scribble her letter

and rush to immediately give it to August? She sounds so serious in that one, but in others she would joke, and sign her name as June-Bug. What happened, between the pages of those last letters, the moments never captured on paper?

"Any new clues?" Nan asks, peering over my shoulder.

I sigh, placing the letters carefully back inside their cubby. "There never are."

During one particularly lethargic summer, I went to the trouble of copying all the letters on Nan's old typewriter, in the order I thought they should be read—like a book. I highlighted every place they mentioned, every street, every name of a friend or family member. Back when Levi and I were still friends, we rode our bikes all over town like kid detectives, searching for answers. He even borrowed his dad's badge.

But we never found anything.

Nan shakes her head. "Let's ask the cards."

I know what the cards will say. I always pick the same ones—I think Nan rigs it, to be honest.

The Lovers.

The Tower.

Death.

I call Dad's cell to tell him I arrived safely. Not that he cares. Dad's a roadie—although it's not really as glamorous as it seems. He works for a big music label, and there are a few regular bands he travels with. No one radio-famous, but big enough that they get to do gigs all across the country. He also doesn't call himself a roadie—he's a sound engineer. Or something. Either way, it's long, late, irregular hours, and pretty much incompatible with raising a kid. He did try, for about a year after Mum died, but eventually he gave in and sent me to boarding school. He tried to make it sound fun. "There's lots of girls your own age," he said. "And besides, maybe it will *help*."

He said *help* so empathically, but I still didn't know what he meant. *Help* me get over Mum dying? *Help* with the string of minor run-ins with the law? *Help* set up a regular routine, one that I hadn't had since we left Warwick?

I started at the Rowley Academy for Girls when I was fourteen, and quickly learned that boarding school is actually really boring: The dorms always smell like BO, and you can't make up excuses not to do your homework because the teachers basically live with you. The cell service sucks, and the internet gets shut off at curfew in the evening. The kids in my dorm had already been living together for two or three years by the time I got there—they were nice enough, but it wasn't home, and they all had their cliques already. I didn't have friends, really. There were people I knew and sat with in class. But I missed Warwick. Plus, the school acronym was RAGs, which just seemed like a glaring oversight.

Dad's phone goes to voice mail. I hang up and text him instead. Home safe. Nan says hi.

Later, when I'm making dinner, I hear the landline ringing. I step into the hallway to answer, but Nan hollers down the stairs that she's got it. When I head up to tell her the food is ready, I hear her cursing out Dad for leaving me to get here alone. I slide down the wall outside her room, knees tucked to my chest, listening to her list of grievances: He didn't even bother to call ahead, and what was he doing, letting me travel alone on a train arriving at night, sending me away with hardly anything but the clothes on my back, does he not take any interest in my education, and most passionately, "for god's sake, Jonathan, get your life together, if not for your sake then for hers." The receiver slams down, and Mabel hisses in response.

I creep down the stairs before she catches me listening, and turn the stove back on just to have something to do while I wait. I tell myself it's the onions that make my eyes water.

She trots into the kitchen and claps her hands. "Smells delicious. Now, I was thinking, wouldn't it be fun if we went shopping tomorrow? Tommy can manage the office—not for too long, mind, poor thing gets a bit confused with the register."

"I really don't need anything, Nan. I've got a few shirts and Dad can send the rest between gigs."

"Well, I'm going anyway, so you'd be doing me a favor. I need new shoes. Let's drive out to Lancaster, make a day of it."

I smile because I know she's lying. She buys her hideous orthotics from the pharmacy. "Sure."

She offers to loan me one of her floor-length flannelette nighties, but I insist my old pajamas are fine. Even if they don't fit over the boobs I didn't have when I first bought them. Fine, maybe I need a *few* things.

We put an old vinyl record on after dinner, and Nan gets into the brandy and reads tarot cards for Mabel, which makes me laugh until my stomach aches, neither of us willing to go to bed until the record begins to scratch with static. Nan pecks my cheeks, tells me "Remember to dream," and drifts upstairs for the night.

I double-check the post office is locked, but I'm not really tired so I open the windows on the balcony, haul out the old patio furniture, and pick up a flaky paperback from Mum's old room. I trace my fingers over the wall, her name still scratched behind the door with faded pencil: *Perry McKellon was here.* "Hey, Mum," I whisper. "Missed you." I don't touch anything else—I never do.

It's warmer tonight; it hasn't rained all day, the stars are out, and it's so pretty I almost don't mind the mosquitoes eating my legs. There were no stars in the city. Too many lights. The only redeeming feature of RAGs was the telescope in the science room, which the teachers let me use whenever I wanted because no one else was interested in it.

When my eyes finally get droopy, I place the book face down and head inside, careful to leave the windows unlocked. Just in case.

I'm halfway between waking and dreaming when I hear the slow groan of a window opening. I blink in the dark, wondering if I imagined it—but it's soon followed by a gentle scuff in the hallway. I sit bolt upright in bed.

And smile.

I pull the door open as a soft knock sounds and throw myself at Elliot. Except, instead of throwing my arms around his tiny shoulders like I expected, my face smacks into the middle of his chest.

"Ew, you got tall."

He laughs, and the sound is deep and unfamiliar.

I shush him, pulling him inside and closing the door. He grins down at me. Seriously, *down.* I almost have to crane my neck to look up at him. He tips sideways to nudge my normal-sized shoulders with his enormous ones. "Missed you too, Red."

I groan. No one has called me that in forever. *Caught red-handed* was a popular phrase in my youth: caught stealing cookies, caught stealing cars. It sort of stuck.

Elliot Maddon is my favorite person in the world. Or . . . he was.

It was hard to stay in touch, after I left. Between the crappy cell service and internet at Rowley, plus his stepdad's tendency to confiscate his stuff for stupid reasons, we missed too many calls and texts to really keep up. We tried for a while. Even wrote each other letters, until it got too hard to fit an entire life on paper. I wanted to see him as soon as I got home, but I couldn't stand the thought of him not wanting to see *me*.

"How did you know I was here?"

"Levi said he saw you. Actually, he said he picked you up from jail."

"I was not in *jail*, I was just walking home. There was a slight, uh, detour."

He laughs, sitting on the edge of my bed. We've spent a lot of nights like this. Elliot lives at the end of the street, in a weatherboard house with a tin roof and weeds growing over the driveway. I heard the yelling one night, years ago, when I was sitting on the balcony. It was the summer of playing detectives, and I knew right away that it was the wrong kind of yelling—the sort of terrible, foreboding screaming that gives you ice-shivers and tells you to get away, to go somewhere safe, to get help. There was a crash, and sobs, and suddenly the screen door banged open and a little kid ran out, backpack thrown over his shoulder, face ruddy and snot dripping down his chin. It took me a moment to realize I already knew him. Our moms had been close, and I'd seen him a few times at the house, though he'd always been too shy to say hello.

I made him a tent out of mailbags in the post office, and sat with him in the Dead Letter room until the yelling stopped. Nan was really mad when she found out—not because I snuck him in, but because I didn't give him an actual bed. He stayed in the study, after that. He'd come in through the balcony window when things got bad at home. Right up until I left.

The memory makes me realize why the sheets on my bed were so clean. Nan's probably been washing them just in case—I know she'd prefer to leave Mum's room as it was, and besides, it wasn't like I was using mine.

"Have I stolen your bed?"

He leans back, arms crossed behind his head. "Nah. Things are all right lately."

I lie back beside him. It might be weird, to have a boy in my bedroom at night, except the one time we decided to kiss—just to get the first one over with—he declared afterward that he thought he would prefer kissing boys and then we both shrugged and went back to playing Nintendo.

He nudges me out of the memory. "So, you back for good?"

Great question. "I guess so. Dad sort of left in a hurry."

"What happened to boarding school?"

"Didn't work out."

"Is that code for 'expelled'?"

"There *may* have been an incident, after which it was heavily implied I would not be welcome back." I'd left a telescope on the gym roof overnight. Unfortunately, nobody realized until the ceiling started to smoke.

"It just got a little singed," I explain when he presses for more information. "In one tiny corner."

"I see we've added 'arson' to the rap-sheet—"

"It was char-grilled, at best. A little smoky."

"Uh-huh."

"I swear! You could hardly tell." I nudge him in the ribs. He's gracious enough to pretend it hurts. "You wanna stay?" I ask. "The spare room is still empty."

"Nah," he says, bouncing to his feet. "I'm actually heading out. Just came to say hello."

I notice that his black curly hair is somewhat styled, which is—or was—unusual. Plus, his jeans are clean and his socks match.

"Date night?" I joke.

He rolls his eyes. "Just Levi and some of his friends."

I frown, surprised, and he mistakes my confusion for curiosity.

"Just down to the lake," he elaborates. "The football team is having a thing."

"Levi and the *football team?*"

"You could come, you know."

"With Levi? Gag. Absolutely not."

He sighs. "You ever gonna tell me what happened between you two?"

"Sure. On my deathbed, maybe."

This is a lie. I will never tell him. I will take it to my grave out of sheer spite. As far as Elliot is aware, Levi and I got into an unspecified fight when I left, and we never bothered to reconcile. Or maybe he thinks we just drifted, after so much time apart. Either way, whatever he thinks, it's probably better than the truth.

"Everything seemed fine," Elliot says, quieter. "And then it just . . . wasn't." There's a strain of sadness in his voice, and I wish I could turn the clock back and set it all right. But that's the worst part: I couldn't fix it even if I wanted to. Blamed for the only theft I *didn't* commit; that's what blew us apart all those years ago. And how do I explain that to him?

I narrow my eyes as headlights flood through the window. I can't really be mad at Elliot—Levi *was* a good friend. Before everything, the three of us were inseparable. I pull him off the bed, pushing him toward the window. "Go on then, can't keep the traitor waiting."

Elliot scoffs, but he lets me nudge him out to the balcony. He's got one foot over the edge when I reach out to snatch his shirt.

"Wait! Did you ever find out who took the Adder Stone?"

"Why? Does that have something to do with you two fighting?"

"No." *Yes.* "Just curious."

He grins at me in the dark. "Still a mystery, Red." Then he winks and drops straight from the second floor to the first. "See you tomorrow!" he yells, running over to the red Jeep parked on the curb.

And for a second, I remember what it was like to be the one running toward that car.

2

The Adder Stone is something of a town legend. There are a few versions of the story, but the most popular one is this: Way back, before Warwick was even really a town, a young messenger was traveling by horseback across the country. He was part of the Pony Express—ye olde way of delivering parcels before Amazon existed. Riders took letters out to remote communities, traveling for months at a time. Anyway, this messenger boy was on his way to sort-of-Warwick when he paused for a drink of water in the local spring and noticed a peculiar stone in the shallows of the riverbank.

It was a curious thing, entirely smooth and perfectly round, with a small hole in the center. He was superstitious enough to believe the rock might be a coveted Adder Stone, an item imbued with magical properties that could grant eternal life or cure any ills. The stones themselves were said to be made of hardened snake venom, calcified by a hundred serpent fangs. You know, normal stuff.

So, the traveler picked up the creepy rock and put it in his pocket. He trotted off on his journey again, until only a few hours later, his horse was spooked by a snake. The rider was thrown from his saddle and bitten on his leg by a rattlesnake. Certain that he was beyond help, the man wrote his last goodbyes and bravely awaited death, the letter in one hand, Adder Stone in the other.

Spoiler alert: He didn't die.

Dude miraculously survived and lived to be a hundred years old. He was so convinced the stone was magic that he added a thick band of gold to the center and turned it into a wedding ring for his sweetheart. That guy went on to become the first mayor of Warwick. His wife *also* lived to be a hundred years old, and her last words are rumored to be "Someone get this cursed rock off my finger so I can finally die in peace."

So. Magic stone. *Allegedly.*

It was handed down for a few generations, but for the last hundred years or so it's been sitting in the Town Hall, on display in a special case surrounded by lasers or whatever.

And *sure*, I talked about stealing it a bunch of times. As a *joke.* I wasn't *serious.* I might have had some questionable history with the Warwick police department, but for the most part, my criminal reputation was vastly overexaggerated.

But the stone went missing the same week Dad told me we were leaving Warwick for good. I had rushed to Levi's house in a fit of tears, and after I'd snotted all over his T-shirt, he tried to cheer me up by pulling out our graduation list. He and Elliot were determined to fit in all the things we'd planned to do over the next three years into that one final week. The list of items included:

- Hot-wire a car from Dwight's junkyard (success)
- Have one last night at the drive-in cinema (success)

- Bury a time capsule in the Rydal Woods (success)
- Skinny-dip at the lake (all three of us chickened out)
- Solve the mystery of the dead letters (failed)

And:

- Steal the Adder Stone.

I didn't steal it. I thought about it, a *lot*. But Barbara told me once that it was insured for squillions of dollars, and there was all sorts of fancy tech protecting it, including a brand-new security camera and motion detector on the case. Plus, I knew Levi would get in so much trouble if I took it. His dad would know it was me, and he'd also know the only way I'd get in that building is with Levi's help.

And then it went missing.

Levi's mum had just been elected mayor, and there was some sort of gala for her at Town Hall. I don't remember exactly. Something boring and grown-up.

I only went to say goodbye. Levi was wearing a black tux that fit him perfectly, Elliot had borrowed a suit that sagged around his ankles, and I was wearing a sweater with holes in the elbows. I didn't feel like smiling for the adults all night, so I snuck in the back, and we all hid in the coat closet and sipped on one shared cup of champagne while people milled around the hall.

The next day, the Adder Stone was gone.

Levi got grounded for the whole summer. His dad had seen me skulking in a dark corner, and that was apparently enough to convince everyone that I was the culprit. Except they couldn't actually *convict* me—first, because no one could find the damn thing, and second, because Elliot lied and said I was babysitting his cousin all night.

The last time Levi and I spoke, he begged me to tell him where I'd hidden it. I listened to his voice on the way to the airport; he said his mum might lose her job and his dad wouldn't even speak to him. I couldn't tell if Levi was more upset because he thought I'd taken it, because Elliot lied for me, or because I didn't include him in the supposed heist. I didn't want him to hear the moment my screaming turned to sobs, so I hung up on him.

We didn't speak again for three years—until he picked me up from the station two nights ago.

I scowl at Town Hall from my bedroom window and contemplate ziplining from one rooftop to the other for the sole purpose of dropping glitter bombs on the stairs. I could wait until Levi's stupid car is parked out front, just to be extra thorough about it. He hates glitter. It'd get stuck in the leather seats and be a nightmare to get out. I look down at the list clenched in my fist: pajamas, boots, hairbrush, socks. I grab a pen and scribble *Glitter?* on the bottom.

Nan raps on the door a second later and soon we're piling into her beat-up station wagon: one panel is red, another is gray, and it stalls every second stop. Still, it gets us to Lancaster, and we spend the morning looping around the boutique stores, picking up clothes we can't afford and setting them back on the rack, running fingers over suede jackets and silk shirts. I don't know why we do this, but it always happens. The stores are overpriced and attended by thin women with sleek hair, each footstep a sharp *click* across white-tiled floors. But we always start here, pause for tea and cake, then rush into the cheaper chain stores on a sugar high.

There's a green jacket that makes me hesitate: the color of the Rydal Woods, and soft like butter. I pick up the sleeve, slipping my hand inside the cuff. Then the price tag falls out, and I sigh, stepping away.

Nan raises an eyebrow. "Time for cake?"

"Please."

The rest of the morning is much more successful. I manage to find a few things, paying with the money Dad left me (of which there wasn't much to begin with), and convince Nan to buy shoes from an actual shoe shop—she complains they're not lined with sheepskin, but eventually choses a sensible pair of black loafers.

We're on our way back to the car when we walk past the boutique with the green jacket. Someone has put it on the mannequin out front and I stop midstep, head cocked, looking in the window.

Nan sees me staring, amused. "Why don't you let me buy it? A welcome home treat?"

I shake my head, turning away. "No, it's silly. I don't really need it. And it's too expensive."

"A good jacket will last you a long time," Nan calls, not moving. "An investment, really."

"Nan—"

"And it will go with all this hair of yours." She pulls on the ends of my browny-red hair and smiles.

I crack. "Fine. Let's just go *look* at it."

25

She tugs me into the store, and soon I'm standing in a pristine changing room, my dusty backpack resting on the floor. I hold the jacket away from my body, hesitating. *Don't put it on. You'll want it too much.*

I put it on.

Nan raps on the door. "Well?"

"It's hideous. Doesn't even fit. I hate it completely."

She starts to laugh, then the sound cuts off. Her voice fades as she turns away, exclaiming in false delight. "Oh, Susan! I didn't see you there."

I cringe with my whole body. Mayor Susan Sawyer. Levi's mum. She's actually pretty nice. Or . . . she used to be. Before I (allegedly) ruined her coronation ball, or whatever the mayoral equivalent is. I'm sure she still thinks I'm suspect number one. How long can I hide in here before one of the saleswomen kicks me out?

Susan's honey-warm voice rings out a moment later, followed by the sound of two wet air kisses. "Delia! How are you?"

"Same as always," Nan says. "Don't see much of Levi anymore; how is he?"

"Tall." Susan laughs. Is he? Tall? I couldn't tell, when he was squashed into the driver's seat. I used to be taller than him and Elliot, and now they'll both dwarf me. The thought is extra annoying, given how much I used to tease them about it.

"Well, hopefully we'll be seeing more of him, now Brodie's home."

Clearly, Detective Sawyer decided not to pass along the details of my homecoming, because Susan makes a choking sound and takes a minute to recover. "O-oh. Well, that's—that's lovely, isn't it. Is she staying long?"

"You can ask her." Nan knocks on the door. "Come say hello! What are you doing in there, sewing it yourself?"

Traitor.

I plaster a big fake smile on my face, emerging from the changing room. "Hi, Mrs. Sawyer."

Her eyes flick from my unbrushed hair to my scuffed shoes. "Goodness, look at you."

That was at least fifty-percent insult.

My smile falters. "I like your pants. They sort of look like the school uniform."

She frowns, looking down at the hanger she's holding. "They're culottes."

They're fugly, is what I want to add. Instead, I start inching toward the exit. "Well, it was nice to see you again. Tell Levi I . . . um, tell him I say hello."

She waves an airy hand. "Why don't you come by the hall tonight; we're having a back-to-school fund-raiser." Guess she's willing to put up with me so long as money is involved.

"Sure. Sounds great. Come on, Nan, the parking meter is about to run out." I reach for her hand, ready to drag her out by force, when the price tag falls out of my jacket. Before I can shrug it off and place it back on the hanger, Susan laughs. "Planning on paying for that?" she jokes. I feel my face fall. "Oh, I'm only kidding," she says. "Nice to see you both."

She takes her ugly skirt-pants into the dressing room, and the door clicks shut. Nan yanks the jacket off my shoulders and thrusts it on the counter. "We'll take that. What else goes with it?"

I walk out with the jacket, a white-knit sweater, the most luscious pair of leather boots I'll ever own, and a pair of silver earrings with moonstone gems that Nan picks out. The number jumps up on the register and I feel my heart stutter.

"Nan," I whisper. "I don't need all this stuff."

"And I won't need money when I'm dead."

She says that when she wants to get her way. It's hard to argue with.

Nan drives home with the radio on high, and I roll the windows down. She takes the long way back, winding through the Rydal Woods. It's always dark here, the sun blotted by sweeping pine branches. It's like the rest of the world can't quite touch the magic here—the silence and the stillness, the morning fog and blue nights. It should be scary, but it never was. Even if some of the kids used to say it was haunted by the Rydal Devil, a trickster demon that preys on young children (literally zero children have ever been kidnapped here, further disproving that myth).

If there's a devil in this forest, it's whoever keeps dumping rubbish for salvagers to find.

Levi, Elliot, and I used to come here after school all the time. We'd start out looking for treasure but would inevitably get bored and end up lying in the clearing. The boys would bring packs of cards or comics, and we'd stay until it got just dark enough that we *almost* believed in the Rydal Devil. When we got older, Levi sometimes brought a girl and Elliot sometimes brought a boy, but none of them ever seemed to find the woods as magical as we did. So it was usually the three of us, inventing games to keep us away from home as long as possible. I wonder what would have happened if

I'd stayed. I guess we would have grown out of it. Or maybe I'd be going to Levi's lake parties with the football team.

Urgh. Never.

Nan rolls into the parking spot outside the post office. Elliot is sitting on the steps, chin resting on his hand. He's not reading a book or scrolling through his phone. He's just . . . waiting. He has an unearthly amount of patience. I asked him once what he thinks about when he daydreams. He just shrugged and said he doesn't think about much at all. It's peaceful, is all he said.

He jumps up when the car stops and bounds over to the door.

"M'lady."

I snort. "I've been accused of being a lot of things but never a lady."

Nan makes a fuss over his hair and his face and him being too skinny, and insists he come inside for lunch. She's just finished plating up snacks when Tommy sheepishly emerges from the post office to say that he counted twice but the till won't balance and he either has too much money or not enough and he's not sure which. She sighs, leaving us with our perfectly cut sandwiches, and disappears downstairs.

I wipe my mouth with the back of my hand, swallowing. "Did you just come to say hello?"

"Yup. Kinda was hungry, though, so . . ." He laughs, but I've seen his pantry and it's rarely full. I resist the urge to stuff granola bars into his pockets. He eyes the shopping bags by my feet and grins. "Don't suppose you got any swimsuits in all that stuff?"

I grin back at him and shove the rest of the crust into my mouth.

My fingers and feet are itching to move, and Elliot can hardly keep up as I fling myself down the stairs, two steps at a time.

"Back by dinner!" Nan hollers as the post office door bangs open then shut, and Elliot tugs me over to his trusty old bike. It's a BMX we liberated from Dwight's junkyard and fixed up—underneath all that rust was a pretty silver frame, and it was worth the hours it took to polish up just to see the smile on Eli's face when it was finished. It's got pegs on the back wheel, but I always preferred sitting on the handlebars.

"Oh my god, my butt hardly fits anymore," I grumble. "This was easier when we were fourteen."

Elliot just laughs and shoves his bike helmet on my head. He kicks off the gravel, and suddenly we're flying down Compton Road, me shrieking in delight, Elliot laughing in my ear. My feet pedal in the air, and I'm both terrified we'll crash and totally sure that I'm safe on these handlebars.

He turns off into the side streets, where we have the roads to ourselves, and sways across from one side to the other, dipping as low as he dares just to see if I'll scream.

But we both go silent as the Rydal Woods loom, and I hold my breath as we cross that invisible line, from the land of asphalt roads and sunny skies to dirt paths and dark leaves. He slows down, easing up on the uneven track, saying nothing as my head swivels back and forth, taking it all in.

"It's exactly the same," I whisper.

"It's a forest, Red. What did you think would happen?"

I thought it wouldn't be magic anymore. I just shake my head and laugh and leap off the bars so I can go as slow as I want, head tilted to the sky. We veer around the walking track, the ground beaten down by joggers and hikers and parents and soccer teams. It's a quiet loop, winding past the lake and a picnic area with tables and water fountains. Elliot locks his bike to the railing, then ducks under and steps into the undisturbed shrubs, waiting.

"Coming?"

I grin and follow, my feet remembering the route without needing to be guided: follow the pepper trees, cross the riverbed, mind the last mossy rock.

I step into the clearing and look around. Above, the leaves are green, red, and gold, a mottled canopy that looks like the jeweled glass mosaics of church windows. It feels appropriate, reverent; this is where I worship. The tree trunks are thick and dark, forming a wall around the clearing. That's the creepy thing at night—looking out into the forest and not knowing if anyone is looking back. Maybe that's why people come here, to leave their strange items. Hard to get caught when no one can see you coming.

Today, there's a couch, a guitar, a world globe, and a stack of books. Pretty standard offerings for the Rydal Devil. Elliot picks up the guitar, giving an experimental strum, wincing when it twangs out of tune.

I nudge the couch with my foot, eyeing the dark corners with suspicion. It looks clean, but . . .

"Wouldn't sit on that. Lizard crawled out last time."

I cringe and sit on the grass instead, twisting the globe with my finger. Where would I go, if I could go anywhere. . . .

August, Winnie, and June mention a place called Treegap in their letters—one of the only places they list by name. I spin the globe, my eyes searching for it amid the tiny cities and riverbanks and mountain ranges. But it's useless—I've never found it, not even close. It doesn't *exist*, according to every single map I've ever searched. Still, I always look.

"What's the best thing you found while I was away?"

Elliot thinks for a moment, trying a chord on the guitar. "Hmm. Either an anatomically correct garden gnome or a framed painting of the Mona Lisa, except her head was one of the Ninja Turtles."

"Stop it. You did not."

He grins at me, switching his grip on the guitar so he can fish his phone out of his pocket, and flicks through the gallery to show me. I jump up, clutching it in my hands like gold. "This is . . . majestic."

"Which one are you looking at?"

"Either. Both. I don't care." I keep swiping between the two pictures, trying to determine a favorite, and accidentally scroll too far. The picture changes, and my mouth drops open at the exact same moment Elliot leaps forward. I dance out of the way, gaping at the photo, shrieking in delight.

"Oh my god, Elliot Maddon, do you have a *boyfriend?*"

"No, you tiny psycho!"

"He looks like a boyfriend."

"He's not—"

"His tongue is in your *ear*—"

His hand closes around his phone, and he holds it directly above his head. I jump for it, but then he locks it and sticks it in his back pocket, so I give up.

"So, who is he?"

"No one you know."

"No shit; I don't know *anyone.*" I mean, we all started high school together, but between the years away and an influx of new students, I doubt I'd know who the mystery boy was even if Elliot gave me a name. And I only saw a flash of cheek in that picture, so I wouldn't recognize him either.

I nudge him with my shoulder. "Does he make you happy?"

Elliot tilts his head back, grinning at the sky. He doesn't have to answer.

"Oh, you are such a fool, I love it."

"Shut up." He elbows me in the ribs. "What about you? You're not totally hideous, I guess. Any boyfriends?"

"At RAGs? The all-girls school where they watched us every hour of the day?"

He pulls another face. "It's not seriously called RAGs. I refuse to accept that."

I sigh, lying back in the grass. "No. Not even friends, really. Isn't that sad? Surrounded by people, and no one to even help braid the back of my hair." I laugh, but the memory stings. All the times I needed someone and didn't have them: When I cried because I forgot Mum's birthday and one of the girls said I should just call her.

When I didn't know how to work the washing machines and shrank my favorite shirt.

When I missed friends no one knew existed.

Elliot lies down next to me. "You're back now. You have me."

I shuffle closer, until our shoulders are touching. It's a strange feeling, having someone so close—close enough to feel their warmth. I didn't realize it was possible to crave touch like this—not kisses or hugs, not hands under shirts or fingers thrust through hair. Nothing so intimate. Just . . . nearness. Friendship. Leaning over and knowing someone will catch you.

He loops a pinkie through mine. We used to sleep like this, when the screaming got bad. *Pinkie swear we'll always be friends,* he'd whisper in the dark. *Pinkie swear you'll always be here.*

It goes quiet for a moment.

"How has it been lately . . . ?"

He shrugs. "The same. Dale's out most of the time. Mum went back to work—that got bad for a while, but I guess the money helps."

My heart pangs. His stepdad, Dale, is . . . a lot of things, none of them good. I think he used to be decent. Must have been, for Quinn to have loved him. Elliot says he doesn't remember the change, just that it was gradual and suddenly home wasn't really happy anymore. "I'm sorry I wasn't here."

"S'not your fault."

"Your mum's okay?"

He nods slowly, like he's thinking about it. "Yeah, I think so. She won't say it, but being out of the house made her . . . I dunno. Different? Better, I guess. Like she remembered how to be human." He folds his spare arm behind his head, quiet for a long time. "She said you should come by sometime. She missed you."

"I'd like that."

We both look at each other, filling in the blanks: *So long as Dale's not home.*

"Did you come over much, while I was away?"

"Sometimes," he says. "Your nan would guilt me into it. Stayed at Levi's a bit too."

"Oh? Tell me, how is the road to Hades this time of year?"

He rolls his eyes. "You guys need to figure your shit out."

"I *did* figure it out. He's a cloven-hoofed demon, and we should all run shrieking in the other direction."

"You're seriously not going to tell me what happened between you? It's been *three years*."

I grunt, rolling away from him, pretending to be interested in a dandelion.

"Brodie?"

"Hmm?"

"If you don't tell me, he will."

I bristle at that—how the story might get twisted. "Unfair," I mumble. "It's just—it's stupid."

"Oh, I'm sure it is."

I sigh, reaching for a new tactic. "It's not important," I say. "Too much has changed. It's been too long. He's persona non grata. The abominable Levi. Brutus at family dinner—"

He waves a dismissive hand. "Yeah, yeah. Judas, right?"

"Exactly."

He sighs. "Just . . . talk to the dude, okay? Maybe you guys can start over."

"Fine. Also, unrelated, how many security cameras are on the

Sawyer residence these days?" I blink at him angelically. He thinks I'm joking, but if I'm going to use those craft-store supplies it would be handy to know. . . .

He gives me a look. Maybe he *doesn't* think I'm joking.

"*Fine,*" I grumble.

"You can start tonight, you know. There's a back-to-school thing happening."

"Oh, I know. Mayor Susan herself invited me." I cringe at the memory. I hope she wears her ugly culottes.

"So come. Talk to him. Meet some people. School starts soon, and it looks like you're sticking around."

"Pass."

"There's free food."

I hesitate. "Still no. The entire Sawyer family would probably drag me out by my feet."

"Funny," he says. "Never took you for a coward."

I bristle at his words, knowing that's exactly why he chose them. "I shouldn't."

"Again, never stopped you."

I *really* shouldn't. Not only do I have absolutely no desire to return to the place where everything fell apart, but I'd probably get hives from being that close to Levi for an extended period of time. I imagine his eyes, boring into the back of my head all night, probably thinking I'd only come to return to the scene of the crime.

Although maybe that's not an entirely terrible idea.

"Maybe I could look for clues. . . ." It's been three years, but maybe there's something—or someone—remaining that could help slam this particular chapter of history closed.

He holds out a hand, looking slightly alarmed. "You absolutely should *not*—"

"Eli, come *on*. If we find any, we can prove who really did take it and clear my name. And, incidentally, really piss off Levi's dad."

"You could also make it worse," he says. "End up in even more trouble."

"O ye of little faith."

He rolls his eyes. "Remember the last time you tried to solve a mystery?"

Rude. He knows how much it bugs me that we've never found the dead letter writers. I try to pull him up, groaning under his weight, urging him back toward the riverbed. "Come on, I'll just . . . sneak a little peek at Barb's computer. Nose around the room a bit."

"If you get arrested, I'm not bailing you out."

"You can't get arrested for *looking*."

"Most people couldn't. You'd find a way."

"That was almost a compliment."

He mutters something that sounds suspiciously like *I bet this is how the gym burned itself down.*

I give him the finger over my shoulder. "I heard that!"

"Felon!"

3

Dear August,

This summer is hot and boring and I'm sick of riding around the same streets. June always complains that her tire is flat, even though it's perfectly fine, and I've checked it myself a hundred times—she'd rather sit outside the ice cream parlor and tan her legs on the sidewalk, reading magazines.

Everyone is on fabulous vacations and I'm stuck here, jumping in the same lake every day. Mum says I shouldn't, but I'm too restless to sit at home and wait—I haven't even gone back to the arcade since you left. Well, I went by once. Even went in and bought a ticket. But I felt silly on my own, and it wasn't any fun playing by myself. I should have told June I wanted to go. I don't know why I didn't.

What did we do before you came to town? I don't remember being bored, but suddenly, I can't recall how we filled the hours. Before the woods, before the lake, before Treegap, before

bike rides and midnight picnics. Warwick never felt small
before. It feels suffocating now.
  I'm itching to go back to school. Isn't that terrible? A whole
summer, and all I want is to go back. I miss everyone—I miss
my friends. I want to see them all.
  I want to see you.
  Because, August?
  I think I miss you the most.

—*Winnie*

I hold the letter in my hand, searching for something. Anything. The leather chair creaks as I shift, hunching over the words. Levi and I tried everything: we looked for cypher codes, invisible ink, anagrams. But they're just letters, hanging on to their secrets all these years later. I sigh, placing the paper back in its envelope. I grab the one next to it, delivered days later.

Dear Winnie,
  I always miss you the most.

That one always makes me smile. I wonder where August went that summer, when the heat and the distance and waiting made Winnie realize he might be more than her friend.

Poor June. She must have sat outside the ice cream parlor, rolling her eyes, waiting for them both to figure out that they loved each other. I shuffle through the earlier letters—some not even posted, just scribbled on lined paper and folded into neat squares. In the very first letter, with its date marked neatly on a wrinkled piece of paper, Winnie had written that they should befriend the new boy in class, since he didn't know anyone in town, and it would be the polite thing to do. And June had replied,

He's scruffy and strange, nobody knows where he came from, and he watches you all the time. That's either terribly romantic or he's an ax-murdering lunatic. Let's ask him to dinner.

—*J.*

I snort. I wonder if June knew all along. Saw the glimmer in Winnie's eyes and *knew* it was something more. "Who are you?" I ask the letters. They don't answer. They never do.

Nan clears her throat. "You sure you don't want me to come?"

I shake my head. Partly because I know there won't be enough whiskey to keep her entertained, and partly because I don't want her witnessing any criminal activity.

"It's fine, Nan. Elliot is going with me."

"Hmm. How's his mum lately?"

"Got a job, apparently."

Nan looks surprised. "Oh—well, good for her. You tell them they're welcome anytime."

I kiss her powdered cheek goodbye. Mabel gives a petulant mew, so I scruff her ears too. "Sure thing. Don't wait up!" I grab my backpack and run out front. I spent the rest of the afternoon fixing my old bike, since I evidently no longer fit on Elliot's handlebars—

40

I have to swap out both tires, plus the brakes are shot, a family of spiders was living in the wicker basket, and the seat is so low my knees are almost perched on the handlebars.

I wait for Elliot's headlight to appear around the corner, then push off the curb, pedaling in sync as we cruise down the hill.

He glances at me from under his helmet. "You look . . . clean?"

"Gee, thanks."

"No, like . . . you look nice."

I give him a look. "Again—gee, thanks."

I'm wearing the outfit Nan bought me, and I'm trying not to fidget because my hands are already sweaty and I don't want Elliot to think I'm nervous.

Truth is, I've been away for a long time. And that aching loneliness still haunts me. I don't think I can survive another year like RAGs. Even though Levi is on my pond-scum list, at least he used to be a friend. Now I only have Elliot, and Elliot has his nonboyfriend and the fucking *football team*.

"Do you play?" I ask suddenly. "Football. You're hanging out with them. And you're . . . sporty, I guess."

"Nah. Fees are pretty high. Plus cleats and gear." He shrugs. "Levi kept trying to give me stuff but . . ."

"But he had sliced holes in all his shirts to make room for his giant leathery bat wings?"

Elliot chokes on a laugh. "That wasn't funny. I didn't laugh. I am Switzerland."

"Ja."

"That's German."

"Does Switzerland have its own language?" We pull up at the Town Hall, slowing to a stop beside the bike stands, locking the wheels and shucking our helmets. "Is it Swiss—is Swiss a language? That doesn't sound right. Or is it French?" I babble, eyeing the doors. I'm not really listening to his answer—I'm watching people I don't recognize walk arm in arm, laughing happily, telling jokes. That used to be me. Elliot's voice jolts me out of the memory.

"Red?"

"Yeah?"

He raps his knuckles gently on my head. "You okay in there?"

"Ja," I answer quietly.

His arm threads across my shoulders, steering me toward the door. "Come on. It'll be fun."

"You could pry my fingernails out of my cold, dead hands and I'd bet it would be more fun than this."

He laughs, dragging me through the entrance. The Town Hall is a multi-service building, with a huge ballroom-type thing in the middle. I mean, logically I know it's not a *ballroom*, but it's a huge wood-paneled room with chandeliers on the ceiling, and they host a bunch of functions here like debutante balls and graduations and whatever. To one side, there's the official local government offices and a small museum, which is mostly a collection of not particularly exciting historical artifacts shoved into one room, and to the other is the police station. There's also a theater next door, the library, and some shared office spaces.

All in all, it's a great place for snooping.

Elliot notices me scanning the building and tightens his arm around mine. "Oh no you don't," he whispers. "Come on. Meet people first. Break laws later."

"It's not against the law to look around," I say innocently.

He steers me to a group of boys who all have that sort of semi-similar look—artfully mussed hair, big shoulders, desperately trying to grow stubble on their cheeks to varying success. I wrinkle my nose. That has to be the football team. They're all so . . . heteronormative. I briefly wonder how Elliot got adopted into their golden circle, but I feel so nauseous the thought gets lost as I look for the nearest safe place to barf. Do I remember what it's like to talk to normal people?

Guess we're about to find out.

One of the guys on the outer edges sees Elliot first, raising his hand to do that weird back-slapping thing guys do instead of real hugs. Elliot lets go of me, and it's like losing a life vest in the middle of a storm.

"Hey, man, what's up?"

Elliot shrugs, smiling. "Not much. Just been hanging around. Hey, do you guys remember Brodie?"

A few curious heads swivel my way. I glance at their faces, but I can't tell if any of these people were here before I left.

"Yo, isn't that the McKellon Felon?" somebody asks, and a few of them laugh.

"I was never *technically* arrested," I object.

A boy with brown skin and dark hair shoves one of the dudes who laughed. "Shut up, Ryan. Hey, sorry, I'm Isaac Adebayo." He holds out his hand to shake, which is weirdly adult, but I take it anyway. "You're the girl who went to boarding school, right? Must have been fun?"

"Oh, no. It's not really like the movies. It's actually pretty boring."

A pale guy with blond hair wiggles a suggestive eyebrow. "Yeah, but you all got in your undies and had pillow fights, right?"

Three of them turn around. "Bro, that's mad disrespectful."

"Yeah it's, like, toxic and shit."

Elliot glowers in a way that I suspect would be intimidating if you'd never seen him put an upside-down daisy on Mabel's head and call her a pretty princess.

"Hey, I'm sorry. I didn't mean it. I'm Ryan." He grimaces. "Sorry. Really."

"He has four brothers," Isaac says. "There's some un-learning to do."

I can't help it. A bubble of nervous laughter forms in my throat. This is not the football team I expected.

Elliot gives me a little nudge. "Anyway, Brodie is back for the year. Figured it would be good for her to know a few people."

"You know what classes you have yet?" one of them asks.

I shuffle my feet. "Er, no. I'm not sure I'm even enrolled yet. . . ."

Elliot nods at me, his pinkie slipping through mine for a second. I take a breath. "But I guess . . . I like English? And history? That sort of thing."

Isaac grins at me. "Take English lit and we'll have class together. Mr. G is actually pretty cool."

"I'm doing world history," says another. "We're studying France this year, I think."

44

One of the guys has been looking curiously at my face. He suddenly perks up, like a memory has jolted him awake. "Hey, doesn't your family run the Dead Letter Office?"

"Mail Redistribution Center," I correct. I eye him warily, not sure where this is going.

"Yeah! That place is really cool. I think I met your nan, maybe? My pops passed away last year; she had all his letters saved up."

I inwardly sigh with relief. "Oh, yeah. We get a lot of that kind of stuff."

"Really?"

"Yeah. Family heirlooms, letters, stuff lost in the mail. Some of it is kind of funny, actually."

The boy grins, totally enthused. "That's *awesome*! What's the weirdest thing you ever found?"

And just like that, my frosty veneer starts to melt. It's easier to talk then, and Elliot stays beside me. A few girls come over to say hello and introduce themselves. I vaguely remember a couple of them, and they smile encouragingly at me. One of them adds me to a school chat, so I'll be able to message people if I need to. She even tells me which of the bathrooms are clean, which ones are filthy and never have toilet paper, and which ones are good for crying "just in case."

And then Levi arrives.

Stupid Levi with his stupid face.

He's wearing a suit, which is way too formal for the crowd, and he keeps tugging at his tie like he's suffocating. His mum swats his hand away, her smile straining as she whispers through gritted teeth. I bet she made him wear it. His blond-brown hair has been brushed, so it's unusually neat, and *oh*, yes, he is tall now. Not as tall as Elliot, but far bigger than the scrawny-shouldered boy I left behind.

"Well, this was fun," I mutter, starting to edge away.

Elliot tilts his head, eyes pleading. "Stay," he says. "You're gonna have to talk to him eventually."

I look at him, and his friends, and I feel the pull of a normal life. These people who have been more welcoming than any of the girls at RAGs ever were. If I stay, maybe we'll talk, and laugh, and I'll have somewhere to sit at lunch.

"I have to pee," I announce loudly instead. *I'll only be gone for a minute*, I promise myself. Ten, tops.

Elliot rolls his eyes. "Fine. Detective Dad is over by the drinks; don't let him see you."

My eyes flit past him, to the bar station set up in the corner. Detective Sawyer is there, in uniform, and he hasn't seen me yet. He's smiling and acting like he's not actually a lizard person in a human skin suit.

I smooth my hair, tuck it under the collar of my jacket, and slip around the edge of the room. The back entrance is unlocked for the parking lot—which makes for a convenient detour as I look for a particular red car—so I duck out and race around the front of the building again, sticking to the shadows. This plan made much more sense in the light of day. Now, skulking alone in the dark, I'm starting to feel much more like . . . well, a felon.

I pay for a raffle ticket at the door, smiling at the grandmotherly woman handing them out. "Excuse me," I ask as she counts my change. "Do you know where the bathrooms are?"

"Of course—just pop around the corner, near the display room."

I feel a twinge of guilt. I already knew where the public toilets were, of course, but if you're ever sneaking around places you shouldn't be, it's always best to point to someone else and blame them.

The corridor is quiet, and I pause at the bathroom door like I'm about to walk in. Then I glance over my shoulder at the empty hallway, and sprint on light feet to the display room instead.

The lights are dimmed, the glass cases glowing with small lamps set into wood-paneled cabinets. It's mostly heritage stuff in here that's not super interesting: the first town planning papers, maps of the original streets. A couple memorial medals, pictures of founding families, a few surviving diaries. There are a few things that are sort of cool, like the wooden leg of a past mayor, who was rumored to take it off and use it as a gavel in court.

And the Adder Stone.

Well. The spot where the Adder Stone *used* to be. The display is still lit, though the lamp only illuminates an empty space—a silver-pronged stand and commemorative plaque. Someone has added a photograph of the ring, with its golden center and rough edges. I can't believe anybody actually wore that—not to mention it was supposedly made of *hardened snake venom*.

Barb said the case was protected with sensor alarms, but I lean down and squint at the little black box to the side. There's no light, no laser. I move to the case next to it, leaning as close as I dare without touching it, and notice the box flickers with a small red dot.

Guess they decided an empty case wasn't worth protecting. I flick the glass lid up, snatch the photo, and dash back to the toilets.

Part one achieved.

Part two . . . slightly more difficult.

I wait until a new group arrives, crossing from one side of the corridor to the other as they pause to take photos and shed their jackets. My heart picks up, stuttering at a hurried pace.

Even though the police station is tiny, it's still, nevertheless, a police station. And even though the double doors are unlocked, it's still breaking and entering. I think? Maybe it's just entering. That's not so bad, right?

There's a young rookie manning the front desk, swinging in his chair, flicking bands on a rubber ball.

"Hey," I say with a small wave. "Um, I don't know if this is a big deal or anything, but some guy just tried to sell me weed from his van? He just drove off—but I think he's going around the block. And you know, all those kids here. . . ."

The guy sits bolt upright, tapping a radio on his shoulder. "Officer Keely, reporting a 207A—I'm gonna go check it out." The radio clicks off and he looks up at me "Miss—what did he look like? Did you get a good look?"

"Uh, yeah. Pale dude, big hair, weird eyes. I think he was wearing a baseball shirt?" *Goes by the name Edward Cullen.* . . .

He jumps out of his seat, running down the hall. "Stay here, I'll be right back."

I wait until the doors swing closed, then I dive for Barb's computer. The login is *Password1*, and if it didn't suit my needs so well, I'd help her change it. It's been the same since primary school, when Levi found it written on a Post-it note stuck to her drawer. Her screen is open to a Google image search of blond poodles, and I have to slam a hand over my mouth to keep from laughing.

Focus, Brodie. I figure I only have a few minutes until the rookie is back, so I jump straight into the local server, typing *Adder Stone* into the search bar.

It brings up the stolen property report, signed off by none other than Detective Sawyer himself. Under suspects, my name is listed at the top. "Hey," I mutter, offended that they didn't even consider other options first. There's a copy of the insurance statement too, and the number of zeros attached makes my eyes bug out of my head for a second. All that for a *rock*?

I print the report, snatching it off the printer and stuffing it inside my shirt. I navigate to the security camera footage section, clicking.

File unavailable.

I frown. That's weird. Did they store it somewhere else? I click around in a few places, searching for the date and day. This is beyond my usual snooping, so I have no idea where to really look, but still—nothing.

I shake out my hands, refocusing. I should get out of here—it's not going to take that cop long to do a lap of the block. But I glance up at the corridor, and it's still empty, so I have some time.

Just one more minute. I open a new page and type.

August, Winnie, June.

No matches. The screen blinks, suggesting I try a more focused search.

August.

Hundreds of reports . . . all filed *in* August from the past god knows how many years. Damn. I try June, and June-Bug. The same thing happens. I lean close to the screen, squinting in concentration. I type their names into the search bar again, selecting *homicide* as the department. In the three seconds it takes for the screen to come up blank, I feel like my stomach will twist itself into irreversible knots.

Nothing. *Thank you, Jesus, Zeus, Osiris, Allah . . .*

But if no one claimed the letters . . .

"What are you doing?" says a voice in my ear.

I yelp, falling off the swivel chair in an effort to put some distance between me and the intruder. Wait. *I'm* the intruder. I scramble to my knees, trying to orient myself. And then I see his face.

"Did you *follow me?*"

Levi stares down at me, rolling his eyes. "Did you *break in?*"

I square my shoulders and quickly exit the page on Barb's computer. The dead letters aren't *ours* anymore, and I don't want him to know I'm still looking.

But the original search remains, and Levi glances down at the screen, realizing what I was looking for—the Adder Stone report is open, and so is the search for security footage.

"Getting rid of the evidence?" he asks.

"No, god. I *told you* I didn't take it."

"Yeah, and this makes you look *real* innocent."

I brush off my pants and muster the patience to explain myself. "I just wanted to see—you know what? Never mind." Patience extinguished. At least I tried. "You never bothered to talk to me, so why should I."

"Brodie—"

I storm out of the office, hurrying to the front steps. I pull out my phone to text Elliot. Satanic encounter, going home.

I realize my footsteps aren't the only ones echoing in the dark. I spin to face him. "What do you want, Levi?" We're alone out here. And yet still too close. How much distance should there be between us? Streets? Cities? States? Seems like it worked last time.

He drops down a few steps, yanking his tie loose in frustration. He doesn't look angry, though, just . . . tired. "Just tell me you did it, Brodie. It's been three years. Just say it."

"*Oh my god,* you psychopath, how many times do I have to tell you—I didn't take it! Why don't you believe me?"

He steps closer. I step back. "We never had secrets before."

"That you know of," I mutter.

"Please," he says. "Why won't you tell me? Are you angry? Is it because of me, because of the—"

I push my fingers into his mouth, stopping him. "Don't say it," I hiss. "I have wiped that memory from my brain. It doesn't exist anymore. It didn't happen."

His shoulders sag. Is he . . . upset? But no, his eyes go cold again, and he backs up.

"I saw you, Brodie."

"You what?" This is exhausting. My hands are cold. The papers

51

shoved in my shirt are slipping. And the longer I stand here and look at him, the more I regret what we lost.

"I know you're lying," he says. "Because I saw you."

"Saw me *where*? Did you hit your head? Are you okay? Are you experiencing some kind of lucid dream—"

"I saw you sneak into the display room. As soon as it went missing, I snuck into Dad's office to check. You got *caught*, Red. On camera. And you're lucky I got there first because at least now there's no evidence."

Oh, fuck . . .

"I—I didn't take it," I say. And that's true. "I—"

Elliot bursts out of the building, rushing down the stairs. "You know you two can't kill each other out in front of the police station, right?" He's joking, but still, he angles himself between us, ready to referee. Not that I'm dumb enough to tackle Levi anymore— maybe when we were kids, but then he went and cheated by actually hitting puberty, and if I dive at his chest right now, I'm pretty sure it'd be like hitting concrete.

"Did you tell him?" Levi asks.

"Tell me what?" Elliot says, looking confused.

I sigh. "Nothing. Because there's nothing to tell."

Levi turns to Elliot. "She got caught on the security cameras, sneaking into the display room the night the Adder Stone went missing."

Elliot looks at me, uncertain. "That can't be right, because—"

"And Levi thinks I stole it."

"What?"

"Even though I *told* him I didn't, but he didn't believe me, and three years later he's *still*—"

Elliot throws up his hands, signaling time-out. "Is this why you two have been fighting?"

"No," I answer at the same time Levi says, "Yes."

Elliot looks between us. "Which is it?"

"No," I repeat. "It's not." *Mostly.* I don't dare look at Levi as I say it. "It doesn't matter. This is stupid; I should never have come."

"Why *did* you come?" Levi asks.

"To prove I didn't do it!"

"Why?"

"Because *I didn't do it.*"

Levi opens his mouth, takes half a step forward—then his eyes cut to Elliot, and he stops. "You got caught," he repeats. "On camera."

"I don't know what you mean. If there was actual footage, then your dad—"

"—never saw it, because I deleted it."

I throw my hands up. "You *moron*, why would you delete it?"

"To protect you! Because we were friends!"

"Did you watch it all the way through?"

"Oh, I'm *sorry*, I was busy aiding and abetting a *crime*, I didn't exactly have time to catch the full show."

"I cannot believe I just wasted three years of my life wondering why—" I groan, exasperated and momentarily at a loss for words. "I didn't take the Adder Stone! I took Ernie!"

There is a moment of complete silence. Levi's face turns white. Elliot just looks blessedly confused. "Uh, guys . . . who's Ernie?"

I feel my cheeks turn pink. "Ernie the Emu," I mutter. "The stuffed giant bird. Remember? I was leaving, and I thought it would be funny if I took him and left him in the Rydal Woods for you to find. And *return*."

Ernie was an oddity in the Warwick display room—nobody quite knew where he came from or what his exact historical significance was, but no one ever had the heart to throw him away, so he sat in the corner of the room gathering dust on his creepy long neck. Kids used to stick things in his beak for fun.

Elliot frowns at me, mouth agape. "You took . . . a taxidermied emu?"

My cheeks burn even warmer. "You would have thought it was hilarious three years ago."

"That's the dumbest thing I've ever heard. Also, how did I forget there was a town emu?"

Levi collapses on the stairs, folding at the knees. He puts his head in his hands, running his fingers through his hair until it sticks up in all directions. "So . . . you really didn't take the stone?"

"No. And please tell me you at least kept a copy of the security footage—"

He looks up, and I've never seen him so pale. "How did you even get an emu out of the building?" he croaks instead.

"Well, if you'd kept the footage, you could have found out."

Levi manages to stand, his mouth half open to ask more questions—just as the rookie cop comes running up the stairs. "No sign of the van, miss." He notices Levi and gives him a salute.

"Evening, Mr. Sawyer. You'll make sure your friend here gets home safe, won't you?"

Levi just glowers at me. "Want a lift, Brodie?"

I clip my helmet onto my head, smiling sweetly. "With you? Not gonna get far with those flat tires."

And then I push off, pedaling wildly up the hill as he curses my name. He starts to chase after me, so I toss his valve caps over my shoulder. I'm not a complete monster.

"See you at school on Monday!"

4

Dear Winnie,

I'm starting to realize this place will feel smaller without you in it. Will you write to me? From the city? Think of me on sunny days, and know I'm down by the lake, in our spot, and thinking of you too. I'll have the shop, at least, and that will keep me busy. Though I can't shake the feeling that the start of this year feels like the end. I shouldn't say that—I'm so happy for you both. It's just the closing of a chapter, June would say. Not the book. And it's not forever at least. ~~I hope.~~ Just a while.

It's worth it, I think. Knowing that the world is bigger. That you'll be out there. I didn't used to think that. My world was a suitcase and this town. But my luck changed the day I met you.

This life might be small, but it's enough now. You were always enough.

Love,
August

I sigh, propping my feet up on the balcony railings. Mabel sits in my lap, raising a lazy paw to inspect the paper. "What do you think, old girl?" It drives me crazy, not knowing. Did he stay? Is he still here? Is Winnie? I rang every store in Warwick, once, and asked if August worked there. It took me three weeks to get through them all, and everyone politely said no, except Dwight who told me I had *some damn fucking nerve calling him after I stole that Jeep*, and honestly, I suppose that was a fair assessment.

Nan taps on the glass. "Don't stay up too late. First day tomorrow!"

My enrollment was finalized over the weekend. I even managed to get most of the classes I wanted, though somehow ended up being forced to take music theater, despite having absolutely no musical bone in my body, because it was the only class that wouldn't clash with the rest of my schedule.

Elliot had come by in the morning, and I thought I'd get a Stern Talking To, but he only asked if we had any pancakes, and the answer was yes, so he sat at the counter with me and cut up strawberries while Nan asked about his dreams. He said they were about clouds, which is just so classically Eli, and Nan said he needed to beware either a controlling force or danger ahead. Then he said the clouds were shaped like Scooby-Doo and that really put Nan in a mood. She swatted him with a spatula and gave him extra toppings.

So it wasn't a terrible day. There was no immediate Levi fallout. Detective Dick didn't come and arrest me for breaking and entering, or for tampering with Levi's car. There were no angry texts or rumors in the school chat.

And yet, my stomach still twists itself into knots.

It's not like tomorrow is my first day at a brand-new school. It's just my first day *back* at my *old* school. I know where most of the buildings are, even if some of them have been renovated, and I vaguely remember seeing a few of the senior schoolteachers around when I was younger.

But . . .

There's a feeling like this is my last chance. For friends, for a life, for something normal. I wonder if that was what August was clinging to. I wonder if he knew that there weren't any grand adventures waiting for him after high school, because there was no money and his grades weren't good enough for scholarships. I wonder if he knew June and Winnie were the best people he would ever meet, and it scared him to know that everyone else would pale in comparison. That he'd live the rest of his life in a memory.

Because that's how I felt, when I went to RAGs. I tried to make new friends. And it sucked. I was just walking around every day, knowing I'd never love anyone as much as I loved Elliot and Levi. Except I didn't love Levi anymore, because I hated him.

So where does that leave me?

I pad quietly to the kitchen, setting the kettle to boil for a cup of ginger tea. I creep downstairs while I'm waiting, restoring the letter to its place in the chest. I take out my notebook, noting the date in a column on the side. Beside it, I write: *No new clues. Never found shop. June at university.*

It's thus far a pretty small list, but I decided to go back chronologically (or as best as we can guess) and reread all the letters with a fresh pair of eyes. Frustratingly, all the things I've written down so far are things I already knew three years ago: June was the oldest, the two girls were local, and August moved to town sometime during high school for unknown reasons. They hung out in the woods and by the lake, like most kids still do, and at an ice cream shop that no longer exists. They mentioned a few classmates, unfortunately only by their very common first names: Mary, Anne, Peter. There are no yearbooks left in the library because it flooded ages ago, so none of the archive editions survived. And without the year, I had to piece together the timeline from the contents of the letters: *Summer is nearly here! Let's go down to the lake and see how far we can float August out on the blowup mattress,* and *This winter is too cold, my tits are frozen right off.* (Both from June.) (Obviously.)

Today is Mum's birthday. It's the first one without her. No. Not that one. I try not to read that one.

I place the letter back in its nook, and head upstairs for my tea.

Elliot is sitting on the balcony when I return, chin on his hand, looking out at the valley. In the distance, I can hear the echo of angry voices.

"Bad night?"

He looks up, as though surprised to see me. "Yeah. Mum put gas in the car and apparently she should have known that Dale spent his paycheck already so now there's no more money for the next two weeks, and it's all her fault."

"You had dinner?"

He nods. "I was at Levi's, earlier."

I bite my tongue and pass him my cup instead. "Tea?"

59

He sniffs it suspiciously. "Is this dirt water?"

I laugh quietly, tucking my knees in close. "You wanna stay tonight?"

He sighs, leaning back until he's lying flat on the bench seat. Mabel emerges to sit on his chest, purring happily. She's always been weirdly obsessed with him. He gives her a scratch, and the purr starts to sound like a motor revving.

"Nah, my books are at home," he says eventually. He looks tired. "Don't wanna be late for first day, going back and forth. Can I just chill here for a bit, though? Until they're done?"

"Sure. Wanna watch *House Hunters* reruns?"

"Sure," he answers, but doesn't move. "Just gimme a minute. I was going to bed when they started."

He closes his eyes, fingers running through Mabel's scruff. I go inside to fetch him a blanket and pillow, and by the time I come back, he's already got one arm over his eyes, snoring softly.

I tuck his legs under the blanket and leave the hallway light on.

"You coming in?" I whisper to Mabel, giving a low whistle that means *you can have food if you do what I say*. She just blinks at me, then tucks herself into a ball, floating up and down his stomach with each breath. I set an alarm for midnight, to wake him up if he needs to, then go to bed to read. I wake up with the book on my chest a couple hours later, the alarm vibrating under my hip. I sit up groggily, ready to wake him, and notice a text on my phone. I open it to a picture of me, drool on my chin in an open-mouthed snore. Came to say good night, but you were already out. Gonna stick this on your locker tomorrow. Night, Red.

Something lands on my feet and whines loudly. It's Mabel, look-ing exceptionally disappointed. "Sorry, girl, it's just me now."

She mews again.

Yeah. I wish he'd stay too.

My day is not a complete disaster. Elliot walks me to my home-room, waits for me in the halls, and powers through the hordes of students to lead me down each corridor. People smile at him, warm and friendly, and he waves as he passes.

"You being popular is deeply weird," I say.

"I'm not popular," he grunts.

I roll my eyes behind his back. He drops me at my last class of the day, English lit, and loiters at the door. The first bell goes, and the few remaining students scatter. I raise an eyebrow. "Don't you need to get to your math tute?"

"Yeah, I will. Isaac is in this class; he said you should sit with him." He presses up onto his toes, scanning through the windows into the room. "He's running late, though. I'll wait."

"Isaac said?"

He shrugs. "Yeah."

"When did Isaac say that?" We didn't eat lunch in the quad—I had to go to the office and spend the hour sorting through my transcripts and signing documents.

Elliot shrugs again. "I don't know. He texted me."

"Huh," I say, eyes narrowed. "Okay, well . . . I'll sit with him then."

"Sure. Great."

"Are you . . . going now?" This was so bizarre. There's a strange look on his face I can't read.

The second bell goes—students are meant to have butts in seats by this stage. His cheeks turn pink.

"I was just gonna say hey, that's all."

Oh. Suddenly, it makes much more sense. I grin at him, watching as the flush spreads from his neck to his ears. "I see."

He shoves me toward the door. "Never mind, you bloody deviant. Go sit. I'll meet you after school."

I laugh, stepping forward, but hesitate as I notice a blue sports jacket in the distance, sprinting up the corridor to meet us. Isaac is panting by the time he reaches the classroom door, wrangling an armful of books. He grins up at Elliot.

"Hey, man," he says, offering a hand. They high-five, holding on a second longer than necessary. Elliot's eyes skate to mine. God, this is adorable.

The door to the classroom is suddenly wrenched open, and a sweater-vested man is standing there, polishing his glasses. "Gentlemen, are we keeping you?"

Isaac just beams at him. "Hey, Mr. G. Have you met Brodie? She's new. Can she be my term partner?"

"Will you sit down and behave if I say yes?"

"I can do at least one of those things," Isaac answers, strolling into the room and sitting front-row. He pats the seat next to him and I cautiously follow. When the teacher turns to close the door, Elliot is already gone.

"Ms. Brodie . . ." He looks down, consulting his class list. "McKellon, is it?"

"*Town felon*," someone whispers in the last row. A chorus of giggles erupts, and I want to hide behind my notepad. The teacher pretends not to hear, focusing his attention on me.

"My name is Mr. Gregory. And from where are you joining us this year, Brodie?"

"Uh, Rowley. In the city. It was a boarding school."

More whispering and laughter in the back row. Emboldened, a voice calls out: "Heard you burned down a building!" The laughter gets louder. I want the earth to open and swallow me up.

"Lightly singed," I object weakly. "It was an accident."

The teacher seems unfazed. "Ah, young Brodie, some of the greatest writers have found themselves indecent with the law. Oscar Wilde, anyone? Mr. Banner, since you have so much to say on criminal matters, perhaps you can remind the class what our dear Irish author was imprisoned for?"

The kid who seemed to be doing most of the heckling suddenly goes silent, as all eyes turn to focus on him. He thinks for a long time before answering. "Um . . . drinking?"

"Um, *no*," says Mr. Gregory, eliciting a few laughs of his own. "Can you perhaps name one of his books instead, Mr. Banner?"

The kid scratches his head, blinking. "Uh . . . like . . . *Pride and Prejudice?*"

The teacher sighs, miming the sign of the cross. "It is *The Picture of Dorian Gray*, Mr. Banner, which you should have already read over the holidays. It is about a conceited young man who slowly loses pieces of his soul—you might find it interesting."

Beside me, Isaac winks. "Mr. G's pretty cool. Just make sure you read the books early."

I start to relax, nodding. Honestly, I'm surprised it took this long for anyone to say something and I expected worse. I feel almost relieved, knowing it's finally happened. And I survived. Maybe everyone will get over it—it'll be fun gossip for a few days, then dropped. New kids are only fun for a few weeks, until everyone resettles and forgets about them.

There's a knock at the door, and Mr. Gregory steps away to answer it. Isaac turns in his seat, taking the opportunity while the teacher is distracted. "Hey, Banner? If you keep talking shit, I'm gonna smack you so hard in the game this Friday you'll be out for the rest of the season."

"We're on the same team, asshole."

Isaac just shrugs, turning back to the board. "Banner's in the reserves—I think he has an inferiority complex," he whispers to me. "Only made the main team 'cause Eli had to drop out last minute."

"You didn't have to say anything," I say, looking down at my hands.

Isaac just grins.

And that's it. That's my last class. Mr. Gregory hands out sheets, runs through the semester course and a few of the other books we'll be reading. Nan has a huge collection, so I've actually read most of them already.

Isaac hunches in his seat, taking careful notes, and taps my sheet of paper when I've spent too long staring out the window. Huh. The girls at Rowley just politely tolerated me. Isaac actually seems . . . to care? He even sticks around when class is finished, waiting for Elliot to come find me. I pretend to have trouble zipping up my bag, so they can have a few minutes to talk, like they both so obviously want to.

"Catch you tomorrow, Brodie!" Isaac says at last, raising his hand for a high five. I raise mine meekly in return, wincing as he slaps it a little too enthusiastically—I really wouldn't want to be on the receiving end of his tackle on the field. I wave until he disappears into the end-of-day throng of students rushing to the parking lot.

"Not one word," Elliot threatens.

"Me? Why?" I blink innocently. I make sure no one is around before lowering my voice and pulling a dumb face. "Oh, you mean because you *loooove* him? Hey, I don't blame you, the dude is pretty."

"I hate you."

"No you don't," I say cheerfully. "Anyway, how was your day?" I'm pretty sure there's more going on between Elliot and Isaac that he doesn't want to talk about, but either he'll tell me when he's ready or he'll just spend a lot of time brooding about it in silence. It's kind of his thing. Everyone has a process, after all.

He shrugs. "Good. Worried I took too many science classes; the exams are gonna be killer. How about you? People were nice?"

"Actually . . . yeah. Isaac, obviously. But there were a couple girls in my theater class—Claire and Emiko?"

"Oh yeah, I know them. Emi's cool, she worked at the movies with me last year."

They were sweet—Emiko had ended up in the class because it fit her schedule, like me, and Claire was a diehard musical fan. They both waved me over to their group when we had to pick trios to work with, and Claire didn't seem to mind much that she was doing all the work. And, actually, most of my classes were like that—some were more interested than others, but they still offered me a seat or chatted while work was handed out. And most important, I managed to avoid Levi all day. There was not one glimpse of his artfully mussed bronze head, or his car in the parking lot. Either he had to walk to school, or he skipped out. Elliot and I didn't have any classes together either, though that wasn't surprising since our electives were so different.

"I think I'll be okay tomorrow," I say optimistically as we walk over to the bike rack.

"Yeah?"

"Yeah, so you might not have to chaperone me so much."

He kicks a leg over his bike, fiddling with the lock. "I don't mind."

I grab my helmet off the bars, shoving it on my head. "Hey, do you want to—" I squeal, shivers rolling down my spine as something cold and slimy trickles across my scalp. I rip the helmet off, pulling at my hair, but whatever it is, it's stuck. "Get it off, get it off!" *Oh god, please don't be a bug, please don't be a bug.*

Elliot's laughing, and I hate him for not immediately leaping to my aid. After a few more seconds of me waving flappy-panic-hands, he steps over—and pulls a purple rubber snake off my head.

"Look, see? It's nothing, just a kid's toy."

I look down at it, confused for a second. Then I grab my helmet and look inside. Two broken pieces of tape are still stuck to the top, where the snake must have been coiled. I pick one up, squinting at the letters.

I'm sorry, it says. *Payback,* says the other.

"Levi Sawyer is a dead man," I declare.

Elliot just tosses me the snake, already pulling away. "Yeah? Then why are you smiling?"

The rest of the week passes without incident. I don't find any opportunity to turn Levi's hair blue, or fill his schoolbag with goldfish, but the rubber snake lives on in my mind. At lunch, I sit with Emiko and Claire to avoid sitting with the football team— and, by extension, the traitor himself. Elliot visits often to say hello, and I eat with the team one day when Levi is in the library. They invite me to another party by the lake, and I decline. It's only after I say no that I realize there's no real reason to turn them down. Habit, maybe? Isaac seems genuinely disappointed by my refusal, and bugs me all through English lit until Mr. G threatens him with detention.

"You should come," Elliot says, riding with me back home on Friday. "Tomorrow. I know you don't have plans. You only know, like, three people."

I shake my head, glad my helmet hides my face—even if I do have to double-check it now for intruders. "I'll see," I lie. "I said I'd help Nan with something."

"What, itemizing her dream journal?"

"Hey!"

He laughs, speeding ahead, and I have to pedal extra fast to catch up. It's a warm day, and I can feel sweat prickling under my collar as my legs work double time.

Elliot must feel it too, because he slows suddenly, eyes on the main road. "Wanna stop for a milkshake?"

"Sure. We can play a few games—still gonna kick your butt at air hockey."

The Archie Arcade is one of the few fun places to go in Warwick. It's an old gaming arcade that's been around forever—there's still pinball machines in the back corner and red leather seats along the prize counter. But it got renovated a while ago, so there's also a drink stand and a café to one side, with outdoor seats that are usually packed after school. It's also the only place we know for sure that the dead letter writers visited, apart from the woods. I always get a tingle up my spine when I step through the doors, wondering where they sat and what games they played.

We pull in and find there's already a line forming at the drinks counter, so we trade some cash for arcade tokens instead. There's a bored-looking guy who makes the exchange for us, counting out the gold coins for the machines. A sign above the counter reminds everyone that FORTUNE FAVORS THE BRAVE, which is a nice way of trying to pretend like half the machines aren't rigged to lose. Luck has nothing to do with it—no one's won anything on the claw machine, ever. And trust me, I've tried. Elliot and I take our place at the air hockey table, trading coins to release the pucks. We worked out a while ago that if you're sneaky, and catch it before it slips through the slot, you can play more games—though once we get going, the game is too vicious to risk smacking fingertips in front of the puck. I laugh as I score a goal, and Elliot has to feed our last coin to play again.

"You wanna swing by tomorrow?" he says. "Dale's out for the afternoon. Mum said she'll make cookies. We can head down to the lake together if you change your mind about going."

"Sure, that sounds good. But I'm still not going to the party."

I like Elliot's mum, and she's always been exceptionally kind to me. When Mum died, Quinn would bake me peanut-butter cookies after school and send Eli to bring them over. She bought me a box of pads, which I was too embarrassed to take with me to Rowley and then later regretted. She taught me how to make fishtail braids in my hair and would paint my nails on Friday nights when Dale was down at the pub getting drunk. She would just listen to me talk; sometimes about Mum, sometimes about school, sometimes just about shows I watched on TV. Nan tried to do all those things for me too, but her daughter had just died, and she was suddenly lumped with a deeply average son-in-law and a preteen grandchild. It took Nan a while before she was *Nan* again, and in that time, Quinn filled the blank spots. Over the years, I've wavered between being bitterly disappointed that Quinn won't just stand up for herself and leave, and sympathetic that she's stuck in such a vicious cycle. It got harder to be mad at her, though, as I got older. When I heard the things Dale said and wondered if she believed them too—and whether the reason she wouldn't leave was because there was nowhere else to go. I've asked Elliot, over the years, if there's anything more, but he says they just yell. Well, Dale yells. He and Quinn listen.

I watch his face now, as we drift to the counter to order milk-shakes, wondering if the circles under his eyes are the shadows of

69

the fluorescent lights or because he hasn't slept again. I tap my card to pay, and he protests, but I remind him that the loser buys drinks, and I lost. He never seems to notice I always lose the last match.

Elliot starts to look around nervously, slurping his empty cup. The obnoxious sound jolts me out of the memory, and he keeps going until I nudge him with my foot.

"Would you *quit*."

He grins, slurping extra loud before setting his cup aside. "So, I've been thinking," he says. "About Ernie the Emu."

I let my head smack down on the table in shame. "What about him?"

"You said you left him in the Rydal Woods, right?"

"Yeah."

"Don't you think it's weird that no one ever found him? Does that mean someone took him home?"

I snort. "Oh my god, poor Ernie. Maybe he's in a better place."

"Imagine, he's just sitting in someone's living room."

I laugh, trying to picture him placed next to a decorative trestle table, maybe adorned with Christmas decorations in December—tinsel around his neck, an ornament hanging from his beak.

Elliot fidgets with his cup, twisting the lid out of shape. "So, you went out there at night? All alone?"

"Where?"

"Rydal."

"Oh, right. Yeah. I mean, not all the way to the clearing. I'm not a complete idiot." I don't believe in the Rydal Devil, but I *do* believe in ax murderers.

He nods, fingertips now drumming on the tabletop. I narrow my eyes at him. "Why are you asking?"

He shrugs again. "Just curious."

"Uh-huh."

"So you and Levi—"

"—my least favorite sentence."

"I'm sorry. About what happened between you."

"It's fine."

"It's not. If I had known—"

"You couldn't have done anything. We were both too stubborn. *Are.* Present tense."

"Yeah," he says. "I was worried about that."

His eyes dart over my shoulder, and this time I turn around. Then I whip back to face him. "You're a goddamn traitor, Elliot Maddon. And I mean it this time."

Levi is leaning against the Pac-Man machine, arms crossed and not even pretending to hide. *Son of a—*

Elliot sighs, slumping low. "I'm sorry! Being Switzerland is hard, okay?"

Levi drops into the seat beside me. He grins, eyes twinkling. "Hey, Red."

"Don't call me that."

"Eli calls you that."

"Elliot isn't the human equivalent of those parasites that eat fish tongues."

He looks vaguely repulsed. "That was . . . specific."

I cross my arms and slide farther into the booth. He smells like

71

expensive soap, and I'm a sweaty mess with chocolate milkshake crust drying in the corner of my mouth. "What do you want, Levi?"

"Look, I'm sorry, okay? You've been avoiding me all week, and I knew you wouldn't talk to me unless Elliot helped."

"*Betrayed*," I correct. "If I saw off my own arm, will you let me out of the booth?"

"Jesus, Brodie." He stands, switching seats so he's not blocking me in. I hide my surprise—I was joking, mostly. He might be a swamp demon, but he does have a soul in there, somewhere.

I glare at him. "You have five minutes before I sage the booth and you get banished to the underworld."

Elliot coughs into his hand, concealing a low snicker.

Levi gives him an unappreciative side eye. "I forgot how you two were, together. . . ." He just shakes his head. "Look, R—Brodie. You didn't take the Adder Stone, right?"

"Was that seriously a question? Four minutes."

"No, just—" Levi rakes a frustrated hand through his hair, recalibrating. "You didn't take the Adder Stone, full stop, end of sentence. But that means someone else *did*."

"Obviously."

"Don't you want to know *who*? Dad is still mega pissed; he's just waiting for you to screw up—"

"Because I just can't help myself? My screwing up is inevitable? Three minutes."

"*No.*" He takes a breath. God, he's so easy to rattle. I forgot how fun it was.

He splays his hands on the table, eyes searching mine. He's quiet

72

for a long minute, trying to find the right words. "Brodie, he's on the warpath. I think he's looking for any excuse to haul you into the station. Mum nearly lost her *job*. But maybe if we can prove you didn't do it . . ."

"Which we could, by the way, if you didn't delete the footage. And anyway, why do you care?"

He looks surprised, mouth dropping open, and I can see all his pretty white teeth in a neat row. Then he recovers. "It's—it's my fault," he says. "You're right, I shouldn't have messed with the evidence."

That *sounds* like a reasonable excuse, but something in his voice doesn't quite ring true. Then he swallows, eyes dropping, and fidgets with pieces of a torn-up napkin. For just a second, I consider his offer. It would make Nan happy, I think, to put a stop to the rumors that her only granddaughter had sticky fingers. Which is, actually, sort of true. Used to be. But I always went back and paid for the things I stole, because it wasn't the price tag that was appealing, it was the thrill of getting away with it—and anyway, this is beside the point because *I didn't take the stupid magical town stone.*

I glance at my watch. "Your five minutes are up. As illuminating as this was—"

"I'll split the reward with you," he blurts.

I pause, hands flat on the table, half rising out of the seat already. My eyes cut between Levi and Elliot. "The—what?"

"Reward," Levi says frowning. "You didn't know?"

Elliot and I look at each other, mirrored expressions of surprise and—fine, I'll admit it—intrigue.

I jut out my chin, trying not to let the shiver of excitement show. "What is it? Like, two hundred bucks and a bag of jelly beans?"

He smirks. "Twenty thousand."

"Dollars?!"

"No, twenty thousand geese and a nice pond to keep them happy. Yes, dollars."

That kind of money is . . . I don't think my family has ever had that much money, not all at once. I could do a lot with that kind of cash. Travel. Run up a tab at the arcade. Not think about next year and the inevitable decline of my fading youth as I avoid any and all adult responsibility. I could get Nan shoes that come from an *actual shoe shop*.

But I would have to split it with Levi. Give him the satisfaction of giving in. I hesitate, knees pushing me farther out of the booth.

Elliot senses my reluctance, because he reaches out a hand, nearly touching mine.

"Let him help," he says gently. "Brodes, you're eighteen in a couple months. The whole McKellon Felon thing was fun while it lasted, but what if something happens when you're legally an adult?"

"I'm not a moron, you know. I wasn't planning on turning to a life of crime."

"I know, but . . . I worry. About you," he whispers.

I close the gap between us and hold his hand. I try not to look at Levi, but it's like ignoring the sun: golden and bright, reaching into the shadows. I remember when I used to turn to him first, when I liked the feeling of sitting under his glow. And I know we won't get that back, but . . .

I glance up at Elliot. He's staring down at me, patient and waiting. We're splitting him in two, making him choose between us every day.

"Fine," I say grudgingly. "Truce. Help me find the Adder Stone, and I won't shove you into a pentagram as a blood sacrifice. And we split the reward, evenly."

"Oh, I don't want any part of this," Elliot says.

"Fine, sixty-forty." I'll just hide the money under his pillow anyway.

Levi grins. *Urgh.* "I was hoping you'd say that," he says, pulling out a notepad and flipping it open to the first page. He has a bunch of notes written down, and I'm annoyed to realize that it looks a lot like my new dead letter investigation, timeline and everything.

"So, November twenty-ninth was the night of the party. You arrived about an hour after it started, so let's say it was seven o'clock. We hid in the coatroom until speeches; that was around eight o'clock."

Elliot frowns. "You guys stayed for the speeches?"

Levi ignores him. "The security camera caught you in the display room at eight fifteen. Then what?"

I shuffle in my seat, reconsidering our truce. "I don't know; it was a long time ago. Do we really need to do this right now?"

"What, so you have time to change your mind?" He shakes his head. *"Please,* Brodie. Try to remember."

I roll my eyes, staying silent.

It doesn't deter him for long. "Fine. You said you went to Rydal after—how did you get there?"

"I walked."

He nods, encouraged. "Okay, so . . . that's usually a fifteen-minute walk."

"Emu on a skateboard," Elliot reminds him. I can't believe he weaseled that out of me last night. "Make it half an hour."

"Good point. So it was eight thirty." He taps his pen on the page. "Let's add some time for you to get through the dirt path. And then you went home?"

I nod. That's another twenty minutes. I can see the wheels turning in his mind—even if I'd doubled back for the Adder Stone, I wouldn't have made it in time. Not on foot, and I didn't have my bike that day because it was still in the back of Levi's car. I flush, wondering if he remembers that specific detail.

"Everybody left the hall around nine," he says. "And nobody noticed until morning that it was gone, but security locked the doors and no windows were broken, so it's unlikely anyone broke in."

Goddamn Levi. He's a half-decent detective when he tries. I look between them and the notebook, summarizing. "So . . . basically, between eight and nine, someone took it?"

Elliot sits up suddenly. "Hey, Red, which way did you walk back home?"

"Uh . . ." It was cold, I was trying not to cry, and I walked home on autopilot, not passing a single soul. I don't really remember anything—does *anyone* remember what they did three years ago? "I don't . . . maybe Compton? I didn't see anyone, though. No alibi."

Elliot shakes his head. "Not from the path. You would have had to double back to town."

"Oh. Sure, I guess." I drop my head into my hands. "All I remember is that my shoes were wet, and I was annoyed that my socks were all packed so I couldn't change them when I got home."

Elliot grins at me. "Walton Road," he says. "The drain always floods after it rains."

Holy shit. "You're right. I stepped in the gutter—it was dark; the streetlight doesn't work on that corner." The memory jolts into place. I was blowing my nose into my sleeve, not watching where I was going—the giddyness of the emu heist had worn off, and it was finally sinking in that I wouldn't see either of them for a long, long time. I stepped right into the overflow, up to my ankle.

Levi frowns. "Why does it matter which way she went home? Nobody saw her."

"Because, genius, the Motor Inn is on Walton Road."

"And?"

"Remember the year your dad found a meth lab in one of the rooms?"

He winces. It was a pretty big scandal for Warwick. "Yeah."

"The owners installed security. *Good* security."

"It's been three years. You think they still have it?"

Elliot shrugs. "Maybe. Sounded like a fancy system—Dale installed it. Reckons it was all wireless, routed back to a secure server. I remember because he complained all week about how it took so long to hook up."

"Is that . . . good? For us?"

"It means the server probably automatically clears the footage from a local computer and uploads it to the cloud. So they might not have the file saved on their desktop, but they could log in and download a specific date to check it. Same basic principle as photos on your phone."

Levi and I sit back at the same time. My eyes snag on his, and for a moment I'm not mad at him anymore. Just stunned. "Why didn't we think of this three years ago?" I murmur. They both give a glare, which I take to mean *because you didn't tell us about this three years ago.*

"I'll get Dad to look into it," Levi says, tucking his notebook back in his bag.

Elliot smiles, delighted. "See what happens when we're all friends?"

Smug little shit.

Levi rolls his eyes and tosses a sugar packet at him. Elliot just grins wider, showing his dimple that I once told him was adorable and he subsequently spent years trying to hide. "This is so nice," he says.

Levi and I look at each other. Maybe we could make this work.

Then he leans forward and puts a hand under his chin. "You coming to the party tomorrow? We can have a cannonball competition." He wiggles an eyebrow. "Loser wears an *I heart Levi* shirt."

And . . . truce over. I grab my bag off the seat, slinging it over my shoulder. "Nope. Bye, Elliot. See you later, Nosferatu—try not to combust in the sunlight." I pull a *I want to suck your blood* face for good measure, because I don't actually think Levi has seen the movie. (Why have I? A cracking case of insomnia and a grandmother with a penchant for the horror channel.)

I can hear someone chasing after me, and I pray for a few precious seconds that it's Elliot. I turn to unlock my bike—no such luck.

"You don't have to go," Levi says. "I'll leave, if you want."

"I have a shift at the post office." Which is true. I glance at my phone—I only have ten minutes to make it back and save Tommy from lockup. Last week, he thought sixty cents made a dollar and I had to recount the whole till.

"Brodie," he says, pleading. I stop, helmet in hands. "How long are you gonna stay mad at me?"

"Hmm. Going rate is three years. That seems fair, right?"

He chews on his lip, wanting to say more. I don't give him the chance. I just pull away, pedaling home. My phone dings in my pocket, but I don't have a chance to check it until later that night.

I am going far away to the land of robbers and ghosts!

Jerk.

He has seen the movie.

5

I have been thinking that we should have a picnic. We can meet in the woods—bring a blanket and flowers and a road map to somewhere better than this. We'll eat pastries and drink cold tea and when it gets dark we can get in your car and drive until we run out of gas. We could do it, couldn't we, August? Just for a while?

A weight lands on my chest. I crack an eyeball open, groaning. Mabel licks my cheek, unbothered by the rather rude awakening. I check my phone—I've slept in longer than I meant to, after I stayed up all night reading the dead letters again. Their words linger, like my own memories instead of imagined ones.

I trudge down to the kitchen, slumping on the counter. Nan is humming an old song, swaying as she tidies the countertop. She beams when she sees me, scowl on my face, Mabel on my shoulder.

"Good morning, my loves. What did you dream about?" she

asks, filling a cup with coffee and sliding it into my zombie hands.

Something that was never mine, I want to say.

"Picnics. Midnight." I rub my face, clinging to the edges of the dream. It's almost gone now. Winnie and August were there, their faces always in shadow. She laughed, and I chased the sound until their headlights disappeared over the Lancaster Bridge. Then I was in the Rydal Woods, all alone, the remains of a tea party scattered at my feet.

Nan frowns, stirring her cup. "I think we need the book for this one." She pulls her dream journal down from the stovetop—where most people would keep, say, cookbooks—and begins flipping through.

"A picnic, hmm? Seems fairly innocuous. 'Carefree,' it says." She eyes me suspiciously, in my brand-new black silky pajamas. I thought they were nice and plain. Nan thought they were *goth* and I had to explain that goths had sort of phased out in favor of emos, and then circled back around to grunge. It was a long conversation that eventuated in a YouTube presentation. "Are you feeling particularly carefree?" she asks, amused. "Or are you *emotional*?"

I don't think the videos helped. "Not especially carefree, no."

"School is good, though? Did you have all your books?"

"Yeah. It was good. Those girls I told you about are really nice; we've been having lunch together."

She seems pleased, turning back to her page. "Midnight. Oh, a sense of new beginnings—and uncertainty about what's to come." She arches an eyebrow at me, and I shrug. She's been pestering me

81

about *what I want to do* next year. Truth is, I have no idea. I don't want to stay in Warwick forever, but I can't picture myself at university either.

"If you ask me about applications before I finish this cup of coffee, I'm going to ask Tommy if I can join his band as a professional triangle player."

"They're called percussionists, darling." She stands, dropping a kiss on my head. "Any plans tonight?"

I hesitate. "Uh . . . I mean, Elliot invited me to a thing, but I don't know if I want to go."

"And what are you going to do instead? Hang around here with your old nan? When I was your age, I had two boyfriends and didn't come home till sunrise." She pauses, pressing her lips together. "*You* have a curfew, though, of course."

"Of course."

Pause.

Her brows draw close. She's drawn them in blue today. "What time do you think it should be?"

"You're asking me to set my own curfew?"

"One o'clock? No, that's too late. Isn't it? Ah!" She snaps her fingers, struck by inspiration. "Midnight. New beginnings. Fitting, no?" The weather vane groans, the sound echoing through the halls. Nan grins. "There, the attic ghost agrees. It's settled."

The groan eases into a slight fluttering, the iron rooster spinning on its axis. "I think that means a storm is coming, Nan. But sure. Home by midnight. *If* I go."

"*When* you go."

"You know, most grandmothers would be delighted to have children who were so well behaved."

"Ha! Most granddaughters have never stolen a car."

I grimace but am saved from having to answer as the doorbell to the post office sounds, and she hustles out of the kitchen. I can hear the faint sound of people chatting, Nan laughing along with whatever they're saying. I go back to my room, trying to tidy the letters. I sort them back in order, hesitating over the ones I'd been reading just before I fell asleep.

Dear August,
Let's stay in Treegap forever. We'll never grow old, and
we'll never get real jobs, and we can travel the world as long as
we want—until we get tired, and come home, and everything
will be the same. How does that sound?

Dear Winnie,
It sounds like a wonderful lie. Tell me another.

Just one question, I want to write back. *Where the fuck is Treegap?*
I'm grouchy as I shower and get dressed, then spend a few hours on shift in the post office. It's quiet on Saturdays, mostly just people coming to pick up parcels they missed during the week. I unpack boxes and stuff the shelves with greeting cards. We should do inventory soon—Tommy's mixed everything up, and he's ordered Father's Day cards instead of Mother's Day cards, even though it's months away. I find myself staring down at a World's Best Dad

83

card, decorated with little cartoons of stereotypical "dad" objects: a wrench and tie. Barbecue tongs. A fancy car and some golf balls. I don't think my dad likes any of this stuff. I realize suddenly that I don't really know *what* he likes. On the few occasions our schedules aligned, he would just come home from work and watch TV. That's what normal people do, right? He was so quiet the rest of the time, though, I never knew if he actually enjoyed anything. Did he like cooking, or did he do it just so we wouldn't starve? Did he like listening to music, or was it just his job? I crumple the card, annoyed, and decide to close up ten minutes early, before I can destroy anything else.

I yell goodbye up the stairs, though Nan is reading tarot on the balcony and doesn't hear, and head down to Elliot's house. The weather vane groans, and I eye the dark clouds on the horizon with caution. Maybe the party will get washed out and save me from having to decide. Still, I hurry down the road, in case the storm rolls in early.

Elliot's house looks the same as when I left: weeds growing in the driveway, fly screen peeling away from the doorframe. There's glue in one corner, like someone tried to fix it and gave up. I raise my fist and give a gentle rap, and the door is immediately flung open. Quinn throws her arms around my shoulders, pulling me close. "Look at you!" she coos. "Look how beautiful you are! Oh goodness, come in, come in."

Inside, the house is warm and cozy, lovingly curated with personal touches. The old couches look a bit worse for wear, sagging in the middle and fabric faded from the sun, but they're decorated with bright pillows, and there's a little vase of flowers on the kitchen table. There was already a plate of choc-chip cookies on the counter, and Elliot is leaning against the cabinets waiting for the kettle to boil. He'd probably seen me coming through the window.

Quinn pulls a chair out for me and looks at Elliot. "You never told me how grown-up she is now! This face—god, you look like your mum." Her hand rests on my cheek for a moment. There are wrinkles that didn't used to be there, I realize. Fine little lines around her lips and eyelids, though it doesn't make her any less beautiful. Her hair is shorter, too, a little blonde bob that curls at the ends, and her skin looks warm and tan. There are freckles on her nose. She looks . . . happier. She fusses over me for another moment, until Elliot blushes a little. "Mum, it's just Brodie."

"Just Brodie—the manners of this boy. Who raised you?" she asks, then pinches his cheek good-naturedly. She helps him pull out a set of mismatched mugs and makes me a cup of tea the way I used to like it when I was younger—two sugars, lots of milk. I don't correct her.

"Goodness, we missed you," she says. "Hasn't been nearly as fun without you." Then she winks, laughing. Quinn was the only one who used to find my antics funny. *She'll grow out of it,* she'd tell Dad. *Let her be wild a while longer.*

"Happy to be home. I missed Nan too."

"Cause any trouble while you were gone?"

Elliot smirks. I ignore him. "Um, a little."

Quinn smiles wider. "Break any hearts?"

"None that I know of."

85

"Ah, bet it won't be long before you do." She looks over at Elliot, ruffling his dark curls. "And what do you know of my boy here? He doesn't tell me anything these days."

He turns beet red, and his eyes cut to mine, a million threats hanging in those dark irises. I smile sweetly at him. "Nothing much," I say. "Yet."

She sighs, wrapping her fingers around her mug. "All right, all right. I'll stop prying. Tell me more about school—did you make lots of new friends at Rowley?"

"Oh. Um. I mean, people were nice, I guess. Not really super close with anyone, though. . . ."

She senses a sore topic and switches tack. "And how's your dad?"

I flinch. "I'm not . . . he's fine, I think. New job. Interstate."

Quinn works hard to keep the pity off her face. "Well. I'm glad we get you all to ourselves for a while."

Elliot mouths *Sorry* at me across the table and slides over a plate of cookies. I shove a whole one in my mouth, appreciating the few silent minutes it buys us. He fills the gap by talking about the football games coming up, and Quinn says she'll have to go sometime after work.

"I heard you got a new job," I say, swooping in on a safe topic.

"Oh! Yes! It's only a silly little thing, at the library. Anyone could do it, really."

"It's great, Mum." Elliot smiles at her, nodding encouragingly. "Tell Brodie about it. She loves snooping."

Quinn laughs. "I wouldn't call it snooping! It's just a collections job, archiving materials and that sort of thing. They got a grant to do some preservation work—old newspapers, artwork, donations, that sort of thing. I just scan it all in, mostly, but there might be an exhibit next year." I watch as her face morphs, filling with pride as she describes the work. Maybe she thinks it's silly, but I can tell she loves it. She's met some really nice women, she tells me, and they like to get coffee after each shift. I don't remember Quinn ever having her own friends. For some reason, the thought makes me happy.

"That actually sounds really amazing," I say, and it's true. I used to love the library—Mum would take me after school. I stopped going eventually, both because it lost a bit of its magic after she died and because it was uncomfortably close to the police station. Just for a second, an old thought raises its ugly head. I wish Mum was the one who lived. I push it away immediately, my stomach dropping with an awful, anxious feeling. Like maybe I'd cursed Dad just by thinking it.

Elliot's phone buzzes, and he glances down at it guiltily. "I'm gonna head off soon. You coming, Red?"

I just shake my head no, and Quinn squeezes my hand. She waits until Elliot gets up, disappearing to his room to grab a jacket.

"Is everything all right?" she says quietly. "Want to stay for a while? I can paint your nails, like we used to?"

I sigh, looking at Elliot's half-closed door. "It's just . . . I don't know. I thought it would be harder than this. Rowley kinda sucked. And then I came back, and I thought Elliot would have moved on and forgotten me, but he didn't. I thought Nan would be annoyed, and she wasn't. I thought school would be awkward, but it's not. I just keep . . . I don't know, waiting for the other shoe to drop. Like, what's the catch? I feel like I'm tempting fate."

"Is there always a catch?"

"Isn't there?" Mum. Dad. Levi. Rowley. It feels like the world's worst game of bingo. One more catastrophe and I win.

Quinn takes both my hands for a moment and holds on tight. "Sometimes, my love, life just gives. And it doesn't happen often, so I suggest you take it and run." She gives a squeeze, then releases me and starts picking up the dishes. I help her clear the table, but she waves me away from the sink, taking the crumb-filled plate from my hands. "Go have fun, Brodie. You deserve it. Plus, I want some gossip about that nice young man my son seems to spend all his time with."

I turn around and find Elliot leaning against the counter, a denim jacket thrown over one shoulder. His ears are turning pink, and he very studiously ignores his mum. "Come on," he says. "If the party sucks we can ditch. I'll even let you steal a car on the way home."

Quinn lets out a gurgling sound, trying to quash a laugh.

"Fine," I say. "For one hour. One. And his name is Isaac."

It's late afternoon by the time we arrive at the lake, the sun glowing pink on the horizon. The shore has been set up with streamers and a low-burning fire, and most of the football team seems to be holding court around a cooler full of soft drinks and snacks. A few people are in the water, swimming out to the floats and diving off.

Elliot puts his elbow on my head, surveying the crowd below and lazing happily until I shove him off. "Did you eat magic beans while I was gone?" I say. "Remember when I could fit you under my chin?"

He laughs, and with an easy swoop, picks me up and tucks me under his arm. One arm. He's not even using two to carry me. "Show-off," I mutter. Lucky nobody seems overly bothered by the scene, since they're just as busy creating their own fun; it's a raucous mix of voices and squeals, music blaring from competing speakers, and one token dude with a guitar. People are laughing and singing, unbound from their slightly more reserved school selves. Elliot heads over to the fire, cutting through the melee, and only puts me down when Isaac waves, grinning as he watches us approach.

"You came!" he says. "Both of you!"

I glance around the blue sports jackets, searching for a neat blond head. Elliot nudges me, reading my thoughts. "Levi's not here yet."

"Obviously. The sun's still up."

Isaac gives me a quizzical look and gestures to a few empty beach chairs. He flops down into one with bright pink flamingos and sticks a drink umbrella in his hair. "So you and Levi. Do I want to know what happened between you guys, or . . . ?"

Elliot rolls his eyes. "Long story. There's a magic stone. And she stole an emu. It was a whole thing."

The CliffsNotes version *does* sound kind of stupid when it's condensed like that. They pull their chairs in close, facing the water. I watch as someone backflips off the float and nearly smacks their head on the wooden platform. They burst through the surface of the water, laughing. "O . . . kay," Isaac says. "Won't ask. Eli, you want a drink?"

I'm such a third wheel.

It doesn't seem to bother either of them, though, and I like the way Isaac always turns to face Elliot, his whole body angled toward him, head bent low, never missing a word. But they don't hold hands, or whisper too quietly, and I wonder again what's going on between them. Enough that Quinn knows him, at least. Not enough that they're into PDAs. Interesting.

They slip into conversations about people I don't know and drama I can't follow. The sun is warm on my face and bare legs, so for a while I just close my eyes and listen to them talk. It's comforting, like the low hum of a television show you've seen before, playing in the background. Eventually, Elliot nudges me with his foot, drawing me back to them. We talk about growing up, and the post office, and my obsession with telescopes. Isaac tells me how he and Elliot finally became friends—years of being in the same classes, finally thrown together in a mock-match during PE. Apparently, Elliot had just gone through his first growth spurt and accidentally threw Isaac over his shoulder midtackle. The football coach saw and begged him to join the team.

We keep watching the swimmers as the sun goes down, bobbing in golden waves. By the time the sky finally turns blue and the lake empties out, I realize it's been much longer than an hour since we arrived and I have no desire to leave. It does get cold, though, and I wish I'd worn something more than denim shorts and a light shirt. Isaac notices me shiver and shucks his sweatshirt.

"Here," he says. "It's fleecy." Elliot's arm is halfway out of his own denim jacket, but he shrugs it back on when I accept.

"Are you sure?" I look around. There're a few girls wearing guys' jackets. I'm not really clear on the acceptable time frame for borrowing clothes from not-really-strangers-but-not-really-friends, but I'm pretty sure I'm too cold to care no matter what the answer is,

Isaac just shrugs. "Yeah, no worries. I'm too hot anyway."

I catch Elliot as his mouth drops open, about to say something that I'm sure would be entertaining, but he sees me watching with a half-cocked eyebrow and swallows whatever reply he had ready.

"Brodie!" a high, cheery voice calls out, and it takes me a moment to realize someone has called my name. I turn to see Emiko bounding along the shore, shoes dangling from her fingertips. "Hey!" she says, waving. "I didn't think I'd see you here!"

Emiko plunks on the ground at my feet, smiling up at Elliot. "And you too! Thank god. I came with Claire but she's snuck off into the bushes to make out with Jenn, and I don't know anyone else."

I pull a face, glancing around at the shrubbery. "I'm fairly certain these bushes are the itchy-rash kind."

Emiko snorts, nose wrinkling, and blows a few strands of loose black hair out of her face. "So, you survived the first week back. How does it feel? Is it weird, or is it all sort of the same?"

"No, it's definitely different," I say. "But not . . . not bad different. I think." I'm not sure if I say that because it's true, or so Emiko doesn't feel bad for me. But when Elliot smiles at me, and Isaac whispers something that makes him laugh, and Emi jumps because something touched her foot in the dark, it starts to feel like it's true.

We talk for a while about nothing in particular, until Isaac rises from his chair. "Hey, I'm gonna go grab some more drinks from the car," he says. "Elliot, do you wanna help? There's a couple boxes."

Elliot leaps up entirely too fast. "You all right for a few minutes, Red?"

I roll my eyes at him, shooing him away. Emi takes his vacated seat, hand slipping into her backpack. "I'm starving," she says. "Let's eat these before the boys get back and we won't have to share." She divides some tiny squares of chocolate between us, most of them adorned with Japanese script, laughing as I bite into the mystery flavors. It's nice to have something else to focus on, something to keep my hands busy, and I listen as she chats happily for a while about her family and the summers she'd spent in Kyoto.

"Do you still visit?"

"Not as much since my grandparents died. But maybe after school ends. It'd be cool to stay for a while—my aunt said I could crash with her." She shoves a chocolate into her mouth and arches a brow. "You?"

"What? Family or travel? Neither, really." I laugh but feel the familiar pang.

"Elliot sort of mentioned. About your mum. Sorry."

I shrug, never having quite figured out what to say in response. But Emiko doesn't dwell or expect some profound observation of grief.

"He also called you Red. What's the story there?"

I groan. "Old name. It's silly."

We sit with our legs crossed, opening the packets one by one, building a tiny tower with the leftover wrappers. Slowly, she pries out the meaning of the old nickname and its origins, laughing particularly hard as I recount the time I was caught freezing a batch of mashed potato to serve as ice cream.

"So the McKellon Felon is actually just a wild child with a bad rep?"

"I guess 'McKellon Misdemeanor' didn't have the same ring to it."

"This is honestly quite upsetting. I thought you were some sort of criminal mastermind."

"No, not really. Just criminally bored, most of the time."

Emiko taps my hand, trading something pink for my last caramel.

"So, they've been gone a while," she says. She doesn't expect an answer, and I don't give one. But she looks up and winks, before turning away. I check the time on my phone, surprised that it's gotten so late.

"Oh. They have been." I frown, wondering if they were just sitting in Isaac's car or if they'd gone for a walk into the woods. "Maybe the Rydal Devil got them."

"Nah," she says. "They always do this."

"Always?"

She snorts, and I find myself pleased to think that Elliot had someone around like her, when I was gone. Kind, quick to laugh. Someone who knew when to let him brood and when to push.

"They dated for a while, last year," she says. "I'm not sure about the rest."

I think she's probably more sure than she's letting on, but I appreciate the tact.

Just as I start to look around in the shadows, searching the surrounding faces for any sign of him, two figures emerge from the woods, giggling. I feel a flicker of relief for a moment, only to realize it's Claire and another girl I don't know.

"Finally," Emiko grumbles. "Claire! Over here!"

Claire's hair is mussed up and her red lipstick is smudged around her mouth, but she still beams happily and keeps her hand wrapped around the other girl's.

"Hey! Oh my god, we got *so* lost," Claire says, taking one of the seats. "Brodie! Hi! This is Jenn."

Jenn waves at me, a little meek and shy. "I think you're in my history class?"

I nod, but honestly, I don't remember much from history except frantically scribbling down timelines and trying to remember all the different Louies.

Emiko elbows Claire in the ribs. "Dude, seriously. Where did you *go?*"

"We were just in the clearing! But the river had flooded, and Jenn didn't want to get her shoes wet so we tried to come back another way. Did you know all trees look the same in the dark?"

"I am so gonna miss curfew," Jenn groans. "My mum is gonna kill me. She's been on a rampage since last time."

Emiko sighs, looking at me apologetically. "Sorry, I think we gotta bounce. Are you going to be okay? We can wait for Eli."

There's so many people around, I feel comfortably invisible in my protected corner. "Go, it's fine. I'll text him to come back."

They wave goodbye, hurrying toward the parking lot. I tuck my legs up to my chest, wondering if I should just bike home and let Elliot have fun. I'd texted Nan a while ago to say I'd be staying later, and she replied with a moon emoji. I wonder if she'll be disappointed when I arrive home with almost two hours to spare before curfew.

I decide to give him ten more minutes and sink farther into Isaac's sweatshirt, glad for the extra warmth. I pull out my phone and play a few levels of Candy Crush, cheeks warming as I realize how I must look to other people. Elliot's ten minutes are nearly up when a thundercloud rumbles in the distance—the storm must have rolled in, down Lancaster way. Maybe that's why the river had already flooded in the clearing. A few people hear it too and look up, waiting for a lightning strike. When none comes, they shrug and continue what they were doing.

I look down at my phone again. As if reading my mind, a text comes through from Elliot—Sorry Red, won't be long. Leave me if it rains.

"You look lonely," says a voice behind me. I glance up and find Levi standing beside me, grinning under his golden hair, teeth flashing.

"Oh, look: night falls and he emerges."

He shoves his hands into his pockets, eyeing the empty seats beside me. "You want company?"

I shrug, determined to ignore him either way. "Just try not to squash your demon tail."

He folds into the nearest seat, eyes narrowing as he looks at me, curled into my own chair. He opens his mouth, then closes it again, clearly bothered by something.

"What?" I demand, suddenly self-conscious about the way he's looking at me. Is there something in my hair? On my face? Did I squash Emiko's chocolate into my two front teeth?

"Nothing." He adjusts his shoulders. But he keeps looking at me.

"What?"

He looks dazed for a moment, like he's in some faraway place. Then he shakes his head. "Nothing. So where's Elliot?"

I roll my eyes. "He went to get more drinks."

"With Isaac?"

"Maybe."

He goes quiet for a minute. A few guys see him and call out, waving. He acknowledges them with that head tilt guys do but doesn't leave. I wish he would. Being alone with him is just so . . . awkward. What do I do with my hands? How did we spend so many hours together, all those years ago? Can I look at him, or should I just keep my eyes on my phone?

I look. I can't help it.

He's wearing his football jacket, and a knit sweater underneath. His hair isn't so neat tonight; it sticks up in uneven clumps, which somehow looks stylish instead of disheveled. Like someone's run their hands through it.

"Brodie?"

"Huh?"

He's asked me a question. He's waiting for me to answer.

"Sorry, I looked into your eyes too long and turned to stone. What did you say?"

"I said, my dad's looking into the security footage at the Motor Inn."

"Oh. Well. Thanks. Are you sure . . ." I hesitate. This not-quite-truce seems so fragile.

"What?"

"Do we . . . trust him? I mean, he doesn't like me very much. What if the footage just goes *missing* all of a sudden?"

"He wouldn't do that." He's not angry. But his words are halting, like maybe he hadn't considered this possibility before. "He wouldn't. Because if you didn't take it, then someone else did. He'd want to know the truth, either way." His voice grows more confident with each word, convincing himself as much as me.

"Okay. Well . . . thanks, I guess."

It goes quiet again. The silence is suffocating, doubly so in the midst of so much life. Beside us, a group of girls are teaching their boyfriends a dance they saw online, laughing as they attempt to mimic their moves. Some people are wading in the lake, ankle-deep, tossing a ball. There's music. People talking.

Then there's us.

"I think I should go," I say quietly. "Tell Eli I said bye, wherever he is."

"He's probably in the clearing. We can go get him, if you want."

"I don't need an escort."

"It's late. How are you getting home?"

"We rode."

He stands, holding out a hand to help me up. "Yeah, not happening. Come on."

I groan, totally indignant. "I'll be *fine*. Pretty sure you're the only stalker here anyway."

"Either you and Elliot ride home together or I drive you. Pick."

I decide to circumvent his ultimatum by texting Elliot an SOS message—except when I glance down at my phone again, the screen is dead. Levi notices it and looks at me like *See? This is how horror movies start.*

I ignore his hand, crossing my arms instead, hiding in the folds of Isaac's enormous sweatshirt—it drops nearly down to my knees, now that I'm standing.

"Didn't you just get here?" I ask, stomping my way through the crowd. I wish he'd leave—I've run through these woods a million times. And sure, usually not alone at night, but it's not like anything is actually going to happen. It's Warwick. *Nothing* ever happens.

He shrugs. "It's going to rain anyway."

Fine. Levi's determined to come with me; that doesn't mean I have to talk to him.

I lead us away from the warmth and noise of the shore, swinging my legs over the wooden fence that surrounds the picnic area, and head down the quiet woodland trail. There's no lights here, and without the flashlight from my phone, I only have the moonlight to see. I can hear Levi behind me, his quiet breath and the slight crunch of gravel under his shoes.

Something rustles in the trees and my spine tingles. I'm tempted for a moment to turn around and make sure Levi is following, but I can't stand to see the look of satisfaction that's surely written on his face.

So I keep stomping. Loudly. In theory, all the things that go *bump* in the night are more scared of me than I am of them. I keep my eyes on the ground just in case, watching for rabbit holes. Peter

Pattison accidentally put his foot in one, during a forever-ago summer. Unfortunately for Peter, the original fuzzy inhabitants of the rabbit hole were long gone, replaced by a supremely pissed-off snake that clamped on to his ankle and wouldn't let go.

I turn past the bend in the path, splitting to the left. It's totally silent out here—the noise from the shorefront has been swallowed by the branches of fir trees, captured in their own little bubble.

Levi's footsteps pick up, jogging closer.

"Hey, Brodie?"

"What?"

It's easier not to look at him in the dark. He's just a shadow figure beside me, nothing but a dark outline and white puffs of breath. "The dead letters . . . do you still have them?"

"Obviously."

"Do you think . . ."

He stops, suddenly realizing we've reached the fence that leads to the river and through the clearing. I don't find out what he thinks, because we pause to duck under branches, and I'm trying not to cringe away from the gossamer cobwebs.

"Urgh!" I squeal, stepping in inches of ice-cold water.

His hands wrap around my arm, steadying me in the dark. "What? What happened?"

"It's flooded," I mutter. "Jenn said it was, but I thought she was just fussy."

He sighs, resigning himself to the same fate. "Here, hold on." He steps into the river, keeping a hand on my arm to stop me from slipping.

"This was a bad idea," I say. "We should just turn around."

Thunder cracks overhead, closer than before.

"*Really* bad idea," I repeat. We look at each other, deliberating. Neither of us is dumb enough to get stuck in the woods during a storm. But . . .

"Elliot's out here," he says. "Let's grab him and go; I'll drive you both out." He checks his own phone and swears. No service. "And let's be quick. Anyone know you're out here?"

"No. You?"

His mouth turns down, and he shakes his head.

"The chances of getting struck by lightning are pretty small, right?" I ask, hurrying after him. He's taken the lead now, long legs moving faster than I can keep up, and I have to jog to keep pace. Even so, I don't ask him to slow down, and neither of us is worried about branches and cobwebs anymore—we're bashing through the dark without grace, trying to outrun the storm. "Plus, you're taller than me, so I'm probably going to be fine."

"Great. Happy to be a lightning rod. You gonna forgive me if I get hit?"

"Maybe. If you live."

He snorts. "I'll do my best."

Thunder cracks again. We're near enough that I start calling their names. "Elliot! Isaac!"

No one answers. Levi calls out, voice louder and deeper than mine. It echoes back in the dark. We finally crash through the tree line and look around the empty clearing. We both swear, turning in circles.

"He was *here*," Levi says, squinting.

"Are you sure? How do you know?"

"Because I was here too. He sent me to go check on you—and *no*," he says, cutting me off, "we don't have time to argue about that right now."

Thunder cracks, and this time, lightning follows. At the next rumble I hold my breath, counting. "How long did you have?" I ask.

"Five seconds. You?"

"Same."

"We're stuck," I say, looking around. The storm is less than one kilometer away—maybe in daylight we'd make it back to the car, but now, in the dark, through the flooded river, we'd be risking getting caught on the open trail—or worse, in the water. "It's pretty dense in here; we should be fine."

Levi looks up, weary. "Could be better. Come on."

He grabs my hand, tugging me back under the tree line. He turns away from the river, heading north, deeper into the forest. "I don't like this," he murmurs, eyes on the treetops. His hand is warm in mine, fingers laced through my own, and in an unspoken agreement, I have my eyes on the ground below to make sure he doesn't fall, while he searches for the thickest covering above.

We've never been this way before, and my heart pounds, nervous that we won't find our way back. But I guess we don't have a choice, and we haven't gone far from the clearing. I realize that he's also leading us farther away from the lake, and hope the kids left behind had the sense to get away from an open body of water.

I used to laugh when Mum would tell me all this, on our walks as a kid. *If you ever get stuck,* she'd say . . .

I once asked who would be dumb enough to be out in the woods during a storm. Guess now I know the answer. As if sensing the direction of my thoughts, the sky opens and rain starts bucketing down.

We move faster, braced for the next thunderclap that's sure to be right above us.

"Hey, Levi," I say, squinting ahead. "What's that?"

I'm looking ahead in the dark, and for a moment my heart races with the thought that I'm staring at a hunched-over person, hiding in the shadows. But I blink and realize the outline is too square, too solid.

Water is soaking my hair, dripping down my spine. It's sheeting down in thick slabs, and the air itself seems to turn gray. The shelter must be a ranger's checkpoint, I realize; too small to be a cabin, too big to be a storage box. "Come on!" I yell, pulling him behind me. He relents, and suddenly we find ourselves looking at a kid's playhouse.

"This is so fucking creepy," he says. "I'm not going in there."

"You're such a baby. What, you think it's haunted?"

"You *don't?*"

I eye the miniature house suspiciously. It's wood, and I can't see much except that the panels look old and splintered. I kick a half-covered doormat in the mud. "I don't think anyone's been here in a while."

He looks around, swearing. We're running out of time and options. A lightning strike flashes, and suddenly, the forest is cast in bright white light.

"What about spiders?"

"Seriously, Levi? What about *lightning*?" I was hoping he wouldn't mention spiders. I'm trying not to think about them, and I cringe away as a wet piece of hair drips down my neck.

More lightning. This time, the sound of it striking the ground is loud and close, my ears ringing with the echo. Levi wrenches the door open and shoves me forward. He dives in behind me, slamming the door shut.

It's suddenly quiet, the thin wooden walls insulated against the worst of the downpour. Our breaths come out quick and ragged, and we seem frozen, waiting for something to crawl out of the corners. Levi fumbles in his pockets for something, and there's a quiet *click-clack*, then a tiny flicker of light. He waves it around the small space, shoulders tense until it's clear we're alone. We don't look up. I'm pretty sure none of the spiders around here are the bitey-lethal kind. Like, ninety-percent sure.

My teeth chatter. Out of the rain, panic slowly slipping away, I realize how cold I am. Still, my eyes narrow on his lighter.

"You *smoke*?"

He pulls a face. "What? No. It's for the campfire. Someone always forgets."

"Good," I grumble.

The storm rattles the branches above, and they scrape loudly across the roof of the shelter. I peer around, looking for clues. "Who do you think built this?" I whisper. Our voices have been hushed since we got inside, like we're observing some kind of reverence.

"I don't know. Not little kids—this stuff would have been heavy. Maybe it's really old."

I hold up an abandoned Game Boy—the kind with a mono-color screen and two buttons. "Yeah, it's not *that* old."

There's not much else in here. A faded sleeping bag and a pillow, both dusty and smelling of mildew. A wicker basket. A book, the cover flaking and yellow.

"Do you think someone lived here?" I whisper.

Levi shifts closer, instinctively moving away from the corners. "I don't know. I don't think so. Maybe they just liked to camp out here." I guess he's right—there's no way to cook, nothing to heat food or draw water. It would be a pretty miserable experience, especially in the pitch-dark night.

I shiver and he edges closer again. "Do you think Elliot's okay?"

"Isaac drove. They'll be fine." *Unless they're looking for us.* He doesn't say it, but it's obvious we both think it.

I groan, dropping my head into my hands. The top of my head brushes his chest, and I feel him inhale. "I should have left earlier," I mumble. "With the others." And then none of this would have happened. I could have texted Elliot goodbye, and the boys would all have gone home, and I would have made it back before the rain. I'd be in my new pajamas, Mabel on my feet, warm in bed.

The lighter flickers out, either because he let it or it ran out of fluid. Either way, it's dark again, and the already-cramped space suddenly feels much smaller. He clears his throat.

"So . . . that's a nice sweatshirt."

"Uh, thanks."

"Football team?"

Has the dark scrambled my brain or does he sound . . . jealous? But no, that's impossible. Levi's heart is made of steel and screws: tough, impenetrable, definitely not beating for me.

"Uh-huh."

"Please tell me it's not Ryan's."

"Considering I just watched him handstand on a keg and projectile vomit, no it's not."

He sighs, obviously relieved. "Just . . ."

"If you tell me to be careful, I will smack you back into the eighteenth century where you belong."

Quiet. Then, "Okay."

"Okay?"

"What do you want me to say?"

"I want you to say, 'Hey, Brodie, I just remembered I have a magic flying car coming to get us and it's stuffed full of dry clothes, and also, I have never seen one single spider in these woods, so don't worry.'"

"Hey, Brodie?"

"*What?*"

"It's going to be fine."

Thunder cracks, and I lean forward, not realizing what I'm doing until I'm inches away from Levi. This is stupid. It's just a bit of rain. And a little dark. And . . . a mystery cabin in the woods that was definitely occupied at some point in time. I take another step forward. We're running out of space, and Levi somehow ends up with his arms around my shoulders. It's not a hug. We're just . . . simultaneously leaning in close proximity. I tell myself it's because there's only a small amount of space where we can stand without our heads hitting the ceiling—the roof is peaked and just barely tall enough that Levi can stand without having to stoop.

"How long do you think this will last?"

He breathes out. I'm so close I can feel his ribs expanding, smell the lemonade on his breath. "I don't know. An hour, maybe? It wasn't even meant to rain tonight."

"Yes it was."

He laughs, the sound unexpected. "Your weather rooster?"

"He's never wrong," I say defensively. "And it's called a weather vane."

"I thought they were just supposed to tell which way the wind was blowing?"

"Well, I don't know what to tell you. He only makes a noise when it's going to storm. Nan says the attic ghost spins him."

We've had this argument before, when we were kids. When the rooster fluttered on his pole, groaning in the wind, Nan would make us pack raincoats and umbrellas—even when there wasn't a cloud in the sky.

The storm carries on, wind howling. Our shoes squelch on the ground, and water drips off our clothes. I shiver again.

"Cold?"

"No."

He sighs. "Do you always have to argue with me?"

"I wasn't arguing. I was disagreeing. It's entirely different."

"God, I just—" He shakes his head. His chin brushes my hair.

"Just *what*? You're in such a weird mood tonight."

"I just . . . really hate that sweatshirt," he mutters.

"You have one *exactly the same.*"

He doesn't answer. I look down at our feet. It looks like we're dancing, from this angle. We did dance, once. The night I left. Elliot had gone to hunt for food, leaving us alone in the coatroom. A slow song came on the speakers, and Levi was so nervous when he asked me to dance that his voice broke twice. Neither of us knew what we were doing, so we just stood together and shuffled, a lot like this.

"Red?"

"Yeah?"

"Do you wish we hadn't done it?" he whispers. His fingers catch the back of my sweatshirt, and I can see his throat bob in the dark.

I know what he means, though I never let myself think about it. Redacted from my own memory. "No," I breathe. The word barely makes a noise, and I wonder if he even hears me. I can hardly hear myself above the blood rushing in my ears.

"No, you don't?" he whispers. "Or no, you do?"

"No, I don't *know*. Do we have to talk about this now?"

His hands have traveled up my back. It takes me a moment to realize mine are on his shoulders. He doesn't say anything. He just stands very, very still, like he's trying not to remind me how close we're standing.

Wind rattles the wooden planks, and the rain comes down so hard it sounds like the roof might cave in.

"No, I don't regret it," I whisper.

He pulls back a fraction of an inch. I dig my fingers into his shoulders, so he's forced to stay there. "I thought maybe . . . you were so mad . . ."

I look down. I can't lie to him while I look at him. "It was just a kiss, Levi. It didn't mean anything."

My stomach somersaults at the memory. The day before I left, I'd gone riding in the forest, to say goodbye to Rydal. My bike tire went flat so I had called him to come get me, and instead of going home we just drove. He was too young, then, to have his license, but he already had the car and his mum was the mayor and his dad was a cop, so who was going to stop us?

We could do it, couldn't we? he asked. *Drive until we run out of gas.* Something Winnie said in one of the letters, a shared joke. But I didn't laugh—I nodded, and instead of taking me home, he drove over the bridge, past Rydal, out of the valley, and kept going. We didn't stop until we hit Lancaster, and realized if we went any farther we'd get in real trouble.

It didn't matter anyway—no matter how far we ran, I'd still be gone in the morning. He turned around, back to the woods, then we climbed into his car trunk to watch the sunset. It was cold, so he got out a blanket and tucked us under, his arm resting over my shoulders. We were huddled together like that when he turned and said *Brodie*, like it was a question and he didn't know the answer—and I didn't either. I hesitated a moment too long, trying not to think about the way his shoulder brushing against mine made my stomach flip, not sure if I'd imagined the way he seemed to keep finding excuses for our hands to touch. He just cleared his throat after that and asked if I was ready to go home, and I wanted to say *no*, wanted to take back the few seconds and turn around when he first said my name. I thought about it all the way home, and when he pulled up to the post office, I leaned across and kissed him. It was too quick and awkward, and neither of us knew where to put our hands but I didn't care. It was Levi, and it felt right. He tasted like strawberry gum, I remembered.

He kissed me again that night, in the coatroom, and I'd cried as he tried to catch the tears with his lips. He promised he would write to me, that he would visit on holidays and call me every weekend, and it wouldn't change anything.

And then the Adder Stone went missing, and it all went to hell.

My voice cracks. I hope he doesn't notice. But I have to know, and I won't ever have the courage to ask again outside of this strange little cabin. "Do you?"

He must. It was stupid. We were just kids. It was just a kiss. Two kisses, fine. He thought I'd kissed him then stolen the stone. I guess now it makes more sense that we were both so angry.

"I—"

I shush him, eyes glancing up at the roof. "Do you hear that?"

"No?"

I drop my hands, eager to put space between us. "It stopped raining."

His eyes flutter closed, and he takes a deep breath. I suddenly want to claw the last five seconds back—I want to redo this moment and stay quiet long enough for him to tell me. Even now, I want to stamp my foot and demand an answer—*do you regret kissing me or not?*

Maybe it doesn't matter anymore. Too much has happened.

With a sinking heart, I back away, fumbling for the door handle. Cold air hits me in the face and I gulp it down like a lifeline. I turn to face him, emerging from the cabin, question on my lips. Ready to throw a grenade on our whole friendship.

And then I stop.

In the moonlight, I can see a sign nailed above the door, carved roughly into a spare plank. The name is a little wonky, etched in uneven italics. Someone has painted a flower next to it.

I can't hear anything. Can't see anything else. Just this one thing. A handful of letters.

Treegap

6

Dear Winnie,

So, you and the new kid looked AWFUL close at the lake last Saturday. And I know you're going to say, "Oh no June it's nothing we're just friends," but I have known you my whole entire life, and I know when you're being a dirty little liar, because your cheeks go pink and your throat does that gurgle thing (it's not embarrassing, it's endearing, don't let your mother tell you otherwise). Oh, and also I saw you kissing. So there's that. LOVE YOU.

—June

I wake up before the sun, shedding the groggy clutches of a dream: the memory of Levi's breath warm on my shoulder, the heat of his body seeping into mine while rain fell outside. *Urgh*, traitorous dream brain. I roll over in the dark and realize Nan is sitting on the end of my bed. I jolt, rocketing back into my pillows. "Jesus *Christ*."

"Just me," she says. "What did you dream about?"

I rub my eyes, banishing the lingering haze of sleep. "Personal boundaries," I mutter.

"Ha! Well, Tommy has that kissing disease and he's out sick. Give your dear old nan a hand sorting the mail this morning?"

I groan, flopping back into my pillows. "Who's Tommy kissing anyway?"

"I think it's that nice young lady with the turtle."

"Yertle?"

Nan pokes me in the ribs. "Be nice! You know her name is . . ." She trails off, searching her memory. "Oh goodness. I give her the paper every Saturday. . . ." She pushes her lips together, trying not to laugh. She's drumming her fingers on her legs, searching for the name. Yertle comes in every weekend. Her backpack is shaped like a shell, she wears different novelty turtle earrings every week, and her phone case says *Let me take a shelfie*. We didn't know her real name for years, because the only thing she ever orders through us is special seagrass that arrives from interstate and is addressed to her turtle. His name is Ralph.

In any case, the sooner I start, the sooner I can slip away. "It's fine, Nan. I can do it. There's not much, right?"

"Just the usual. And there's a fresh cup of coffee waiting for you."

I grumble, slightly less annoyed about being awake. I'd fallen asleep with a million questions swirling in my mind and had planned to wake up early enough to sneak back on my own—without *him*. My whole body cringes at the thought, and my mind flashes to Levi last night in the forest. We scrambled out of the

112

woods as quickly as humanly possible and found Elliot and Isaac waiting in the parking lot, both rushing out of the car to make sure we were okay. It wasn't anyone's fault—we must have *just* missed them on the trail, and Elliot had tried to text me to say he'd meet me in the lot. If my phone hadn't died, I would have seen it before the first raindrop fell. I thought about a lot of *ifs* on the very silent drive home.

I banish the thought by throwing off the blankets and welcoming the early morning chill. Sundays are mostly just inventory, so usually I don't mind it much: mindless, easy work. Today, however, I wish I had something to occupy my wandering mind. *Levi's hands. The letter writers. Treegap. Do you wish—*

Urgh.

Nan plods after me as I head down to the post office and start sorting through the tubs with more force than strictly necessary. We have a pretty good system: Nan handles letter envelopes, I do parcels. It's not super exciting, except that Mr. Harris—our kindly old neighbor with a face like Saint Nicholas himself—has a suspiciously shaped package from *Café Kinky*. I slap a stamp over the return address before Nan sees it.

I sort through the rest of the PO boxes, methodically scanning everything in by number, running down the length of the counter, hardly even needing to check the numbers—I know these names like old friends. *601: Anna Owens. 602: Lionel Nelson. 603: Yula Ivanov.* I try to yank open the next locker, but groan as my fingers jam in the handle.

"Seriously, has no one fixed 604 yet?"

113

"It's cursed!" Nan calls. "Bloody thing can't be opened."

Short of blasting it with a flamethrower, I think that might be true. It's been stuck this way for as long as I can remember. There's no name assigned to it, the master key is useless, and we have heaps of spare boxes anyway, so mostly we forget about it.

Elliot appears at the door, scrubbing his face with the ends of his sleeves. He taps with one knuckle, waiting until I climb over the mountain of tubs to unlock the front door. "M'rning," he mumbles, taking a seat at the register, fingers snaking out toward my coffee cup.

"You touch that mug and you'll lose your fingers," I threaten.

Nan hands him a novelty cup straight from the counter display. There's a jolly yellow slug on the side with an envelope in its mouth, and it says *Snail Mail* on the side. He pours coffee from the pot, eyes bloodshot and weary. "Why are you awake?" he asks between slurps.

"Office duty," I answer. "Why are *you?*"

"Dale lost his work shoes. It was an argument that apparently needed to happen predawn. Should I be helping, by the way?"

"Nah, I've got it. Go nap on the couch; I'll come get you when I'm done."

"M'kay," he says, but he doesn't move. Mabel comes downstairs and sits on his lap, practically vibrating with joy. They end up semi-slumped on the counter, breathing loudly in a way that could *almost* be considered snoring except that every time I whisper, "*Elliot, are you awake?*" he says, "*Please shut up I am sleeping.*"

By the time we've sorted through all the boxes, Nan declares that it's a respectable enough hour to start drinking, so she goes upstairs to make herself a mimosa and spy on the neighbors. Elliot's breathing has evened out, so I let him nap a little longer while I get a head start on the register for Monday morning: swapping in new rolls of receipt paper, double-checking the coin float, sorting the pen display into a vague sense of order (there's a massacre in the glitter section, thanks to the twelve-year-old kids who get dragged in after school with their parents).

Elliot is still asleep when I'm done, so I sit back at the counter and doodle a sketch on the notepad: a peaked roof and a darkened doorway. I don't know why we didn't tell him about Treegap last night. I guess that would have involved talking to each other. Me and *Levi*. Who I have managed not to think about for a solid seventy-three minutes.

My pen presses into the paper and ripples in a neat tear.

The cabin was deep in the woods. How did they even cart the wood in? The letters are old, but they're not pre-*tree* old—they couldn't have driven them in with a car. Maybe they did carry it all, in pieces. Didn't we have the same idea when we were younger? Build a tree house, bit by bit? It's strange to think there is so much missing in the letters, three lifetimes that we know so little about. I dig through the letters, trying to find more, something we missed the first time.

Dear Winnie,

There are a family of cats living in the trunk of my car.

Still, it's better than rats in the ceiling. I guess one problem has solved the other. There's one particularly feral cat that won't let anyone touch her. I've named her June. Don't tell.

The loft isn't so bad. Better than being in the house, at least. A little cold at night, but Human June came and dropped off some woolen blankets. Hand-knitted, too. I tried to refuse, but she said they looked like a Rorschach test and gave her nightmares. Guess that's her way of being subtle. And when it's too cold, I can hike out to Treegap. If we ever finish it. If it's ever more than just a dream. Cat June would like it there, I think.

Love,

August

If we ever finish it. They *must* have built it. For August? I frown, rereading the letter. Was he running away from home? Or just running to be with Winnie? Although, we don't know if they ever ran at all. I sigh, shoving the letters back. They've never given me the answer before—don't know why I thought they were going to start being helpful now.

I resolve to go back as soon as I can. There must be clues, I decide. *Helpful* clues. It was their place; they must have left more than an old blanket and a Game Boy behind. Maybe I can tell Elliot today, and we can go together. Either way, I need to see it in the daylight, to know it wasn't just a dream that manifested in the middle of a storm.

Elliot suddenly jolts, and Mabel shrieks in displeasure. "I'm awake!" he says, blinking rapidly.

116

"Seems like," I say. "Hungry?"

"Always."

"Pancakes?"

We trudge upstairs, delighted to find the scent of maple syrup and warm flour already filling the kitchen. Nan is standing at the kitchen window with a pair of binoculars raised to her eyes. "I think Shelly Newborn is having an affair. Quick, pop down and look inside that silver Camry out front."

"Nan! No!" I peek over her shoulder at the young man in question. "Also, that's her *brother*."

"Oh," she says, squinting through the binoculars. "So it is. Well, you can't blame me; he used to be bald." She sniffs the air and her nose wrinkles in displeasure. "And go bathe—you stink. You've got ten minutes before breakfast is ready."

I sniff the ends of my hair and cringe. After our adventures last night, I was so tired I'd come home and fallen straight asleep—my hair smells like wood smoke and damp, and my T-shirt was sticking to the back of my neck.

I hold up a warning finger at Elliot. "If I'm not back in ten minutes, you must protect my pancakes from Mabel."

"Why? Mabel loves pancakes." He grins, and Mabel's tail flicks over his lap.

I sprint to the bathroom and scrub my scalp with more vigor than strictly necessary. I close my eyes and imagine I can still smell Levi's strawberry breath, then lather up the lavender soap to cleanse my mind of the thought.

Do you regret—

117

I slam the water off, the old pipes shrieking in protest.

Elliot is sitting at the breakfast counter when I return, water still dripping down my spine.

"Did you know that my very large hand apparently means I also have a very large brain?" he says, palm held hostage as Nan carefully inspects it.

"More like a very large ego," I mutter, sitting beside him.

Nan *tsk-tsks*. "I said you are a *thinker*, Eli Maddon. But you could be thinking about rocks for all I know. But here, your heart line is high and strong, toward your Jupiter finger. That's good. Lots of love to give. Hmm, but this line—a controlling emotional presence."

"Nan, I think that's *you*," I say, pulling Elliot's elbow so she's forced to drop it. He winks at Nan, but his face changes when she turns away to boil the kettle.

"So," I say, pulling apart a baguette with my fingers and shoving it into my mouth. "Are you taking Isaac to the dance?" Emiko had mentioned it last night—the school hosts a big Valentine's dance every year. They open up all the classrooms and have different activities in all of them: marshmallows roasting over Bunsen burners, book clubs in the library, sleeping bags and snacks in the geography portables. Except they don't actually let anyone stay overnight anymore, because . . . you know. Teenagers, hormones, confined spaces. *I should know.*

Elliot rolls his eyes.

"That's not a no," I say.

"It's a 'mind your own business.'"

"Jeez, just asking. Someone's cranky today."

Nan putters around the kitchen, banging cupboards and drawers. I glance at her, waiting until her head is stuck inside the pantry, then lower my voice.

"What's with you guys? I can't figure it out."

"What's with *you?*" he shoots back.

"Me? Nothing."

"You and *Levi*," he clarifies, looking awfully smug.

My heart gallops, then stops dead. "Nothing. There's no thing. There's no *us.*"

"Uh-huh."

"Uh-huh *what?*"

He arches a brow, giving me the *are you being intentionally obstinate or are you actually just stupid* look. "You guys just disappeared into the forest, hid out in a cute little cabin in the middle of a storm, then came back all wired and blushing—"

"*I* wasn't blushing."

"—and now you're back to not talking to each other. What gives?"

I square my shoulders, determined not to acknowledge any of his questions. "It wasn't cute, you know. More like murdery and dusty." *It was theirs,* I want to scream.

Elliot rolls his eyes again. "Right."

Nan pops out of the pantry, triumphantly holding up the cinnamon sugar. "Ah-hah! Now if you are done colluding, my dears, please set the table." We both look at each other nervously, but Nan's hearing is pretty questionable, and I doubt she'd mind much even if she had heard everything.

We eat while the record player skips over a jazz track, and by the time we're done washing up, Nan fixes herself another mimosa to take out on the balcony.

"I wonder what Mr. Harris has been up to lately. . . ." she says, drifting up the stairs.

Elliot insists on drying everything and putting it away, because he is a Good Houseguest, even though Nan and I are total heathens and just leave everything to drip in the rack until we need it again. We each take a towel and work in companionable silence.

As the kitchen fills with midmorning light and the record player fades to a static echo, I feel an urgent tingle working up my spine, the seconds ticking away on the kitchen clock filled with urgency.

"You all right, Red?"

I jolt, turning away from the sink. "Yeah. Just tired."

"Because you and Levi were out so late?" He wriggles his eyebrows. "In a romantic cabin in the woods? Did you guys kiss or something?"

"Ew. *No*. Why would you even think that? Also a) it was *not* romantic, and b) *you* are the reason I got stuck there in the first place!"

"I'm sorry," he says earnestly. Which he already said a million times last night. "Bad friend moment."

"It's fine, it was an accident." I squeeze his hand because I can see him getting stressed again, and it's not his fault Levi and I got stuck with dead phones. "So," I say, working hard to keep my voice steady. "What did Levi say, exactly?"

"About the murder house?"

"I *told* you it was creepy!"

Elliot ducks a spray of dish soap bubbles, swatting them away till they pop. "He didn't say anything. He said he was pretty sure there were spiders, and you were a pain in the ass."

"Oh."

He nudges me. "Why? What were you hoping he'd say?"

I sit up, smiling sweetly. "I was hoping he'd been bitten by one of those spiders and at least three of his fingers had fallen off."

"Liar."

"I think we found Treegap," I blurt instead. "The cabin. That's what it is."

He pauses with a plate halfway to the rack, dripping water on the floor. "What? From the dead letters?"

"Yeah."

"It's a real place? After all this time?"

"I think so."

"Right," he drawls. "And what makes you think it's Treegap, exactly?"

"There was a sign on the door."

"You should have led with that." The surprise fades, and a slow grin forms instead. "I mean, that's pretty major. Can I see it?"

"Sure. I was going to go back anyway."

"Can Levi come?"

I groan. *Must* he? Besides, he's probably off somewhere taking fake candid photos of his letterman jacket and, like, polishing the scales of his true succubus form."

"I thought only women were succubuses. Succubi? What's the acceptable plural, do you think? Is it like octopuses?"

"I don't know, ask Levi."

He rolls his eyes. "All right. Tell me more about this cabin."

I try to describe the path we took, but it was dark and raining, and my mind was occupied by wondering about lightning strike survival rates and whether my foot was about to end up in a snake hole. Elliot grabs a stack of napkins from the counter and has me draw it up instead. I map out the usual route we take to the clearing, then trail my pen away from the river, toward the approximate location of the cabin. Elliot flips the image around and makes a few amendments.

"You'd have hit the townie bike path if you'd gone that way; it must have been farther north." He points an arrow slightly to the left of where I'd drawn it and raises both eyebrows. "Look about right?"

"I guess. I'm pretty sure I could find it again on foot, though."

"Pretty sure?"

"Like, ninety percent."

"What about the other ten percent?"

I shrug. "Bring a flare gun and some snacks."

He leans back in his seat, eyeing the drawing. "We're gonna need supplies."

Typical Elliot. Always so cautious. This is why *he* never gets arrested for trespassing with his pants stuck to a fence.

I snatch the map away before he can protest, grinning. "Don't worry, I have a plan."

We pedal down to the forest on our bikes, pulling into a half-full parking area and already sweating from the bright afternoon sun.

It takes us a while to pick our way through the usual trail: the

122

path is muddy, the riverbank burst, and the branches are coated in slick moss. By the time we make it to the clearing, we're both panting, and I toss him the water bottle from my backpack while I consult the smudgy map. I look between the points we drew up in the kitchen and try to remember exactly how we'd found it last night. I double-check my position in the clearing, and orient myself north, an arm held out in front of me.

"That way," I say, more confidently than I feel.

"You sure?" We both double-check our phones to make sure they're fully charged, and I drop a pin on our location. If we *do* get lost, at least I can follow it back: a digital bread crumb trail.

"Yep," I say, marching ahead. "And I brought yarn, just in case."

"Oh good. When we get lost out here, at least we'll have time to make a nice sweater."

"For *navigating*, moron."

"That's"—his nose scrunches up—"not the worst idea, actually."

He follows me away from the clearing, and when we start to lose sight of the sun in the grass field beyond, we tie red wool around tree trunks to guide us back.

But we shouldn't have worried, because it's exactly where I remembered: Treegap, standing in the Rydal Woods, a little splintered and beaten but *real*.

Elliot lets out a low whistle. "Holy shit. You weren't kidding."

I run my fingers over the sign, nails scraping over the carved-out *T*. "I thought we might have imagined it," I whisper. Then I laugh, throwing my head back, watching as Elliot loops around the tiny building.

"Can I go in?" he asks.

I shrug, because it's not like it's mine to decide.

He knocks, out of habit, then eases the door open and ducks low under the threshold. I sit on the miniature porch, wondering who painted the sunflowers and how many days they spent here together.

I can hear Elliot making small sounds of exploration inside: shuffling the sleeping bag to one side, picking up and putting down the wrappers and tiny debris, a quiet "*Oh*" voiced to no one in particular.

In the light of day, I can see a few signs of people who must have discovered the shack over the years—some initials carved in the windowsill, dated almost a decade ago. Some chocolate wrappers and a beer can, both too new to have been theirs. It feels like sacrilege, that someone walked where they did, not knowing or caring what this place meant.

"They didn't leave much behind," he says, flipping the Game Boy over in his hands.

"Almost like they weren't planning on coming back."

He looks up, contemplating. "Maybe," he says, placing the console back on the windowsill. He comes to sit beside me on the porch, legs bent over the railings. "I wonder where they all went when they were done with this place."

"Well, June went to university. Winnie was supposed to follow, but the letters stopped after that."

"August?"

I shrug. "He was supposed to stay. Maybe he's still here, somewhere. Managing a bank or something atrociously boring."

Levi and I used to play this game, *Where are they now?* We'd take turns making up stories, finishing the chapters they left out of their letters. *June is a helicopter pilot, never touching down for more than a day. Winnie knits bespoke handbags for poodles. August is a taxi driver by day and hit man by night—it's the perfect cover story!*

I'd settled on my favorite fantasy a long time ago: I liked to imagine August and Winnie moving away somewhere distant and glamorous, like Berlin. They'd live in an apartment, and August would be a carpenter, and Winnie would illustrate picture books for children, her art drying on their walls. June would fly in to see them sometimes, bringing exotic wines and bags of gifts.

Back at RAGs, on those long, miserable, lonely nights, I'd close my eyes and picture them like that, and it would bring me some comfort to know that they had grown up and moved on. Survived the small town and found their place in the world.

Elliot just jumps to his feet, brushing off the cobwebs from his hair. "Come on, let's walk back. This place is giving me the creeps."

I sigh, closing the door to their cabin, promising to return. We end up back in the clearing, shucking our shoes and wandering through the ankle-length grass. Someone has left twenty-five cactus plants and a life-sized cutout of *Hannah Montana*. The blue couch remains, seat cushions chewed thin by a small woodland creature.

Elliot picks a spot half in and half out of the sun. I lie down beside him, and his eyes flutter closed.

"Tired?"

He murmurs something in the affirmative. "I was up late, with Isaac. After we dropped you home. . . . Anyway, then Dale woke me up early. I need at least three more coffees before I feel like a human being today."

"I see. And what were you and Isaac doing, exactly?"

He opens an eye and squints at me. "Driving," he answers, one side of his lip curling up.

"Right."

He sighs, tipping his chin away slightly. "I just . . . we just . . ."

I wait. Elliot's fingers drum a pattern on the earth while he thinks. He doesn't say anything until he's ready, and when he does the words are halting and unsure. "He wants to be my boyfriend," he says, very intently avoiding my gaze. "He introduced me to his family. You know they have a German shepherd that's a literal, actual show dog? It's won prizes. It met Oprah. And his house is huge, and his sister goes to a select-entry school, and his dad grows prize-winning pumpkins."

"Okay. They seem like they might keep bodies in their basement, but otherwise that sounds nice. Right?"

"They're great. And *we* were great, you know, for a while. But then he wanted to come inside one day, 'cause he saw Mum at the window. And that was okay, because Mum knows everything, and she's always been great about it. But Dale was home. And he doesn't know—I mean, it's fine, I'm used to it, but Isaac is, like, the *one* person who thinks I have a nice, normal life, and I don't want Dale to ruin this thing that is actually good and just mine. So I said I had to think about it, and now it's this weird thing between us. Like he's all in and he thinks *I'm* not, but I am, I just . . ."

I grab his hand and squeeze. "Maybe you should talk to him about all this," I say quietly.

He just laughs, blowing out a lungful of air. "That is great advice from the world's biggest hypocrite."

"Hey!"

"Red, you and Levi have had three years to talk about stuff. That's a long-ass time to hold a grudge."

"That's different. He *hates* me."

"Do you seriously think he hates you?"

"Why else did he ignore me for three years?"

Elliot sighs, running a hand over his face. "Is it really *just* about the stone?"

It takes me too long to answer. The silence becomes answer enough. "He never called," I say instead.

"You ignored him too, you know."

"*He* was the one who accused *me*—"

He waves a hand, cutting off a tirade he's heard a hundred times now. "All I'm saying is, maybe there's a reason that he found it hard to talk to you, after everything."

I roll my eyes, then kick my boots in the dirt. "What's your theory, then?" I mumble.

"Maybe he was upset. Maybe he thought you blew out of town in a hurry and tossed a grenade as you left. Maybe he thought you lied to him, and neither of you would stop screaming over the other long enough to have a sensible conversation. Maybe his feelings were hurt."

I look up at Elliot, eyes narrowed. "That's a very specific theory."

"Yeah, well, I've had a lot of time to think about it."

I slump down in the grass again, dandelions tickling my ears. "Why didn't he tell *me* all that, then?"

"Would you have listened?"

"I . . . maybe." I don't want to say what I actually feel. That the spot Levi used to occupy in my heart has ached ever since I left. That I wanted to call him every day, but I was too stubborn to be the one who caved first. I cycled through emotions like dials on a clock: sad, angry, indignant, lonely. After a while I managed to not think about him at all. Now it's all starting to feel like wasted time.

"He could have tried," I insist.

"He's a seventeen-year-old hetero dude who doesn't know how to express his emotions." Elliot shrugs. "Maybe he needs a little help."

I snort. "I sincerely hope you're not implying that I use my soft, womanly intuition to help atone for his mistake."

"Jesus, I can't win with you two."

"Would it be any fun if you did?"

He flops back, eyes on the sky. "Maybe I'd get a fucking minute of peace. *Eli, does Brodie have a date to the dance? Eli, how many security cameras does the Sawyer house have?* I'm not a messenger service, you know."

I frown, looking down at his black curly head, an arm tossed over his eyes. I tug on his hand until it comes away and kiss him on the cheek.

"I'm sorry, Elliot." Sorry not just for this, but for everything.

That he works twice as hard to have half as much. That he can't bring his boyfriend home or sleep in on Sundays.

He shrugs again. "I was only joking."

I settle under his free arm, my head in the crook of his shoulder. "No, you weren't. You're our favorite, you know that, right? And we shouldn't put you in the middle so much. Though now would be a really convenient time for you to confess that you've been *Parent Trapped* and actually have a backup twin so we can have one each."

He laughs, the vibrations of his chest rumbling along my spine. "Just me."

"Fine. I guess we can learn to share."

"I don't know why," he says quietly.

"Why what?"

"Why you love me so much," he whispers. I roll over and see tears in his eyes and throw my body weight on top of his. I hold him tight, arms around his neck, and feel his tears soak the collar of my shirt.

"You are *good*, Eli Maddon. Good all the way to your soul."

He just rocks me, huge arms wrapped around my waist, until I don't know who is clinging to the other anymore.

Dear August: I call a truce. The terms are thus: We agree that Winnie loves us equally, and that we get to share her. And when you two run away to the city, you have to tell me which one, so I can come and visit and never leave. Ha! Also, I get to pat Cat June. Yes, she told me.—J

129

As a general rule, I avoid the football oval at all costs; it reeks of body odor and heteronormativity, the grass is always churned up and muddied, and there's no phone signal. Plus, it's Levi's area. We have perfected our distant orbit, two stars drifting in careful synchronicity, never to collide lest we implode. I sit with Emi and Claire at lunch, browse the library stacks, sit on the drama building steps. He has the quad and the oval, and sometimes the cafeteria. Elliot bounces between us, like a pissed-off meteor shower.

I take a seat on the bleachers and watch the boys' team chase their little ball around until they inevitably collide with each other, with no particular rhyme or reason. The coach yells, they follow. Occasionally, a boy calls foul, and the team resets.

Isaac runs circles around them all—I don't even need the name stitched on the back of his shirt to pick him out, since he towers over everyone else. But then he stops to wave at me and gets viciously spear-tackled from the side.

"Dog move, Ryan!"

A high-pitched whistle shrieks and they all stop. Words are exchanged, and Ryan slumps off the field to start jogging laps around the oval.

The rest of the team claps hands and brushes their sweaty hair away from even sweatier brows. Honestly, no wonder the whole place stinks like Mabel's fermented hairballs. They drift toward the changing rooms, voices snatched away on the wind. Except for one lone body, which makes its way across the field toward me. I clench my fingers in my pockets, watching as Levi jumps up the few steps to join me.

"Want a hug?" he says, holding out slick arms and a soaked shirt.

"Gag. Absolutely not."

He pulls his shirt up to wipe his face and I get a glimpse of his stomach. Unwillingly, obviously.

"So," he says, sitting a good two feet away. Was he avoiding me? Or did I just not notice? Maybe I was avoiding him too.

"So." I clear my throat, suddenly feeling very, very stupid. "I came to propose a truce."

"I thought we already had a truce."

I roll my eyes. "You ambushed me, asked for my alibi, then agreed to split the reward money *if* we find the ring. That wasn't a truce. That was a hostage situation."

"I see."

I fidget with the end of my zipper, feeling my cheeks burn. He's watching me with that half-cocked smile, waiting for me to say something, which is ironic, given how long we spent ignoring each other. Three years. What a waste. "Do you hate me?" I blurt.

Surprise registers on his face, the corners of his smile dropping. "What? No. Why would you think that?"

"I just—I was talking to Elliot, and he said—" I shake my head. "It doesn't matter. Forget it." God, what was I thinking?

This is all Elliot's fault. I should never have listened—I was perfectly content hating Levi and pretending he hated me too. *Knowing* it. God, what a mess. Warning signs are blaring in my mind: Get out, red alert, go directly to jail and do not pass go, evacuate now. Minimize damage.

The soles of my shoes slap against concrete as I stand, turning away.

131

He grabs my fingertips. I try very hard to ignore the way that small brush sends a river of nerves up my arm, but it's hard when he's left his hand there: knuckles pink and the pads of his fingers rough, thumb pressed against the thin skin of my wrist. All the feeling inside my body seems to pool there and it's screaming *run* but also *more*.

I have never thought about someone's hand as much as his.

"Red? Talk to me."

I squeeze my eyes shut, counting the galloping beats of my heart. He's still holding my fingers—so gently, like he expects them to slip away. Like he let me, once.

I snatch my hand back. "You never called."

"What?"

"At Rowley. You never called. I waited. For a year. You never called, and you never wrote, and you never emailed, and I only knew you were still alive because Elliot told me." I fix my eyes on the top row of the bleachers, watching the treetops rustle. Anywhere but him.

"I was fourteen, Brodie. And really, really stupid."

I shake my head, stepping away. "I shouldn't have come. This was a bad idea."

"You're not listening—"

"I know. Okay? It's fine. We were young and stupid—"

"I think technically we *are* still young and stupid—"

"And you regret everything and it's *fine*. I just came here to say that it's fine." *Liar, liar, set the house on fire.* "Let's just never talk about it again and call a truce. Okay?" An excess of honesty makes the hair on the back of my neck stand up.

132

I turn back to him and hold out my pinkie. Pinkie swears used to be our most sacred pacts. "For Elliot," I add, replacing that shield between us that the honesty had worn away for a few precious seconds. I will not think about his hands and the things they might do. This is Levi, and I hate Levi. Yes, that's the way this works.

He doesn't take it. He's looking at me, eyebrows furrowed, mouth half open.

"You didn't call me either, you know."

I frown. Elliot said something similar, and at the time, my being morally correct seemed very important. Now I let my gaze lower to the scuffed toes of my shoes. "Would you have answered if I did?"

"Always," he replies, without hesitation. I remember the night I came back to Rowley, his car idling on the curb. It's a ten-minute drive from the station to his house—he made it in five.

"Elliot said you got in a lot of trouble when I left."

He nudges my toe with his own. "I got in a lot of trouble *before* you left."

"Because of me?"

He shrugs. "Wasn't exactly stealing cars before I met you, was I?"

"That was *one time*. And you got to keep the car!" A small fact that most people seemed to forget when that particular story was retold.

"I also had to wash all of Dad's squad cars for six months after that."

Graciously, I do not respond with any disparaging comments about his parents. "Nan just told me I should have driven faster," I admit. "Wouldn't have gotten caught."

"Does that mean she's taught you how to drive properly, then?"

"Oh no, those privileges are long gone. Dad's orders."

He grins. "Worth it," he says. "All of it."

How did we get back here? Friends-to-enemies back to almost-friends again? This is probably the longest conversation we've had since I got back. Has too much changed since then? Since he was hiding toothpaste in my Oreos and I was sneaking salt into his coffee? But I'm too afraid to ask that question aloud.

"Truce, then," I say instead, willing my fingers to stop trembling.

He ignores my outstretched pinkie and takes my hand instead. "Have you been back?" he asks, voice rough. His thumb brushes across my knuckles.

I blink, brain sluggish and confused. His hand is so warm. "What? Where?"

"Treegap."

"No," I lie. "Why?"

He clears his throat. "We should go back. Together." He hesitates. "All of us. With Elliot—obviously."

"Obviously," I repeat.

He lets my hand slip away for the second time. I turn away, blink away the fury-tears. That's what Mum used to call them. *Petal, you only cry when you're angry. You get that from me.*

I take a breath to say something else, then realize there's nothing left. "Okay, then," I whisper, and rush down the stairs, hugging my jacket tight so my hands don't shake. I've already hit the grass by the time I hear his voice again.

"I don't regret it," he calls out. "Just for the record."

I turn around. He's grinning at me. *You hate him, Brodie. Remember?*

I think of the house in the woods. Elliot's hug. Levi's car and the last sunrise.

No, you don't.

Goddamn you, Levi Sawyer.

7

Dear June,

Thank you for your letter, direct though it may be. I'm happy to answer your ~~interrogations~~ questions. To start: No, I am not, nor have I ever been, an ax murderer (though isn't that what I would say if I were, in fact, an ax murderer?). I moved here from the city. I don't have ~~much~~ family in Warwick. I like to read. I cannot do a handstand (sorry). My "intentions" with Winnie are only to be friends—you, too, though perhaps less so after this letter (that was a joke). I can't remember the rest of your questions—music? I don't listen to the radio much, except when I'm driving.

Thank you for inviting me to dinner. I had a nice time. Please thank your mother for the leftovers. ~~She reminds me of my mum.~~

Oh. The woods, you said. Sure. I'd like to see them.

~~Kind regards,~~

~~Sincerely yours~~

From,

August

I consult the letters again, tally more clues in my journal. If I'm going to accept Levi's help, then I'm going to make damn sure I'm the better detective. Eager to prove my innocence? Perhaps. Eager to prove him inferior? Absolutely. He sends me a flurry of texts, which I ignore, mostly because I don't trust myself to talk to him anymore. I might say something deranged, like *I actually saved this one voice mail you left me for three and a half years because I liked the way you laughed.* Or worse.

Much worse.

And that I *would* regret.

But it turns out ignoring Levi is harder than I thought.

The truce lasts exactly four days before a water balloon explodes in my bicycle helmet. I freeze in shock as ice-cold water bursts on my head and trickles down my shoulders, while Elliot's face quickly morphs from concern to surprise to laughter. A few kids streaming out of final-bell classrooms stop and stare, though thankfully the snickers come to a grinding halt as Elliot glances up. Oh, to be so menacing. If only they knew he wasn't the one they should be afraid of.

I rip the helmet off and stare at the note taped inside. *Truce doesn't mean we can't have fun, right, Red?*

"I'll kill him," I declare, pushing wet hair out of my face.

Elliot takes the helmet from me, glancing inside, a crooked grin lighting his face. It makes me want to kill Levi a little less, if Elliot will keep smiling like this. He tries to swap mine for his dry helmet, but I shake my head. I'm already wet, so what's the point?

He reluctantly passes it back and tries to suppress a giggle. A *giggle.* "Come on, Brodie. You guys used to do this stuff all the time!"

"Yeah, and I also used to shove glue sticks up my nose and show Nan the mold it made."

We used to spend weeks in prank wars. Maybe we never grew out of that phase—maybe this is the only way we know how to be friends now.

I snatch the helmet and ease it slowly onto my head, half expecting another rubber snake or balloon to appear. I double-check my tires, but he's evidently not as petty as I am. *I'll have his car towed. I'll sprinkle icing sugar all over his bag so he gets ants. I'll—*

Emiko halts as she walks past, doing a double take. "What happened to you?"

"Sabotage," I grit out through clenched teeth.

She looks between Elliot and me, him trying to mask his amusement, me still clutching my bike handle with one white-knuckled hand.

"I sense tension," she says cheerfully. "You want a lift somewhere?"

Oh.

And just like that, I start feeling a whole lot better. "Hey, Emi, you have a car, right?"

"Yeah. Where are you headed?"

Enemy territory.

Elliot steps between us, palms up. "Oh, no. Brodes, come on, it was a harmless prank."

I smile sweetly up at him, batting my eyes. "I have no idea what you mean. I am but an innocent maiden with honest and good intentions."

"That has literally never been true. And you have the Felon look in your eyes."

I shrug. "It's genetic."

"Brodie, it was a *prank*."

I tuck my wet hair as primly as I can behind one ear. "No, Elliot," I say, tossing my helmet at him. "This is war."

The Sawyer house is a big colonial-style mansion on the horizon: rooftop dotted with dormer windows, porch wrapped in wrought-iron lace. It has *wings*, not levels, and they have two kitchens so they can pretend they don't make human mess or eat human food. There's a gargoyle head over the doorway and faux-Grecian columns along the side.

It is, obviously, completely hideous.

Mrs. Sawyer personally oversaw the renovation, and whenever someone would come to visit she'd tell them it was inspired by "the most darling provincial country home we used to summer in before the kids." *Summer*, as a verb. What a dickhead.

I liked it better before they renovated. It had a brick chimney and an attic we'd pretend led to Narnia. Levi's room was wall-papered with different shades of mismatched blue, and if you laid on his bed looking at the ceiling it felt like you were underwater. But everything got boarded up and painted over, and now it just looks like a house that's too big and too empty.

In summary: It's a pretty easy place to break into.

"Okay, well," Emiko says, eyeing me suspiciously. "Here we are. Wherever *here* is."

"This is Levi's house," Elliot says from the backseat. Our bikes were both still locked up at the school, and it was going to be a pain to go get them tomorrow, but I promised him double milkshakes and breakfast fries.

"Ohhhh, *Levi*'s house?" Emi repeats, cooing his name. Her eyes are suddenly alive with mischief, and she folds her hands in her lap. "Pray tell, what are we doing here?"

Elliot leans forward, sticking his face between the front seats. "Yes, Brodie, what *are* we doing here?"

I twist so I can poke him in the chest. "We? Nothing. *You* are going to go knock on the front door."

He frowns, unsatisfied. "And what will you be doing?"

"Just sitting here. Watching the world go by. Chatting about the weather. You know, normal, innocent things."

He rolls his eyes. "And what about *after* I knock on the door? Are you going to toilet paper the house?"

"Ew, so unoriginal. No." Still funny though—shelve that one for Halloween. "I just thought we'd hang out for a minute. Came all this way, you know." I wave a hand around the manicured street, like I might just stroll around and look at garden gnomes. I actually stole them all, once. Drew mustaches on every single one and put them back the next day. The real tragedy is no one noticed, since they all pay other people to clean their yards.

"You're being weird," Elliot says, a touch of accusation in his tone. Hypocrite—he helped me *carry* all those gnomes.

"You're being paranoid," I reply, smiling sweetly.

Emiko clears her throat. "Just to be clear, I don't want to commit an actual crime. Like, crime-adjacent, sure. Something I can be charged for, no thank you. The movie theater does not pay well enough to make bail."

"You're just the getaway car, don't worry."

She bounces in her seat, apparently quite pleased with this responsibility.

Elliot looks horrified. "You said—"

"Hmm? What? Oh no, look at the time." I reach over and unlock the door, shoving it open. "Well, bye-bye now. Call you later."

He grumbles as he steps out, and I duck low in the seat. "Wave!" I say to Emiko.

She holds out a hand and waves, right as he steps on to their lawn and the motion-detector light comes on, spilling across the dashboard.

I count the beats of his footsteps. "Did he ring the doorbell?"

Emiko's still waving like a beauty pageant queen, beaming wide, speaking through closed teeth. "Yep. I think they have one of those bell cameras."

I grin at her. "They do. Now back up a bit like you're going to reverse—right up to their side gate."

She backs up and angles a bit like she's about to do a three-point turn. "This is very exciting," she says. "How long have you been planning this?"

"You don't want to know." The first night at RAGs. I was so mad at him, I made a whole list. It was scrawled in my diary under the name *The Rowley Revenge Papers*.

Emi side-eyes me, a quirk in her lips. "You guys have a weird way of flirting."

"It's not—" My cheeks burn bright red, and I shove her baseball cap low over my face. I check my reflection in the mirror, tucking my hair under my collar. Still wet, by the way.

"Uh-huh." She checks her watch and hunkers down. "All right, steal whatever it is quickly and let's go. I gotta babysit at seven."

"Hey! Why would you just assume I'm gonna steal something?"

She gives me *the look*. "Aren't you?"

I open the car door and ease it shut behind me, leaning through the window.

"I'm not *stealing* anything."

"Uh-huh," she repeats, unconvinced.

"Besides"—I grin—"It's not stealing if you plan on bringing it back. I'm just . . . borrowing."

Emiko drops me home to an empty house, waving as she pulls away. I let myself into the post office entrance, flicking on lights as I go, and spend the rest of the night with a bubble bath and a pot of sencha green tea that Emiko gave me because, and I quote, *You need to chill the fuck out.*

A wet tongue licks me on the face, and I glance down. It's possible she has a point.

Nan has bridge club on Friday and usually comes home late, pretending not to be drunk and babbling to the attic ghost. It's just as well, since I'm not entirely sure she'd approve of my latest heist.

"What?" I say, letting the freshly washed fluff ball nudge my hand. "You like popcorn? Can dogs eat popcorn?" I google it and the internet says yes. Mabel mews from her perch on top of the bookshelf and glares at me, eyeing my new companion with utter distaste. She spent the first hour alternating between hissing at him and trying to catch his tail, neither of which Pudge seemed to care about. He stares at me with those enormous dopey eyes, and I feed him more popcorn. He slobbers on my shirtsleeve, but I figure that's fair.

My phone dings about twenty times, all text messages coming in rapid succession, but I'm suddenly too chicken to look at them. The dings gradually decrease, until eleven p.m. when the distant sound of a car rumbling to a stop echoes through the house and Elliot climbs over the drainpipe, looking disheveled and flushed. He heads straight for the living room, coming to a stop in the doorway.

He looks at me.

He looks at the couch.

"So Levi's dog has gone missing," he says.

I toss a piece of popcorn into my mouth. "Interesting."

"Also, there is a dog on your couch."

"You know, it was the strangest thing, I just found him walking around. Figured it would be cruel to leave him out there."

"I see."

"And there's no way to know that *this* dog is Levi's dog. Pudge could be anywhere."

Pudge's tail thumps against the couch. Tiny traitor.

Elliot clears his throat, folding his arms across his chest. "I see," he says again. "Brodie?"

"Yes?"

"Why is Pudge pink?"

"Oh. That." I look down at his fluffy pink body. His head is still dark and there's a few gray spots on his coat, so he looks a bit like a watermelon. "Because . . . I found him that way?"

Elliot's head drops to the side, as if to say, *Really?*

I throw my hands up in the air, revealing my red-stained palms. Really should have worn the gloves that came in the pack. "Fine! But he likes it, I swear. Who's a pretty boy, Pudge? It's you, yes, it is." His tail wags triple time and he gives me a dopey grin. "He's very secure in his masculinity, you know." I comb the fine hairs around his ears so they'll dry all nice and fluffy, and he rolls in my lap showing off his fat little belly.

Elliot points a finger at me, aiming for intimidation, but the effect is somewhat ruined by the fact that he has to bite his lip to keep from laughing. "You get to be the one to tell Levi about this. He's gonna lose his shit. His *dad* is gonna lose his shit. This right here is the stupidest thing you will ever go to jail for."

"Oh please. Detective Dick isn't gonna arrest me for giving his dog a bath. Do you know how embarrassing that would be?"

"Exactly! You would be—"

"Oh no," I say, waving a dismissive hand. "Embarrassing for *him*. What kind of detective just lets someone steal their dog from their own house?"

He raises his eyebrows. "I thought you found him."

"Eh, semantics." I *found him* in their yard. That's basically the same thing. Pudge eases himself off the couch, rubbing up against Elliot's legs. Pudge looks like a wiry mophead: The shelter said he was crossed with a lot of things, and they could only guess about three of them. Usually, he has a white-gray coat and soulful brown eyes that could convince you to drop roast chicken right on the floor. Tonight, the eyes are still soulful, but he's also a blindingly vibrant shade of magenta pink.

144

Pudge does a lap of the room, then shoves his head into my lap, whining quietly until I pick him up again and sit him next to me on the couch. I scruff his ears, my heart giving a tight squeeze as I notice the paling fur around his snout. "You getting old there, Pudge? You've got a beard now. Very distinguished."

He tries to crawl into my lap, so I sit cross-legged, letting him squish me as he gets comfy. Pudge used to come on all our adventures: He was Aslan in the attic, the Rydal Devil in the woods. He walked the streets between our houses too many times to count, and he only once tried to eat Mabel on the way. I was there the day Levi brought him home.

"Did you miss me?" I murmur. "Who's a good boy? Who's the *best* boy?" His tongue lolls out of his head in agreement. Mabel hisses from the shelf and jumps onto Elliot's shoulder. Such a disloyal tramp.

"I'll take him back in the morning," I say to Elliot. "He'll be there before they wake up."

Elliot looks up from his phone, ears turning red. "Might be a bit late," he says.

My stomach drops. "You didn't!"

"You took his *dog*, Brodie!"

"He waterbombed my helmet! He *started* it!"

"Oh my god," he says, raking his hands down his face, horrified.

I try to bundle Pudge up into my arms, but his tail is flailing around like a windmill. Mabel is screeching, and Elliot is holding out one hand to stop me from falling, and there's a thumping on the balcony, and then a bronze head pokes through the window. Levi's weathered brown boots land on the floorboards, and he's

145

standing there, frozen, looking at me clutching the dog that I stole. Found. Whatever.

His mouth drops open. Closes. Opens again.

Everything is silent for approximately two seconds, until Pudge gives a single yap and the spell is broken. "You *took my dog*."

"Found!"

"He's pink!"

"Is he? I'd say it's more of a peach color. Rosy, even. Hardly noticeable." This is a lie. Pudge looks nuclear. If we turned the lights off, I am entirely sure that he would glow.

"Pink, Brodie. *Pink!*"

"Calm down, dogs are color-blind. He probably thinks he's a very nice shade of green."

"Why is he a color at all?!"

"It's beetroot dye. You can eat it. Wanna try?"

"PINK!"

"Want me to do yours? A little bit in the front? This curl right here—"

He gives a strangled cry, cringing away from my fingers. Then he slumps against the wall, head cradled in his hands. Pudge whines until I set him down, and he runs over to lick Levi on the shoulder. I discreetly wipe my palms on my pants—this all seemed very funny before Levi arrived, but now I am worried this prank has fallen into the *way too far* basket.

"Yes, Pudge," he says grudgingly. "You're a very handsome boy."

Pudge seems pleased by this and begins to roll over the carpet to show off as much of his fluffy pink body as possible. I wasn't kidding when I told Elliot I thought he liked it—he's been preening ever since I scrubbed him dry and fluffed him up with Nan's blow-dryer.

"Anyone else think he looks like a Teletubby?" Elliot says, rocking on his heels, looking completely smug. Just because *he* didn't do anything wrong.

Levi peeks out between splayed fingers. "He looks like Kirby."

I tilt my head. "Kinda looks like a Powerpuff Girl if you squint a little."

Elliot snorts, then slams a hand over his mouth.

"My mum is gonna kill me," Levi says, glaring at me.

"Oh please, like she'll even notice. Remember when she wanted that ring-tailed Appalachian dog?"

"Afghan Hound," he corrects.

"That's what I *said*." It looked like a skinny ghost and cost seven thousand dollars, but Levi was adamant he wanted the mop-looking creature at the pound.

"I can't believe you stole my dog."

"Found."

"Jesus."

Honestly, it wasn't even hard. Pudge was so happy to see me he walked straight out. I made him salmon for dinner and brushed out his tail. It was basically a free spa service.

Really, this is all Levi's fault. We could have just navigated this new truce like mature, grown-up people. Even if I don't really know exactly how mature, grown-up Levi and Brodie would be friends—or how we'd even start.

Maybe we're doing this to pick up where we left off: fourteen and confused.

Maybe it all too late, and this is all we'll ever have.

"So," Elliot says, flopping onto the couch. "What are we watching?" For a moment, I'm jolted by the memory of a night just like this—the three of us crowded on the couch, arguing about what to watch. Except back then, Elliot's legs weren't long enough to touch the coffee table. He nudges a foot toward me, and the corner of his lips twitch up in a hesitant smile. *Please*, it says.

I can never say no.

I grab the popcorn and fold in next to him, while Mabel settles on his shoulder like a second head. "*Halloween*," I answer, studiously ignoring Levi and telling myself that I don't care whether or not he stays. The screen flickers, then rights itself—the internet gets patchy in the evening, so all I have are Nan's old DVDs.

"I hate scary movies," Levi says mournfully. Notably, he does not say, "*Brodie, I'm going to have you arrested*," or "*Brodie, now I regret kissing you because you are obviously an insane person*."

"Then don't watch," I snipe.

"Pudge wants to stay," he says, and I do a very good job of ignoring the flush of relief in my chest. "Besides, I can't go home now. My dog is *pink*."

Elliot elbows me in the side and I kick him in the ankle. "Whatever," I say. "You can sit in the beanbag chair."

"The beanbag chair smells like wet beets."

"Pudge had a nap."

"Shove," he says, sinking into the space at the edge of the couch, and hugs a cushion in front of his face. "Tell me when the creepy kid is gone."

"That is literally the entire premise of the movie."

"He's gone," Elliot lies.

Levi looks at the screen and groans. Elliot laughs. Levi smacks him in the head with the pillow. Mabel leaps into my lap and presses her claws into my bare thighs. I yell, Pudge barks.

Nan appears in the doorway. She looks at me wedged between the two of them. Looks down. "Is that dog pink, or am I drunk?"

"Pink," we all confirm.

"Oh good. Still room for a nightcap, then." She turns away, and I can hear the *pop* of a champagne bottle in the kitchen.

Elliot smiles, tilting his head to rest on my shoulder, and clicks *play* on the remote. "Feels like old times," he says.

I look at Levi and he's smiling too. *Truce*, he mouths.

I roll my eyes, but I don't move away from the warmth of his body, or his hand when it brushes mine, and when they climb over the balcony later that night I stand there looking at him, watching as he lowers the Pink Pudge into Elliot's waiting hands.

"You know, you can use the front door," I say, crossing my arms against the chill night air.

He grins up at me, shaking out the rain droplets fallen in his hair. "Nah, that wouldn't be any fun." He hesitates for a moment, feet pressed through the railings, elbows hitched over the balcony. "Hey, Brodie," he says.

"What?"

"Come here." Smiles wider. Dimples. *God I hate his face.*

I nudge slightly nearer, closing the gap between us. Below, I hear the quiet scuff of Elliot's shoes as he disappears around the front of the house.

"I was serious," he says. "We should go back. To Treegap. Together."

"All of us?"

He swallows. Nods. "Right. All of us." He reaches out for me. "Hey, come here."

Another step. Warning bells rattle in my head, so loud I can hardly hear him over the sound of blood rushing in my ears.

"I can't believe you stole my dog," he whispers.

"Found."

"Whatever."

He laughs, a quiet sound that sends little gray wisps from his mouth. "Are we gonna keep doing this forever?" he says.

"What?"

"This. You and me."

I hesitate. "The pranks?"

"Sure. The pranks."

I want to tell him that I don't know. I don't know how else to be us, after everything else. Don't know how to get past this uneasy half-friendship, the unsettling feeling that I came home to feel whole again, but the pieces don't fit like they did before. What else is there, if not *this*? His hand knocks mine on the balcony, and a flush of goose bumps runs up my arm. It's the cold, I tell myself, and hesitate a step back. *Retreating*, I think before I can shake the thought away.

His breath still smells like strawberries. He leans in close. His nose is almost touching mine. I can see his freckles, the ones he thinks no one notices. "You started it," I mumble, and know from the flicker of disappointment on his face that it's not the answer he wanted. *The pranks are easier than talking* is what I should have said. But he recovers so quickly I wonder if I imagined it, and all he says is "Okay."

Cold water explodes on my head.

He rockets back, laughing, holding the burst edges of a balloon. I screech, wordless sounds, shaking off the rivulets dripping down my shoulders. "Oh my *god*."

"Now we're even," he says, voice fading as he drops away, landing on the ground below. He rolls neatly to his feet, straightening the edges of his jacket. Doesn't even have the decency to sprain his ankle or break a leg.

I lean over the railing, shuddering in the suddenly freezing air. "You're a dead man, Levi!"

He takes a bow, dipping low, and waves as he sprints back to his car—the car *we* stole—Elliot already in the front seat with the engine running.

I stand there for a few moments longer, plotting my revenge, except I can't seem to hold a train of thought long enough to consider anything truly evil. Instead, I watch the space where he fell away, thinking about the way he said *together*.

8

Dear Winnie,

June said I should write a poem, and I tried, but they weren't very good. So I'm writing you a letter instead and telling myself it's not the cowardly thing to do. ~~I don't think I could have asked, in person, if I had to look at you while I did it.~~ Perhaps I should have grabbed a bigger bit of paper though. I would have—never mind. I'm running out of room. So here it goes: Will you come to the school dance with me? I just want one dance with you. Actually, several. But this seems like a good start.

~~From~~
~~Yours~~
Love,
August

It is my least favorite time of year: red hearts and sappy cards, boxed chocolates and tacky teddy bears. The time of year when love-drunk morons stumble in, sending pre-written sweet nothings to their honeys, repeating the same inane Hallmark quotes over and over again, like *I love sharing life with you.* Gross. It sounds like two people just constantly breathing into each other's mouths until the oxygen turns into carbon monoxide.

"Isn't it too early for this?" I protest, holding up a bunch of nearly identical cards featuring fuzzy dogs.

"February is next week," Nan singsongs from the register. She holds up a banner, beaming at me. It says LOVE IS OUR TRUE DESTINY, and it's covered in hundreds of tiny pink hearts.

I throw my hands up, shielding myself. "Stop, it's blinding."

"Oh pish—come help me hang it; my knees don't bend that way anymore."

I abandon my box of cards to help Nan set it high over the register, so that anyone walking in can't help but be overwhelmed by the sight of it. Valentine's Day. One of the busiest times of the year for us, with people rushing in to spend twelve dollars on a card that opens with confetti and hearts and the blistering light of a thousand blessed angels, or whatever else they expect to find inside.

Mum loved Valentine's Day.

She used to buy me flowers, every year. "Petals for my petal," she'd say. I woke up covered in gerberas, once.

I push the memory aside, hopping down from the counter to appraise the store. The usual smell of warm ink and musty paper is gone, and the wall of local postcards has been obscured by twin card racks right by the entry. The curated displays of historic maps and collectible stamps have been switched out for tasteless gift fare: the aforementioned chocolates and teddies, plus socks with weirdly sexual innuendos printed on them, novelty mugs, and fake silk flowers. I don't know who buys this crap, but we sell out, every year, without fail.

Nan also sets up her tarot table down here during February. She charges double what she usually does and wears a silk scarf on her head that she insists was hand-knitted by blind Italian nuns, but I'm fairly certain is just from Target. She reads cards and predicts loves lost and found, nodding solemnly at proffered palms, muttering about omens and lifelines. When she's done, she sends them over to buy a heart-shaped card "just in case" the right person comes along. I've never decided where she's fallen on the line between *scammer* and *opportunist*. She even whips out the old crystal ball, which usually lives the rest of its life as a paperweight in the study.

Nan waves a card at me now, red-and-gold writing shining on the front. "And will *you* be sending any cards this year?"

My whole body cringes at the thought, and my mind flashes to Levi standing on the bleachers. *Truce?*

"Only the vinegar kind," I answer.

Nan snorts, ever entertained by the strange custom that our family has maintained for years.

Vinegar Valentines—or Poison Valentines, as I prefer—are a delightfully niche tradition that started in the nineteenth century. They're small cards with scathing insults on them, usually accompanied by disparaging illustrations. For the lonely and spiteful who have no lovers to woo, these cards can instead be mailed to their dearly despised. Not many people actually purchase them for their intended purpose—they usually get picked up as a collectible item, since the vintage drawings are fun to look at. There's only one artist who supplies them now, and every year she curates new limericks so that those with long-running feuds don't have to repeat their insults.

I'd forgotten all about it, until I gleefully ripped the box open to unpack the stock.

The first card is a pretty standard vanity blow: *For all your wit and endearing grace / there is no escaping your miserable face.* The one below that reads: *You do not set my heart aflutter / for you stand no higher than the gutter.*

Nan peers over my shoulder, laughing as she looks at the illustrations—they're beautiful, if you don't look too closely. But once you really notice, it's hard to unsee it: how grotesque the characters are, their wide grins a little too manic, their elegant petticoats hiding donkey hooves. They look like storybook characters, or pirate tattoos—thick bright lines, not-quite-human faces. I have a whole scrapbook upstairs with my favorites.

Nan leaves me to sort through them, heading upstairs to start dinner. I hear the scratch of a vinyl record, and the steady beat of a waltz floats into the post office. I look up and glance out the window; the sky is purple-orange, still an hour of daylight left. If I work quickly enough, I might be able to make it back to Treegap before nightfall.

I've been thinking about it ever since I went back with Elliot: Treegap meant something to the writers. There must have been something we missed—a clue they would have left. A memory. Preferably, a date-marked diary outlining their exact movements for the last twenty years or so. *Something.* We must have missed *something.*

I drag the open carton over to the far corner, shoving my sleeves up while I work. We always set up the Poison Valentines along the back wall, so I start by shelving the thin orange-spined classic books we keep for travelers and dusting off the counter. Then I unroll the posters that accompanied the cards with a flourish. It looks like a circus blowing through town, with pinup girls flashing garters and witty comments. Someone complains every year that it's *indecent*, and Nan just tells them that back in her day she didn't even bother with garters. I try very hard not to think about my free-loving nan forgetting her underpants, and instead turn to wade my way through an ocean of stacked boxes in the storage room to retrieve our antique mailbox. It's a pretty majestic thing that reaches almost to my shoulders: blue-painted brass, its coat worn thin to show off the golden metal underneath, the letter slot etched with rearing horses. Mum found it at a garage sale when I was little, and nearly wet herself laughing as she struggled to fit it in the back seat of our tiny hatchback. We haul it out in December, too, for kids to post letters to the North Pole. Or . . . we used to. I guess it's too heavy for Nan now—the top is coated in a layer of thick dust.

I set the letter box up in the corner and reach back into the box for the last set of cards. *Oh what a pretty Valentine / I shall celebrate that you were never mine.* I frown down at the cover, feeling the words sting—flaying the edges of a wound I'm determined to ignore. The artist has painted the silhouette of a woman on the front, and Cupid above her, his arrows falling helplessly to the ground, never quite striking his target. I shove them roughly into the stand and crumple the box with more force than necessary. Maybe it is a stupid tradition after all.

Someone knocks at the door, ignoring the opening hours sign clearly plastered on the front. I ignore them, focusing on the display, until the sound comes again, more impatient this time.

"We're closed!"

"Then open," calls a voice in response. "I'm wearing the wrong shoes for balcony climbing."

I freeze, wondering if I can run upstairs and hide.

"Elliot's here too. He's hungry!"

Eli's muffled indignation comes a split second later. "Hey!"

"You just *said*—"

"Yeah, but—"

I sigh, wrenching the door open. Eli looks over my shoulder at the pink confetti, spewed over every flat surface in the post office. "What happened in here?"

"Welcome to the Warwick Post Office," I drone. "The home of all your holiday needs. May I interest you in a cupid's card or a romantic rose?"

Elliot screws up his face. "Stop that. It's creepy."

I start to close the door, but Levi's hand rushes up to catch it. "If you kick us out now, you'll never find out the good news." He grins, knowing the curiosity will kill me.

I narrow my eyes, grip firm on the door. "What? The dollar store is having a sale on water balloons?"

"I'll have you know Pudge had three baths this morning and he still looks like a deranged Furby."

Elliot gives me a subtle nod, so I sigh and throw the door wide, letting them in. "At least be useful—I need that *I Love You Beary Much* stand to fit under the window."

Levi holds up a novelty mug from the counter. It has a little green drawing and says *I Think You're Turtley Awesome.* "How much is this? I must have it."

I smack his hand. "Stop it—that's for Yertle."

"Who?"

"Never mind," I say, brushing the edges of sweaty hair out of my face. "What do you want?"

He jumps up to sit on the counter, cradling the mug. "My dad no longer has you pegged on his corkboard of Warwick's Most Wanted."

My brain is still struggling to process the fact that he's both *here* and willingly engaging in conversation. Was last night a turning point—a way back to what we were? The three of us, here, gives me a strange sense of déjà vu.

"What?"

He waits for a more intelligent response apart from *What?* but since none is clearly forthcoming, he carries on. "The Motor Inn had that footage of you. Tripping into the gutter, just like you said. And at first Dad said it didn't mean anything, since the Adder Stone could have fit in your pocket, and you could have taken it when you took Ernie—which, by the way, he's *kinda* pissed about, but not, like, *super* pissed 'cause it's a bird and honestly, I don't think anyone actually noticed he'd gone missing."

"Oh," I manage. *Oh* meaning *thank you* and also *why* and also *sorry*.

"Right, so he's like 'That damned McKellon kid is all trouble; this doesn't prove anything,' et cetera et cetera—I'll save you the tirade."

"Gee, thanks."

"But then, Barbara swoops in—she comes over for brunch, sometimes, I think she's lonely without her kids, did you know they moved—"

Elliot elbows him. "Today, Levi."

"*Anyway*, Barbara says that my mum actually took a group into the room right after you left to *specifically* show them the stone, and she remembered because someone asked if they could try it on, and they touched the display, and the alarm went off, and the security dude had to come in to deactivate it."

I stop, very suddenly, mouth gaping open. The box I'm halfway unpacking tips over, but I hardly notice. "I'm sorry . . . *what?*"

Levi grins at me, shoving his hands into his varsity jacket. "Right? So that means—"

"That your mum definitely hates me because it's awfully convenient she didn't remember that detail three years ago?"

His nose scrunches up, clustering the freckles in his cheeks. "Uh, I guess that too. But it means you're innocent. Name cleared. You're welcome, by the way."

Urgh. I hate him. I hate him and his stupid freckles and his stupid jacket and his stupid smug smile. I inhale a calm breath, nails digging into my palms. "Well, thanks, I guess," I say, shaking my head. "Wait—so who did take it? Did Barbara say anything else?"

"Just that the stone was still there when she left."

"Holy shit," I whisper.

"Exactly."

And now we're one step closer to claiming that reward—*if* we can find it. *If* it even exists. I'd searched online for any mention of the reward. There were a few local articles about the theft, and a video of Levi's mum urging anyone with information to contact police. But not much else. I glance at Levi, wondering if he made the whole thing up. But that's not him—he usually relied on my fabrications rather than inventing his own. And whether it's a rumor or it's real, someone out there has the stone that ruined three years of my life.

"Can someone grab the bear end of this sign?" Elliot grunts, twisting over the counter to pin it.

I rush over to help him, scrambling onto a chair to hold it, ignoring Levi as he stands beside me and holds my knees so I don't fall.

"So, are you going to the dance?" he says, and I nearly topple off my perch because that's not what I expected him to say. He keeps surprising me. I don't know this version of Levi, the one who says what he thinks.

"Definitely not," I answer. Emiko had been bugging me about it too, but even the promise that she'd let me spike the punch wasn't appealing enough to drag me to an organized school event.

"You should come," Levi says. "It'll be fun. Elliot's going."

"No, I'm not," he grumbles.

Levi looks scandalized. "But Isaac asked you!"

Elliot drops his arms, crumbling the *Beary* part of the sign. He realizes and tries to smooth it out, using the excuse to avoid looking at either of us. "He just—it's weird, okay? He'll want to come over and pick me up—"

"What a monster," I say.

"Chivalry is dead," Levi agrees.

Elliot throws up his hands. "Whatever. Never mind. I'm not going. And I liked it better when you two hated each other, by the way."

"No, you didn't."

He just grunts, and he's saved from having to explain any further by Nan reappearing at the bottom on the stairs.

"Ah, the gentleman callers return," she says, clapping her hands.

"Nan!"

She fluffs a hand, ignoring me. "Remember to cover the crystal ball before you come up."

"Ooohh, why?" Levi asks, interest piqued. "Is it haunted? Will the evil spirits escape?"

Nan's brows raise into her gray coiffed hairline. "No, but it'll burn the bloody house down when the sun hits it in the morning."

"Oh."

Elliot grins. "Hey, Mrs. Mac."

Nan pats him on the cheek, then licks her hand to smooth back his dark curls. He has the decency not to look completely repulsed. "Hello, darling," she says. "I've made your favorite for dinner and Mabel's looking for you."

"*Actually*," Levi interjects. "I was wondering if we could borrow Brodie for a few hours?"

Nan looks at me. "Well?"

"I thought you told me not to hang out with bridge trolls?"

"I also told you not to get arrested, and look where that got you."

"Hey! I wasn't *technically*—"

But Nan's not listening. She's already retreating up the stairs. "I'll pop dinner in the oven if you're late."

I turn to look at them both: Elliot looking bashful, Levi looking pleased.

"Fine. Where are we going?"

Treegap looks different under the half-twilight sky. Less murdery, more mysterious. Levi walks laps around the outside, searching for some kind of clue. I hate that we both thought the same thing: They spent so much time here. They must have left *something* behind.

He checks the roof and the stoop, yelping when all he finds under the stairs is a pissed-off possum that scuttles into the trees.

I unload my backpack, setting out cans of bug spray and a solar lamp. When Levi is done crawling around under the stairs, we play rock/paper/scissors to decide who has to drag the old sleeping bag outside. Elliot loses, and he looks inside the cabin with forlorn eyes.

"What if there's a body in there?"

"It'd be all lumpy," Levi says. "Right?"

For some reason, he looks at me for confirmation.

"Are you implying that I should understand how to dispose of a corpse?"

Levi cocks an eyebrow. "I mean, of the three of us . . ."

I roll my eyes. "There's no body in there. Here, I'll do it, Elliot's starting to look green."

He's standing in the doorway, looking at the sad scene below. A few games and scraps of food wrappers. The sleeping bag torn in one corner.

"It just feels weird," he says with a shudder. "Maybe we should leave it."

"Shove," I say. He ducks outside with Levi, and when they're not looking, I give the sleeping bag a few good stomps, checking for bones and snakes. The blanket doesn't jingle or hiss, so I take a breath and grab the closed end with gloved hands and drag it outside.

The boys look down, waiting for something to crawl out. Nothing does, except a few moths.

"Well, that was underwhelming," Levi says.

"What were you expecting?"

"I don't know. A cloud of smoke. Bloody handprint. The Rydal Devil with a fiddle of gold to trade for souls."

We look down at the sleeping bag. Nothing happens.

"Just a sleeping bag," Elliot confirms. "Plus, you don't have a soul to trade."

"Hey!"

I leave them bickering and venture inside, inspecting dark corners and running my hands under the windowsill. There are etchings on the wall, some scratched in and others written in fading markers. Names twined in hearts. Initials roped together. Snatches of song lyrics. I run my fingertips over their words, recognizing their writing.

August was here.

I trace the lines, wondering about the day he carved these words. Was it warm? Did he come here, bored and alone? Or were the girls with him? Where did he go after—where did they all slip away to, when the letters stopped?

On a whim, I take out a pen and write a reply below.

Where'd you go, August?

I brace my hand against the wall to stand, boots sliding over slick moss below. The sleeping bag covered a section of floor that's damp and green, clearly weathered by years of rain dripping through the roof and slowly rotting away. I take a step back and the floorboards groan underfoot.

"You can't even play the fiddle," I hear Elliot argue outside.

"It's four strings, how hard can it be?" Levi replies.

"You got kicked out of orchestra because you couldn't play the recorder in tune."

"That was ten years ago!"

I frown at the floor. My boot eases down. It groans again, but the sound is strange. Hollow. "Hey, guys," I call out.

"—bet I could do the dance, though. The little jig. See? Elliot? Are you watching? Look—"

"Please stop before you hurt yourself—"

"Hey!"

"—Am I doing it? I'm totally doing it."

"That's more of a shuffle—"

"What *is* the difference between a jig and a shuffle?"

"HEY!"

They both turn to look at me, pausing midsentence. Levi stumbles out of something that looks halfway between an Irish high-kick and a country line dance.

"Do you hear that?" I say.

"What? The sound barrier shattering? That's just Levi trying to sing."

"No." I stomp my foot on the dry floor, then on the rotting boards. A hollow echo fills the cabin again. "That."

Levi frowns and surges toward the cabin, crouching beside me. Elliot trails after, leaning against the doorway. I knock on the floorboards, searching for the sound again, until we've mapped out a few loose boards. Levi tries to pry the board up with his fingernails, but curses under his breath when he can't get a proper hold—the water has bloated the planks and they won't budge.

"Anyone got a pocketknife?" he asks.

They both look at me.

"Move over," I grumble. "And for the record, I use it to open boxes at the post office."

"Sure you do, Red."

I wiggle the blade between the rotted edge, grunting in surprise as it splinters into wet green chips. I pick up a section that's come loose, the edge coated in gray film. They're not just water damaged. . . .

"It's glued shut," I say, passing the fragment to Levi.

"Huh," he says. "Guess they really didn't want anyone getting down there."

I peer into the tiny hole we've created, pressing my eye as close as I dare. "Elliot—hand me the lamp. There's something down here."

He doesn't answer for a long moment, and I glance over my shoulder to find him ghost-pale. "You okay?"

He jolts, spurred into action. "Yeah. This place just gives me the creeps. You don't feel it? Like someone is still here?"

I shake my head—trust Elliot to start believing in ghosts *now*. Or maybe he means an actual someone. The thought makes me shiver.

He passes me the lamp while Levi moves back to give me more room. I work on the driest section of the board, sliding the blade under and up. It sticks, stubbornly refusing to budge—then suddenly it springs free and clatters between us.

"Holy shit," I whisper.

They both press close, leaning over my shoulder. Levi whistles low, then settles back. Elliot just swallows hard, waiting.

"Ladies first."

"Chicken."

"Criminal," he mutters.

I pull a face, but now we're just delaying the inevitable. I shake my fingers out, trying not to cringe as I stick my hand into the dark, praying it doesn't come out covered in spiders. But all that's down there is an old shoebox, wrapped in a plastic bag that's dotted with brown muddy droplets.

I cradle it in my hands, like it's precious cargo, and wordlessly carry the parcel outside. We stare at it for a long time before I start peeling away the plastic layers, working away the edges of wrapped duct tape. Whoever boxed this up knew they weren't coming back for a long time, and they definitely didn't intend on anyone getting in.

"I feel like we're robbing someone's grave," Elliot mutters. "Maybe we should put it back."

Levi frowns. "I didn't seriously expect to find anything."

"Why'd you make us all come out here then?"

Levi glances up, eyes locking on mine. The corner of his mouth lifts. "Adventure. For old times' sake." He winks at me. *Winks.* "Open it, Red. It's your mystery."

My heart hammers a chaotic beat against my ribs. Years of wondering who the dead letter writers were—was I holding the answer in my hands?

Only one way to find out.

I take a breath, holding it until my lungs ache, and ease open the lid.

Crinkled yellow pages are stacked in neat bundles, along with a few small tokens, a pressed flower, the frayed remains of a friendship bracelet, a movie ticket stub.

I flick through the letters, searching for their names. Their *real* names. But they're all the same as the ones in the post office: Winnie and June and August.

Something falls into my lap. A black-backed square that I don't quite understand until I flip it over: a Polaroid photo. A boy standing at the lakeshore, grinning at the camera. The edges are faded blue and white, the details a little fuzzy, his face not quite in focus. It looks like a dream you can't quite remember, hardly even a glimpse, just a feeling that's slipping away.

Levi looks down, mouth dropped half open. "Who is that?"

They crowd over my shoulder again, peering at the boy in the photo. Elliot responds, reading the name scrawled below. "That's August."

I can hear them, whispering reverently, theories rapidly unraveling. But I can't hear the words, can't focus on what they're saying. Because that face, those curls, the tilt of his smile.

"I think I know this kid," I say.

The woods fall dead silent. I can feel the weight of their stares.

"What?"

"How?"

I shake my head. "I can't . . . I can't remember. But I've seen him before, I know I have." I grasp the edge of memory, as useless as trying to spool gray mist in the mornings. *His face.* I've seen it. But where?

Levi sighs. "So you don't *know him*, know him?"

I hold the picture up to the sun, squinting. *Think, Brodie.*

I tilt the photo, searching for some kind of clue, anything that—

Suddenly, I clutch the photo close, pressing it almost to my nose, sure that I've imagined it. But no, there it is and—

"There's something else," I say, flipping the Polaroid so they can see. "He's wearing the Adder Stone."

Levi tosses a popcorn kernel into the air and catches it in his mouth. "Semi-famous game show host?"

"Nope."

"Town pervert?"

"Nope."

"That one guy at the grocery store who always wears a three-piece suit?"

"Please stop."

"The illegitimate love child of a distant relative?"

"Oh my god, Levi, stop."

Levi swings his legs off the edge of the couch, sitting up. "I'm sorry, but how can you just *not remember* where you saw someone?"

I pull a face at him, and Elliot shoves him in the shoulder. "Dude, chill."

We're in the attic of the post office, the air stale and warm, dust blowing through sun traps and settling on every flat surface in a gray film. Elliot tried to wrestle a window open earlier, but it remained stubbornly closed and so now we're all sweaty and irritable. Levi's sprawled on an old settee, boxes of abandoned photo albums at his feet. We'd trawled through every box in the attic, carefully looked through every photograph, and I still couldn't remember where I'd seen August. I was starting to think I'd dreamed it—maybe I just *thought* I knew the dead letter writers. Had read their words and known their thoughts so intimately that I'd imagined their faces and convinced myself it was real.

Levi looks incredulous. "How is this not bothering either of you?"

I groan, tipping my head into my hands. A dolphin-shaped candelabra stabs me in the ribs. "It *does* bother me, but you aren't helping."

"Okay, fine. Next question," Levi says. "How did he get the Adder Stone? He must be someone in town, right? Brodie remembers him,

169

and the stone went missing three years ago. That can't be a coincidence—and at least that means they're still alive. Right?"

Elliot looks unconvinced. "Maybe the stone is unrelated. The picture is so grainy, how can you even be sure?"

"I'm sure," I repeat. It took all afternoon and I had to pay fifty dollars for a proper Photoshop program, but it's definitely the Adder Stone: blown up and slightly pixelated, but it's definitely that ugly hunk of rock strung around his neck with a piece of leather twine. Why did we want to steal this thing so badly again? More important, why did *he*?

Something else about the Polaroid bothers me, but I can't quite place it. Something about the letters and his clothes, out of place with the recent disappearance of the stone. How did it all fit together? Are the letters not as old as we thought—are they still out there, right now, still writing? But that doesn't make any sense, because the letters have sat in the post office for years. Unless these are more recent, mildew aside?

I hold the Polaroid up to the light again, half expecting to see something new. But I've stared and stared, and there's nothing else. Just a boy at the lake, smiling at the camera.

Elliot leafs through the letters, pulling them out so gently, like he's worried they'll flake away. "August," he says, the same way you'd say *hello* to an old friend. "I wonder if it's his real name."

"It has to be a code name," I answer. "They all do. We looked for them everywhere."

Although August's and June's names *did* make it hard to search, I think, remembering back to that night in the police station.

"Also, what kind of names are they?" Levi adds. "Two months and the Pooh."

"Okay, one, rude. Second, maybe they're just nicknames?"

"Or maybe this is a very elaborate prank and they never existed at all." Restless, Levi starts prowling around the attic and flips open random boxes. He recoils from one, vaguely disgusted. "Why do you have a bag of bones sitting in a salad dish?"

"It's a scrying bowl. Nan went through a pagan stage."

He gingerly replaces the lid and moves on to the next box. He pulls out a silk scarf and a bowler hat, donning both.

"Would you come to the dance with me if I dressed up like this?"

I peer over the letters, still inspecting the way they wrote *August*. "You look like the babadook."

Elliot snorts, handing me more letters, and stretches until his joints pop. "I'm getting hay fever up here. Wanna go for a swim?"

I wrinkle my nose. "In the *lake*?"

He chuckles, crossing his arms. "McKellon Felon, scared of a little water."

"First of all, I'm not scared of the water, I'm scared of what's *in* it, and secondly—"

My phone buzzes. It takes me a moment to realize it's my phone, because nobody ever calls me, and just about every friend I have is standing in this room.

Elliot tilts his head. "Gonna get that?"

"Uh . . . it's my dad."

He manages to only look surprised for a second. "Come on, Levi, show me those chicken bones."

171

"But—"

"Come *on*." He muscles Levi over to the other side of the attic, distracting him with a box full of theater swords with retractable blades (Nan went through a thespian stage after the paganism).

The phone vibrates again. I close my eyes and hit *answer*.

"Hey."

"Hey, kiddo. How's things?"

How's things. So casual. No, *Hey, Brodie, sorry for basically kicking you out and shoving you on the midnight train with hardly a backpack full of clothes.* No, *How's school, do you have everything you need?* I can hear the low hum of traffic in the background, the slight static of a car phone. The call was probably an afterthought on the way to somewhere better.

"Fine, I guess." Pause. Silence. "How's the new job?"

"Good, real good." Another pause. More silence. "I've been meaning to call. I know we talked about you staying for a while, but . . ."

A while. Actually, what he said was *I need you to go stay with your grandmother for a few days.* That was almost a month ago now. God, I hope he's not calling to tell me I have to go back to RAGs. Though at this stage, to take me he'd have to claw me out of Nan's hands without getting hexxed into the next century.

"—finish up the school year?"

I blink, trying not to concentrate on the cold sweat gathering on the back of my neck. "What?"

"With the new dates added and the shows all sold out, things are gonna be busy for a while. You can go back to Rowley if you want—"

"*No!*"

172

"But you've got friends there, now, right? Plus, your nan likes having you around. How is she?"

Mad at you, I want to answer. "She's fine. But Mabel has been—"

"Well, good," he says, not bothering to let me finish. "So you'll stick out the school year there, and I'll see you soon. Right?"

"Right," I agree.

"Thanks, Brodes. You're a good kid."

I shake my head, sinking onto the closed lid of a leather chest. *You're a good kid.* That's what he said when Mum died, and I managed not to cry at the wake because it made everyone too upset. It's what he said the first time he went on tour—just a few days, then, the fridge stocked with microwave meals. It's what he said before he closed the door and drove away from Rowley, leaving me with a bunch of kids staring at the girl with a suitcase at her feet and no one to help carry it upstairs. And suddenly I'm so angry: angry that he left, that he never bothered to try, that I never even really knew him at all—not since Mum died. I think of that stupid Father's Day card, with the golf bag and the cars and the barbecue tongs. I blink back fury-tears, angry that my voice shakes when I speak.

"Hey, Dad?"

"Yeah?"

"Do you even like cooking?"

"Cooking?"

"Yeah. You used to do it all the time, but I didn't know . . ." Suddenly, I lose my nerve. The phone droops in my hand. What's the point? "Actually, it's stupid. Never mind."

The line goes quiet for a while. For a moment, I think he's hung up. When he speaks, his voice is colored with surprise. "Sure, I like cooking. Started when your mum got sick."

Oh. "Really? I don't remember that." I was nine the first time she got one of her headaches. We were driving, and she pulled over to vomit out the window.

He huffs a laugh. "Both of us were hopeless cooks—lived off takeout, sandwiches, cereal sometimes. But then she couldn't eat so much, and when she was hungry she always wanted your nan's spaghetti, so I learned how to make it. She got tired of that eventually and wanted soup instead, so I learned to make that too."

I frown, trying to remember. Sure, there was the occasional family meal. But it was mostly plain pasta or fish fingers, something thrown in the oven. I remembered being so excited to move in with Nan because she made roast dinners on Sundays, and Mum promised me when she got better she'd teach me how to make the bready pudding that went with it.

"You okay, Brodes? Everything all right?"

I swallow, nodding, then realize he can't see me. "Yeah. Yeah, I'm fine. I was just wondering. Hey, Dad—did Mum leave any photos behind? I'd like to see them."

"A few, sure. I think there's one of Perry's albums back home in the city. Any reason?"

Damn. If it was in the city, I'd have to wait for Dad to finish up the tour before he could send it to me. "Just curious," I sigh, feeling defeated.

"Ask your nan, there must be a few hanging around in the attic."

I stare at the cluttered attic, boxes half open and spewing twenty years' worth of memorabilia. "Yeah, I will."

"I'm turning onto the freeway—can I call you back in a minute?"

"Sure, Dad. Bye."

"Talk soon," he says, and I know he'll forget to call back and we probably won't talk again for a few weeks.

I sigh, and the exhaled breath makes dust dance around the curtains. An album back home—had I ever seen it? Dad mostly kept her stuff wrapped up, worried that I'd accidentally ruin something too precious to replace.

Elliot settles beside me, nudging my shoulder with his own. "You good?"

"Yeah. Always am."

"He loves you, you know." Elliot's fingers drum a nervous beat on his legs. "I know he's not there enough. And he's kind of a crap dad. But he loves you. At least he tries."

I lean my head on Elliot's shoulder, reaching down to clasp his fidgety fingers in my own. "You're very wise, you know, for a teenage boy."

"It's my heart line," he says, holding his palm flat. "Huge brain."

"Huge head," I correct. "Starting to think it's full of your own ego."

"I'm bored and dusty," Levi whines from across the room, reappearing from a cupboard that Elliot appears to have shoved him in. "Let's go swimming."

The weather vane groans.

"Gonna rain," I say.

Levi presses his face flat against the window. "There is not one single cloud outside."

"Gonna rain," I repeat with a shrug.

"How do you *know*?"

175

"Attic ghost," Elliot says, steepling his fingertips and giving a sage nod.

Levi rolls his eyes. "It's not going to rain."

"Fine. But I'm not getting in that water."

We swim.

It rains.

9

The new letters consume my waking hours. I read them and read them again. I search for names and places and dates and little inside jokes: *anything* that might lead me to them. But these letters are more personal than the others—there's hardly any mention of their lives, the real world. They give me absolutely nothing that is, objectively, useful in any way.

But *oh*, how I love them.

These letters, which were loves given and promises told. They make me laugh, and I watch August and Winnie fall in love—*really* in love, not just crushes and sideward glances—and I catch myself so engrossed that my fingers are clutched around the pages and my nose is nearly pressed to the ink. There's so much that we missed, so many in-between moments, and I read them all until I've nearly memorized them.

I cannot see with only this ridiculous candle burning—it gives me a splitting headache to squint in the dark; how can you stand it? Though I suppose you and August are probably just waiting until I'm asleep so you can go pash in the library, but I'm not tired and I'll stay awake just to spite you both. Ha!—J

You are such a quarrelsome creature, you know that? And we're not going to "pash," June.

Oh no? Not like your paperback Fabios? Does he have a rippling bodice?—J

A) Only women wear a bodice. I believe you meant body and B) could you please keep your perverted thoughts to yourself.

I think men should be allowed to wear a bodice if they want. Don't you think he'd look cute all trussed up like that?

You are utterly incorrigible. Go to sleep so August and I can go pash in the library.

Thought you weren't going to—

The letter breaks off suddenly, pencil running erratically off the page, like it was snatched away midsentence. I run my hand over the corner of the page, smoothing the crease. I like to imagine June and Winnie in the dark, trading letters, giggling and whispering and writing down what they didn't want August to overhear. I imagine Winnie peeking over June's shoulder, watching what she wrote, then finally giving up and whacking her on the head with a pillow. It makes me laugh, and I keep it in my lap as I reach in for the second letter.

Dear Winnie,

I would like to say that I sent this letter of my own volition, but actually, June frog-marched me to the post office and forced me to buy this particularly hideous card so that, and I quote, "you could stop mooning over each other and just go snog already." Who says snog, anyway? Ow, June just hit me on the head. ~~Go away, June, I know you can see me writing this. You're making it weird. This card cost five dollars, and I'm wasting all this space writing to you.~~

Anyway. This seems silly now. I've ruined it, haven't I? Should I buy another card? Although the line is quite long. I guess I'm stuck with this one. And maybe I should just ask you myself. That seems to be the done thing. It's only, I tried. A few times. And I got so nervous. And I'm still nervous, but at least I can't run away from a letter.

Maybe I should, actually. This letter is a mess. This is the worst letter, this one right here. Please throw it out. But I guess I'm not so much afraid of sending it as much as I am of not sending it.

Anyway. This is all squashed. Probably illegible.

I just wanted to ask you to dinner. If you wanted. Just the

two of us. It would be a date—June said to add that. She says
I don't get to the point often enough.
She also says you'll say yes.
Please say yes.

Love,

August

I flick through the next letters, trying to sort them into some kind of sensible order when the post office bell dings and a throat clears at the counter.

"Excuse me, do you sell any turtle cards?"

I look up. Bleached blonde hair and wide red-rim glasses look down. Yertle is clutching her hands nervously, fidgeting with the clasp of her turtle-shaped coin purse.

"Oh, hi Yer—Yula. How's Ralph?"

"Slow."

"More than usual?"

"No, that was a joke," she says with a frown.

I cough, setting the letters down and jump to my feet. "Well, actually, Nan saw these on the supplier form and ordered them for you just in case. What do you think?"

"*I shell always love you*," she reads. "Oh. Ha! Oh goodness, how funny." She sets the card down on the counter and gives it a gentle pat. "Thank you, it's perfect. I'll take it."

I take her coins and bite back a smile—Tommy was *in love* then. Explained why he kept missing his Saturday morning shifts.

"Do you want to take your seagrass today too?"

"Please."

I reach behind for her locker with my eyes still on the register, blindly stumbling over the jammed door of 604 before correctly recalibrating to 603. The seagrass smells like damp butts, as Nan says, and it always soaks through the bottom layer of cardboard. Yula looks pleased, unbothered by the stench, and tucks the card in her pocket. "Thank you! Happy Valentine's Day."

I pull a face as she leaves, wrinkling my nose.

"I saw that, young lady!"

I lean over the counter, eyeing Nan at her tarot table. "You look like the Zoltar machine."

"The manners on you, child, I swear. Who raised you?"

"You, mostly."

"Explains a lot."

The bell dings. Nervous Ms. Fieldman from down the road walks in, towing her little white dog. She comes every year, hoping the cards will predict that she'll soon capture the attention of a young suitor. Seems like it would be a lot easier for her to find love if the monster at her feet didn't chase them all away.

I duck behind the counter again, leafing through the letters until another customer enters. Working retail would be so much more enjoyable without actual people involved.

"I'd like to mail this, please."

An obnoxious red envelope lands upside down on the counter.

"Dollar for stamps," I say, holding out my palm, not bothering to look up.

"Trade you for a kiss." Levi smirks, leaning down to set his elbow on the counter. "Whaddya say, sweetcheeks?" he adds, aiming for an old-Hollywood drawl and landing somewhat south on a weird country twang.

"Who's the unlucky lady?"

"You wound me, Brodie."

"Stamps are two dollars."

"You just said one."

"Whoops, did I say two? Five dollars for you, *bucko*."

"Bucko?" he asks. "Really?"

"Sweetcheeks?"

"Point taken." He hands me a dollar. "So. Any luck?"

I sigh, pushing the letter pile forward. "None. Mostly what we already knew: They went to the lake, the arcade, the cinema. Treegap, though I guess now that makes more sense." And absolutely zero mention of the Adder Stone.

"That's it? Nothing new?"

"Well . . . I think Winnie had a brother," I say tentatively. "I went back over the other letters, and he's never mentioned again. But look, here: *Dear Winnie, your darling bub simply will not leave me alone. I knew I shouldn't have gone on that date, but you said it would be fun, and I believed you because I'm an idiot. Honestly, you got all the charm in that family. Poor Charlie: pretty face but such a bore. He talked about football for an hour then tried to kiss me with garlic-milkshake breath. Remind me which university he's going to so I can never, ever go there.*

Levi reads it and looks up. "Bub?"

I shrug. "People use all kinds of nicknames. For instance, I saved your number in my phone under 'Satan.'"

"You saved my number?"

"Okay, bye now." I whip his envelope off the counter and stuff it into the local mail tub, while Levi protests. A very annoying part of me wishes I'd checked the address before I stashed it.

"I'm sorry! Brodie, please. Tell me more about the brother."

I cross my arms and glare at him.

He pouts and holds out his hands.

Silently, I hand over the very last letter. The one that was buried and folded, the lines deep and soft as though it had been agonized over and over again. I watch him read in silence, his lips moving slightly as he skims over the words until he reaches the very end.

"*Tell Charlie I'm sorry?*" He looks up. "What does that mean?"

I blow out a breath, and spin around in the office chair. "I have absolutely no idea."

"Interesting."

"Do you think . . ." I chew on my lip. Shaking my head.

"What?"

"It just . . . I don't know. Doesn't that letter sound sort of *final?* And we've never found any trace of them. . . . Maybe . . ."

Maybe the worst. Maybe the thing that we never dared say when we played Where are they now?

Levi reads the letter again, frowning. "No way," he says, but his voice gets tight, and I can tell he's lying. "It's just a—a fight. A misunderstanding. I bet Winnie gave this to June and went home right after and they all had shepard's pie for dinner."

"Apple pie for dessert," I mumble.

Levi chucks me on the chin, then flashes a broad smile. We used to do this. Beg and tease until the other smiled back. "Then played Monopoly until June cheated, and everyone got annoyed."

"So they made hot chocolate."

"Snuck out to the woods—trying to summon the Rydal Devil."

"Got bored when nothing happened."

"Went to Treegap."

"And then . . ." I trail off. *And then disappeared forever.* "You're right. It's probably nothing."

There's a sharp rap, then a loud throat-clearing "AHEM." We both look at Nan, her decorated head scarf sitting slightly crooked as she stacks a new tarot deck, eyes narrowed in our direction. "Apologies for the distraction, Ms. Fieldman," she says, turning back to her customer. "Pick a card—the one you feel drawn to. . . ."

Levi flashes another smile. "Better bounce," he whispers. "See you around, Red. Don't forget to mail that card."

He slips away to the sound of bells jingling, the post office door closing behind him with a heavy clatter. I sigh and spend the next ten minutes eavesdropping on Nan's reading.

"The Hermit card. Interesting—no, no, you're not going to die alone. Collect yourself, woman! A journey to self-discovery, yes, see? Maybe you should take that trip to Italy after all. . . ."

Levi's red card pokes through the stack of boring white envelopes. *Technically*, intercepting mail is a federal crime. But is it *really* intercepting if one *happens* to work for the post office? And it's not as if we don't already read every heartfelt, tragic, slightly erotic postcard that comes through here.

I stare at the upside-down envelope. Who's Levi been flirting with? No one that I know, which isn't saying much, since I avoid him at school like the bubonic plague. It's really none of my business who he flirts with.

Really.

None.

But it's not like he can just *hand* me this and *expect* me not to look. Or is it a trap? One of those exploding glitter envelopes everyone thought were hilarious a few years back?

I snatch the envelope up, shaking it beside my ear. Those cards really had some horsepower behind them—I accidentally set one off and was picking glitter shards out of my hair for a month. The card quietly shuffles inside, sabotage-free.

I flip it over to the front and frown. He's forgotten to address it. And I should call him back. Yes, that's what I should do.

I peek at Nan again, but she's bowed over the deck, now fully immersed in the reading. "Ace of cups—upright, a lovely card. A moment of reflection, new feelings—love, perhaps . . ."

I look at the ceiling and pray to the gods of postmasters past. "Whoops," I whisper, sliding my fingernail under the thin tape stuck to the back (tape! Practically *begging* to be snooped on. If he really wanted to keep me out he should have slobbered on it).

I knew you'd read this letter,
(still on that revenge vendetta?)
So I thought I might as well ask:
Come with me to the dance,
I'll promise zero romance—
And you can think of it as a daring task.

185

I frown at the rhyme, then crumple it in my lap, panicked by the sudden shuffle of chairs. *Shit, shit, shit.* I try to smooth the letter under the palm of my hand, voice squeaking as I wave Ms. Fieldman toward the guidebook section. Sweat beads against my collar as she retreats to the rear of the store, and I flip the card over.

Addressed to: Brodie McKellon, my favorite felon.

Son of a—

I bet he had to use a rhyming dictionary to make that poem. I read it again, then notice the tiny postscript at the bottom. *Truce, remember? It'll be fun. Elliot's going.*

I grab the office phone and dial Elliot's number from memory. It's the only number I know by heart.

"What?" he answers, clearly awoken by the call.

"It's eleven o'clock."

"Thank you: I do, in fact, know how to tell time."

"Did you tell Levi you'd go to that dance?"

Silence. "No . . ."

"But?"

". . . I said I'd go with Isaac."

"So you are going?"

"Technically, I will be there, yes."

"Traitor. I'm really happy for you. But *traitor.*"

"I'm hanging up now," he says, voice muffled by pillows.

"Bye, Brutus. Come by when you're ready for pancakes."

"You are mildly psychotic, you know that, right?"

"Love you too."

"Get the maple syrup ready, I'll be there in ten."

I hang up, still clutching Levi's letter. For a minute, I think about sealing it up and marking it *Return to Sender*. Then I remember the Vinegar Valentines card sitting up in my room. If Levi wants a vendetta, then that's what he's going to get.

I toss his letter into the bin, then frown. There's another envelope in there, even though it's only been me on the desk this morning and so quiet I haven't had to clear anything away. A bright red stamp peeks out from under Levi's card—those stamps are usually the important ones, and I worry for a second that I've accidentally thrown away someone's mail instead of filing it. I reach down to grab it, finding it addressed to Delia McKellon, in neat, official typewriter face. You learn a lot about mail working in the post office—like how to tell the difference between a bill and a birthday card without needing to open the envelope. With its gray-printed insides and clear plastic address window, this letter screams *bank*.

The seam is ripped open already with rough, jagged edges. I frown at the red stamp that caught my attention. *Final bill*. It's none of my business. Nan is an adult, and a forgetful one at that. She forgets to pay bills all the time; half the time her phone doesn't ring because she can't be bothered topping up the credit.

I peek inside, mostly so I can remind her to pay whatever is due. But I frown at the letter, not understanding for a moment what it means. There's a *lot* of zeros—and they're all in the owing column. I scan the details and a kernel of dread settles in my chest: Nan hasn't paid the mortgage for a while. And unless we can find almost fifteen thousand dollars in a few weeks, they want to claim *collateral.*

They want to take the house.

The entire school is obsessed with the Valentine's Day dance. I don't know who decided it was a good idea to toast marshmallows over devices we use to boil chemicals and let a bunch of horny teens roam free with minimal supervision, but there has been a serious error in judgment here. Even when Mr. Gallager reminds us that "the boys and girls will be monitored" on the dance floor for "inappropriate relations," Claire and Jenn just snicker quietly while Emiko rolls her eyes.

"Please come," she says. "The dance is actually fun, but I really don't want to be alone on the sidelines while Claire and Jenn are canoodling."

Claire pulls a face. "We do not *canoodle.*"

"Well, you do *something,* because last sleepover I heard—"

Claire thumps her on the head with a stringy wig from the prop basket. Emiko just laughs until the teacher walks in and the room takes on a sudden, reverent hush, a low murmur of whispered voices instead of the usual clamor and chaos.

"What's going on?" I whisper to Emiko, hoping I hadn't forgotten an exam or—worse—some kind of performance.

"They're announcing which play we'll be doing this year," she whispers back. "The thespians are about to pee themselves with excitement."

Claire elbows her in the side. "It *is* exciting, but I will throw myself into the river if they make us do fucking *Cats.* Again."

"I like *Cats*," Emiko says, looking up with a frown. "The moonlight song. It's cute."

"It's 'Memory,' you heathen,"

"Snob."

"Urgh—just—" Claire shushes her with a hand over her mouth, which makes Emiko giggle, which makes *me* giggle, until the teacher walks onstage and makes a show of unfurling a prop scroll.

"Hear ye, hear ye," he says, and the theater goes silent. "I see you are all excited, so let's get straight to it. We are very impressed by the class talent this year, and so I'm thrilled to announce the school has approved a musical created this side of the century. Don't get too excited—no, Elloise, they will not let us perform *Bat Boy*, please stop asking—we are still restricted to the bargain division of licensing fees, so this year's musical—"

"Fucking *Cats*," Claire whispers.

"—is *Tuck Everlasting*, based, of course, on the novel by Natalie Babbitt. Have we all read the text?"

Emiko looks at me and shrugs, while Claire nods enthusiastically.

"I'll take that as a resounding no. Well, that's this weekend's homework sorted. Track down a copy, have a read, start thinking about sets, costumes, props, and we'll begin brainstorming production next week."

Claire is practically vibrating with excitement. "This is perfect!" she whispers. "God, I want the lead so badly. Except *ew*, who's going to play Jesse? They won't really make us kiss, will they? Maybe I can convince them to put Jenn in a hat. . . ."

Emi and I squeeze her hand, and I can practically feel her heart-beat drumming. When was the last time I'd wanted something that badly? I grin at her, her eagerness contagious.

"I could live with Mae, I guess. She gets her own song. . . ."

The teacher shushes the room, trying valiantly to continue with the class plan despite the entire rear half of the room now scribbling possible cast arrangements on bits of loose paper.

Claire bumps me on the shoulder, whispering quietly, "So, are you auditioning?"

I look up at the stage. So far, musical theater has actually been bearable. Usually, I get to help coordinate the lights or music for the mock performances, and only occasionally have I been subjected to reading lines in front of the class. It helps that the lights are so blinding you can't really see anyone in the seats below. Now the class is getting ready for an actual performance, and the room is full of nervous jitters.

"Absolutely not," I say. "I'll just . . . be one of those wing people."

"Stagehand," she corrects.

Emiko shoves the blonde wig onto her head, slightly off center. "Is this cute or no?"

Claire glances over. "You look like Glinda the Drunk Witch."

"Hey! Just because I said *canoodling*—"

The bell finally sounds, and we all rush to stand, but the teacher calls us back. "Hang on! I have a reminder from the office that ticket sales for the dance are now available. Buy a dollar heart to invite a special someone!" He raises his voice, calling out to be heard above the end-of-day melee. "Remember that Hamilton wrote fifty-one Federalist Papers, so you can write one poem!"

The entire hallway is filled with them—it looks like the Hall-mark factory exploded mid-production. Notes are stuck to lockers and passed between friends, pinned to shirts and trampled on the floor. Claire buys one and writes to Jenn *"Come canoodle with me."* Emiko buys another and tries to stick it to my forehead, but I duck, and it flutters to the floor.

"Well, if that isn't entirely symbolic of my love life," she mutters.

I laugh, watching as she runs after it in the wind.

"Hey!" Levi glowers at me from across the quad, and for a moment I think of turning and running back into the end-of-day fray, losing him in the sea of students flowing out the doors to freedom. But no, I stand my ground, and square my shoulders as I spot the card in his hand. I had settled on simplicity in the end:

> *Roses are red*
> *Violets are blue*
> *Your Jeep is stupid*
> *And you are too*

He leaps over a low-level brick wall and nearly takes out a tiny junior student as he comes level with me, face-to-face on the steps. He holds up the card, lips curled back.

"Don't hate on the Jeep," he says.

"Really? *That's* the part you're offended about?"

"You helped me steal that car, if memory serves."

My cheeks heat at the memory. "Yeah, and then your mum paid for it."

"So you wouldn't get arrested!"

"So *you* wouldn't get arrested," I correct. "Whatever—you should be grateful I didn't go for the pink Beetle."

He makes a sound somewhere between a strangle and scream. "You are infuriating," he says.

"That's one of the nicest things you've ever said to me."

"Uh, guys." Emiko gives a meek wave, stepping between us. "People are starting to stare. As entertaining as this is—whatever this is—do it in private, maybe?"

Levi's mouth drops open to say something else, but I give him a pat on the shoulder then bounce down the stairs, arm slipped through Emiko's elbow. She squints at me, giving me the look.

"Don't say it," I warn.

"*Such* a weird way of flirting."

Tommy finally emerges from his love bubble to do a few shifts at the post office. The till doesn't balance when he closes—apparently, he lost all the receipt paper, so he started giving people handwritten notes and scribbling tallies in the margin of an old notebook, and then Mabel shredded it all anyway. Nan makes him a cup of tea and asks if he really has his heart set on working retail for the rest of his life.

"I always thought my band was gonna *make it,* you know? But our drummer is an accountant now, and Gav's got two kids. . . ."

I shake my head, trying to ignore Tommy's existential crisis as I continue tabling a list of inventory beside me.

"I dunno. I've been thinking of, maybe, like, reptile breeding? You know a turtle costs a thousand dollars? And you can just grab those little dudes from the lake, so . . ."

There's a sudden crash, the sound of glass shattering and something heavier, something *wrong*, and Tommy yells out. "Mrs. Mac! You okay? Brodie, help!!"

My stomach clenches, ice-cold dread flooding my veins. *Not Nan, not like this—*

I scramble out from behind the counter, finding Tommy leaning over Nan, sprawled on the floor beside a smashed teacup, a dark spot blooming on her side. I drop beside her, hands racing over her chest, useless and terrified.

"Nan? Nan! Can you hear me?"

She sits up suddenly, waving me off, straightening her cardigan. "Stop your fussing! I'm fine!"

I exhale a long breath, all of the worst-case scenarios melting away just as soon as they'd formed. My fingers brush against the warm liquid on her side, and I realize it's just spilled tea, nothing worse. I help her to her feet, ignoring the gnawing feeling of barely averted disaster. "What happened? Are you okay?"

She curses, kicking off her loafers. "It's these damn *fashion* shoes. Got caught in the rug, is all. Why do you both look like you've seen a ghost? I'm not dead yet, and trust me, you'd know. I'll haunt this place good and proper."

Tommy and I look at each other, uncertain. Nan settles back in her chair, ignoring our fussing as she checks her hair in a pocket mirror.

"Maybe I should—"

"I'm fine," Nan says again. "Though if you want to be useful, Brodie, I was really looking forward to that cup of tea. Go be a pet and boil the kettle? Now, Tommy, you know you can't just *take* a turtle—"

I hesitate, and Tommy and I stare at each other for a long moment before I sigh and turn away, trudging upstairs toward the kitchen.

Trying to forget the terrible sound of a body hitting the floor.

The shatter of glass.

I set the kettle to boil with shaking hands, breath hitching in my throat. *She's okay, Nan's okay, nothing happened.* I slide down to the floor, my back pressed against the cupboards, hand pressed against my mouth. *She's not Mum. It's not the same.*

She was just standing there. Singing a song about dancing in the mud with alligators while she mixed together a batch of packet cupcakes. Holding Nan's favorite blue bowl.

"Shit, it was only meant to be two eggs," she said. Mum was excellent at a lot of things; baking wasn't one of them. Then she looked up at me, a strange look on her face.

"I feel . . ."

The bowl dropped first. Shattered.

And she was gone. Just like that.

The doctors said it was *cerebral arteriovenous malformation.* Her brain was just wired the wrong way. They'd tried to help her over the years, shaved one side of her head and stitched it back up again. But she still got the headaches, and then one day, *that day,* her luck ran out. A time bomb counting down that none of us had heard ticking away, suddenly detonated.

Collateral damage.

The kettle shrieks, and Mabel crawls into my lap, bumping her head against my chest. I hold her close, keeping her balanced on my shoulder as I pour Nan's tea.

"What do you think, old girl?"

Mabel mews quietly, a sorrowful sound. She was Mum's cat. We don't talk about that much.

"I miss her too," I whisper.

I take Nan's tea down and watch as she shifts in her seat—waiting for something worse, a flinch or a tremble. Like Mum. But every time she catches me staring, she just raises an eyebrow and eventually shoos me away.

I clean up the glass shards and make an excuse to retreat upstairs and pull my phone out to call Dad. The line rings until his voice mail catches. "Hey, Dad, it's me. Can you call me back when you get this? Nan—she—um . . ." I sigh, rubbing my eyes. This is stupid. It was nothing. What would I tell him? She tripped on shoes I made her buy? She hasn't been paying the mortgage for a while, could you maybe chip in with all that money you *don't* make as a roadie? I take a breath, making sure my voice doesn't shake when I speak again. ". . . it's her birthday soon. I wanted to buy her something nice. Could you maybe send some money? Um, that's all, I guess. Miss you. Bye."

I crawl under my bed and take out a few of the letters—looking for one in particular. The one I usually avoid. It's the only letter that's not addressed to anyone. I think it was never meant to be read at all.

Today is Mum's birthday. ~~*It's the first one without her.*~~
She loved her birthday. She always got up before anyone else. She would bake herself a cake, and we'd have it for breakfast.

195

I baked her a cake this year. Took me three hours to figure out how, but I made it. I was going to light the candles for her and say a prayer even though I don't really believe in God, because if there was a god Mum wouldn't have died, but it seems like that's what people do, and I thought she would have liked it. Then Dad came home and said men aren't supposed to make cakes, and men aren't supposed to be crying over their dead mothers.

~~*He threw the cake in the bin.*~~

I was already packing my bags when June knocked on the door. Don't know where I was going. Just somewhere that wasn't here. June took one look at the kitchen and declared it was a sleepover night. I don't know how she does that—knows when she's needed. But she always does. I think she might be my best friend, actually. And Winnie is—

There's a break in the page, a few inches of empty space. Then the writing resumes, a little looser, a few water stains dotted at the edge.

I wish you could have met them. You would have really loved them. They're the only things keeping me here, now. Anyway. Happy birthday, Mum. I miss you.

Love,

August

I hate this letter. I hate that I know how it feels, the first year, alone. The moment just before you open your eyes in the morning and you forget, just for a second, that they're not here anymore. Glancing down at the date in class and wanting to say happy birthday. Walking past pink floral birthday cards and thinking you ought to buy one—then realizing you don't need to, ever again. I think of that first year, when I was alone at RAGs. At least August made his mum a cake. I didn't bother—I had no one to share it with anyway.

Below, I hear the shuffling of seats and feet, the sign in the door flipping to *Closed*. I stuff the letter back under the bed as Nan makes her way up. She makes a show of stowing her shoes in the buffet cupboard and starts pulling out pots and pans. I jump to my feet, grabbing the chopping board and the boiling pot. "How about I cook tonight instead?"

"I'm *fine*, Brodie."

"I know, but I have a craving for box mac and cheese, and you just don't have the knack for the fake stuff anyway."

We eat in silence, and eventually she takes a bottle of sherry upstairs to watch her shows and drunk dial Mr. Harris down the road. An alert pings on my phone—the bank app letting me know Dad has sent fifty dollars to my account. No call back. Just the transfer. Set and forget.

I creep into Mum's room, whisper *hello*. Trail my hand over her old pillowcase, though it's been washed so many times, it no longer smells like her. I think sometimes that I'm forgetting her: the exact pitch of her laugh, the chip that might have been in her right tooth or her left. I walk to her old closet, half full with Dad's unwanted shirts and a few boxes of junk. But there's a few things, still. A knit sweater with her lipstick stain on the collar. A pair of overalls with said lipstick in the pocket. A leather jacket I'd probably wear, except I'm terrified of ruining it. I hold it close and pretend I can smell her perfume in the fabric. But I'm scared of using it all up, this lingering piece of her, so I set it back, close the doors, and convince myself that I might have come in here to do homework. I glance at her shelves, searching for our drama text, but there's a gap between Austen and Brontë where the book should be—or would have been, if we had it. Instead, I crawl out onto the roof beside my window, watching the stars twinkle to life. There's a clattering on the balcony, and soon Elliot heaves himself up beside me.

"Would you rather have no elbows or no knees?" he says by way of greeting.

"Depends. Can I have robot legs to hold me upright?"

"Can you *afford* robot legs?"

"Why am I giving up my kneecaps if I don't get money for it?"

"Because I'm pretty sure the black market for illegally trafficked kneecaps is pretty slim."

"Actually, I think you can live without kneecaps. Can you live without elbows? Or would you get spaghetti arms?"

He laughs, folding an arm under his head. "Where's Delia?"

"Bed," I say, terse.

He checks his watch. It's early, but he doesn't say anything. "I think Mum's gonna get promoted to that curator job at the library. For the display?"

"Really? That's amazing."

"Yeah. She's pretty happy. Said to tell you hi."

"I'll come by soon. I want to see her in action. I'm picturing Rachel Weisz in *The Mummy*."

"I mean, it's mostly old newspapers and scanning, but sure."

"No mummies?"

"Nope. Also, she's going to be a curator, not an Egyptologist, so even if there *were* mummies she wouldn't let you poke one."

"I don't want to poke one—"

He swats me away as I poke him in the ribs. Mabel must sense his presence because she drops down and nestles on his stomach.

We lie together in silence, watching the sky, listening to Mabel's low rumble. Elliot waits. So patient, unhurried by life.

"Nan fell today," I whisper. "Like Mum did. She was fine, and then she wasn't."

Elliot stills, hand freezing on Mabel's spine. "She okay?"

"She's fine. Said it was her shoes. But just that moment, the sound . . . and seeing her . . . I thought . . ."

His pinkie loops through mine. "But it didn't. It wasn't."

I blow out a breath. "Yeah. I know."

"Do you believe her? That it was just a fall?"

"I guess? Usually I can trust her, but . . ." I think of the letter in the bin. The zeros on the arrears notice. "I found a bill today too. She's behind on payments for the house."

"How much?"

"A lot," I mumble. "She never even mentioned it. I mean, we've never had mountains of gold or anything, but this is different."

"Did you ask her about it?"

"She'll just say it's fine. She always does."

199

"Yeah," he says quietly. "Life would be easier if adults didn't lie, hey?"

I think of Dad. *Call you back soon.* "Yeah," I agree. "Mum never lied, though. Sometimes I wish she would have. She would just blurt out so much truth I didn't know what to do with it." When she was sick, I had asked if she was going to get better. *I'm going to try,* she said. *Try.* And I knew then that maybe I wouldn't always have the life I'd thought; that maybe Mum wouldn't pick me up from school again, watch me graduate. Wouldn't bake school cakes and paint my nails. Wouldn't read to me at night and kiss me goodbye in the mornings, the print of her lipstick always stuck to my cheek.

"My mum said she was leaving Dale," Elliot chokes. His voice hitches and breaks, full of hope and despair. Wanting it to be true and knowing it wasn't.

"She loves you," I say, squeezing tight. "She's trying." It happens every few years: Quinn builds up the courage to leave Dale, and then she doesn't. Or can't. Sometimes, it's the same thing: can't or won't. Where do you go when you have nowhere left to run?

He nods, throat bobbing, blinking hard. "Isaac met her."

I grin at him in the moonlight. "Yeah?"

"Yeah."

"Did she love him?"

"Obviously."

I laugh, and his chest hikes up and then down, tension melting. "Sorry about the dance," he mumbles. "I know you don't wanna go. You don't have to."

"It's fine; it's not your fault Levi got the idea to make it happen."

"Actually . . ."

I jolt up in time to watch a warm red blush spread across his cheeks. "You didn't!"

"I sort of might have, sort of . . . *suggested* he should ask you."

The sound that comes out of my throat is hardly human.

"As a group hang!"

"Group. Hang?"

"Look, I wasn't planning on going, but Isaac wore me down and I thought—I thought maybe you and Levi were getting past things. Maybe we could go back to the way things were. Before the stupid stone, and whatever happened when you left."

I kick my foot at the railing, tracing the wrought iron, pushing until I think it might buckle. "I don't know if I know how to do that," I say quietly. Then, louder: "I do, however, look forward to taking three hundred photos of you and Isaac all dressed up."

"You will not."

"We'll see."

"No."

"Hmm? Maybe? Yes? Unrelated: Do you own a bow tie?"

"You're incorrigible."

"Incorrigible? That's a good word. Did you help Levi write his poem? I didn't even think he could spell *vendetta*, much less use it in a sentence."

Elliot laughs, a deep happy sound that bounces Mabel on his stomach. She sticks out her claws to balance, and Elliot grabs her to hoist her away from his sweater. "Damn, Mabel, chill."

She mews petulantly. He scruffs her head.

201

"Any big Saturday night plans?" he asks, tucking her in under one arm.

I grin at him, suddenly inspired. "Wanna go put a turtle in Levi's bathtub?"

"Where does one even acquire a turtle around here?"

"Oh don't worry. I know a guy."

10

Dear August,

I've been thinking about devils.

Mum has been sending us to church every Sunday since that night. You know the one, where we—well, you were there. I'm sure you remember.

The minister goes on and on about temptations and devils and sin. And they get such a bad rep, but really, isn't THE devil just a fallen angel? Isn't temptation just something we want, that someone else has decided we can't have?

And devils can't all be bad. I think they're just bored. Wouldn't you be bored, sitting around in the clouds all day, doing everything you were told?

I am. I'm bored, August. Without you and June. I think they're planning to keep me grounded forever—at least until university. Maybe I should wander out to the nearest crossroads and see what happens. What should I wish for?

Actually, I already know. I've thought about this a lot. I'd
wish for you and June to stay. For every year to be just like this
one, even the boredom. The summer days and the lake and
Treegap. Even being grounded forever and ever would be okay,
if I got to re-live it all again. It was worth it, just so you know.
The thing. That we—maybe I shouldn't write that one down,
actually.

I'll sneak out tonight. Through the window—Mum won't
notice. Meet me at the crossroads. Let's have some fun.

Be my devil, August. And I'll be yours.

—W

"They made it up!"

Levi refuses to look up from a stack of textbooks, so I can't entirely tell if he's happy to see me or not. He seems to raise his chin a fraction of an inch, so that his hair falls artfully in front of his eyes in a manner that I'm sure he's rehearsed in the mirror. Then he turns back to the book.

I wait for all of thirty seconds before repeating myself. "Are you listening? They *made it up*!" I slap the letter down on the table. "Look! I've heard it before, that phrase! *Be my devil.* They were just bored! The Rydal Devil is a rumor *they* started."

Somebody shushes me from the stack and then gasps when I give them the finger. Who actually studies in the library anyway?

Levi stares at the letter for a long drawn-out moment, then shoves his bangs out of his face. He looks less than thrilled that I'm disrupting his designated study period.

"Brodie," he says, leaning back in his chair and crossing his arms. A muscle ticks in the corner of his jaw. "Did you know that some turtles urinate from their mouths?"

"I—what?"

He leans forward, lowering his voice. "I found three turtles in my bathtub on the weekend. And the little bastards kept chucking up pee, and I thought they were *dying*, so I had to call my mum, and she called the ranger, and he was *not* happy—"

Turns out, turtles are surprisingly transportable. They didn't mind a little detour on their way back to the lake.

"—and then the ranger came over, and he's all 'Hey, kid, there's only three turtles here, where's the fourth?' and I'm like 'What fourth?' And then I look at them, and I'm like *Oh shit, Pudge ate a turtle*, so we're looking for *an hour* before the ranger thinks to ask where I got them from and I realize *Oh wait*, what kind of *asshole* would just leave turtles in my bathtub—"

I had considered breaking in and leaving them in Levi's bathtub with no explanation, but then I decided it would be more fun to label their shells with the numbers *one*, *two*, and *four*. There was no *three*. Figured it would take a while before he worked that out, though.

"Mr. Sawyer!" A cry of outrage cuts through the quiet library. Levi's head snaps up in time to watch the supervisor stomp over to our table and hiss: "Watch your language, young man!"

I raise an eyebrow at Levi, who scowls at me in chastised shame, waiting until Mrs. Vickers is out of earshot again. "Language, Sawyer," I whisper. "Is that any way to talk to a young lady?"

"Depends, have you seen one?"

"Urgh, you're so—" I grab him by the edge of his jacket and march him toward the stacks, pushing him into the shadows until we're cornered in the old reference section. Encyclopedias slump on the shelf in a defeated heap, their spines cracked and pages yellowed. The stacks have been built over the windows so the light is dim, and it still smells like mold from that one time the library flooded a million years ago. All of which is to say: This is a very un-sexy place to be, and yet, Levi looks at least twenty percent less annoyed now, and smirking in a way that makes me want to yank off his jacket and strangle him with it. Or wear it forever until it smells like me and it's soft enough to sleep in. I'll decide when I get there.

"Look, I'm sorry about the turtles, okay?"

"Are you?"

"I mean, no, not really, but—" I shake the letter in front of him again. "*Come on,* would you *look!*"

He takes it, fingers brushing mine. I concentrate on the book beside his head so I don't actually have to look him in the eye. *Evolution of the Octopus: Alien or Animal?* I frown, staring at the title, wondering if someone took it from the science-fiction section just to see if Mrs. Vickers would notice.

"I'd ask you to be my devil, but you already haunt me," he says sarcastically. "This isn't a clue, you know. Really, it just proves that they're pathological liars."

"I don't care, it's *something*. We never really knew if everything in the letters was real. We don't know if their names are real. Until we found Treegap, we thought that might be made up too. The devil rumor, and all the stuff that gets left in the woods—maybe

206

that's why August took the ring? Maybe it was just a joke." An elaborate prank—isn't that why we wanted to take the Adder Stone for ourselves, all those years ago?

He looks down at the letter and frowns as he repeats my words. "Maybe it was all a joke. . . ."

Somehow, it's worse when he says it. "The photo wasn't." I snatch the paper back. "The letters are real. *They* were real."

"Fine. Good work."

"Why are you so pissy?"

"Nothing. No reason." He rakes his hair, refusing to meet my eyes.

"Okay. Well. Good chat. See you later, Mr. Hyde."

I turn but he catches the edge of my sleeve. His voice rumbles low and close to my ear. Closer than I thought. "Hey, Brodie, there wasn't a fourth. Was there?"

I pretend to count on my fingers, *one, two, three* . . . "Hmm . . . maybe? Or maybe not. I don't quite remember."

He glowers at me. I push my finger in the frown between his brows. "Cheer up. Pudge doesn't have enough teeth left to eat a turtle anyway."

He grabs my hand, pushing it away from his face, but he doesn't let go. "Wait. I wrote you another valentine. Want to hear it?"

"No."

He sticks a pink heart to my shirt. "Wrote it before the turtles," he mutters. Then he turns and stalks off, accidentally bashing into the corner of the atlas section in his hurry to leave. I stare at him until he slips away back to his desk, then I keep staring when he's gone.

What the . . .

I know you think it's a dull affair
And would rather stay home in the attic chairs
But I thought I'd ask again
In case you'd be willing to attend
With your (exceedingly handsome) friend?

I flip the card over and start to write *You're not as handsome as you think you are*, with the intention of smacking it down on his notebook before fleeing the library. Instead, I look down at his cramped scrawl, and tuck the note inside my diary. Then I sit for the rest of the day, wildly oscillating between anger and confusion, until I can pedal home after school, snatch up one of the Vinegar Valentines, and convince Nan to drive me across town. I shove the card into his letterbox just as the sun sets, shoulders sagging with relief. There. Missive delivered. We're even now. Right? His was a joke, and I've sent one right back. But then why do I feel the urge to peel open his mailbox and steal the letter back? I should have used a different card—the one with the snake head. I run through my selection again in my mind, picturing the woman with a bustled ball gown ignoring a kneeling lover:

On poetry and gush he is very strong.
And he tells her the same worn-out song:
He's so soft and sappy
And he'll make her so happy
But the madness won't last very long.

"Brodie?" Nan calls, poking her head out the window. "Isn't this the Sawyer house?"

I try to stick my hand through the slot but it's too small and my fingers get stuck. "Hmm? No."

"Remember, mail fraud is a crime, darling."

A frustrated scream strangles my throat, emerging as a defeated groan. I yank my hand out, fingers red and skin scraped, and jog back to the car.

Nan's still squinting at the Sawyer porch when I slam the door behind me. She used to drop me here, sometimes. Back when it still had a brick chimney and a soul.

"Didn't this place used to be prettier?"

I drop my head into my hands. "Just drive, Nan. Please."

She pats my knee and the car shudders to life. I turn back to see the curtains peeling away from Levi's room and I shrink down in the seat.

"Want to talk about it?" she offers.

"Absolutely not."

Nan drives in slow looping circles for a while. She likes driving, even if there's no destination. She wears white leather driving gloves, and hums along to the radio that will only tune to one station. I think, again, of the bank notice in the trash.

I clear my throat, needing a distraction. This one seems as good as any. "Hey, Nan, I've been thinking. Maybe I could get another job, when school ends. Stick around for a while, help pay the bills?"

She raises her eyebrows: Today she's drawn them in with blue pencil between her gray hairs. "Now why would you want to do a thing like that?"

I shrug, as though I haven't spent the last few nights wondering how to come up with a serious amount of cash—after all, the Adder

209

Stone is starting to seem like a dead end, and reality is setting in. "I just thought maybe you could use the help for a while. Could take a few days off from the post office every so often?"

"Uh-huh," she says skeptically. "You've been snooping, haven't you?"

"No, I just—" I take a deep breath. "Are we okay?"

"We're fine, darling, I'm fine. That fancy private school of yours charged a pretty penny, but if you're not going back—"

I frown at her, confused. "You paid for Rowley? I thought . . ." Dad had always acted as though he was the one forking out for the payments.

Her bright pink lips purse together. "Never you mind. I was happy to do it."

"Nan, I—"

"*Tut-tut*," she says. "This is what you get for snooping. If this was the olden days, I'd chop your left hand off and send you to market. But as it turns out, you make a decent cup of coffee and you can reach the tall shelf in the pantry, so I think I'll keep you around," she says with a wink. "Enough worrying. We're doing just fine, I promise. Now, if you're not going to tell me why you were snooping at the Sawyer house, you might as well tell me where you're heading—it's my turn to bring the vodka to book club and I can't be late."

She drops me off at the Archie Arcade, where the blaring welcome sign reminds me once again that *Fortune favors the brave*, except today it feels vaguely insulting since I just fled some mail in my grandmother's getaway car. Sneaking up his stairs with three turtles hidden in my backpack while his mum is in the kitchen unboxing food she pretends to cook? Cakewalk. Sticking around to watch him open a Valentine's Day card? *Nope.*

I bang my head on the booth as Elliot slides in opposite me.

"Easy, you'll knock those last two brain cells right out."

"Ha ha. Shouldn't you be on a date with Isaac?"

"I am. We stopped for snacks."

I turn back to the counter. Isaac waves. "I'm third wheeling your date."

He shrugs. "It's cool. You want fries?" He nudges a plate toward me, and my hand snakes out to steal a few and shove them in my mouth.

Elliot eyes me suspiciously. "You okay there, Red? You look kinda . . . wired. You been watching those videos of shelter dogs being rehomed again?"

I shake my head. "No. I'm fine."

Genuine concern crosses his face. "Is it your nan?"

"No, she's okay." Mostly. Aside from money problems, evidently. "It's nothing. You should go, Isaac is waiting for you."

Elliot responds by turning around and waving Isaac over to our booth. I see them squeeze hands under the table, and for a second, I am slightly less miserable.

"Hey, Brodie, what's up?" Isaac grins. "You wanna come to the movies with us?"

"No, you guys should go, I don't wanna crash your date."

Isaac tosses a fry and catches it in his mouth. "Invite Levi then, it'll be a double," he jokes. *Jokes,* because I know he's not serious. And yet, I feel my cheeks turning crimson, and my mouth drops open, suddenly incapable of any intelligible noise.

Elliot laughs, then looks up. Sees my face. "No way. Actually? You and *Levi*—finally . . . But wait, then why are you sad? What—"

"What do you mean 'finally'?!"

"Are you and him, like, a thing? Is this an *official* thing?"

"It's not a thing at all!"

Isaac just tips his head back and laughs, holding his hands up in surrender. "Hey, I was just kidding, thought you guys were friends. None of my business."

"*Nothing happened,*" I manage to hiss. "But don't—you can't—don't say anything to him."

"Say what?" Elliot asks. "I saw Brodie and she looked weirder than usual?"

"Hey!"

Isaac nudges Eli in the ribs. "I'm sensing this is a best-friend conversation, so I'm gonna just go hang out by the Pac-Man machine. See you later, Brodes."

I seize Elliot by the wrists. "Swear it, blood oath, right now, you can never, ever say anything."

"Okay, first of all, I'm not making a blood oath with you; I'm pretty sure you've had rabies at one point—"

"Spit in your hand then."

"How about a traditional pinkie swear and a bit of trust?"

Grudgingly, I hold out my pinkie "Fine, pinkie swear that you don't know anything, because nothing happened."

"Right. Obviously."

He holds our hands like that for a long moment, until I start to tug away, and he loops his fingers tighter. "Hey, Brodie?"

"What?"

"It's okay if something does happen."

"Very funny."

"I'm serious. You guys were always . . . I kind of assumed . . . anyway. Whatever. Do your thing." He coughs, starting to rise from the table. "Big brother talk over."

"You're not even a year older than me."

"Still counts."

He ruffles my hair, and I slap him away, and Isaac watches us with a shake of his head. "Go," I say. "It's rude to make your boyfriend wait."

"He's not my—"

"Yeah, yeah, whatever you say." I wave them away and walk home as a fine mist falls from the sky, dampening my hair. Nan's gone out for book club, so I watch horror movies until my eyes get heavy. I must fall asleep, because the doorbell rings at midnight, waking me.

My heart races for a moment until I realize it's probably just Nan forgetting her keys. But then an engine throttles to life as I creep down the stairs, and there's a shadow behind the frosted glass door, too tall and too broad.

An envelope slides under the door.

I read it as headlights flicker through the windows, lips quirking at the image he's printed off. It's a vintage-style card, drawn to show the vampire Dracula sucking on a bag of O+ blood. Below, the script reads *You're my type.*

And for some reason, my heart sinks and my veins run cold.

This worn-out song of ours suddenly doesn't seem as funny as it used to.

Maybe, I think, *but how long would the madness last?*

"Did you tell Levi my blood type?"

Elliot looks up from the bleachers, his eyes tracking Isaac as he bounces the ball into the goalposts. End zone. Whatever. "What?"

"My blood type."

"How would I *know* your blood type?"

I sit down heavily beside him, the metal seat groaning. "I don't know. That eighth-grade science test we did?"

"Uh-huh. That was four years ago."

"Yeah, but you have a freaky brain that remembers everything."

He just shrugs.

"That's not a no."

He shrugs again and opens an arm so I can lean into his side. "Gonna go to the dance?"

"Nope."

"Okay," he says. "Gonna break the poor dude's heart, though."

"Levi doesn't have a heart. He's like a . . . a . . . I don't know. A jellyfish," I finish lamely.

Elliot's chest rumbles as he laughs. "Feeling a little off today?"

"Shut up."

"How are the letters going?" he says. "Any clues?"

"Maybe. I don't know any Charlies, though, do you?"

He shakes his head. "Not any with siblings. How about August? Remembered anything new?"

I sigh, leaning back. "Nothing. Dad won't be back in the city for at least a month, so if it's with Mum's stuff we won't know for a while." And that means the reward is a dead end too. Our only clue leads nowhere. I watch Levi crash into Ryan, sending them both sprawling. He looks up, and I duck my head before he sees me. "I wish we had yearbooks. Records. *Something.*"

"You should go see my mum," Elliot says. "She said a lot of stuff gets donated to the library. I know the flood wiped out the school records, but someone might have had a spare yearbook and dropped it off. Or a newspaper photo. You never know what people find in old cupboards. Long shot, but it might be worth it."

"That's a good idea. Levi and I looked back when . . . before. But it was a few years ago, so if they're digitizing everything maybe something new might be there."

"Don't get too excited. She also said someone donated a pressed banana and a hundred-year-old book about Kama Sutra. I mean, technically it's an antique, but . . ."

I snort, bouncing to my feet. "I better go," I say, hurrying to shrug my backpack over my shoulder as the coach below blows their whistle, calling an end to practice. I intend to be nowhere near this field, or Levi, ever again.

Elliot chuckles quietly, though true to his promise, says nothing.

I rush into the theater just before the bell rings, squishing myself between Claire and Emiko. It's audition day, so most of the class is clutching plastic folders and eyeing the piano like it might be planning to sabotage them. Claire is sitting ramrod straight, unusually

215

quiet. I squeeze her hand in solidarity. Emiko takes a more direct approach.

"Bet you'll smoke them," she says. "Phillipa Soo who?"

Claire gives her a sideways glance.

Emiko is not discouraged. "They're gonna call you Kristin Claire-noweth."

"Stop it."

"The rest of the competition is going to have to Cynthia Eriv-go."

"How do you know these names? Did you . . . learn musical theater for me?"

"Babe, I swear I could pull off a jazz square right now."

Claire snorts, then laughs, then hiccups in quick succession.

"Ladies!" the teacher calls out. "Perhaps you would like to get us started?"

Claire jumps up, white-knuckling the sheet music in her hands. "I'll go," she says. She angles her hips, sets her feet, squares her shoulders. She turns back once, winks, then saunters to the stage. "My name is Claire Barnes and I'll be singing 'Seventeen.'"

Unlike Emiko and I, Claire can actually sing. Her voice carries across the theater, clear and strong. Emi cheers the loudest when she's done, jumping to her feet for a standing ovation. We spend the next hour huddled into the back row of the theater, watching the rest of the students warble through their songs (two students sing "Defying Gravity," which Claire mutters is boring and cliche, which makes Emi call her a snob, and then we get shushed again).

When the auditions are done, the class sprawls on the floor, a palpable sense of relief in the air. The teacher takes the stage again, giving a sharp clap to get our attention. "Thank you, everyone!

You're a talented bunch this year. Casting will be posted on Monday next week."

The whole theater groans.

The teacher grins. "I know, I know. But we're trying to make it fair so that everyone who auditioned gets a speaking part. All right, on to this week's class. Shakespeare! The school wanted us to study *Romeo and Juliet* ahead of this week's Valentine's Dance, though they have clearly forgotten the part where two teenagers die at the end for lack of patience and modern postal service. Remember, kids: Don't drink and marry your underaged paramour. Now, who can tell me the components of iambic pentameter. . . ."

We spend the rest of the class not really paying attention, thumbing through sheet music we pretend to read (well, Emi and I pretend. Claire points at little blobs on the page and says things like *upper register* and *high C*).

The bell finally rings, signaling the end of the day, and they both plead with me again to come to the dance on the weekend, but I shake my head.

"At least come shopping with us," Emiko says. "I want shoes. Something shiny but sensible. Although, I will settle exclusively on shiny if needed."

I laugh, about to shake my head. But why not? We pile into Emi's car, and I send Nan a quick text to let her know I'm going out. She responds almost immediately:

Don't come home till midnight.

We shop until Emiko gets hungry, and then she insists on making us stop for dinner—we end up sharing pizzas in a sketchy shopping center café, where the kitchen looks like it hasn't been cleaned since the nineties and the food is just greasy enough to disguise any mold. Emi didn't end up buying shoes, but she *did* make us wait half an hour while she pored over the true-crime section of the local bookstore. Claire lingered over a dress in one of the glittery expensive boutiques, but eventually let it go with a sigh.

They drop me home, but I'm not tired and it's still early—part of me wants to come home at midnight just once to see what Nan would say. I consider trudging upstairs anyway but turn at the last moment and walk down the road to Elliot's house. The lights are on and Dale's car isn't in the driveway, so I knock on the door and wait.

Quinn beams at me, wrapping me in a warm hug. "Oh, what a lovely surprise!"

I hug her back, smiling. "Thought I'd see if Elliot was around. I accused him of being a traitor at lunch and now I feel bad."

Quinn snorts, patting me on the head. "He's gone to Levi's; you just missed him." She must notice my face drop because she hesitates a moment, then adds, "Do you—do you want me to drive you over?"

I struggle to keep my eyebrows from shooting up into my hairline. Here's the thing: The older Maddons and the Sawyers do *not* get along. No one knows why. Well, I think Nan knows why, but she won't say anything. Quinn never even steps foot on their side of town if she can help it—honestly, I was surprised she took the library job, given how close it puts her to the police station. When

218

we were kids, the boys either rode, or, if we all had to go somewhere together, Dad would take us, muttering how ridiculous it was that grown adults couldn't get their shit together long enough to be civil to each other.

I heard an argument, once. When I was too little to really understand it. Mum and Quinn, drunk and whispering in the kitchen. Giggling, then not.

Elliot had gotten sick at Levi's sleepover party the week before. Thrown his guts up for hours until they had no choice: Detective Dick drove him home, carrying him straight to Quinn's door.

"The fucking nerve," Quinn had said, banging her glass down on the counter a little too hard. Quinn never swore. She didn't even say *damn* when she jammed her toe that one time and broke it. "He just couldn't leave it alone," she continued. "The house, Dale, Elliot—his dad."

His dad.

I'd frozen then, at the top of the stairs, foot hovering in the air, not even daring to breathe.

"Richard's just—"

"I know. But you didn't see him, standing there, judging me. Asking if we were *okay*, if Elliot was eating properly. And getting pissy when I told him we were just fine, and to shove it up his—"

Mum barked a laugh, slapping a hand over her mouth. "You didn't! Tell me you didn't. Good, he deserved it."

I sneezed then, the sound echoing down the stairs, and suddenly the voices stopped.

And that was it. The first piece of the puzzle. One of the only pieces, really. Whenever Elliot asked about his dad, Quinn would tell him that they could talk about it when he was older. That he was a good man, but he made a mistake. That he wanted to be here but couldn't.

She's looking at me now, waiting for an answer. "Oh—oh no," I manage. "That's okay, I can ride."

Her eyes narrow at the darkening sky and the streetlights starting to flicker to life. "I'll take you. Really, it's fine."

"No, it's all right. Actually, I think I'll just go home after all."

"Are you sure?"

"Yep," I say, with false cheer. "All good. I'm—I'm really tired anyway." I force a yawn for good measure, which isn't overly convincing. I turn to go, then pause. "Hey, Quinn—Elliot mentioned you might have some digital records at the library."

She smirks, bemused, and leans against the doorframe. "We have a lot of records—what were you looking for in particular?"

"Old school yearbooks? From before the library flooded? A few years got lost then, and I thought maybe . . ."

Quinn frowns, a touch of concern or something like it on her brow. "I suppose we might—any reason you're looking?"

"I just thought—" I can't tell her about the letters, I'll sound like a crazy person. Besides, it was *our* secret—Elliot's and Levi's and mine. "I just wanted . . ."

The frown drops all of a sudden with an "*ohh*" of realization. She reaches an arm out to touch my shoulder, her eyes softening. "Oh, of course. You want to see if your mum is in them?"

I nod, ashamed that I hadn't even thought of that myself. Was she there, in those pictures? A girl that wasn't a parent yet—wasn't sick yet. Did we smile the same, like Nan always said we did?

"Yes," I say honestly. "I'd really like that. I think maybe she kept some, but they're stuck back in the city with Dad."

"Of course, of course I'll help. Come see me next week; I'll dig through the latest donations. I'd give you mine if I had it, but it's . . . well, long gone now."

I give her another hug. "Thank you," I whisper, about to slip away when she grabs my hand.

"Brodie, wait—Elliot said you weren't going to the dance?"

I shake my head *no*, then try to find the words. "I'd feel—I don't know . . . it seems silly."

"Your mum loved dancing."

That makes me laugh. Mum would dance anywhere: the supermarket, the car, the hairdresser—coming home with lopsided bangs because she'd wriggled too much.

"And it's not silly, you know. To want to go. Sometimes, you have to make the good moments happen."

I smile at her, glad that I had come even if I didn't find Elliot after all.

"Thanks, Quinn."

She winks and watches me walk all the way home before she closes the door.

Nan's sitting in the kitchen nursing a glass of sherry in her hand. She glances at the clock on the wall. "It's not even nearly midnight," she says in a droll tone. "Go back and try again."

I take a breath. "Actually, Nan . . . I think I need a dress."

221

It doesn't mean I'm *going*. I just want options.

Or at least that's what I tell myself.

I go again to Elliot's the next day—Dale's car is in the driveway, and he spots me before I can creep away. He turns from tinkering under the hood of his car to face me, tugging on the corner of a frayed cap. "Well, damn—you the McKellon girl then? Got tall."

"Hi, Dale. Nice to see you," I lie. Also, I've been the exact same height since I was twelve, which Dale would probably remember if he didn't drink his way through a case of beer each night.

"He ain't here," he says, exhaling a cloud of cigarette smoke. "With that fancy kid again."

"Levi?"

"Yeah, that's the one." He gives me a look up and down that makes my skin crawl. "So, how's your mum?"

I feel my eyes narrow, the blinds of politeness shuttering closed. "Still dead."

"Ah shit," he says, taking a step closer. He smells like whiskey sweat and nicotine. "Meant your dad."

"He's fine."

Dale nods, smiling in the way he thinks is charming. Probably was, once. He looks younger than he ought to, and those icy blue eyes might be appealing if you don't know what kind of hatred his lips were capable of spewing.

"You two together, then?"

I frown, not following. "Who?"

"You and the kid."

My stomach churns into a tight knot as I try to decide on the best response—I don't know whether he means Levi or Elliot, but I know it's none of his business either way.

"Bye, Dale," I say, backing away. "Tell Quinn I say hello."

He waves a hand, suddenly bored with me. "Yeah, whatever."

I don't breathe again until their house disappears from view, wiping cold sweat from my hands against my jeans. My fingers tremble as I text Elliot, and for the millionth time I wish I could take him away from here—hide him in the attic with our ghosts and secrets.

Elliot replies almost immediately: Busy—at Levi's. Can't talk, call later.

I frown at his reply. *Can't talk?* What does *that* mean? I consider being a reasonable person for about ten seconds before snatching my bike and pedaling to Levi's house before the rational part of my brain can catch up to my body and start screaming about unanswered valentine cards and personal boundaries.

Their driveway is empty when I arrive—which means his parents aren't home. Which is even *weirder*: What are they doing alone that's so important that Elliot can't respond? Neither of them is really into video games, and they don't have any classes together. I peer over the back fence, but they're not playing football either.

There is, of course, a small part of me that acknowledges this is straight up unhinged behavior. They're busy—maybe they're baking red velvet cake or watching *The Vampire Diaries* again. I'm not their whole life anymore. But I used to be.

Before I left.

Before things changed.

And I guess . . . it was starting to feel like maybe we were going to be that way again. We found Treegap, we found the letters—together. We were supposed to track down the Adder Stone, together. It was the three of us against the world again. *Jesus, Brodie, they're just hanging out. Get a grip. You left three turtles in Levi's bathtub, so no wonder he doesn't invite you over anymore.*

I turn to leave—and then I realize that the blue light on their security doorbell is flashing and has already recorded me snooping around. It's worse if I leave now. They'll think I came to case the house and steal their garden gnomes. Or their dog. Again.

I muffle a silent scream into the cuffs of my sweater and groan.

Then I take a breath, smooth my hair, and knock. I'll just say hello—I was in the area, how funny. No need for them to know I was in the area because I rode *directly here.*

There's a thundering of footsteps on the staircase inside, then the door blows wide open. Levi blinks, looking down.

"Brodie?" He frowns. Then smiles. Dimples. "Brodie," he repeats, crossing his arms and leaning against the doorframe. "Finally succumbed to my effortless charm? Come to pick me up for the dance? You're a bit early, and I'm not sure we'll both fit on that bike, but I'm willing to try."

I roll my eyes. "Firstly, you try way too hard to be considered effortless—"

"—does that mean you still find me charming?"

"Secondly, for the *millionth time*, I'm not going to the dance with you. I was looking for Elliot. I just . . . came to ask about some homework."

"Sure you did. I'd invite you in, but I'm going to need to check your backpack first for turtles and other amphibians. You got frogs in there? Frogs give me the creeps—"

"Is he here or not?"

"The turtle? I told you, the ranger came—"

I take a breath, determined not to screech at him like a banshee. "Elliot. Is Elliot here?"

"Why?"

"That's not an answer."

He shrugs. "He's not here," he says. "Just left. Doesn't mean you have to, though."

"What were you doing?"

He shrugs. "You know. Stuff."

"Stuff?"

"Yeah. Guy stuff."

"Guy stuff?" I repeat, unconvinced.

"I'm sorry. If you come back later—"

I throw my hands up, exasperated, and he flinches. "I'm not here for you, Levi!"

Hurt flashes across his face—there and gone so quickly I think I've imagined it. "Fine. Whatever. Wait here, I'll call Elliot back and tell him you have a girl emergency."

"I don't have an emergency. What even *is* a girl emergency?"

"I don't know. Do you need—"

"I swear to god, if you offer me tampons—"

He frowns. "Then why did you come?"

"I don't—you're just—your stupid doorbell and—it doesn't

225

matter. Whatever. Bye. See you on Monday. Have fun at the dance."

There's no *way* I was going after this. I turn and march back toward my bike, wishing I'd just stayed home in the first place.

He runs a hand through his hair, setting it loose in frazzled waves. He takes a step forward and I take one back. "Can you just talk to me for a second?" he pleads. "What's wrong?"

"Why can't you tell me? You're both acting weird. Do you not—do you not want to be friends anymore?"

"Jesus, Brodie, not everything is about you."

My mouth drops open, the shock hitting before my brain can even decide how offended I am.

"I'm sorry," he says immediately. "That came out wrong. I *meant* to say: I can't tell you because it's not my secret to tell, okay? It's got nothing to do with you, it's just . . . private."

I blink away the fury-tears building behind my eyelids. "Whatever. Bye, Levi."

He keeps following me, watching as I shove my helmet on over my hair, but I'm so angry my hands shake and I can't get the clasp to catch. He reaches up and eases my hands out of the way, clipping it on, fingertips lingering a few seconds on my chin.

"You left," he says quietly. "And I know that wasn't your fault, but you weren't here. It's been three years. He's been going through a lot. He'll tell you when he's ready. Can you just . . . give him some time?" One hand has inched across my chin to rest on the back of my neck, where I'm sure he can feel my pulse humming.

"Is he okay?"

"He's fine. All in one piece, promise."

I nod, but there's worse ways to hurt. Levi must realize it too, and his eyes soften. He gives a small shrug, and that movement says: *mostly*. And it takes everything in me not to fling myself up Compton Road, knock on Elliot's door, drag him home, and wrap him in warm blankets. But Elliot wouldn't want that. Not if he's not ready to tell me, just yet.

"Hey," Levi says. "Do you want to go for a drive?"

"What?"

"A drive."

"With you?"

"With me."

"Now?"

"Ideally."

The anger and confusion flushes from my body, making way for red-hot panic. "Why?"

He shrugs. "You said no one had taught you. I thought maybe I could show you. If you want."

"I can drive," I say defensively. "Technically."

"'Technically' got us caught."

"I didn't realize it was a manual!"

"The clutch wasn't a giveaway?"

I glower at him—we were so young, too young. And so stupid. Young, and stupid, and wild. What an intoxicating combination.

Everyone makes a big deal about the Jeep. And, sure, we did sort of remove Dwight's property from the location in which he left it, and yes, some people would call that theft. But two points in my defense: The first is that we always intended to put it back. The second is that Mum had only covered the theoretical components of driving with me—she used to let me use the steering wheel while I sat on her lap, sometimes even letting my foot rest on top of hers to press the pedals.

I hadn't realized how stubborn the car would be—we basically bunny-hopped a few blocks down the road until we got caught. Dwight kept making noise about the mayor's son being a thief, so Susan offered to buy the car in exchange for a no-charge deal. It wasn't the thing that tore us apart. There was no one moment when it all went wrong. But it didn't help—his parents already thought I was a bad influence, and suddenly, they had proof. And even though Levi jumped into the passenger seat, I wonder if it also fractured the trust between us: that I wouldn't ever do something so wild it couldn't be undone. Maybe that's why he was so quick to believe I could have stolen the Adder Stone.

Maybe that's why I find myself saying, "Fine."

Levi drives us out to the outskirts of the Rydal Woods, winding down one of the unused fire trails—empty this time of year apart from a few lazy hikers trying to cheat their way to the lookout point. He pulls over on the widest section of road, parking the car, and opens his door.

"Where are you going?"

"Well, to drive the car, you gotta be in the driver's seat," he says, voice dripping with sarcasm. "We're swapping."

"Now?"

"We could try while the car is already moving, but that seems like skipping a few steps."

"Very funny. I just meant—shouldn't there be a theory component to this?"

"Sure," he says, pointing at his feet. "Clutch. Stop. Go." He pauses, seeing the hesitation on my face. "Have you driven much before? Aside from, you know . . ."

The car you stole?

"Sure," I answer. "Bumper cars."

He winces. "Okay, well, just do the complete opposite of that. Try *not* to hit things."

I allow myself a few moments of panic while he walks around to the passenger side, and I awkwardly scramble over the gearbox. This is a terrible idea. This whole day, start to finish—awful idea. Why did I go to his house? Why did I say yes to this? Why don't I just run away, right now, into the woods. I'm one small person in a big green space—bet it would take him ages to find me and he'd eventually give up. *No, he wouldn't,* says a small voice in the back of my mind. I clip my seat belt in and ignore that voice—that, and the flush creeping up my neck that's making the back of my hair itchy.

"Ready?" he says, watching me expectantly.

"Nope."

"Good start. Oh wait!" He pops open the glove box, looking for something.

"What are you doing?"

"Checking my insurance."

"Very funny."

He grins at me, nudging the compartment closed with one knee.

I roll my eyes and twist the key in the ignition, feeling the engine rumble to life. "Okay. Shut up and be helpful." He waits a moment, while I check my feet again, and I feel the blush creeping higher. "I don't actually know how to do this," I admit.

"That's okay," he says patiently. "I didn't either."

He points at each of the pedals in turn, encouraging me to start with both feet on the clutch and brake, easing both until the engine catches and the car crawls forward. Well, less of a crawl, more of a shuddering leap. We do this for half an hour, creeping up the road in tiny increments, coasting a few yards in first gear until the motor inevitably stalls again.

"Stop saying I'll feel it! I can't feel it!"

"Jesus. Okay. Foot on the brake—it's that thing in the middle you've hardly touched." He shifts the gearbox into neutral and sighs. "Let's try this again."

He puts one hand on my knee, the other on the wheel. I glance down at his hand, surprised by the casual touch. But it seems like he hasn't even noticed, because his eyes are glued to the pedals, frowning slightly.

"This foot goes down, all the way. Okay. Turn the key."

I press my toes against the pedal and twist the key, waiting for the engine to catch again.

"Good. Now go to first."

"I think we did that already," I quip. "In a coatroom." I don't know why I say it. Probably because I'm tired and pissy and his hand is still on my leg.

There is a brief flicker of surprise on his face, though he recovers quickly. "First gear," he clarifies.

I grudgingly shift gears, and the car begins to rumble.

"Good, now slowly move your feet—lift and lower."

The car shakes as I ease my left foot off the clutch, Levi's fingers gripping my knee a little tighter.

"Feel that?" he says. "That's the biting point."

His hands are warm. His skin grazes mine through the rip in my jeans.

"Mmm-hmm."

"It feels like a shiver."

I can't tell if it's the car starting to tremble or me. Levi doesn't seem to notice. He's just waiting for me to let go of the clutch completely, focused entirely on the task at hand. Why can't I?

I clear my throat. "I got it."

"Okay, now go."

And I'm driving. Very, very slowly. But smoothly.

I grin at the open road, picking up enough speed that the wind ruffles my hair through the window. We stick to the back roads—the fire trails and the dead ends. Levi doesn't say much, just tells me where to turn and when the clutch needs a little more give. I catch his eyes in the rearview mirror, just for a second, and wonder if he's smiling like that because he's laughing at me or something else. Eventually, we nudge into second gear and it feels like I'm speeding. I laugh, my heart ticking faster, a beat in my chest that throbs just loud enough to be felt.

"I'm going to steal this car from you."

"I'd probably let you," he says. He turns the radio on softly, not loud enough to be distracting. Eventually, we loop back closer to town, though he doesn't tell me to stop. Not yet. But all too soon, the parking lot comes into view, and he tells me to pull over in an empty corner so we can switch seats.

"I'll drive you home," he says, but I shake my head. I'd thrown my bike into the back before we left—a girl always needs a getaway plan, after all.

"It's okay. I can ride."

"I don't mind."

"It's fine."

But I don't get out of the car. I stay there, seat belt clipped in, staring out the windshield, eyes fixed on nothing in particular— roaming the treetops, the footpath, a purple shoe left on the ground. Anywhere but at him.

I clear my throat to say goodbye.

"Why'd you do this?" I say instead.

Levi just laughs, a soft, breathy sound. Like he's not surprised at all. "I think of you, when I drive," he says. "Out here. And I always thought you'd like it—windows down, music up. Nobody chasing you. I used to picture you like that. When I missed you."

Goose bumps rush up my arms, a shiver down my spine that's all my own and nothing to do with the silent engine. "You missed me?"

He shifts in his seat. Hand under my chin. Lifting my eyes so I'm forced to meet his when he replies. "Every day."

"You didn't call."

"Neither did you."

"Once," I whisper.

He frowns.

"My birthday. I wanted to—I don't know. I was sixteen. It felt like it should mean something."

"But?"

"It didn't." It was just another day, in the end. Nan had sent a card, of course, but it had arrived two weeks earlier and was already open on my dresser. Elliot texted. Dad forgot. And Levi—god, I'd missed him so fiercely in that moment, it *ached*. I wanted him to be the one voice I heard that day, the person to say "Happy Birthday" like it mattered. Because I knew it would—to him, it all mattered.

"I should go," I say again.

Neither of us move. My eyes burn for no good reason.

"Brodie?" I can't look at him again. He reaches for me but stops short and tugs the corner of my sleeve instead, the back of his hands skimming over the crook of my elbow. "I'm sorry I missed your call."

I almost tell him. Almost.

Hello? Who's there?

His voice. Deeper than I had remembered. I'd thought it was his dad, just for a second, when he first picked up. And the realization that he had changed so much—that I didn't even recognize my best friend—rendered me mute.

Hello? Is this a prank?

Always, I think.

"Come to the dance," he says suddenly.

"I can't."

"Why not?"

I blink at the windshield, so angry and confused and lost in a way I can't even put into words. "I don't know how to do this."

"Do what?"

I sniff, turning to face him. "Be friends. Be people. I left three turtles in your bathtub!"

His lips quirk. "I know."

"I'm sorry."

"I forgive you."

"I don't want to be forgiven."

He sighs, and his hand is still on my neck. "What do you want?"

"I don't know." But I lean into his skin, just for a moment. Letting myself enjoy the warmth, the rough pad of his fingers, the wild thought: *What if.* What if we hadn't ruined it all? What if I stayed?

But I don't say anything, and his hand falls away.

"Fine," he says. "I'm very cross about it. Better?"

"Yes." *No. Maybe.*

"Can I drive you home now?"

I shake my head. "I said I would ride."

And before he can say anything else, I open the door and walk around to the back, pulling the bike toward me. His door closes, and then he's there beside me, lifting it effortlessly above my head and setting it gently on the ground. I settle in the seat, clipping my helmet in place.

"Thank you," I say. "For today."

Levi gives my helmet a gentle rap with his knuckle. "I'll save you a dance," he says. "Just in case."

And then he lets go of the handlebar—I didn't even realize he was holding it, and the bike wobbles beneath me now that he's not keeping it steady. And it kind of feels like the whole world shakes under me as I ride home, a little less sure of the ground underneath my feet than I was this morning.

11

Dear Winnie,

There is not one single piece of taffeta left in the whole country, because it is all currently pinned to my body and this dress is going to look fucking FABULOUS, unless all the pins holding it together manage to poke me to death before I can actually sew it shut. And anyway, in answer to your question, yes I can fix that hideous monstrosity your mother bought you. By the time I'm done, you'll look so amazing August won't know what hit him. He'll be too polite to say so, of course, but I want to see the look on his face when his eyes bug out of his head anyway.

Love,
June

I don't mean to end up at the dance. Really, I don't. I just went to Elliot's house to take a bunch of pictures of him and Isaac, making them pose twice each time so I could take photos on my phone and on Mum's old camera that we'd unearthed in the attic in lieu of any *actual* clues.

Quinn stood in the kitchen, trying to contain a beaming smile, sure that her pride would make Elliot blush (which it did), and I spent a long time convincing the boys to pose until the Polaroid film ran out. And then Isaac was making Elliot laugh, his head tipped back and the sound coming from his chest bright enough to fill the house with a contagious joy that sends us all a little bit silly: Quinn put on some dance music, and then she started braiding my hair while Isaac polished his shoes and re-did Elliot's bow tie. (*"Did you know they make the show dog wear a tie to competitions?"* Elliot whispers, which Isaac then yells is a lie.)

The boys are whispering and giggling in the kitchen, and I can see the way they lean in close, heads nearly touching shoulders, hips bumping as they lean against the counter, hands brushing against hands.

"Why don't you go?" Quinn whispers. "It's not too late."

I shake my head, ears turning pink as I realize she's caught me staring at them with a pang of longing. "I can't," I say, searching for an excuse. "I never found anything to wear."

I feel Quinn tugging at my curls, fluffing the ends into loose waves. The braid wraps around my crown, keeping the loose strands away from my face. She's done it the way I like it without me having to ask—out of my eyes, but still free at the back.

"Rubbish," she says. "If I know Delia McKellon at all, that woman hasn't thrown anything out since the sixties. I bet there's something."

I chew on my lip. "Levi . . ."

Quinn raises an eyebrow. "Levi?"

I shake my head. "No, never mind. Nothing."

She laughs and envelops me in a hug. "Never mind Levi then. Go with the boys. You can always come home if you hate it—but you'll never get the moment back if you miss out."

Elliot turns at that exact second, chin tilted over his shoulder. He grins, cheeks dotted pink and hair a little messier than it was a few minutes ago. He *winks*, which is so uncharacteristic it makes me snort.

"Go," Quinn whispers. "I'll keep them here a few more minutes."

I make an excuse to head home, and sprint up the stairs to find Nan holding my boots in one hand, mascara wand in the other. "Quinn called," she says, and for some reason, I throw myself into her arms and hold on tight for a few long moments.

"Okay," I say, pulling away. "Do your worst."

And just like that, I'm shoved into the green velvet dress she'd already steamed, my nicest pair of black boots, and I hurry on a flick of eyeliner in the reflection of our kettle. Elliot and Isaac are idling in the car, both clearly confused as to why Quinn is standing in the driveway with her eyes glued to her watch. I grin at her and haul myself into the backseat.

"No making out while I'm in the car," I say, buckling my seat belt as two pairs of surprised eyes lock on mine.

"Ew, Brodie."

Isaac just laughs, pulling away as we all wave goodbye.

Elliot turns in his seat and gives a low whistle. "Gonna give me a spin later?"

"Absolutely not," I say. "*You* spin."

Isaac smirks. "Please do."

I pretend to gag but smile when they're not looking.

Ten minutes later I am deeply regretting my decision. The gym has been turned into a pink-and-red glittering nightmare of hearts, while one lonely disco ball throws light across a row of chairs pushed up against the walls. I start to back away, but Elliot and Isaac flank me on either side and seize my hands. "Oh *no* you don't." They each take an elbow and lift me into the air, until my feet are dangling over the ground.

The music thumps loudly enough that I feel it in my chest: a deep, heady beat that has most of the students dancing on the floor. Some are awkward, some are silly, and very few are actually talented, but no one seems to care. Isaac jumps straight into the fray, leaping around in total abandon. Elliot commences a vaguely rhythmic side-to-side shuffle, while I oblige his earlier request and give a quick spin, laughing as the dress blooms out from my waist.

Claire and Emiko spot me from across the room, and rush to throw their arms around my shoulders in a chorus of squeals. "You came, you came!" Claire says, clapping her hands. She's dripping in a sparkly pink dress, while Emi has gone the complete opposite and is zipped into a sleek black jumpsuit.

Emi waves at Elliot, mouthing *You look hot*. He blushes so fiercely he has to tuck his head against Isaac's shoulder to hide. I tug his sleeve in a quiet moment, between the dancing and the drinks.

"You okay?" I ask, hoping he knows that those few words span everything from *I love you* to *I'd lie to the police for you.*

239

But he just smiles, wide. "I'm great," he says, and for now, I believe him.

I find myself anxiously looking around the room for a particular bronze head, but so far, he's nowhere to be found. I try to peer over Elliot's shoulder when his phone pings, but the screen is dark, and anyway, I remind myself, I don't really care what Levi Sawyer does.

The song changes, something upbeat, and a rush of bodies crams onto the dance floor, filling the space with loud voices and loose elbows. Isaac is dancing with the guys from the football team, forming a huddle that eventually devolves into a circle for showing off. I dance with Emi and Claire, until a fine sheen of sweat beads on my hairline, smiling as the boys drift toward the edge of the room for a moment alone.

The girls take turns to teach me dances they made up during long-ago holidays and sleepovers. Claire is halfway through declaring me completely, hopelessly uncoordinated when she suddenly breaks off and darts to the doors to retrieve a reluctant-looking Jenn.

The songs are slowly turning into old cheesy mixes, so we end up gathering around the drinks table with a few other stragglers, gulping down cups of off-brand fruit drinks. I flop down on one of the little plastic chairs and watch the lights blink on and off, a fuzzy feeling settling in my chest that I begrudgingly admit might be something like happiness.

Elliot returns a while later, looking thoroughly mussed and happy, his hair sticking up at odd angles and his neck sporting a few suspicious red patches. "Came to find you—may I have this dance?"

I laugh, taking hold of his outstretched hand. "Having fun?" I ask, as he attempts to whisk me away to the dance floor. In reality, it's a bumpy, half-walk half-shimmy, and we end up awkwardly staring at each other for a moment before laughing.

"Uh, I guess . . ." He holds out his arms, trying to work out how to hold me.

"Elliot, *you're* meant to lead."

"You're gonna boss me around anyway, you might as well do the dude arms."

In the end we both wind up holding shoulders, which probably looks silly, but we're not really dancing anyway, just sort of shuffling side to side. "I'm glad you came," he says, shouting over the music.

"Me too," I answer, trying not to stand on his toes.

"You look . . . clean."

"Gee, thanks."

"I like your hair thingy."

"Braid?"

"Sure."

I laugh, leading us away from a group of rowdy guys who are just jumping up and down and screaming the wrong lyrics. "You look pretty good in a suit, by the way. Very dashing."

He rolls his eyes. "No one says *dashing*."

"Fine. Stupendous. Debonair. A total hunk show."

He screws up his nose. "I take it back. *Hunk show* is worse than *dashing*." He looks at his feet, making sure he's not stepping on me in return. "Anyway, it's Levi's."

"What is?"

"The suit."

"Oh." Awkward pause. We haven't talked about Levi since the diner. "It looks better on you anyway. Did you have to stitch up the holes from his leathery demon wings?"

"Ha ha."

I bite my lip, chewing down on the question I desperately want to ask: *Is that what you were doing at his house this morning? Is that all it is?*

"Ow," he says suddenly, looking down.

"Sorry, I'm a terrible dancer."

He laughs. "Want to stand on my shoes and let me lead after all?"

"Pass. That would be humiliating, even for me."

"At least we're not doing *that*," he says, pointing to a shadowy corner where one of the guys from the football team appears to be vigorously twerking and snapping his suspenders.

I laugh, tipping my head forward on his shoulder, solid and comforting. He squeezes my hand, and it's one of those moments that makes me feel ten years old again: just the two of us against the world, pinkies intertwined, whispering secrets and promises in the dark. And I swear, right then, that whatever is haunting Elliot won't have the chance to drag him down.

The music changes, the lights start flashing overhead in technicolor beams, and I'm jostled out of Elliot's arms. I take that as my cue to escape, leaning on my tiptoes to get his attention.

"I'm going to get some air!" I yell in his ear, and he nods. The gym is stifling at this point—between the crammed bodies and the complete lack of ventilation, the air feels warm and heavy, and

I can feel a bead of sweat on my spine. I've wriggled halfway to the door, when someone grabs my hand and I thump into a solid chest, nearly losing my balance.

"Nice of you to run into me for once," Levi muses, wrapping an arm around my waist.

"Accident. I'm much quicker when I'm running *away*," I say, tugging on my hand, but he won't let go.

"One dance," he says, rocking side to side. "Please?"

I hesitate.

"Brodie McKellon, town felon," he taunts. "Braves guard dogs and barbed wire fences—terrified of a waltz."

"This isn't a waltz," I grumble, to which he responds by lifting me into the air, high enough that I squeak and clutch his shoulders to keep from falling. His mum made him take lessons as a kid: annoyingly, they seem to have stuck.

He sets me down and we end up closer than we were before, resuming a subdued shuffle. It doesn't match the music at all, but he doesn't seem to notice.

"I wouldn't have dropped you," he says. "For the record."

I realize my hands are still clawed into the collar of his jacket, and I force them to relax and rest flat against his shoulders instead. I dare a glance at a few of the other couples and note that the way we're standing is hardly the most scandalous. Nobody would even look twice. So why does it feel like one of those dreams where I'm naked in front of the whole school?

"So," Levi says, clearing his throat, "you look nice."

"Thank you," I reply in a clipped voice. "You do too. Though

I've always wondered how you manage to style your hair when you can't see your own reflection in a mirror."

"I don't think I've ever seen you wear a dress before." His eyes find mine, and I hold them for a few moments before letting my gaze drift to our feet.

"It's old. Probably smells like attic."

"Sexy. Do you mean vintage?"

"Same thing."

He steps a little closer, so my nose is nearly touching his shirt. He smells like strawberry gum and fresh laundry. I could close that gap, just half a step. Lean my head against his chest, let my limbs go heavy, and give in to the stupid voice in my head that whispers *What if?* I have a sudden flash of what we'd look like: my feet between his, trying not to stand on his toes. His arms around my waist, holding tight. Like two people who are definitely more than friends, like people who don't leave turtles in bathtubs and water balloons in helmets. How did we get *here*?

I remember when I was taller than him and thought boys had cooties.

I remember when I threw my bike in his car and drove away from it all.

Levi clears his throat, and I can feel his palm warming in mine. His fingers thread between mine, and I let them. "I thought you weren't going to come," he says, voice thick.

"I wasn't."

"Why'd you change your mind?"

"I just—" I look over my shoulder. Elliot and Isaac are dancing together, so wrapped up in their own world they're not even keeping time to the music. They laugh, and whisper, and I think about how I nearly missed it all.

"I just didn't want to miss out," I say, but that's too honest, so I smile and add: "Elliot's wearing a bow tie. It's a momentous occasion."

I wait for him to joke back, but he just nods, and his fingers run up the velvet material of my dress until his hand is cupped over my shoulder, pulling me ever-so-slightly closer. He must not have realized, because he shakes his head and mumbles an apology, dropping his hands. *Don't stop*, I think wildly.

"I have to—I need some air," I say, and grimace. Coward.

I turn and—well, it's not *exactly* running, but I rush to the doors and shove them wide open, gulping down lungfuls of fresh air.

The doors blow open behind me a few seconds later, and I cringe, but it's just two girls, laughing and taking pictures on their phones. I need to move, and my feet seem to be acting totally independent of my brain: I hurry past crowded classrooms, ignoring squeals and laughter and faces that are vaguely familiar. I end up in the courtyard, now filled with floating lanterns and fairy lights. I hear footsteps in the dark and squeeze my eyes tight. Because I want it to be him, and I don't. God, what a mess we've made.

The footsteps fade, and I'm alone again. My ears ring slightly, echoing from being so close to the speakers all night. My dress sticks to my back, my feet are sore, and my heart is thundering in my chest like I just ran a marathon. So why do I want to turn around and go right back?

I text Emi instead, relieved when she replies almost instantly, and make my way over to the library where rolls of yoga mats and cushions are being set up and groups have clustered around card games and board games—most abandoned and merely a gathering place for friends to meet, though some seem to be more competitive than others.

Claire pops up and calls my name too—loudly, her cheeks looking suspiciously flushed. "Brodie! Here!"

She grabs my hands and pulls me toward the rear of the room, where Emiko, Jenn, and a few others are gathered in a circle. Ryan is there too, doing a very poor job of concealing a small flask. He grins at me, but I ignore him and sit beside Emi, leaning my head on her shoulder.

"Too much fun?"

"Just bogeyed out," I reply. "Have you been here long?"

Emiko rolls her eyes and waves a hand at Claire. "Long enough for One-Drink Wonder over here to start feeling silly," she says, then leans in close and whispers, "Don't worry, it's mostly cordial. He tipped in half a seltzer and is calling it sangria."

I giggle, refusing when Ryan offers said flask. Irritated, he attempts to draw me into the game I had apparently interrupted. "We're playing truth or dare," he says. "Which will it be?"

"Truth," I answer, resisting the urge to roll my eyes. I hadn't played since I was kid, and the most outrageous dare was when I made Levi wear a saucepan on his head for a whole day.

Ryan smirks. "Is it true you burned down a building at your old school?"

"Gently grilled," I object. "Ryan: truth or dare?"

"Dare," he says, all bravado. A few of his friends snicker, waiting for him to be caught out. I think for a moment, though the lack of saucepans really puts a damper on my initial plans. "There's a book on the back shelf called *Evolution of the Octopus: Animal or Alien?* Go stand at the podium and read the first chapter."

Genuine trepidation crosses his face, and for a minute, I think he won't do it. Then he gets up, making his way to the back stacks. A few of the guys wolf whistle and make a general ruckus before turning back to their conversation, Ryan quickly forgotten.

Beside me, Emiko squeezes my hand. "Hey, are you okay? You seem kinda peaky."

I think of Levi's hand on my back. The way he looked when I turned away. "Yeah," I answer. "Weird night. I think—"

A wave of ear-piercing static suddenly rips through the library, causing everyone to throw their hands up over their ears. Ryan taps the microphone and clears his throat. "The octopus," he reads. "Animal or alien? This author has cause to believe that the creatures we know as underwater wonders, are, in fact, descendants of extraterrestrial life-forms. This research has been undertaken in the—"

"*Ryan Turner!* You get down from that podium *at once!*" Mrs. Vickers storms out of her office, face bright red and full of fury. "Get down! And what was that drivel you were reading—"

She snatches the book from his hand and covers the microphone as she delivers a verbal serve. I can only catch snatches of conversation, though definitely pick up on the words, *irresponsible* and *detention.*

He stands there for a few minutes longer, nodding periodically.

The game continues without him, harmless questions like: *truth, have you ever peed yourself laughing? Dare, lick an encyclopedia of your choosing.*

A weight drops down beside me and I stiffen, not needing to turn around. Emiko's face brightens and she beams just over my shoulder. "Hi, Levi. How's the dance?"

"It was pretty good, until my dance partner ran away."

"I did not run," I object. "It was a brisk stroll. My shoes hurt. I needed a break."

Emiko drops her gaze down. "You're wearing boots."

She waits.

"Don't you ride home in those boots?"

I still don't answer.

"Come to think of it, I've watched you scale a fence in those boots."

"Whose side are you on?" I mutter. Unable to delay the inevitable, I turn to face Levi. "Hello."

He looks halfway between bemused and disappointed. "Hello."

"What happened to Elliot?"

"He was having fun."

I fold my hands in my lap. One errant curl is sticking up by his ear, and I would very much like to reach up and smooth it down. "I see."

"He and Isaac are still dancing."

"That's nice."

"Neither of them ran away."

"Where's the fun in that?"

248

He sighs, pushing his hair back, and the curl settles. "You're impossible, you know that?"

"I'm not—"

"Levi! My man!" Ryan has evidently escaped Mrs. Vickers and rejoins the circle. He slaps Levi on the shoulder and tosses me the octopus book. "Sawyer—truth or dare?"

Levi shakes his head, but Ryan harasses him until he answers. "Fine. Truth."

Ryan blinks for a long moment. "Um. What's your favorite . . . holiday?"

His eyes cut to mine. "Easy," he says. "Valentine's Day."

I roll my eyes. "Seriously? Whose favorite holiday is Valentine's Day? What about birthdays? Halloween? Christmas!"

"Christmas is overrated. The tree gives me hay fever. And there are people everywhere."

"Okay, Krampus."

Claire hiccups. "Levi, it's your turn," she says helpfully. And at that moment, I want to reach across the circle and give beautiful, kind, lovely Claire a good throttling because I know exactly what's about to happen.

Levi's eyes alight with mischief. "Is it now? Hmm." He drums his fingers on his chin, pretending to look around the circle. As if he might choose anyone. He takes his time, dragging out the decision as long as possible. "I think I'll choose . . . Brodie."

Fuck.

"Truth or dare?" he says, and I could murder him right there for how smug he looks. Because he *knows*. Ever since we were kids, I would never choose truth, not with him. There's too much power in truth. Most people avoid dares because they're worried about being embarrassed, but those people have never attended an all-girls boarding school where truth could be completely, utterly ruinous.

I nearly did it. Just to spite him, but I was worried about which truth he'd demand so I stuck out my chin and answered "Dare."

The grin that consumes his face makes my toes curl.

"Brodie McKellon: I dare you to break into Dwight's junkyard. And steal something."

If my dress snags on this fence, I will be so extremely pissed off.

I stand in front of the junkyard, breath wisping in the cold air.

"Brodie, come on. This is stupid. I'm sorry."

I whirl on Levi, crossing my arms. "This was *your* idea," I remind him.

"It was a dumb idea! Let's go back."

I ignore him, facing the fence once more. My phone vibrates, stuffed down the front of my dress. I pull it out and open the group message to find Emi has said, *Steal me a souvenir* and Ryan has added *Make it something weird*.

The first time we broke into Dwight's junkyard, all we did was look around. We'd snuck out of Peter Pattison's sleepover party and walked until the yellow glow of the junkyard lights made Dwight's place look like a wonderland. Back then it wasn't so hard to break in: We jumped a two-meter fence and walked around the maze of twisted old metal and tangled wires, nudging rickety

250

old furniture, and took turns sitting in the driver's seat of rusted-out cars.

Levi's car was a contender, but it wasn't our favorite—back then, we only had eyes for the Mustang set up on jack stands in Dwight's old workshop. We'd crawl in through the open passenger-side window, not even daring to open the door in case someone heard us. We sat there making the start of our graduation list and telling ghost stories until we had to go back to the party and tuck ourselves in, pretending we'd been on the back porch all along. In the quiet, and the dark, it became one of our magic places, like the Rydal Woods. Elliot rarely came with us, always complaining he couldn't afford a criminal record, even though we'd quickly discovered Dwight had no interest in bothering to secure the yard. Most of the valuable stuff was sorted when it first came in, shuffled into the locked-up warehouse we'd never even tried to enter—it was the only new thing on the whole property, and we knew Dwight slept in there most nights. And if some of the junk got stolen in the night—well, what did he care? Saved him paying to have it destroyed.

The Jeep was one of the few salvageable cars, and it came to life over time: windows replaced, seats upholstered, wheels instead of cinder blocks. It was a little rusty and dusty, but it had charm. And then I sort of, you know, stole it.

Anyway, then came the six-foot fences and the floodlights and the slobbering feral dogs.

"*Bad. Idea,*" Levi hissed again, bringing me back to the present.

"If we get caught your mum can just *buy you another car,*" I snipe, walking sideways along the fence searching for a gap in the links. We were at the very back of the junkyard, one edge lined by towering oak trees; the streetlights didn't quite reach us here, and I could hardly see but for the sliver of moonlight above.

Levi crossed his arms, leaning against the fence. "Why do you have such a thing about my car?"

I throw my arms up in exasperation. "I don't have a thing about your car, okay? Now *shush* and give me a boost."

"Since you asked so politely: no."

"Then turn around; I don't want to flash my knickers," I say, with as much dignity as I can muster.

"For the record—"

I slap a hand over his mouth. "If you have any sense of self-preservation, do not finish that sentence," I threaten. He nods, eyes a little wild. He grabs my hand as I pull away.

"Let's go back," he whispers. "I'm sorry. I'm a stupid vampire jock demon, or whatever it is you usually call me. Let's just go."

I think about it for a moment, the warmth of his fingers bleeding into the cool skin of my wrist. But answering feels too much like *truth*, so I turn away. "Dare's a dare, Sawyer."

He swears under his breath, and just as I stick my boot in the fence, I feel his hands around my waist lifting me up.

I swallow a yelp and grab the hem of my dress in a panic.

"My eyes are closed," he says as my hand blindly knocks his head. "Tell me when you're over."

In answer, I land with a light thump on the opposite side of the fence, dust billowing out like mist.

"Open," I say. "There you go, I broke in. Happy now?"

He leans on the fence, fingers laced through the chain links. "You're impossible, you know that?"

I don't answer, because I am, indeed, aware that I'm an impossible girl. My mum used to use that exact phrase.

I open my phone to take a picture to post in the group chat, throwing up a peace sign as Levi looks on, slightly forlorn, from the other side of the fence.

"Was it so terrible?" he murmurs, watching me click *send*.

My phone buzzes again, a new message from Elliot that makes my stomach clench: Why did Emiko just tell me you left the dance to go commit a crime?

"Was what terrible?" I ask, irritable and paranoid, glancing around at the shadows. *You are such an idiot, Brodie McKellon.* At least I'm a self-aware idiot. God, this was so stupid. Suddenly, all I want is to be back in the very place I ran away from: dancing under the mirror ball with Elliot and Isaac and, *urgh*, even Levi.

He's gone so quiet I turn back and watch his throat bob in the moonlight. "School. Driving. The dance." Pause. "Us."

My mouth drops open, about to demand what *us* there was left, force him to say something that mattered, ready to finally let the unsaid words tumble out. And then.

"Did you hear that?" I hiss.

His head tilts, listening. Then he shakes *no*, and shrugs.

But he hasn't lived in a creaky old house where the shadows are filled with ghosts, waiting for hallway windows to open at midnight.

I strain to focus on the sound I thought I'd heard, blocking out the low rush of distant cars, the slight ruffle of leaves in a quiet wind. Levi's breath, steady and strong.

There. "Dogs. Incoming."

Levi swears, eyes skittering to either side of the stacked-up cars behind me. "Quick, come back now."

I latch onto the fence, shoving a boot into the warped holes. I climb for all of three seconds before my shoe slides out and I crash to the ground, my knee cracking on the dirt and the air blown out of my lungs. I'm so stunned for a moment that I just stare at the graze, blood beading on the surface.

"Brodie, get up," he says, voice tinged with panic. "Are you hurt?"

I open my mouth to answer, but the air won't come back—I try to suck in a breath but it's like my lungs are seized in iron and can't expand. *Shoes*, I mouth, clutching my stomach, lungs aching. Oh god, Nan will kill me if this is how I die: She will resurrect my ghost, and screech obscenities into the afterlife until I issue my sincerest apology via Ouija board.

Levi swears again, shucking his jacket and tossing it on the ground, lurching himself over the fence. I finally manage to catch a breath, stumbling to my feet.

"What are you doing?" I wheeze.

"I'm not going to let you get mauled to death, Brodie."

"Because you're, what, immune to teeth?"

He lands beside me and grabs my hand, taking off at a run. "Less arguing, more fleeing."

We round the corner, the dogs sounding like a gallop of horses, their barks echoing in the night.

He tries to turn toward the warehouse, where the main entrance is, but I yank his hand and pull him toward the old shed instead.

"There's no exit that way," he hisses.

"And the front gate is padlocked. We just need to hide long enough until they lose interest." Floodlights kick on one by one, blinking to life overhead. I cringe, shying away from the beam. "Also, Dwight is that way."

We are so screwed.

I tug Levi toward the shed, occasionally doubling back to confuse the dogs that can't quite seem to catch up as we hurtle through gaps in piles of scrap metal and clamber over the hoods of broken-down cars. Finally, we tumble through the wonky side door of the old workshop—it's pitch-black inside and it smells like engine oil and the metallic tang of forgotten parts, but the darkness is now a welcome friend.

Levi hesitates a moment in the dim, but I shove him toward the ladder from memory. I feel my way through the room until my palm hits the rung and feel gritty charcoal against my fingers— fire damaged. I say a small prayer that it doesn't collapse under our weight and haul myself up, straining to hear Levi follow. We used to do this all the time, back when we'd sneak in to visit the Chevy— but we were smaller then, and the rungs didn't groan as we climbed, threatening to snap at any moment.

Luckily, they hold under our weight, and I collapse on a bed of mold-scented straw, trying to suffocate in silence, and wipe the sweat from my brow. There's a quiet shuffling, and I feel Levi's body come to rest against my arm. His fingers find mine and I cling on tight. "You okay?" he breathes, as quietly as possible.

"Fine," I answer. "Shh."

We roll back into the farthest corner of the loft, peering through cracks in the wood as Dwight stalks across the yard, flashlight sweeping through the shadows. "Enough! You idiot dogs, better not be another fucking possum."

He pauses at the edge of the shed, light drifting through the open door. We hold our breath, counting the long seconds as a pale yellow beam sweeps over the shadows.

Finally, he turns away and trudges back to the warehouse, two dogs at his side, until a door slams shut in the distance and the flashlight disappears, and finally, the floodlights go dark.

Levi exhales, the air tickling my ear. He starts to stand, but I pull him back down. "Wait. Dwight's a drunk but he's not a complete idiot."

Sure enough, two minutes later, there's a soft padding of feet below, and I spy Dwight through the planks of wood, quietly stalking around the perimeter of the junkyard. No dogs this time, no lights. "He knows we're in here somewhere," I whisper, feeling a ripple of goose bumps up my spine.

Levi peers through the crack, watching Dwight stumble around the fence. "He's half full of whiskey; he doesn't know his own name."

"Okay, well, off you go then. Hey, does he sleep with a shotgun or a teddy bear? Gosh, I just can't seem to remember. . . ."

Levi groans, pushing the heels of his hands against his eyes. "Why do I let you talk me into these things?"

"*Me*?!" I whisper-screech in the dark. "This was *your* idea!"

"Oh," Levi says. "Yeah. Habit. Uh, sorry."

"Habit?!"

"Please be quiet," Levi says. "I really don't want to get shot on Valentine's Day."

"I'm sorry, is there a *better day* to be shot?"

He grumbles something about Christmas and eventually settles next to me. "I, um, I'm sorry. For ruining your night. It was a dumb dare."

I settle back into the mattress, cringing away from a slightly damp corner. My eyes adjust to the dark, shadows taking form. There are a few things scattered around—a sweater, bits of crumpled paper, a rolled-up pair of socks. I reach out to gingerly poke the cover of a book, the title smoke-stained and illegible in the dark. "Do you think someone used to live up here?" I whisper.

"Sure," he answers, leaning close. "The children stolen by the Rydal Devil."

"*Urgh.*" I sigh, pulling out my phone to shoot Emi a quick message: Got stuck. Might be a while.

She messages back almost immediately, offering to be our getaway driver if needed. I click the screen off, nervous that the brightness could make us a target, and stuff it back into my dress.

Me and Levi. Levi and me. Alone. In the dark. This is fine. Dwight *is* a terrible drunk—eventually, he'll fall asleep, and we'll tiptoe away into the night. Maybe even make it back to the dance.

"Brodie?" Levi says, close enough that his breath is warm on my neck.

I cringe away from him, leaning into the spiky straw. "What?"

"Are you going to ignore me the whole time?"

"Probably."

He sighs, rolling away. I see the slope of his shoulders illuminated by moonlight as he sits up, looking down at the space where the Chevy still sits. "Remember when we planned to save up all our pocket money to buy that car and drive it across the country?"

The corner of my lip quirks, unbidden. "The great pancake tour."

"We could still do it," he says quietly. "Graduate. Drive out of town and keep going."

My heart pangs, stuck somewhere between longing and regret, for what we had, and the fact that we can't quite seem to get it back. "I don't know," I say. "Warwick isn't so bad."

"Yeah?"

"Sometimes I think it's my favorite place in the world."

"Did you miss it?" *Did you miss me?*

"Sometimes." *Every day.* I think of Rowley, and the dorms at night, quiet and lonely. How on particularly bad days, I'd take the telescope up to the roof and point the lens north, pretending I could see all the way home. "Anyway, we couldn't leave, because your car would have a breakdown on day one. Drives like a supermarket trolley."

I'm sure he rolls his eyes—I feel that eye roll in my bones. "You didn't seem to mind so much, this afternoon."

"I was being gracious."

"Uh-huh."

"We should honestly just ask Dwight if he wants it back. Scrap it for parts."

"Why do you have such a thing about my car?"

"I don't have a thing about it," I snipe in response. "I just—"

"Just *what?*"

"Nothing. You just—why are we even talking about this?"

"Fine, let's talk about something else. Why did you run away from me at the dance?"

I grimace in the dark. "Maybe not talking is better." Although, honestly, it's easier like this. Not having to face him. Saying words and not having to watch as they land. It goes quiet for a few minutes, until I can't stand the silence anymore. I chew on my lips, my brain screaming to *just shut up for once,* but it comes blurting out and I can't stop it. "It's just that you drive that car around, acting like it means something, when we all know your mum would buy you whatever car you wanted. I bet she's offered; I know she hates that thing. You would never have picked it, and you only have it because Dwight threatened to press charges unless your family made it *worth his while.*"

Silence.

Then.

"She wants to buy me a Tesla," he says.

"Of course she does." It's the Afghan Hound all over again. "I don't get it, that's all. It's like you're playing at being poor or something. Like you think it somehow makes you more . . . like us. But you get to go home to your nice family and your nice house and your room with your nice things. And your stupid old car parked out in front."

It goes quiet again. I regret every single word I just said, and I want to stuff them all back in my mouth, but it's too late, always too late.

He lies down beside me again, staring straight at the ceiling; I can see the peak of his nose cast in the shadow, the curve of his lips. I'd know Levi anywhere, even without light; he smells like strawberry gum and freshly mowed lawn, and his arm lying next to mine makes my skin ache.

"Did you know," he says flatly, "that car is one of the only things I ever chose for myself? My mum picks everything for me. She still buys my *clothes*, Brodie. She chose my classes this year. My university next year. The nice house and the nice room and all the things in it—none of it is really mine."

I want the earth to open up and swallow me. I *knew* what his mum was like—all shiny surfaces and hollow insides. Somehow, three years away had been enough to make me forget. My finger twitches and touches his, a moment longer than I could call an accident. As close to *sorry* as I can get right now.

"You're wrong, though," he whispers, after a long time. "It does mean something. It's the last piece of us, that summer. I kept it because it was the last of *you*. Or at least, I thought it was," he says, voice hoarse. "But now you're back."

"Oh."

"Yeah, well," he says bitterly. "Maybe I'll trade it for a fucking Telsa." He rolls to one side, facing the empty shed below. Still close enough to touch, but now the years stretch out between us.

260

And for the first time, I think that maybe Levi was lonely too. In a different sort of way, but lonely just the same.

I make a face in the dark, kicking myself for starting an argument I don't even care about. "Levi?"

"What?"

"I—I hope you don't get shot on your favorite holiday." *Chicken.*

"Gee, thanks." He rolls back.

But the quiet doesn't last. I'm addicted to it, this honesty and the darkness. I think back to that first night in Treegap. *Do you regret it?*

"Hey, Levi?"

He sighs. "Yes, Brodie?"

"What else did you choose?"

"You." Pause. "And Elliot."

"And Elliot," I agree.

"And Pudge. He's still pink, by the way."

"Blush."

"Magenta."

"Was that all?" The ball is clearly in my court: He gave me something true and I gave nothing back. I'm in debt, and he's sick of cashing me out.

"I . . . yeah. Yeah. That's all."

I can see just enough that I watch his eyes flutter closed, disappointed. He's not watching me anymore, and I haven't had such a good opportunity to just *look* at him in years. The slope of his nose, the shape of his brow, the peak of his cheekbones, and the square of his jaw. The neck I'd like to lean into, lips I once kissed. And eyes . . . open again.

"Sorry," I mumble.

He shrugs. "I don't mind."

I take a breath, emboldened by the dark and his nearness and the fact that I have already colossally screwed up already and *surely* it can't—statistically—get any worse. So I reach out, tracing a line from his cheek to his collarbone, watching as he shivers under my fingertips, not breathing at all. Goose bumps flush down his neck, ridges peaking under the trail of my fingers, disappearing below the buttons of his shirt. I feel my heart thundering in my chest, nervousness bubbling through my veins, worried I'll lose my mind and keep going. Worried I'll stop. We'd never done *this*. Both of our stolen kisses had been quick and awkward, cut short. And then I'd left. There had been no time to linger. I watch my fingers resting on his throat, like they belong to some other person. He'd let me keep going, I realize, heat flushing my face. I could run my hands down his arms or unclasp that button and he'd let me.

I come to my senses and snatch my hand away.

"I didn't—sorry," I stutter. "I don't know—" I shove my hands into my lap, not trusting myself.

He pushes onto an elbow, leaning close. "Brodie . . ."

His fingers are brushing away my hair. His hand comes to rest at the nape of my neck. And he's going to kiss me, I know he is, and there is a sick feeling in my stomach because I have only right now, *this second*, decided that is exactly what I want, and suddenly it's all I can think about. Levi and his strawberry breath, and his lips tipped into the tiniest smile, and—

262

Light floods the loft. The sheer brightness of it burns my eyes and I jolt up, flinging one arm over my face and using the other to shove Levi down. When we aren't immediately shot, I dare to squint between splayed fingers and find myself looking down at a supremely pissed-off Dwight.

"Brodie fuckin' McKellon," he says. "Shoulda known."

I want to be clear that, once again, I was not technically arrested. *Detained* is not arrested. Though the semantics of police involvement aren't exactly doing me much good right now, since Dwight seems to be delighting in spontaneously yelling "Throw her in the slammer!" as he works through the report.

"She robbed me! Again!"

Detective Sawyer sighs, and his eyes drift halfway closed as he silently mouths *one, two, three. . . .*

"They haven't taken anything, Dwight. It's a trespassing charge at best."

Dwight spits tobacco into a nearby bin, a metallic *clang* echoing through the police station. "Like hell. She's a thief! A THIEF," he yells, spinning around on his swivel chair. "Bet she took a car again. Have you checked they're all there?"

I lean between the bars of the cell, rolling my eyes. "Where would I have put a car, Dwight? Under my dress? Let me look, maybe the Hadron Collider is in here too."

The detective grits his teeth, taking a steadying breath. "Ms. McKellon," he bites out. "You do, in fact, have the right to remain silent. I would advise you to utilize it."

I give him the finger when he turns away, and Levi swats my hand. "Hey! He's still my dad."

"He *arrested* us!"

"Detained," Levi corrects.

"Oh, whatever. Where's Barbara?"

He shrugs.

"Why are you not bothered by this?"

He shrugs again.

"You are a terrible accomplice."

One arm starts to lift.

"*Do not* shrug at me," I hiss.

He scrubs a hand through his hair, taking a seat on the bench. "Look, it's fine. You're still a minor, Dwight's still an idiot. You didn't get charged last time, did you?"

"Well, no, but—"

"It's more paperwork than it's worth. Dad will fix it."

I grudgingly take a seat beside him, only because I've been half hanging through the cell bars for the last thirty minutes and my adrenaline levels are slowly waning. Apparently, heckling a police officer for their inferior office supplies can be considered "interfering with an investigation," but I'm pretty sure Detective Dick made that up. Either way, I've hardly spoken to Levi since his dad came and hauled us away in a police wagon. The most insulting part is that Levi got to sit in the front seat, and I had to sit in the back, behind the cage.

We sit in silence, at opposite ends of the bench seat, studiously avoiding each other's gaze. God, why did I say yes to this stupid dare? Why did Levi look like he was going to kiss me and why did I *touch him* like a massive creep? Seriously, I *felt him up*. There are no other words. It cannot be phrased politely. I'm going to have to move. Skip town, not speak for three years, come back and try again. That seems to be the only way to salvage our friendship.

"McKellon!"

I jump, surprised to find myself half dozing on Levi's shoulder. I discreetly wipe the drool out of the corner of my mouth and squint up at the detective. He looks sweaty and tired and disappointed, and his eyes linger a little too long at the spot on Levi's shoulder that I'd been sleeping on. He clears his throat, hooking thumbs through his belt. "Misdemeanor charge, sealed and wiped on your eighteenth, penalty fine only. Best I can do."

Levi's spine straightens, and I see him scowling from the corner of my eye. "That's bullshit."

"That's trespassing," his dad says, sounding tired.

"And me?"

Detective Sawyer hesitates for a second. "You're off. He won't charge."

Levi blinks up at him for a long moment, then strides across the cell and grips the bars. "Hey, Dwight! Remember when someone filled the crush cars with lake water and hermit crabs? That was me!"

The indignation is immediate. "You sonofa—"

Levi rockets back, and I realize suddenly that he no longer has to look up at his dad. They're the same height, shoulder to shoulder, glaring at each other. "Do better," Levi says, then drops down beside me.

The detective mutters something that sounds like *"Getting too old for this shit,"* then saunters back to his desk. "Dwight, let's take a walk. You like cigars? Thought so. . . ."

Footsteps fade as they walk down the corridor, leaving us alone. I whirl on Levi, looking at him for the first time since the loft. "You're so stupid, why would you do that—"

I grab a fistful of his shirt, intending to shove him, but somehow end up pulling him closer. And I'm so angry at him, for making that ridiculous dare, and then for getting himself in more trouble, for thinking I took the Adder Stone, and for not talking to me for three years because he's *an idiot*—and mostly, because I can't seem to get Levi Sawyer out of my head, and I think I've dreamed this before, the two of us standing like this, because it feels so easy, so familiar. I've seen his face tilted down like this, his brows pulled close, and his lips parted in surprise. I've seen him turn toward me exactly like this, and I hate the way my body hums when he looks at me, like he's the sun and I'm the last stars in the sky, and the freckles on his nose are a constellation I'd like to explore with my mouth and—

I am kissing Levi Sawyer.

It's an accident, I think. I wanted to tell him I hated him, but I somehow end up shoving my lips on his instead, the words lost when he opens his mouth and says *Oh* and then Levi is kissing me back. His hands are in my hair and on my waist, raking up my sides, and I shudder without meaning to, pressing myself closer, wanting to crawl inside his skin and claim it as mine.

He pushes me against the back wall, and *Levi is still kissing me.* It's all wrong for a moment, not the kiss I remember, which was quick and awkward: Back then, I had to duck a little bit, and it was just lips pressed against lips, and I think I sort of spit on him accidentally. But now, *now.*

I tilt my head up and open my mouth, wrapping my arms around his shoulders. There's a rhythm to this kiss, and it takes me a minute to catch up, my brain emptying of all thoughts except this: We must look obscene, two criminals pressed against each other in a jail cell. I can feel my cheeks burning, the hem of my dress lifting as I reach up, but I don't care—and then my feet aren't on the ground at all. Levi lifts me up until I'm standing on the bench seat, placing us nearly eye to eye. "Much better," he mutters, and I'm about to say something but I can't remember *what* because his lips are on my neck. He kisses a trail to my shoulder and it burns; I am burning, my skin is on fire. He mutters my name, and it's both cool dousing water and fresh flame. Damnation and salvation, all at once.

My eyes drift open for a second, bleary and blissed. And then I blink.

"August."

Levi leans back, hand coming to rest under my chin. He frowns, puzzled. "What?"

I shake my head, forgetting how to make words. I point over his shoulder, at the poster my eyes had snagged on. "Look. I remember now, where I knew him from."

Levi turns, shoulders sagging the moment his eyes land on that crumpled old poster, still tacked on the very back wall, the edges curled and yellow.

Nearly twenty years old, the kid they never found and no one had the heart to take down.

Missing: presumed dead.

"It's him. It's August."

12

Dear August,

I made so many plans, all laid out in neat, lined books.
We used to play that game, where will you be in five weeks,
five months, five years. And for a long time, the answer was:
Warwick, Warwick, Warwick. But for the first time in my life,
I don't know the answer. Where will we be, August?

"Brodie McKellon!"

I bolt awake in bed just as my bedroom door bounces off the wall, bits of plaster cascading to the floor.

Nan fills half the frame with her silk-dressing-gowned body, hair in hot rollers, cat on her shoulder, and she's still more terrifying than a Texas chain-saw-wielding psychopath. "Why was Detective Sawyer just in my living room explaining to me that you were arrested last night?"

I stumble out of bed, feeling the need to be upright for this conversation. "Uh . . . detained, actually—"

Nan just stares at me for a full minute, then *hurumphs*. "Is this why you snuck in after midnight?"

I hold a finger up, pausing. "Technically, I snuck in because I lost my key. I was *late* because of the whole . . . detaining thing."

Nan sighs. Mabel mews. "No pancakes for you," she says, then closes the door. It opens again a second later. "And the next time you come home stumbling in after midnight from the police station, remember to take your makeup off. Terrible for the complexion, darling. And you're grounded! Until lunchtime, at least!"

The door closes again.

I collapse on the bed, throwing an arm over my eyes. Last night feels like a fever dream, ripped from the throes of a strange delusion. The dance and Dwight's loft and *I kissed Levi*.

All of it blurs together, and then I feel my breath catch.

August.

His poster, there all along. And I *saw it*, the very first night I came back to Warwick. I didn't pay much attention at the time—had assumed it had only remained after all this time because no one could bear to pull it down and put it in the trash. So old and sun-bleached it was barely legible, his surname lost in a torn corner. And I'd hardly even caught a glimpse last night—there was no time to analyze it between the detaining and the kissing and Dwight eventually drinking himself into a near coma before being convinced to drop the charges.

Of all people, it was Quinn who'd come to collect me.

The doors blew open, she stormed in with fury on her face and soft pink slippers on her feet, Elliot sheepishly lurking behind her.

270

Guess they'd figured out the whole dare went to shit when no one could actually contact us—plus, I'd used my phone to text Elliot from the back of the police cruiser, begging him not to let Nan find out if it could be avoided, right before Detective Dick saw it and snatched it off me.

I've never seen Quinn like that. Her face set, no tremble of hesitation in her voice. She stood in the glow of the exit sign, eyes bright with fury. "I will be taking Brodie home. Now."

Detective Sawyer opened his mouth to protest, but she didn't even let him speak.

"*Now*, Richard."

If she was surprised to find Levi in the cell with me, she didn't let it show. She waited for *both* of us to scurry out and drove us home in silence. Levi and I sat in the back seat together, hands splayed in the middle seat, fingers nearly touching but not. I'd hesitated when she pulled up at the post office, and eventually just murmured my thanks to Quinn. She surprised me by letting out a sharp laugh. "Ah, kid, it's not the first time I've picked up a McKellon from the station."

I yank a pillow over my head, screaming into the feathers. What is wrong with me? Why couldn't I just go to the dance and have a nice time—spike the punch like a normal delinquent?

Maybe I can stay in here forever. Join the ghost in the attic, the memory of a girl who was brave enough to break into private property but not brave enough to face a boy she liked.

But *August*.

If not for that poster, I would have spent the day wallowing in bed. Instead, I force myself to shower and dress and eat, and work in the post office until Nan sighs and declares me un-grounded.

She holds my chin, and smiles. "Too much like your mother, sometimes."

And although she's forgiven me, I still see the tight lines of stress around her eyes. I wrap my arms around her shoulders, breathing her tea-leaf-and-talcum-powder smell. "Sorry, Nan."

She shakes her head, patting my back. "So long as you always come home when you're done." She steps back, sweeping an arm across the post office. "Now, do you think you can get this place cleaned up before tomorrow? Alas, love must wait another year. . . ."

I groan, looking at the red-and-pink sea of hearts. I bite down a complaint, figuring I deserved it. Nan is halfway up the stairs when I call out, "Hey, Nan . . . did you know that kid who went missing?"

Nan halts on the staircase, peering over the top of her half-rim glasses. "Why do you ask?"

"His name was August. He was one of the letter writers—I saw his poster last night."

"Oh."

Importantly, *oh* is not *no*. I frown, wondering if perhaps Nan has known more than she had let on all along. "Do you know what happened to him?"

Nan hesitates a moment, and I wonder if she's really trying to remember or trying to settle on a version of the truth. "It rained," she says eventually.

"What?"

272

"I remember the day he went missing. It rained."

"Is that—is that all?"

She shrugs, and Mabel curls around her feet. Nan flaps a hand and recommences her shuffle toward the kitchen. "I'm old, poppet. It was a long time ago."

And I think, as she walks away, that her answer still wasn't *no*.

I want to thank Quinn again for bailing us out last night, so I pick some flowers from Nan's garden and bike across town to the library. I find her tucked away in a dusty corner, picking through old newspapers and occasionally setting some to the side to be labeled and stored. I remember that I'm supposed to ask about August, but right now, all I want is forgiveness.

She's so focused on her work, squinting in the dim light, that she doesn't see me coming until I'm standing right in front of her.

"Good morning, jailbird," she says with a smile. "Are those for me?"

I nod, handing them over, feeling like a chastised child even though she's been more gracious about the whole situation than I really deserve. "Sorry again," I say, feeling my cheeks turn pink. "About last night. It was really stupid."

She sighs, picking up the flowers to admire. "Just don't go making it a weekly occurrence. Do I want to know what you were doing in that junkyard?"

I feel my cheeks turn an even deeper shade of pink. "It was dumb. It was a dare, and we got a bit carried away. I'm really, really sorry."

"Just glad you called," she says.

"Well, technically, I called Elliot and swore him to secrecy, but I guess he's always been the smart one," I joke. "You should be proud."

Quinn smiles at me, tucking a piece of hair behind my ear. Mum used to do that too. "You call me, anytime, okay? I'll never be angry, not if you need help."

I nod, feeling tears prick behind my eyes. "Thanks, Quinn."

She pulls me into a hug and holds on tight. "Love you, kid."

"Love you too," I mumble. It reminds me of Nan this morning, and I can't help but think back to RAGs, when I accidentally burned that hole in the gym roof and everyone voiced their disappointment at me for two days straight, occasionally interspersed with all-out yelling. The loneliness shrinks a little more—and I think it's been shrinking for a while now, and maybe I just hadn't noticed as it was slowly patched over with the people who'd made themselves part of this new little world. Nan and Quinn, Elliot, Emiko and Claire, and Levi . . . *Levi*. But that will have to wait.

Quinn finally releases me and invites me to her office for a cup of tea. "I have something for you," she says, with a sparkle in her eye.

I follow her through the stacks, and wave hello at the people she introduces me to. They all light up when she says my name, as if they've heard it before. She beams at me as she holds open her office door, looking sheepish. "Did I embarrass you? Sorry, I brag about you kids a lot."

Her office, as she explains, is not so much an office per se, but a carrel tucked along a row of similar desks, all laden with mountains of paper and a few occupied by harried-looking librarians.

"Here, make some space. Just watch those photos, they're hanging on by a hope and a prayer."

I leaf through some of the more stable collections while she fetches the teapot—it reminds me of the Dead Letter Office, these pieces of history. There are newspapers and photographs and a few Kodak slides I have to hold up to the light to see. I pick through a row, finding tiny negatives with old Warwick preserved: the arcade back when it first opened, a couple kids in skates and kneepads, the flooded lake and the ruined library, roof collapsed from the rain. There's even one of the post office that makes me smile. I hold it up to the light, squinting at the negative.

"Those things are the bane of my life," Quinn says, hustling back. "I spend half my time scanning them into the archive. Is that the post office?"

I nod and she smiles, holding out a hand so she can look at it herself. "That's a good one, but actually not what I wanted to show you."

She reaches into the bottom drawer, carefully pulling out a leather-bound book. It's large and square, and for a moment I think it's a photo album until I see the gold-foiled lettering on the front.

"Is that . . . ?"

Quinn runs a hand over the cover, tracing the letters. "Your mum's yearbook—well, not hers, exactly, so you can't keep it, I'm afraid—but it's her year. Someone donated it, to replace the ones we lost," she explains, tapping the photos from the flood. She flips through, clearly looking for something, then turns the book to face me, opened to a black-and-white spread. But Quinn's not looking at the photo: She's watching me, gently pressing the book into my open hands, smiling still, but a little sadder now.

I recognize the girl on the left immediately as Quinn: She looks remarkably the same, with short, cropped hair and a self-conscious half-smile. The photographer has caught them mid-conversation, arms slung around shoulders, crowded on a single seat.

And the other girl . . .

"That's Mum?" I whisper, reaching out to touch the picture, as though I could feel her reaching back.

Quinn nods, and I feel the tears return with a vengeance. She looks so young, younger than I've ever seen her. Head thrown back, eyes crinkled shut, mouth wide and laughing. Her hair is pulled up, the way she used to like mine, away from her face so I can see the freckles scattered across her cheeks. "She looks like me," I say, surprised. I always thought she was so beautiful; I never saw any of myself in her. But here—with her smile just like that, tilted toward the sun—no wrinkles yet around her mouth, a little less refined, a little less adult . . . here I could see the similarities.

"You can hold on to it for a few days," Quinn says. "There's a few more in there too. I think your nan would like to see."

I nod silently and clutch it to my chest. "I'll look after it, I promise." My cheeks are wet, but I don't care. She hands me a tissue and I swipe at my eyes.

"You need anything else?" she asks gently.

I flick through the pages, looking for more photos. The page immediately after has a short, rough edge, like it's been torn out.

"What happened here?" I ask, running a finger along the tear.

Quinn peers over my shoulder. "Ripped out."

"I wonder why."

She shrugs, turning away.

I run a finger down the damaged edge. Fair enough, I suppose. If I'd *had* any photos of Levi when I went to Rowley, I would have torn them to pieces and burned them under a full moon. I close the book and hug it tight to my chest, smiling at her.

"Thanks, Quinn."

"Anytime," she answers. "And hey—stay out of trouble, okay?"

I start to say *I promise*, but the words die on my lips. "I promise to try," I answer instead, and I walk away to the sound of Quinn's laugh, thinking that it's been a long time since I heard that sound.

The ride home is long and lazy; I take the back roads, winding through Rydal Woods, until the sun gets low and the air turns cold. I open the yearbook by the lake's edge, looking for more photos of Mum. There are a few scattered across the pages: lurking in the background of an art exhibit. Throwing bunny ears behind Quinn as she wins an award. Cartwheeling across the finish line of a running race. The last one jolts me—with her hair across her face, only her smile visible, I'd almost mistake the photo for one of me. I inspect the ripped-out pages, because I'm nothing if not criminally nosy. No clues, really, though there's another tear within the graduate portrait shots: Whoever it was has been neatly erased. It's the kind of petty thoroughness I admire.

The lampposts startle me, sputtering to life above the lake edge. The sky has turned dark without me realizing, and when I check my phone for the time, the battery has died—I never charged it after I stumbled into bed last night.

I gather my things and pedal slowly back to the post office, not bothering to compete with cars and gravity. I'm nearly home when I see it: the red and blue lights, flashing all too close to home.

Not *close* to home.

At home.

I drop my bike in the gravel, running to the doors with my heart in my throat, pleading with the universe, *Not Nan, not Nan.* It takes me a moment too long to realize it's not an ambulance like I first thought; it's a police car.

I burst into the post office and find chaos has exploded. Detective Sawyer is there, sitting beside Levi and leaning over someone wrapped in a blanket. Nan is on the phone, repeating over and over again, *He's okay, he's here, he's okay, just come quick.* She sags with relief when she sees me and waves me over.

Levi looks up when I walk in, and I can't read the clouded expression on his face until he steps to one side and I see him: Elliot, clutching an ice pack to his cheek, a bruise flourishing under one eye.

I push my way to him, dropping to my knees, gripping his hands in mine. His fingers are ice-cold and he flinches when I reach for him.

"What happened?" I ask, willing my hands to be still, not to run over him for cuts and bruises.

"You should see the other guy," he mumbles, but his eyes are

278

red and a tear drips down his cheek. I throw my arms around his shoulders and hold on tight, waiting until he stops shaking. Levi sits on his other side, adding his arms to mine, until we've built a safety net, hanging on while Eli falls apart.

Nan gently clears her throat, patting his shoulder. "Your mum is on the way, hon."

Elliot nods and we slowly peel away, though neither of us can bear to let him go completely. We adjust slightly to sit on either side, Levi holding one hand while I have my arm looped around his elbow.

Detective Sawyer gives us a nod, muscle ticking in his jaw. "I'll give you kids a minute. Delia?" He inclines his head toward the door and Nan follows, leaving us alone.

"You don't have to say anything," I whisper. "But we'll listen if you want."

Elliot just shakes his head. "S'okay. They already know."

I glance at Levi and finally I understand the look on his face: rage and despair, competing in equal measure.

"It was Dale," Elliot says.

I squeeze his hand tight, waiting.

"It was so stupid. I'd been out with Isaac. It was a good day. It was *supposed* to be a good day," he says, and his voice is rough with grief. He's lost a lot of good days. "Dale was just . . . just drinking, all afternoon, sitting and stewing, getting drunker and drunker. Pissed off that he got fired from his last job and that he'd run out of money for more booze, asking me to buy him shit, then getting angry that I had cash in my wallet. He stood up to grab it—to take it right out of my hands—and he tripped. Spilled his beer every-where. And it was like he just *snapped*. Screaming at me, because it was all *my* fault, all of it. . . ." He breaks off, shaking his head. "And I just . . . I don't know. I realized that I was taller than him. Does that sound stupid? But I was thinking that I didn't have to look up at him anymore, and that he wasn't this huge giant, he was just some fucking loser that lived in my house. And I was just standing there, thinking that I was taller than him, and he lost it. Like me not being afraid of him just worked him up into this frenzy. He started yelling—I don't even know, just rubbish, just whatever he could think of, and somewhere in the middle of all that he threw his bottle at the wall and my face got in the way. I don't even know if he meant to hit me. . . ." He trails off, looking out the window at the shadow of Nan and Levi's dad. "I hit him back, in fairness."

"What?"

"Not proud of it. Don't wanna talk about it."

I squeeze his hand again. "Okay. That's okay. Do you need any-thing else right now?"

His chin jerks up and down. "Yeah, I just—" His voice breaks. "I just really want my mum."

Levi squeezes his shoulder. "She's coming. She'll be here soon."

We sit like that until Quinn bursts through the door, and her eyes are red like she's been crying, but she holds it together for Elliot: takes him upstairs to Mum's old room and they stay there for a long time, just talking. Nan drifts up, footsteps creaking on the old floor, and their voices are quiet but purposeful. The kettle is set to boil.

Detective Sawyer comes back after a while, muttering something into his radio. He looks at me and Levi and shakes his head. "Eli doing okay?"

"Yeah," Levi answers. "Think so."

"What—what's going to happen to him?" I ask, not even sure that either of them will answer. Not sure I want to know.

Detective Sawyer sighs, pinching the bridge of his nose, and he looks tired all of a sudden. "Jail, if I had anything to do with it. But most likely a restraining order. Doesn't do much, but it's a start."

His radio fills with static for a second, then a voice comes through clear. *"Suspect located: Detective Sawyer, do you copy?"*

He turns away to answer the call, responding in codes that I don't quite understand. I realize after a while that I'm leaning into Levi, and even then, I don't bother to move away.

"Are you okay?" he whispers.

"Me? Yeah, I'm f-fine," I say, teeth chattering. Is this shock? I'm shivering and I need him to stay warm. That doesn't seem right. It's not my trauma. I wasn't even there. But I think of Elliot in that house, and it takes me a minute until I can breathe right again.

Detective Sawyer eventually leaves some papers with Levi, and Nan comes back downstairs to sit with us. "Elliot and Quinn are going to stay here for a while, okay?"

"Okay, sure."

"I mean, they're going to move in."

"Okay."

"We might have to put them in your mum's room."

"Nan, it's fine. She'd—she'd want that."

It's almost midnight when Elliot comes downstairs. He's had a shower and Nan has dug out one of Dad's old shirts, and his cheek is still purple but less angry than before. Mabel is wrapped around one shoulder and she hisses when anyone gets too close, her claws needling his shoulder.

"I think Mabel is mine now," he jokes, and of all people, it's Levi who has to turn away to hide the tears.

We sleep in the post office that night, dragging down mattresses and air beds, flipping the CLOSED sign on the door and wheeling out the old television that only plays local TV stations. We snuggle under blankets and watch a terrible telenovela, ending up tangled together, but Elliot always wedged between us and Mabel grudgingly letting us share him but never far from his lap.

It's one a.m. when Quinn comes down, kisses him good night.

Two a.m. when he first laughs.

Three a.m. when we make popcorn and spend an hour talking about nothing.

Four a.m. when he finally falls asleep.

Five a.m. when I get up to grab a spare sweater, and Levi kisses me in the kitchen because I ask him to.

Six a.m. when Nan wakes up and declares that no one is going to school today.

Dawn when it's a new day, and the house is the same but everything's changed.

Elliot and Quinn move in on Monday, and it feels like the house was built for them. Elliot takes Mum's old room, Quinn sleeps in

282

the study, and Mabel sleeps on Elliot. Their voices fill the quiet spaces, and the hallways don't seem to echo like they used to. Isaac learns to climb the balcony, sneaking in at night until Nan catches him and tells him to use the front door.

She never catches Levi.

On Wednesday, Detective Sawyer comes to sit in the kitchen to have a private conversation with Quinn, and they pretend not to notice as we sit on the stairs and listen as he explains what will happen. Turns out Levi's dad was never a Dale fan: He's booked him for every offense possible, and just to be thorough about it, had his car towed for collateral. Jail time seemed unlikely, but Dale was heavily encouraged to leave town. Something about demonstrating good behavior. Besides, there was nothing here for him now. That's the thing about small towns: word travels fast. I don't know how to feel: Victory, for Elliot. Grief, for Quinn, that it took so long. Anger that Levi's dad is a pretty shit cop until it suits him. Guilt. Gratitude. Relief. All of it.

"You didn't have to come," Quinn says, when he's done.

There's a long silence until Detective Sawyer answers, "Yeah, I did." And then: "It just should have been sooner."

He leaves after that, and Quinn watches his car until it disappears over the hill.

And even though their house is safe now, Quinn and Elliot only return long enough to pack more bags and clean clothes. Quinn stops me one afternoon to ask if it's okay, and I don't know how to tell her how much I love them being here, so I ask her to braid my hair instead.

And Elliot: Elliot comes alive.

He makes pancakes with Nan every day, dances with Quinn in the kitchen, teaches Tommy basic math in the post office. He laughs so easily and often I realize how starved we were for the sound.

He still creeps into my room at night, and we lie head to toe whispering in the dark.

"Hey, Red?" he says, on Friday. "I think I'm gonna be okay."

And on Saturday we find the Adder Stone.

13

Dear June,
    I wish you were here. You always know what to ~~say~~ *do.*

                                         —August

Yertle comes in on Saturday morning to pick up her wet-butt-smelling seagrass. Levi and Elliot are sitting at Nan's tarot table, learning how to read the cards, and both are failing spectacularly.

"Ten of wands: Wands are good right? Who doesn't love wands?"

Nan grumbles at Levi, flipping the card face down again. "Ten of wands is a terrible burden. Pain, suffering, inevitable doom. Pick again."

"Ah . . . Death? Is that bad? That seems bad."

"Nah, dude, you picked it upright—that's just a change. Fresh start. Right?"

Nan is going to pee herself with excitement. "Perfect, Eli! I tell you what, next Valentine's Day we'll make a killing with you at the deck. Now hold on, I'm going to go get the turban. I want to see if it fits you."

I roll my eyes, trying to suppress a smile, and turn to locker 603. And stop.

"Is everything okay?" Yertle asks, peering over the counter. "They haven't sent the kikuyu grass again, have they? It gives Ralph the most terrible runs."

I jolt, fumbling over the lockers and pulling out her parcel. "No, sorry. All good; here you go."

My hands shake as I pass her the bundle, waiting until the door clicks shut.

"You okay? You look like you've seen a ghost." Levi is twisted in his chair, watching me. He does that a lot, I've noticed. Though in fairness, I only noticed because I watch him too.

I wave a hand at the drawers behind me. "Did either of you come back here this morning?"

Levi just frowns and shakes his head, looking at Elliot, who shrugs. "No, why?"

"There's a key here. In the PO box."

"It's a post office, Red, there's a lot of those."

"No, you don't understand. It's 604."

They look at me blankly.

"604 has always been locked," I explain. "It's *cursed*."

Elliot sighs, looking back at the deck. "It's not cursed, it's just stuck."

But Levi bounds over, coming around the swinging side door to inspect it. "You gonna open it?"

"I don't know. Should I?"

"How long has it been stuck? I mean, cursed?"

286

"Forever. Always. As long as I remember."

And now there's a little silver key sticking out of the lock, a bit rusted and tarnished, and otherwise totally inconspicuous. Not that there's reason for it to be suspicious, really. Like Levi said: There's a lot of post boxes here.

"Maybe Tommy left it," I say, staring at it.

"You're being so weird about this," Levi says. "How are you not dying to know what's inside?"

"Honestly, I always assumed it was empty."

"Maybe it is. Or maybe it's filled with severed toes."

"Well, thank you for that image."

"You're welcome. So now it's Schrödinger's box: both empty and filled with toes until you open it."

"That's not how it works!" Elliot yells.

Levi looks at me again. "Jesus, Red, if you don't open it I will."

"No! Just . . . give me a minute. I'm having a moment." He waits a few seconds. Nothing happens. I sigh. "Fine. Moment over."

I twist the key and it sticks before the lock springs loose. I have to jimmy the wood a little to pop it open, but finally the door swings out and we peer into a dark, empty space.

"Oh. Well, that was underwhelming." Levi starts to turn away, but I squint.

"No, wait, there's something in here."

"Is it toes?" Elliot asks, interest piqued and now loitering at the window.

I pull out a small yellow envelope, no bigger than a credit card. It's nearly entirely flat but for a tiny bump in the middle.

"Maybe it's diamonds," Levi says.

"Maybe it's a very small toe," Elliot says.

I tip it into my hand, and it takes me a moment to realize what I'm looking at. "It's . . . it's the Adder Stone." The golden band glimmers as I twist it in my fingertips, and I frown.

"No," Elliot says, face ashen. "It can't be."

I glance around, but the post office is empty and the street is quiet. "It's fine," I whisper. "No one saw."

"No," Elliot repeats. "It can't be here."

I hold it up again, squinting in the dim light. "I'm pretty sure it is."

"It can't be here," he says. "Because I took it."

There are a few long seconds of total, complete silence. And then—

"You what?"

"When?"

"How long have you—"

"When you say, 'took it,' does that mean—"

He slaps a hand over his mouth, wobbling uncertainly on his feet.

"It's okay," I say. "Sit. Levi, grab him that chair. And pinch Nan's coffee; he needs some booze."

Elliot sits heavily, turning whiter by the second. "I'm sorry, I'm so sorry—"

"It's fine," I say, reaching out to wrap my hands around his. His skin is icy cold. "It's okay. Just start at the beginning."

"The night you left," he says. "I found a picture in Mum's room. She didn't keep important stuff at the house, because

Dale—well, he's Dale. But this wasn't a proper picture, it was a bit underdeveloped, and you couldn't really see who was in it, but I knew Mum was there because she has this cross that she used to—" He shakes his head. "It was Mum and a guy with his head sort of out of frame, but he was holding the Adder Stone."

"Okay . . ."

"And I asked Mum about it, and she got all weird, and I asked if it was real, and she got weirder—"

"Right . . ."

"And then she said just to forget I ever saw it, and to leave it alone, and that I shouldn't tell anyone what I found."

"*Definitely* weird."

He nods. "And then I tried to ask her more questions, and she just started crying, and it was so strange because she'd never ever mentioned the stone, and I couldn't figure out why she had a photo of it, somewhere that definitely wasn't the museum, with a guy I'd never seen, and when I got to the Town Hall I was pissed off, and upset, and then I had to say goodbye to Brodie, probably forever, and I was sort of crying, so I went into the stupid display room, and I don't know—I just wanted to see it, a bit closer, to make sure it really was the one in Mum's picture, and then I sort of . . ."

"Stole it?"

He covers his face with his hands. "I'm sorry. I'm so sorry. I was holding it, and someone was coming, and I put it in my pocket because you're obviously not meant to *touch it*, and I went home, and then I woke up, it was a big fucking deal, and I didn't know how to take it back without admitting what happened, so I just sort of . . ."

"Kept it?"

"In my sock drawer," he says miserably. "And now it's here. But I swear to you, I didn't put it there!"

"Right," Levi says. "Okay." Except he says it in a strange way, the way a doctor does when you're getting really bad news, but they don't want you to freak out just yet.

Elliot looks up, fresh horror on his face. "And you two—I swear, I didn't know that's why you were fighting. You never said anything! If I'd known, I wouldn't have let it—"

"It's fine," I say, gently wrapping an arm around his shoulders. "It's our fault, right, Levi? We should have told you sooner."

"Old news," he agrees. "And look at us now—it all worked out."

We glance at each other, over the top of Elliot's head. Confused, surprised, at a total loss for words—but he nods, and in the one gesture promises not to let any of it slip in front of Elliot. Not when he's already been through so much.

"I tried to fix it," Elliot grumbles. "When I realized. To get you to look for it, so Levi would believe you. And I wanted to just give it to you, when I found out about the reward, but I didn't know how to do that without telling you I'd had it all along."

We all look at the ring, on the counter. A twenty-thousand-dollar find.

"We could claim it now," Levi suggests, but I shake my head.

"No. Not if it links back to Elliot."

"It's fine," Eli says. "You should. I can tell them—"

"No," I repeat. "We wouldn't do that. We'll find another way." The reward is worthless if it puts Elliot in the firing line, if it was even real to begin with.

"I'm sor—"

"Elliot, look at me: I've stolen worse things." He laughs—a sad, wet sound. "And if you hadn't taken it, I probably would have. Eventually. I'm sorry we made you feel like you couldn't tell us. All we care about is you. And a little bit about why your mum—never mind. I love you. We're not mad. We'll never be mad, not at you. That's all that matters. Okay?"

I hold out my pinkie. He loops his finger through mine. "Okay."

I squish him into a hug, and Levi wraps his arms around both of us. "My little thieves," he whispers, and Elliot laughs again, properly this time.

"Hey," he says, picking the ring up, shuffling out of our embrace. "There's something written on this. I never noticed."

He squints but can't seem to make out the words and passes it to me.

Levi hovers over my shoulder. "What does it say?"

"It says . . ." I stare dumbly at the inscription, frown deepening as I read it aloud. "It says: *dent fort vat.*"

Levi and Elliot stare at the ring, then at me.

"Just one question," Levi says. "What the hell does that mean?"

Treegap sighs in the wind and it sounds like *Welcome home*. The little house seems happy to be filled with people again and the meager offerings we have left it. Hazy afternoon sun streaks in through the tiny windows, dust traps dancing in the light. The floor has been swept, and we brought an old rug from the attic that Nan said we could have because *your grandad chose that one and it looks like the funeral home had a garage sale.*

I'm lying in the doorway, head undercover, legs in the sun. Elliot is nobly attempting to repaint the patterns on the outside walls, and Levi is disconcertingly quiet. Every so often his eyes flicker to me then scatter away. We haven't actually talked since *the kiss.* Well, since *the second kiss.* But that was an emotional distress kiss, and it doesn't count. I mean, we've talked, obviously, about the weather and turtles and missing boys, but not about . . . *us.*

"Does this look like a peony or an axolotl?"

I sit up, inspecting Elliot's handiwork. He's frowning at a pink-shaped blob, which does indeed look mildly amphibian.

I mash my lips together, determined not to laugh. "How exactly did you get the two confused?"

He sighs, wiping excess paint off his arms. "Well, I don't really know what a peony is meant to look like, in fairness."

Levi pokes his head out the window. "Nice. I like its antennas." He waves his hands next to his ears, trying to demonstrate.

"Do you mean gills?"

"No, like this." He flaps more aggressively.

Eli and I frown at each other. "Whiskers?"

"No—you know what, never mind. Elliot, it's a very nice flower. Maybe something simpler next time, though, like a daisy. Or a . . . circle."

Elliot rolls his eyes. "Ha ha. Why don't you come help?"

"Because I failed eighth-grade art class when Mrs. Hampton made us do those clay statues, and I conceded any creative talent thereafter."

"In fairness, your interpretation of the subject was very . . . phallic."

"It's not my fault! I was making a skyscraper! They're all sort of penis-shaped if you think about it." Levi looks to me for assistance, and I just raise one eyebrow in response.

"Therapy, Levi. What you're looking for is therapy. Wouldn't have picked you as particularly Freudian, though."

He throws his arms up in surrender. "Just—fine, give me a brush. What's this? A squirrel?"

Elliot sighs. "Tulip."

Levi lets his head bang gently against the planks.

I look at the piece of paper in my hands, scribbling some more. "Maybe it's an anagram?"

"What?" Levi asks. "Tulip? *Lit up*?"

"No—the message. In the Adder Stone."

Here's the thing: I wanted to take it to the police station. I really, really did. We had it in our possession, we could have taken it in and claimed the reward. Twenty thousand dollars is enough to make my head spin. But I can't work out how to manage it without somehow linking it back to us—if Levi takes it in, they'll assume it was me. Even if my name has been technically cleared, there's no way Detective Dick won't think I'm involved—especially since the ring has somehow made its way into my home, *and* there's the small matter that we have no idea how it got there. That means someone, somewhere, knows that we have it. And I won't risk that, not until we can figure out how all these pieces of the puzzle fit together.

It's too much of a coincidence: the missing stone and the missing boy. And nowhere, ever, has there been a mention of an inscription on the Adder Stone.

Levi drops his paintbrush for a moment, thinking. After a few long moments he sheepishly concedes defeat and pulls out his phone. "I can't do this in my head," he grumbles.

Elliot frowns at the ceiling, tongue between his teeth. "None with all letters," he says. "Not, era, one? Torn, raft . . . um . . . rodent? Seems unlikely. Trove? Atoned?"

"Nerd," Levi mutters.

"Hey!"

"What?" Levi says innocently, holding up his screen "It's an anagram." Levi looks back at his screen, typing. "Battlefront? Except we're missing a few letters."

I roll my eyes. "I highly doubt someone stole the Adder Stone only to engrave it with the incomplete and jumbled letters of a *video game.*"

"You never know. What kind of person steals someone's dog? People do all sorts of insane things." He squints at me for a second, thinking. "You know, it is kinda weird that we found the stone in the post office. . . ."

"It wasn't me!"

He holds his hands up in defeat. "Just checking!"

The list of suspects on that front is pretty short: How many people can slip behind the counter unnoticed?

Levi turns back to his painting, adding some greenery. "I guess the message doesn't really tell us much, though, does it?"

I frown. "Technically, no, but don't you find it odd—"

"Sure," Levi answers. "It's interesting. But it's probably just some old scribble from the dude who first found it. He turned it into a wedding ring, right? I bet it's some lovey-dovey nonsense."

I glance back down at my sheet of paper. No matter how I twist the words, the only sense I can make of them is in their current form. "I guess," I say, feeling deflated. But something about the words bothers me. The ghost of a memory, a black-and-white film with no sound. *What is it, Brodie?* It's the sensation of seeing August all over again. *I know this, I know this.*

"I just feel like—" I start to explain, then stop. Elliot's bruised cheek catches the sun as he turns, and I sigh, shoving the paper into my pocket. This is stupid, solving a mystery when we have real problems. "I feel cold," I say instead. "I'm gonna go grab the spare blankets."

We'd stacked Levi's car with a bunch of stuff for the cabin, so I run back to where he's left it unlocked. I open the back door and rummage for supplies, cursing as I drop one of the thermos jugs, reaching under the front seat to retrieve it. My fingertips brush a paper envelope, and I snatch it up, worried coffee might have leaked on whatever it is.

It takes me a while to realize what I'm looking at. Elliot's birth certificate. I frown, looking at the words scribbled out next to parent information: mother *and* father.

It's a copy of a copy, clearly. The original could still be intact, but this one is blurry and incomplete. Without really meaning to, I flick to the next page.

It's a spreadsheet, something like a telephone directory for the entire state—every single person with the surname *Maddon*. The first page is entirely crossed out, struck through with blue pen.

I slam the folder shut, feeling like I've intruded.

Elliot is looking for his dad—from the number of pages jammed into this folder, I'd say he's been looking for a while. And Levi's helping him.

Except . . . why was Quinn's name crossed out, too?

Carefully, I grab the thermos and replace the folder exactly as I found it. Heart in my throat, I glance over my shoulder, feeling the sensation of being watched, and toss the backpack over my arm. I slam the door shut and find a man standing there, and scream.

He grins.

"Isaac! Jesus, you scared me."

"I called out your name. You okay?"

"Yeah—sorry, I was, um, daydreaming."

He holds out an arm. "Want a hand with those?"

"Oh, sure. I mean—where are you headed?"

He waves down at his sweat-soaked shirt and running shoes. "Just finished up." He wrinkles his nose. "Sorry about the smell."

"You forget, I lived at boarding school. You ever smelled a bunch of teenagers who haven't figured out washing machines yet?"

He laughs, taking nearly all the bags and leaving me with the lightest one. We start toward the trail, and chat about nothing much until we reach the clearing.

Isaac clears his throat, looking intently at his shoes. "Is he . . . okay? Do you think?"

"Have you guys talked?"

He swallows, still not able to look up. "Yeah. He says he's fine. But I don't know. It's like I'm just on the other side of the door— does that make sense? He's there but not." He scrubs a hand over his face. "Sorry. Rambling."

I pat his shoulder and give him a tight smile. "I'd hug you, but you stink," I say lightly.

He laughs. "Thanks."

"Give him time. He's there. I promise."

Isaac nods, then looks around the empty clearing. "Where is everyone?"

"Oh. About that . . ."

Isaac takes the news of dead letters and a secret hideout pretty well. He seems skeptical until he actually sees it, a real-live place with the name nailed in over the door. Elliot grins as he approaches, and they kiss while Levi and I pretend to suddenly find unpacking the bags incredibly interesting.

"You know, you can start kissing me hello too," he whispers. "I wouldn't mind."

I throw a moth-eaten pillow at him, hoping he doesn't notice when my cheeks turn pink. "*Shh*, someone will hear you."

He catches it, setting the cushion down beside him. "So, we can kiss but we can't talk about it?"

"Pretty much."

"Fine. Kiss me then."

My mouth drops open. He just grins, standing, and takes the cushions inside. There's a couple from our attic, dusty and discolored, and a few liberated from Levi's house. These are feather-filled and thickly woven, and I'm sure one pillow costs more than my entire bed. Isaac valiantly offers to de-cobweb the roof, using a stick to wrap around the gossamer edges. The solar fairy lights I left during our last visit are now charged, and they begin to glimmer to life as dusk falls. Levi has added the smallest fold-out camping table I've ever seen—just big enough to hold a deck of cards.

Elliot trades paintbrushes for a bottle of cider, and I venture outside to pick up where he left off. In the fading light, I find tracing over the old patterns to be strangely soothing, my hands where theirs have been, not erasing what they built but bringing it back, brighter, remembered.

"You're pretty good at that," Eli says, leaning against the side of the cabin.

I shrug. "Steady hands is all." *From picking locks*, I think, but don't say out loud.

He smiles, offering me a sip from his bottle. "Thanks for bringing Isaac."

"Felt like it was time to share this place." I look up at him and give him a half-smile. "He's worried about you, you know?"

Elliot sinks a little deeper into the wall. "Yeah. But I'm doing good. Just not ready to . . . you know. Talk about everything. Kinda kills the mood," he jokes, but his eyes look a little sad, so I wrap my arms around his shoulders and give him a tight squeeze.

"Love you," I say, just to remind him.

"Love you too, Red."

"Come on, you can drink and paint. Maybe tipsy Elliot is a better artist."

We sit together until it gets too dark to see what we're doing, giggling in the grass. Elliot tries to paint us together, little stick figures on bikes, Levi's red car beside us, the pink Pudge trailing behind. I add stars and the lake, which he says looks like a black hole about to suck us into its orbit, so I try to add trees, which he says look like aliens.

"We're ruining it," I groan, wondering if we should just paint over it all.

"Nah," he says. "Just making it ours."

Footsteps pad around the corner, and Levi clears his throat. "It's getting dark. You guys wanna come in? We're playing spit and I'm pretty sure Isaac is cheating."

"No I'm not!" Isaac calls out, thumping the inside wall. "You just have terrible reflexes."

"Wait," I say. "It's a full moon tonight. Doesn't Levi have to go home and lock himself in the basement?"

He rolls his eyes, holding out two hands to pull me up. I grudgingly accept, and he takes all my weight as I stumble to my feet, toes numb with pins and needles. He holds on a moment longer than necessary.

"Interesting," Elliot says, sipping his cider again.

I snatch my hands away, poking Eli in the side. "Come on,

I bet I can beat you at least three times before you need to be home."

"I actually *don't* need to be home. No more curfew. McKellon family perk. Although did you know your nan feels very passionately about midnight?"

Isaac deals another hand as we walk in, four each, and winks. "I have some ideas about what we can do until midnight."

Elliot chokes on his drink, ears turning red, and says nothing as he drops down into Levi's fancy pillows. I dig into the last unpacked bag, drawing out a sack of Maltesers and popcorn.

"So, Isaac," I say, swooping in to save Elliot from a rather impressive blush. "Wanna hear more about the letters? We've all read them too many times. Might be good to have fresh eyes. Ears. Whatever."

"Sure. Hit me."

Levi folds down in the last remaining corner, between me and Elliot. There's not much room left, so he ends up half pressed into my leg, and when he leans over to steal the bag of chocolates, his shoulder presses into mine, and I remember what they felt like when he lifted me up in the police station. I lose my train of thought for a second, mouth turning dry, until I snap out of the memory.

The story unravels in starts and stops—trailing off while we play, laughing and watching each other lose in turns, groaning when Levi wins three rounds in a row. Isaac asks questions. One of us answers, depending on who best remembers.

"Man, how long have you been trying to solve this?"

"Too long," I groan. "Five years. Six?" It's nearly eleven o'clock, and we're all tired now. The exhaustion colors my voice, a groan for the unsolved mystery.

Elliot is wriggling and his eyes are starting to droop. Isaac adjusts his legs and gently pulls him down so he can lie in his lap. Elliot smiles, letting his eyes close. "Someone wake me up when it's time to go home."

I smile at the way he says *home.*

We play a few more rounds of spit, though Isaac starts to lose because he's only playing with one hand. Elliot's fallen asleep on the other, and Isaac seems happy enough to live without it. Eventually, he gives up and it's just me and Levi.

"My mum went to our school," Isaac muses after a while.

"Oh," I say, confused, not understanding what has inspired this statement. "That's . . . nice?"

He laughs, shaking his head. "Nah, I mean, she might have some stuff left over. Maybe knew August, even. I think she'd be a few years older, but if the kid went missing, she'd probably remember."

I think about the yearbook in my room. The surprise of seeing Mum had eclipsed any thoughts of August. "Would she have photos, maybe? From school—like the old yearbooks and things?"

Isaac shrugs. "I can ask."

I never told the others about the book. The missing page. But it wasn't a clue, was it? Just an anti-clue, if anything. I'm about to say something when Levi tosses his deck down. "All right, I'm done. Any longer and I'll fall asleep. You want a ride home, Brodie?" he says, overly casual, searching for the keys in his pocket. "Or are you gonna stay for a while?"

The offer throws me, so unexpected that I just blink at him.

"I can give you a lift if you want to stay," Isaac says. "I haven't had anything to drink, obviously."

I look at Elliot, who opens one eye. "I'm comfy. Don't make me move."

He rolls over and gives an exaggerated snore.

"Well, that decides it then," I say. "It's fine. Just get him home before curfew."

Isaac gives a mock salute, all bravado and rebellion, but then ruins the illusion by quickly scrambling to set an alarm on his watch.

Levi and I walk back to the car in silence, picking our way through the path and the riverbed, occasionally stalling and waiting for the other to catch up. There's a humming in my veins, the waiting for something to happen, and I can't decide if I want it to or not because I don't know how to be *us* when there's *more.*

The parking lot is empty except for the two cars, strangely quiet for a Saturday night. Warwick sparkles in yellow-white light on the hill, the post office nearly visible from here. Our footsteps echo on the pavement, and Levi lopes around the passenger side to open my door.

"Thanks," I mumble, stepping under his arm.

His fingers loop through mine, his head ducks low. "Brodie . . ."

I want to turn around. I want to tilt my face up and let him kiss me. I want to tell him that his strawberry gum haunts my dreams. I want to tell him that I missed him every day at Rowley and that's why I was so mad at him.

302

I click in my seat belt and stare straight ahead.

He sighs, closing the door.

The silence presses in around me. It whispers *coward*. It whispers *what if*. In the seconds between, the moments of *then* and *now*, I see a diverging path, and the road is murky but demands to be trod. I throw the door open again, my feet dropping to the pavement.

"You can't just *Brodie* me, you know."

He turns, trunk halfway open. He drops the backpacks he was holding, brows furrowed close. "What?"

"Why didn't you kiss me at Dwight's? Or ever since? You keep saying my name and I don't know what that *means*." Is all of this in my head? Oh god, the embarrassment would kill me—if it was all one-sided and he didn't feel the same. He kissed me back—but maybe that's just a reflex? Like when cashiers ask how you are, and you say *good* even if your world is slowly falling apart. Kissing someone back is just polite.

Levi leans against the trunk, crossing his arms. "Honestly, Brodie, I thought it was a fifty-fifty chance at getting slapped. And I did kiss you, in the kitchen."

"Because I *told you* to."

"Fine. Is that what you want? Because I really don't know. Half the time you're ignoring me, the other half we're arguing."

"I don't—I don't know—" The path shrinks in my mind. It's barely a trail, a one-way ticket to nowhere.

He shakes his head. "Let me know when you figure it out." He pushes off the trunk, grabbing the bags and throwing them in.

I frown at him. "So you're just, what, going to wait for me to decide?"

"Pretty much."

"Why?"

His hand drops away and his eyes lock on mine. "Figure it out, Red."

"I don't understand," I say. Except there's something strange happening in my chest, a live wire humming, and it's making my hands tremble, this jolt of electric *something*.

He takes a step forward, nearly touching but not. "Do you remember the day we met? First day of school. We played tag and none of the other kids could catch you."

I do remember. I remember my feet hardly touched the ground and it felt like I was flying, and it was only when I had reached the oval, totally alone, that I realized no one else was chasing me still—until Levi hurtled around the corner and the game went on and on and on.

"I've been chasing you ever since, just trying to keep up," he says. "So, if you say wait, I'll wait. I don't care anymore, I'm done pretending. I'll take anything you give me, Brodie, because all I ever wanted was to be near you, and I didn't ever care if that was as your friend or more."

His hands come to rest on either side of my jaw, stroking my cheeks. The live wire flashes and dies, leaving me bare. "I wanted to be the person you called when you got home. The reason you were late for dinner. I wanted to be the one who fought monsters in the woods with you and chased fairy tales in the attic. I wanted to drive you to the beach, and kiss you in closets, and walk you to your door afterward. I just wanted to be there. And then you left."

His lips are hovering close to mine, and my chest hurts because I don't think I've taken a single breath since he started talking.

"But you came back, and I don't want to ruin it again. So tell me what you want, and I'll want it too."

Oh.

I pull on the collar of his shirt—the barest of movements, but we're so close it's enough. His lips are on mine. His hands in my hair. Our first kiss was careful; this one unravels. I want to be hard and distant and full of thorns, but all of that is stripping away as I push my body closer, whisper *more*, hands running over his shoulders and chest because I can't decide where they want to rest, where they want to still and sigh *home*.

He is strawberry and fresh-cut grass and childhood memories, warm and sweet, and it hurts just the right amount. His teeth graze my lip, and he pulls back, says *Sorry*, until I return the favor.

The back of my knees hit the open trunk and we crash down; I remember another Brodie, another Levi, just like this, our first kiss on our last day. Something sharp digs into my side.

"Ow. Bag."

He yanks it out from under me, laughing against my lips. His chest presses down on mine and it's atrocious how much I enjoy that weight, the feeling of him pressed against my skin and burning bright. I push and he rolls, and now I'm looking down at his face, his swollen lips and mussed hair and *god*, I think this boy might love me.

"Hi," he says, fingers brushing over my lips.

"Hello."

"You okay?"

I nod.

"I'm going to kiss you again," he says.

"Thank you." See, I can be polite too.

He laughs into my mouth and we stay like that, tangled together, kissing and exploring and hands in safe places, mostly, until my lips feel bruised and my head is fogged with *him*, and I pull away. "We should probably go," I whisper. "It's almost midnight. I turn into a pumpkin."

"I turn into a werewolf," he deadpans.

He walks me back to the passenger door, and I grin awkwardly—cheeks too full and too warm. He kisses me on the cheek as he plugs in my seat belt, and we drive home with the windows down and his fingers wrapped around mine. He glances down, every so often, as though not quite believing the sensation. Needing to check I'm there, eyes flicking to my face, smirking just a little when he catches my smile.

"Stop that. Your ego will crush us to death in this car."

He chuckles and walks me to my door. Kisses me good night. Waits until I've locked the door behind me. I listen for the rumble of his car as I flop face down on my bed, and Mabel trots in to give me a judgmental glare.

"Oh stop it, you trollop. I've seen you with the tabby next door."

She leaves a dead mouse in my shoe the next morning. And Levi leaves me a letter.

I've been in possession of many letters—but this is the first one that's *mine*, and suddenly I understand why August and Winnie

and June kept every word they wrote. This moment, preserved forever, his voice on paper, indisputable proof that we were *here* and
we *mattered*. At least for a moment—long enough to write a letter.

I rip a sheet of paper out of my own notebook and begin.

Dear Levi . . .

14

Dear Winnie,

Thank you for inviting me to dinner. And for your letter. I'm not used to writing letters. It's nice, I think. Although your friend—June?—has impressed upon me the importance of not being an ax murderer. I promise I'm not. Just in case that was a factor in determining our ongoing friendship. She's very ~~loud~~ ~~scary~~ protective. It's rather ~~intimidating~~ ~~alarming~~ sweet of her, to care so much.

You asked, last night, why I was at the station alone. I'm sorry I didn't answer. It's only that you were all being so nice, and I didn't want to ruin it. My dad was supposed to pick me up. He forgot, I think. We aren't really close. But it's okay. I'm used to being on my own. It used to be me and my mum, but she died recently. ~~It's fine.~~ You don't need to write anything back about it, it's okay. I have enough sympathy cards for ~~a lifetime~~ now. Anyway. If he'd remembered, you might not have seen me. Or asked me to dinner. And I'm very glad that you did.

Your friend,
August

Dear Winnie,

"Sweet"? Ha! I like him. I think you like him too. No, I think you <u>like</u> him. Winnie and August, sitting in a tree, K-I-S-S-I—

June, you do not need to sing the song out loud when you are also writing it down. And I don't think any such thing—I was only being polite! You would be unfamiliar with the concept, so I don't expect you to understand. Stop singing. Stop it. Stop—

Levi and Elliot leave on Sunday to watch a football game, valiantly attempting to convince me to accompany them, but since we ended up skipping out on nearly a whole week of school, I have homework to catch up on. Also, I cannot look at Levi without my face flaming red. I delivered his letter in person and he accepted it with an outrageous grin, tucking it safely in his coat pocket.

I spend a good portion of the afternoon furiously scribbling on a sheet of paper, trying to decipher the message from the Adder Stone. Levi had suggested maybe the anagram was in another language, which was helpful, but then found the only halfway reasonable translation was *strong teeth* in French, which was not.

Elliot got nervous about walking around with the stone, so we ended up putting it back into locker 604 and pocketing the key. Plus, it meant I could keep an eye on the locker, if anyone tried to come back for it. The key was currently looped around an old hairtie in my pocket, and I kept patting the fabric of my jeans to make sure it was there.

I look down at my sheet of paper again and sigh. Backward it was *tav torf tned*, which was just more nonsense. Any possible way I tried to unscramble them, I always came back to the original inscription. I throw my pencil down in frustration and concede defeat; the words have to be a code or cipher or were just flat-out written in another language.

Emiko texts me that Claire got the lead part in the school musical, and warns me to come prepared on Monday, so I bust out my borrowed copy of *Tuck Everlasting*, drag a blanket onto the balcony, and make a pot of coffee. I crack open the spine and read the first line, feet kicked up onto the railing.

The first week of August hangs at the very top of summer.

A shiver runs up my spine. I hadn't expected to see his name. Not that it's his name in this context, but the coincidence is strange.

. . . three things happened and at first there appeared to be no connection between them.

The words hit me like a spray of bullets. Every page, every word; it seems that the years unravel, right here in this book.

Winnie.

Treegap.

August.

My feet drop off the railing and I stare down at the open pages. "Fuck." My palms turn slick with sweat, and I fumble for my phone. Why didn't we figure this out earlier? Why didn't we know? It takes me a few tries to pull out my phone, but I don't know what to write, so I just stare at the screen, cursor blinking.

Because I've found them, they're right here, but we're missing something. We're missing one piece and it's driving me crazy, like the memory of something hovering just out of reach, a word on the tip of your tongue.

There are too many coincidences here, especially the fictional Winnie and the everlasting home they run back to, Treegap. It's clear the letter writers took inspiration from this book—or at least one of them did—but how much?

They were real. We know they were real. We found Treegap in the woods, we found August.

Except . . . we didn't, did we? He's missing. All we found was a poster and a picture—the ghost of August. Maybe he was never real at all.

Maybe none of it was. Maybe they just took their nicknames from this book and the rest was all a game. I think of what Levi said that day in the library—what if it was never real?

I shake out my hands, shove my phone back in my pocket, and read. I read, because I cannot stand the thought of it being over—the letters and the magic and the thread that binds us all. Of it not being real, not being ours.

I read until the air turns shivery cold and it's so dark outside I can hardly see the letters anymore.

I read until I'm crying for Winifred and Jesse, who missed each other for a cruel trick of time. Crying for their Treegap, left behind and eternally perfect but never the same. Crying because I know the notes of this song, but I can't quite feel the beat and it's thrown me off course.

"Where did you go?" I whisper. Mabel answers with a petulant meow, and the attic ghost rattles the weather vane, but I still don't know. I close the cover on the book, the spine sighing with relief, and try to shake off the feeling, tipping my head back to watch the stars.

Maybe if I don't think about it, the answer will come.

Except that trying not to think about it feels an awful lot like thinking about it.

I close my eyes instead, trying to meditate, visualizing the strings between each clue. August and Winnie and Treegap and June. The letters and his photo and the Adder Stone.

"How long have you been sitting there?" Elliot threads his legs through the window, sitting on the sill.

I groan, throwing my arms over my eyes. "Too long. You ever read this?"

He takes the book and flicks through the pages. "Nope. Should I have?"

"No, never mind." I don't want to stress him out more this week—there'll be time for clues later. "How was the game?"

"We lost."

"Sorry."

He shrugs, curling himself into the spare chair. Mabel appears, making herself at home in his lap. Elliot leans his head back, resting against the brick, and smiles. "Doesn't matter. I actually had a really good weekend."

I smile, setting the book to one side. "Yeah?"

He keeps his eyes closed, and his hands are running methodically through Mabel's fur. He's nodding for a minute before he speaks again. "Yeah. I don't think I'd ever noticed how much we adjusted for him. Don't make noise early in the morning, don't leave any mess out, don't forget to buy food, don't buy too much food. Get out of the house for a while but not too long. I spent so much energy, every day, just trying to predict his moods, to avoid stupid arguments. Here it's just . . . I can breathe, you know?"

I nod, even though he can't see me, nudge his knee with mine, letting him know I'm there, but I can tell he has more to say so I leave the space open.

"Mum's just . . . kind of devastated, I think? She's so happy to be here, to feel free, sort of. But she's realizing it could have all happened so much sooner. And that it happened over ten fucking dollars. . . ." He trails off, shakes his head. "I don't know. She's kind of losing it a bit. But also doing really well? I don't know. It's weird."

"Stay as long you want," I say. "Stay forever, both of you. I just want you to be happy."

He swallows, and his throat bobs up and down. "Yeah. She's . . . she's talking about moving, maybe. As in, moving far. Away. Said she doesn't want to stay in this town forever; it feels too small. I think she's felt like that for a while. Every time she talked about leaving him, it was pretty clear the plan was just to *leave*."

I straighten in my chair, glad he's not looking at me because of the selfish expression of grief and disappointment slashing across my face. "You could stay here," I whisper. "If you want to."

He opens his eyes, then smiles. "I know, Red. But she's my mum, you know?"

I drop my head, because I do know: If my mum were here again, there's nothing I wouldn't do to keep her beside me every day. I reach out a hand and he loops his pinkie through mine. I am thinking of sunshine and puppies and rainbows. Leather boots on sale and perfect lake days and sweet gum and all the glitter bombs in the world. I will not cry.

"Hey, Red . . . there's something else I want to tell you. I should have, a while ago, but I didn't know how." He pushes himself up, shoulders pressed into the brick as though he needs the support to stay upright. "I've been looking for my dad. And Levi's been helping me. The software on his dad's home computer isn't as good as the one at the station, but it's still got a pretty decent database."

I nod, remembering the folder I found yesterday in Levi's car.

"Mum always said she'd tell me more when I was older, but I don't even know his first name. Every time I ask, she just cries. Honestly, I don't even know if Maddon was his surname or if Mum just made it up. Could have been either."

Those reams of paper, crossed out. Maybe he'd run out of Maddons to find. My tongue is thick, and I'm trying to figure out what questions to ask without giving away what I already know. "Why do you think that? Why would she lie?"

He's playing with Mabel's tail now, and she's purring contently, pushing into his chest. He smiles into her fur for a second before taking a deep breath. "Remember when I said I had to quit the football team? Part of it was the cost, sure, but the team has finals all over the state. So I figured, I could get my license and Levi and I could split the drive. I had to take my birth certificate to the test, and a bunch of other documents. But they wouldn't accept it, because it was a copy, and because it was 'incomplete.'"

Quinn's name, not included. It's making more sense now.

"Do you think . . ."

He shrugs. "I don't know. I went through all the options—maybe Mum wasn't my mum. Maybe she found me in a train station somewhere. Adopted, maybe." He tries to laugh but the sound is hollow.

"Have you tried to ask her about it?"

"Once," he says. "Right after the test, when they wouldn't give me the license without the original. She just got this . . . haunted look. And I realized, I sort of don't care. She's my mum, I'll love her anyway. Plus, I've seen the pregnancy photos, so I'm pretty sure I'm hers," he jokes. "But Dad . . . I just want answers, either way. I don't know anything about him. Not a name, never seen a photo."

I nudge his shoulder with my own. "You could have told me."

He nods, and his throat bobs. "Yeah," he says, squinting at something in the distance. "It's just . . ."

I wait, knowing he's trying to settle on the right words. Letting him find them.

"I guess I didn't want to tell you, because not having my dad around was one thing, but knowing for sure feels like it might be worse. Like, what if it turns out he's just some dropkick who doesn't even know I exist? Or worse, what if he knows but doesn't care? Or if he's . . . god, I don't know. What if he's in jail. What if he's—"

Dead. Neither of us says it, as though speaking the words out loud might make them true.

315

"I think about what's worse, sometimes," he says softly. "Like the worst game of would you rather."

I squeeze his hands tight. "Your dad would be so lucky to love you, Elliot. No matter what. And if he didn't see that . . .'"

I don't know what to say. Don't know how to make up for a lifetime of self-doubt. I just squeeze tighter. "He'd be an idiot, for not knowing you."

He smiles, bumping my shoulder. "Thanks."

"Besides, if he's in jail I bet it's for a really good reason. Like, he holds all the information about Area 51 and tried to leak it to the press. No, better: He's a benevolent thief, robs from the rich and gives to the poor."

"Are you implying my dad is literally Robin Hood?"

"That makes your mum Maid Marian. She's hot, in that fox movie."

He laughs, shoving me gently. Something glimmers in the back of my mind. I remember suddenly that I am not supposed to be thinking of the writers and the stone and the missing book. Strings pull taunt then fall loose. The edge of something slips away. . . .

I squeeze my eyes shut, willing myself to snatch the thought from nothingness—but it's gone.

Elliot gives me a weird look. "You okay? You had that look on your face like in seventh grade when you were convinced you could levitate."

"No, I just—nothing," I sigh. I scrub my face, and the thought turns to dust. "My brain hurts."

"It's all this book learnin'," Elliot says with a thick fake accent, tapping the pile of books beside me. "You know what we need? Fries. Also, milkshakes."

I laugh, stretching my arms above my head. Nan made soup for dinner, but she won't mind us ducking out for dessert if we're quick. "Sure. Do we want to invite . . . um . . . Levi?"

He bounces to his feet, his eyes sparkling bright with mischief. "Yeah, we can invite *um Levi* if you tell me what's been happening with *um you two* lately."

I want the earth to open and swallow me whole. When this doesn't immediately present itself as an opportunity, I sigh. "Fine. Fries first, interrogation second."

"Deal."

Elliot rides us down to the Archie Arcade, this time with me standing on the back pegs, and he waits until I'm stuffed full of ice cream and three games down on air hockey to ask again.

"Nothing!" I say reflexively. But what's the point of hiding? Why am I running from *more* when all I really want is to dive headfirst into it? I check over my shoulder, glancing at the kids running rampant on sugar and pink lemonade, the machines blaring loudly, music distorted on old speakers. Levi texted to say he had to finish Sunday night family dinner before he could come, and even then, not for long. "Fine," I say, turning back to Elliot, deciding the coast is clear. "We kissed. Twice. Three times."

"Like . . . a peck?"

I use the lapse in his attention to slam the puck into his goal,

317

hoping the blinding red *score!* lights that flash above our table will hide the flush in my cheeks. "No. Like, *kissed.*"

"Ah," he says, grinning.

"Please stop."

"Are you going to be in the Sawyer family Christmas card this year?"

"Oh god, stop."

"Did you know I had a bit of a crush on him when we were kids? For, like, a week, until I realized he was already totally in love with you."

"He is not in love with me."

"Sure, Red. Hey, who did you go dressed as for Halloween the year before you left?"

"A sailor. What does that have to do with anything? It was pirate themed!"

"You made him go *as a mermaid.*"

"I had the hat already!"

Elliot's shoulders are shaking, and he's got a fist pressed into his mouth. "You are the dumbest smart person I know."

"Unfortunately, it's not the first time someone has told me that."

I retrieve the puck and start a new game, welcoming the distraction. We play for a while until my spine tingles, and I can feel someone standing behind me. I turn and tilt my head up, and find Levi watching, warring with a tiny smile on his face.

"Hi," he says, voice breaking. He coughs, tries again. "Hi."

"Hey," I say, unconsciously leaning back a little bit, enjoying the warmth of him so close. Then I remember Elliot and break away, snapping my attention back to him.

"You guys can kiss if you want," he says.

Levi winces. "Thanks, man. Real smooth."

I drop the paddle on the table. "We're out of tokens. I'll go buy some more."

Elliot calls out his apology, but I wave him off, happy to have a moment to collect myself. Not that I ever imagined I would be a person who needed to "collect myself." But here we are.

The guy at the counter looks up from playing a game on his phone, not even bothering to mute the sound effects. Little candy pieces dance across his screen. "Welcome to the Archie Arcade, where fortune favors the—"

"Yeah, yeah, I was here earlier, I know the drill." I hand him ten dollars and he shrugs, stabbing at the counter with one finger until it springs loose. He tips five game coin tokens into my hand, the gold flashing as an alarm suddenly sounds through the store and a kid starts screaming in ecstasy, everyone crowding around one of the brightly colored machines.

"I have a master's degree," the guy mutters. "Two years in graduate school. And what do I get?"

He ducks under the counter and emerges with fake gold glasses that say *jack* and *pot* over each eye, wielding a life-sized purple bear. "Drop out of school," he tells me, then wanders off to present the prize.

I start walking back to Levi and Elliot, jumbling the coins in my hand. The threads in my mind pull tight again. I stop, under

319

the flashing lights, squinting at the coins. Have I ever really looked at them before? We've played here a million times, used to stop in every day after school. The coins are heavy and gold—not real gold, obviously, just yellowish brass. They're stamped on each side with a cursive *A*, and smaller font around the edges. I pull the coin close, realizing the words run into each like an ouroboros, but they're not the same—each side is different.

Fortune Favors the Brave, says one side. I turn it slowly, recognizing the Latin. *Audentes Fortuna Iuvat.*

Dent fort vat.

Not an anagram. Not a code. Not a message.

I sprint back to the table, holding up the coins.

Levi notices me first—*always* notices me first. "What's wrong?"

"We have to go home," I say. "Now. Right now."

Elliot frowns, setting the game paddles aside. I shove the coins into his hands, and he looks down at them, perplexed. "What's going on?"

"The Adder Stone," I force myself to say. "I think it's a fake."

The house is dark when I bolt up the stairs, footsteps quick and sure, guided by a lifetime of creeping in the dim. Levi and Elliot follow awkwardly—too loud and stumbling and slow.

Nan is upstairs and the light under Quinn's door is on, but thankfully neither emerge from their rooms. I make it to my room, clawing at the floorboards under my bed, feeling for the loose panel and the contents hidden inside: old diaries and the dead letters. And the photo.

A strangled sound escapes me as I stare down at the picture, blinking fast, not quite believing my eyes. But it's true, I was right.

"I was right," I repeat out loud, holding the photo up to the light just as the boys burst in, both looking at me like I'm a lunatic. But I was *right*.

Elliot steps forward first, gingerly taking the photo from my hand. He frowns at it, twists it in his hand, and holds it high under the light bulb.

"Fuck," he says, head dropping back.

I slap both hands over my mouth, silencing a hysteric bubble of laughter. Levi leans over Elliot's shoulder, looking at the photo: the one I'd taken from the museum, sitting in the display where the Adder Stone used to sit. I'd mostly forgotten about it, given it had no real use except that Elliot had suggested we should be collecting clues, and this seemed like a good one. For the very first time, my unchecked predisposition for kleptomania has served me well.

"I don't get it," Levi says.

"You're a terrible detective," I answer. "No wonder we never found the letter writers. *Look.*" I hold up the Polaroid of the Adder Stone from the display case, then flick through my camera roll to find a picture of the version we'd found in box 604. I hold them side by side, watching as realization dawns.

"*Fuck*," he repeats, seizing the Polaroid. He holds it close to his nose, as though straining to catch sight of the script inside. But it's not there.

It's not there because *our* stone is a *fake*.

321

Well. One of them is a fake. Probably the one made from melted arcade brass, but who knows anymore? Maybe both of them are.

I press the Archie Arcade coin into Levi's palm, and his lips soundlessly mouth the Latin words. *Dent fort vat*—no wonder we couldn't make them mean anything. They *don't* mean anything, not on their own. They're just melted down words wrapped around a cheap imitation.

Levi sits heavily on the bed, scrubbing his hair. "Okay. *Okay.* This is a clue. I don't know what to *do* with it, but still a clue." He looks at me with a rueful smile on his face. "Jesus, Red, you got a photographic memory or what? You creep me out sometimes. You're gonna commit a major crime one day and slip away into the night. Probably frame us for it too."

"Don't be silly. I'd never frame Elliot." I shove his shoulder and dig through the mess under my floorboard for the second clue: August at the lake, wearing the stone around his neck.

"What are you thinking?"

The truth is, I don't know what to think. I feel like we keep finding these half-clues, pieces of a puzzle with no picture.

I squint at the photo in my hand, looking for something that's not there. I've looked at this photo a hundred times, and every time I flip it over, hoping to find words on the back that will lead us to him. To all of them. I sink farther to the floor, the adrenaline I'd felt in the arcade slowly wearing off, as I realize once again that this doesn't tell us any more about the writers; it just feels like two more steps back from what we thought we knew. "I guess . . . August took it? No," I say more firmly. "We know August took it.

He's wearing it. So he must have taken it and . . . made the fake to cover his tracks?" I lean my shoulders against the bed frame, staring at the Polaroid. I run my hand across the script at the bottom, the unfamiliar writing. I scrub a hand through my hair, and I can feel it—the thread is right there, but it keeps slipping loose. The answer is *there*, I can feel it. *Winnie and Treegap and August, June and*—

"Okay," Levi says. "But why would he *leave* a fake?"

They both look at me. I try not to be offended by the implication of that. "I'd only leave a fake if I didn't want to be caught, I guess. It's a lot of effort. And it's a good copy, so I don't even know how he would have managed it." I wonder, briefly, if this is why they used code names. Can't get caught if you've signed off your crimes under the cast of *Tuck Everlasting*. I think of Levi's barb all those weeks ago in the library—that the writers might have been lying all along. So what does this make them now? Liars and thieves? I almost tell them, but I don't know what any of it *means*.

"He had a shop," Elliot says. "In the letters. August says he's going to inherit his dad's shop. Business. Whatever."

I raise one eyebrow, impressed. "Could have been a jewelry store," I theorize. "Or . . . a blacksmithery?"

Levi gives me a look. "Twenty years ago, Red. Not two hundred."

"Whatever. And I guess maybe . . . they sold the original for the money? The gold alone would have been worth something." But why would they *need* money? Winnie and June, at least, mentioned bikes and holidays and fancy dresses. Those things all cost money, and it seemed like their families were willing to put up for the expense.

I spread the clues out on the floor: the stone, the picture of August, the museum Polaroid of the original. And the letters, cast to one side in a jumbled heap. I frown, my hand reaching out for something, the memory of—

Tell Charlie I'm sorry.

I lunge for the letter, rereading the line again. Levi reads over my shoulder and lets out a low sound of realization. "Oh," he says, reaching for it when I'm done. "You said it sounded final. I just didn't believe you."

"Shocker—"

"—but what if you were right? In a way."

Elliot takes the letter, reading it next.

Dear Mum,

Please read this carefully, and don't tell Dad. Not right away. I'm leaving this note because, despite everything, I love you, and I hope that one day you'll understand why this is the choice I've made.

I wish we could have talked. I wish it were different. I wish you'd given him a chance, and maybe I could have stayed.

Tell Charlie I'm sorry. Don't look for me.

Love,
Winnie

"This is a goodbye letter," he says. "It sounds like they're running. Like it was planned."

"I thought maybe—when I first read it—" I shake my head. "I don't know what I thought."

Levi frowns at the letter. There's a date stamp in one corner, the day and month. "This is only a few days before August went missing. The sign at the station, it had *last seen* on it."

"So if they planned it . . ."

We're quiet for a few, long seconds. The unfinished sentence hangs there, the words we're all too scared to say out loud: *What went wrong?* And for that matter, what were they running from to begin with?

"I wonder what happened," Elliot says softly, clearly reading my thoughts. "I wonder if they got out after all." My mind flashes to the poster in the police station, yellowed and peeling. Gone on a rainy day, according to Nan.

"Maybe they did," I say, pushing the thought away. "Maybe they got so far away that no one found them, and they lived happily ever after."

"Committing an annual jewelry heist," Levi adds.

"To pay for their apartment in London," I agree.

"I thought it was Berlin."

"Only for a while. They'd get sick of the cold."

Elliot rolls his eyes. "It's cold in London, idiot."

"Oh. Fine. Paris. Lots of jewelry to steal in Paris."

I smile, relaxing my fingers that clutched the picture of August. If they had the original stone, if they had enough money, it was possible. Wasn't it? And June was already in the city, as far as I can figure from the other letters. Maybe they met her there and never looked back.

Just then, I hear the soft echo of footsteps in the hall, and I have just enough time to shove all the papers under the bed before there's a soft knock at the door and Quinn sticks her head in. "I thought I heard voices," she said. "Just wanted to make sure you were home okay."

"Yep," I squeak. "Just got back."

Elliot nods in agreement. "Just saying good night," he adds.

"I'm also leaving," Levi says. "Because I don't, uh, live here." He stands up, realizes Quinn is blocking the door, and sits down again. "I'll wait."

Quinn looks skeptical but seems to let the weirdness slide. "Isaac came past," she says instead. "He was looking for you both. Anything important?"

Elliot glances at me, raising a quizzical brow, and I give a small shake of my head. Both of us? Maybe he was just embarrassed to tell Quinn he was there to see Elliot on his own—they still didn't know each other very well. He shrugs, moving to the door, effectively herding Quinn out of the room. "Thanks, Mum, I'll text him now."

She hesitates a moment, but Elliot smiles and she relents. "It's late," she says, winking as she pulls the door closed. "Don't stay up too long."

It's not like Quinn makes the rules in the house, and it's also not as though Nan ever had rules to begin with, but I'm pretty sure having a boy in my room this late at night is nudging the very loose boundaries that have been set, and I know she'll probably wait to hear Levi's car leaving before she goes to sleep. Which means we should probably hurry to put everything back under the floorboard as quickly as we can.

But then I turn to face Levi, who looks extremely pleased by the situation. He turns a full three-sixty degrees, as though he's just now appreciating the fact that he has unfettered access to my room. "*Don't,*" I threaten. "Not one word."

"I would never. But also, I totally thought you'd have a dartboard with my face behind your door."

"Took it down last weekend."

He grins. "Any particular reason?"

"Wore out the bull's-eye."

"Uh-huh," he says, taking a step closer. "I haven't been in your room since . . ."

Since before.

I clear my throat, turning away. I still don't know how to do this, whatever we are. "We should clean up," I say. "She might come back."

He's still for a long moment, then comes to kneel beside me, peering at all the loose sheets of paper. I can feel him looking at me, and my cheeks turn pink as I think how easy it would be to just stand up and throw him on the bed. Well, not that easy, he's heavy. But I think he'd let me. Instead, he just shakes his head and says, "You sort, I'll stash," and wriggles under the bed to pry open the floorboard again. I pass him the letters and the Polaroid, the picture of August, and he tucks it all in safely.

"I'm sure there's a joke to be made here about the monster under your bed," he says, voice muffled under the sheets.

"Baba Yaga," I agree. "You do sort of have chicken legs."

"Hey! Also, are these sushi pajamas? These are made for a child, surely?" He holds up the pants I'd discarded after my first night here. "This is adorable. You'd look far less murdery in sushi pajamas."

"I do not look murdery!"

His head emerges to gives me a *look*.

"Also, why do you have a list that says, 'glitter bomb: Levi's car'?"

I snatch the piece of paper out of his hand. "None of your business."

"Seems like my business."

"Nope. None."

He scuffles around, extracting himself from under the bed, mumbles *ow*. "What do you keep in your schoolbag? Bricks?"

"Glitter bombs. Zip ties. Abseiling equipment. Three hundred tampons. The usual."

"Sounds like a good time. What about this?"

He slides something across the floorboards, nudging it out until I can see a corner of blue leather. I recognize the yearbook that Quinn gave me, surprised that I had somehow forgotten it in the madness of the past week.

"Oh," I say. "It's one of the old yearbooks. There's a picture of my mum in there." I guess it's probably not true to say that I entirely *forgot*. In the quiet, dark hours of night, I'd considered pulling it out again, to find her. But something about seeing Mum looking so young and healthy brought tears to my eyes, and I couldn't bear to open it alone, looking at a version of her that looked like me.

I lean over the bed and pick it gingerly off the floor. Levi sits beside me, gives my shoulder a reassuring bump with his own. I flick through the opening pages, smiling at the dorky outfits and dated hair. I don't recognize any of these faces—Mum didn't have a lot of friends from school. She seemed to collect friends like some people collect teaspoons, picking them up in strange locations, bringing a piece back to be part of her life forever: Lara from her first plane ride, Angela from the bookstore, Patrick from the community garden. None of them really stuck around, though, not after . . .

Just *after*, I guess.

I turn and find myself looking down at Mum and Quinn again. My heart tugs but doesn't break. I was expecting it this time, so it's okay. Her smile, her crinkled eyes. The way she and Quinn are locked together.

"So that's where you get the felon look," Levi says, smiling. "She looks like you. Or you look like her, I guess."

"You think?"

He presses a brief, soft kiss against my hair. "Definitely."

I turn the page, and he leans closer, peering over my shoulder. "What happened there?" he says, tilting his chin at the ripped-out page.

I shrug. "There's a page missing."

"What do you mean 'missing'?"

I roll my eyes. "What do you think? Missing, vacant, gone. Not present. The absence of a thing."

"You are such a pain in the—"

"It's been torn out," I clarify. "Someone donated it. Quinn said she didn't know why."

He touches the edge, as though willing it back. "Well, just a guess, but maybe it was a picture of a missing boy with a stolen historical artifact?"

"What do you mean?"

"Missing," he repeats in a droll tone. "Vacant, gone—"

"Shut up, Levi."

He grins at me, then turns somber. "Just seems a bit convenient, is all. All the yearbooks go missing, August goes missing, the Adder Stone goes missing, and then suddenly, what? We get a piece of the puzzle but half of it's missing?"

"Or . . ." I frown and flick the page back. "Not missing? Maybe . . ."

"Sabotaged," Levi finishes for me. "Did Quinn say who donated it?"

"No. But I'll ask, in the morning." I have half a thought to sprint down the corridor right now and bang on her door, but Levi's leg is pressed against mine, and he's braced one arm behind my back, the warmth of his body radiating against my own, and it's making my heart do weird things in my chest.

I close the yearbook and place it to one side, curling my hands to stop them from trembling, and look up.

"Thanks," I say. "For not giving up on the letters. Or . . . me."

"Even after the turtles."

"Even after the turtles," I agree.

"And you stole my dog."

"Found."

He closes the gap between us. Kisses me as he whispers, "Whatever." And we stay like that, for a while, until I remember Quinn is probably listening, and he reluctantly drags himself away to disappear over the balcony.

"Hey, Brodie," he says, one foot hanging over the ledge, hands wrapped around iron edges. "Promise me something? If you ever leave town, tell me first. I don't want to wake up one day and find a letter. I don't want us to end up like . . ." *Like them.* Like us, again. The sting of three missed years smarts in my chest.

"Don't worry," I answer, stepping closer. "If I ever leave town, I need you to drive the getaway car."

And I fall asleep that night, dreaming of midnights and lost girls and the boys who loved them.

15

You should go, Winnie. There's a whole world waiting, and it's yours—all yours—if you'd just have the courage to take that first step. Just be brave for a moment, for a minute, for an hour. Let August drive you out of that town and start over somewhere new. And you can be as scared as you like when you get there, but it won't matter, because the hardest part will be done. Treegap will be there if we ever decide to go back. Isn't that the magic of it? Isn't that what you told us? So there, the decision is all made. And you know how stubborn I can be, so really, it would be much easier if you started agreeing with me now.

I'm serious, Winn. I know I'm not very often, but this time I am. And no matter where you land, I promise I'll find you.

So go. Find a life that's yours, and we'll follow.

You deserve a home that's real.

Love,

June-Bug

I wake up to find Quinn has already left for the day, and resign myself to waiting until the afternoon to ask about the donated yearbooks. Not content to simply sit in class, however, I get to school early to rummage through the library, looking for copies we might have missed—nothing, not a single one left after the flood. Elliot had stumbled down the stairs this morning to gulp down a cup of coffee and ride half asleep beside me, and now sits slumped over a table, grumbling that he doesn't know why he had to come with me because we don't have any classes together, and I remind him that I didn't ask him to, and he says, "*Oh*." Levi breezes in early because he's always early, and spreads out his already finished homework to double-check the answers.

I screw my nose up. "I can't believe my boyfriend is a nerd."

"What happened to 'I can't believe my boyfriend is a jock.'"

"That's worse, don't remind me."

Elliot seems to jolt half-awake. "Are you seriously just going to start calling each other boyfriend and girlfriend, like that's not deeply fucking weird for the rest of us? What happened to archrivals? Nemeses. Nemesi? Hey, Levi, by the way, what's the plural for—"

The bell rings, and the boys start to pack their things away. I glance down at my phone, eager for Isaac to reply. I'd messaged him to let him know I'd be in the library early—though I'm not even sure why he was looking for us to begin with. Maybe it was nothing after all, and he really was just looking for Elliot. Square one all over again.

Elliot and Levi split off toward the science block, while I dawdle toward the drama theater, dreading another day of soprano solos. But when I turn onto the quad, I spot Isaac waving a frantic arm in the distance and calling my name.

"Hey," he says, picking a careful path through the throes of students. "You didn't call me back last night."

"Sorry, it was late when we all got back. What's up?"

"It's about August," he says.

I stop dead, another student bumping hard up against my shoulder. When we'd told Isaac about the letter writers, I wasn't really expecting him to come up with anything, let alone so soon. "What? Really?"

"Yeah," he says. "Turns out my mum *does* remember him."

The second bell sounds, but no earthly force could drag me away right now. We slip between two portables, not really hidden but at least off the footpath.

Isaac grins at me, clearly excited to share whatever he's uncovered. "Man, I don't know how this town keeps secrets, but this one got buried *deep*."

"Wait! Have you told the others yet?" It feels wrong to find out without them, but I'm not sure my limited patience will stretch until lunchtime.

He shakes his head. "You're the first; I haven't seen them yet."

I should wait. I *should*. But . . . "Okay, go. Tell me. *No wait, don't*." I shove my hands over my ears, then let them flop. "Sorry, I'm freaking out. It's been so long. Okay, *okay*. I'm really ready this time."

"Okay, so," he begins, lowering his voice. "Mum's a few years older than August would have been, but she remembers that he was a student. I tried to ask who he was friends with, and she said she really didn't know—it's not like you pay attention to every single person in the school, you know? And besides, it sounds like he didn't even rock up that often. But she remembers seeing him around."

"Oh," I say, feeling strangely deflated. "Is that all?"

"Not even close. So, she said it was all pretty normal until a few weeks before graduation. She drives past the school one day on her way to work, and the police are there, waiting for someone. And she's like, What's going on? And they don't want to say anything at first, but then this rumor goes around—"

"*Isaac.*"

"Fine, fine. Not interested in the dramatic preamble, got it. Turns out August burned down some building, and he was wanted for arson. But they never found him, because he skipped town." He finishes his story with a dramatic flutter of his hands. "Never to be seen again," he says, then raises an eyebrow, clearly waiting for a response.

"Why would he burn down a building? That makes no sense, he would never . . ." But what do we really know? Some words on paper? That's not the whole story, clearly. Maybe the kind, quiet August we thought we knew was a lie all along.

"Oh, that's the best part. It was *his family's building.* They apparently had some huge argument, and everyone thought he burned it down in retaliation. There was a massive search, but then the flood hit town the next day, and *boom*, everything's underwater, people have bigger problems. Kid slips away in the night."

335

"And takes the Adder Stone with him," I say, nodding. "Makes sense now." I wonder if that's why August's poster is still up in the station: It's not sentimental, it's because he's still *wanted*. For arson? I try to reconcile this new information with the August we know. But maybe we never really knew him at all. . . .

"One more thing," he says, unshouldering his backpack. "She had a yearbook, like you mentioned. I don't know if it's any help, but—"

He hasn't even finished the words before I snatch the book out of his hands, staring down at the cover. "It's the same one," I say, dumbfounded by the sheer luck of this discovery.

"Oh, so you've seen it already?" He shrugs. "Never mind, I thought it was a long shot anyway."

"No. No, mine is—damaged. There was a page missing. . . ." I start flicking through the book, scanning the faces I half recognize. And then—

I slam it shut, clutching the spine in a white-knuckled grip.

"Did you look through this? Last night, when your mum gave it to you?"

He shakes his head. "No, I honestly didn't think it would do any good."

A breath hitches in my lungs. "I need—I need to go," I say. "I'm sorry." I start to walk away, then stop. I face Isaac, brows pulled tight, wringing my hands together. "Can you find the others? Tell them—I don't know what to tell them. But Elliot . . ."

The amusement dies in his eyes. "What's going on? What am I missing?"

"I'll tell you—I'll tell him—I *promise*, I just need some time. Give me a head start." Maybe I'm wrong. Maybe there's a better explanation. Maybe . . .

Isaac, always so easy to smile, so sunny and warm, turns dark, serious. "I'm not going to lie to him," he warns. "He's been through enough lately. What's going on?"

"I don't know. Not for sure. Tell them to meet me at the house. But—" I glance at my watch. "Give me an hour. They're both in the science block; you can find them at second period."

A muscle in his jaw ticks. "Fine. For the record, I don't like this."

"I know. I'm sorry."

"One hour," he repeats. "Then I'll tell him."

"Thank you," I say, and turn to run.

Running to the past. Running to the truth.

Running home.

Quinn isn't at the library. I check in the collections room, her desk, and walk through every inch of the building looking for her before I think to ask reception and they just shrug and say they haven't seen her. I bike home again, wondering how mad Nan will be that I've skipped school. I decide not to find out and climb up the balcony instead.

"Ah," she says, looking up from a cocktail glass as I hurl one leg over the railing. "It is nice to see you return to regular truancy."

I groan, unable to believe my own cursed luck. "Would you believe me if I told you the school sent us all home early out of the goodness of their hearts?"

"Not in the slightest," Nan says, taking a sip of her drink.

"Why aren't you downstairs?"

She cocks an eyebrow. "Why aren't you in school?"

"I—felt sick?"

Nan *harrumphs*. "Fine. Go on then. Bring me a fruit salad and I'll forgive you."

"I don't think we have fruit salad."

"No, but we have olives for the gin. That will have to do." She thrusts her empty glass at me.

I go and fill up her glass, topping it with a dash of water, which I'm sure she'll complain about, but hey, that's one way to hydrate.

And then I turn to find Elliot at the kitchen counter, and Levi standing beside him.

Goddamn it, Isaac.

Elliot is looking between us, shoulders slumped. I remember, for some reason, the first day I saw him; the day he flew out of that house with his backpack slung over his shoulders and looking impossibly small under its bulk. "What's going on? He just said you'd left, that it was about August, but it seemed important?"

I glance at Nan's silhouette on the balcony and tilt my head toward my room. I lead them to where I'd dropped my bag on the floor, and pull out the yearbook, handing it to them in silence. They turn the pages until they come to the one I'd marked: Mum, and Quinn, and—

"August," Elliot says. "They knew each other?"

He looks just like he did at the lake: shy smile, messy hair, eyes focused somewhere just off camera. But that's not all. . . .

I wait, heart thrumming in my ears.

"But it says—" Levi's hands fall still on the page, and I hear the hitch in his chest as he draws a sharp breath. He skips all the way to the back of the book, where each student is pictured with their school photo and name below, tearing through the classes until his fingers pause next to a tiny, grainy portrait.

His hand clenches again and he tries to slam the book shut but it's too late, I've already seen it.

Richard Sawyer, his dad. He looks like Levi, a little. Same sandy hair and sharp nose. It's a nice photo, but otherwise unremarkable.

Except, below that . . .

It's Quinn, but it's not her name: not Quinn Maddon, not some unknown maiden name I've never thought to ask.

It's typed right there, in neat little font, alphabetical order: *Quinn Sawyer.*

I want to ask if he knew all along, to demand he tell me the truth right now, but his face is alarmingly pale, and I know right away that he had no idea. He shakes his head, staring at the page. "I don't know what to say. . . ." He looks up at Elliot, helpless, and just as dumbstruck. "I don't . . . I didn't know. . . ."

I don't know what to think of the roiling emotions competing for attention: shock and grief and the worst of it all, a pang of *jealousy*. They're related, bound for life, a bond I can't ever touch. But I push it all aside, looking at Levi.

"My nan calls him Charlie," he chokes out. "I never—even when you asked—I didn't think . . ."

The letters.

Tell Charlie I'm sorry.

Suddenly, the strings fall into place: woven and tied, a tapestry finally complete. And now there's only one final question to ask.

"Where is she?" Elliot asks, sitting heavily on the bed.

"I don't know. She's not at work, I already checked."

He pulls out his phone and dials. It rings, and rings, and rings. He hangs up, dials again.

I shake my head, backing away. "I can't sit here." I can never sit. Every day my body screams *run*, and every day I have to ignore the urge to listen. Not today.

Levi reaches out a hand, but I duck away. "Where are you going?"

"I don't know. Anywhere. I need to look."

I turn and stride down the hallway, about to slam the window back open and ask Nan where the hell Quinn is right now. But then I pass her room—Mum's room—the door open just a crack. And I hesitate. Because there's a book on her nightstand, a letter shoved in the middle, used as a makeshift bookmark. It's *Tuck Everlasting*.

I let out a sharp exhale, my ears thrumming with a rush of blood—the strings pulling so tight they might snap. I pick up the book, and the folded-up letter falls out. *Dear Winnie: Fairy tales are stupid, but you're not. I hope you find your forever. Love, June.*

There's a noise in the hallway. The quiet pad of footsteps. I look up to find Quinn in the doorway, wrapping the edges of a worn cardigan around her shoulders. Her smile falters. She notices the book in my hand. And I watch as the emotions cycle behind her eyes: uncertainty, understanding, guilt. Grief.

340

"This is Mum? June?"

She nods, taking a step into the room, reaching for the book.

"She gave it to me because I liked the story so much." She runs her hand over Mum's handwriting, her fingertip tracing the swooping *J* across the page. "I loaned it back to her when she was sick. And after . . . I couldn't bear to have it in the house."

"She's June. From the letters. I never . . ."

Quinn nods. "She always thought her real name was, pardon the phrase, 'hippie-dippy nonsense.' She used Perry, mostly. Especially when she got older. But I always thought June suited her best."

Nan clears her throat from the doorway. "Juniper is a perfectly acceptable name. I wish she hadn't changed it, but she couldn't be told."

The boys emerge behind her, crowding the room.

Quinn just nods, chasing the memory of something, I think, wishing it hurt less. Agreeing with someone in the past, a voice she can still hear.

Elliot has a strange look on his face: despair and hope. He slumps forward, like he can't bear to hold himself up anymore. I shift closer, letting him lean on me. Holding him up even when he can't do it himself. "Mum," he croaks. "Who's August? Is it . . . is he my dad?"

Nan turns away, scooping Mabel into her arms. "I'm sorry. I can't hear it again." She pauses, reaching up to touch Elliot's cheek, then retreats up the stairs. She turns back once and meets my gaze. She touches her fingers to her lips and holds them out to me. I watch her go, and I know this story doesn't have a happy ending.

Quinn looks at the ceiling for a long moment, a prayer for guidance, for strength, for anything. She swallows. Straightens her collar. Clears her throat. And finally:

"I guess you have some questions," she says. "I suppose we should start at the beginning."

16

"June and I grew up together; our parents knew each other. Delia and my mother were close, grew up together, went to church together, husbands got drafted together. Even got pregnant together.

"I don't even remember meeting June, she was just always . . . there. Every memory. I grew up in this post office: every weekend and afternoon, crawling around the floor while our parents sat for tea on the porch. She called me Winnie—she could never get the Q sound right. Mum liked to tell me it was her first word. We were practically sisters.

"And then June's father died. I think Delia lost faith then, and after a while she stopped going to church altogether. But my parents were . . . devout, I suppose. They believed every loss had purpose and every struggle brought strength. I don't blame Delia for walking away. It was too much, in the end.

"But even then, our parents weren't unfriendly. They never tried to keep June and me apart, so for us, not much changed. Not for a while, at least. We went to school, we spent weekends down by the lake, summers at the arcade. It was the way things had always been, mostly; we might have been a little bored after a while, but we were happy. And we knew that Warwick wasn't forever—June had been planning to move since she first discovered an atlas. And I only wanted to be where June was, so I figured I'd follow where she went.

"And then August came to town. The first time I ever saw him, he was standing at the train station with a bag slung over one shoulder, waiting in the rain. I didn't know who he was, but he looked so sad, standing there, waiting for no one. I never told June that—that I saw him that day. And when I saw him at school on Monday, I remembered that look, and so I wrote her that first letter and said we should invite him to dinner. I think it's the first thing I ever decided on my own—she was always the wild one, the impulsive one. But that day, that letter, I suddenly felt this . . . urgency, I suppose. It felt like something I just needed to do, and it was such a strange feeling to me that I followed it.

"He was quiet, at first. We brought him here, and you know what that's like—he hardly knew what to do with himself. Barely managed to say *yes ma'am* and *no ma'am* while he watched us running around like lunatics and couldn't even look us in the eye. Then a few days later, June had the idea to show him Rydal and it was like something just clicked, like the forest was so still and so silent he finally had room to speak. He told us his mum had died, and he didn't have any family left, so he ended up here, with his dad. They weren't close. Had hardly ever spoken, actually, apart from the occasional Christmas card. But it was Warwick or foster care, so here he was.

"I loved him right away. I tried to keep it secret, but I think June knew. She always knew that sort of thing. He was so kind, so endlessly patient—he would listen to us talk for hours, and sometimes I'd think he must be bored, but I'd look over and he'd be smiling to himself, just happy to be near us. And I was so naive about the world back then, but he never made me feel silly about it. He would just wait for the right moment, ask the right question, and then he'd listen while I talked myself in circles, knowing I needed time to put the pieces together. And him and June— god, they were a mess. Too much the same and, yet, somehow, too different. I spent so many afternoons wedged between them, listening to them bicker, feeling their laughter pressing into my sides. They could spend all day scheming and running around, concocting crazy plans and inventing wild stories, but in the end, she was reckless without limit, and he knew there was no safety net waiting to catch him if he fell. But still, even if he didn't dare to dream of it for himself, he made me believe that there could be . . . more than all of this. More than the life my parents had planned for me.

"My parents didn't like him, of course. He was the 'wrong kind of people,' not the boy they had imagined for me. They wouldn't say it in so many words, but he was the stranger in town, the poor kid with a dead mum and drunk dad and destined for nothing. They tolerated him for a while, partly because they knew forbidding us from seeing each other would only backfire, and partly because Delia thought so highly of him. They thought I was safe, especially with June around.

"I guess that's why we ended up at Treegap. It was suffocating, knowing they were always watching. It started as a joke—just something to do on the weekends, instead of walking the same laps around town. Then it started to mean something, to all of us. It was this tiny piece of the world that was just ours, a thing created from nothing more than determination and friendship, and we swore, right then, that we would all be friends forever. That this *place* would be forever.

"I kissed him the night we finished it. I watched him hang the sign above the door, and June complained she was cold, so she'd started walking back to the bikes. I just couldn't take it a moment longer. I loved him so much already. And we fell into that love so easily. We became inseparable, finding reasons to sneak out at night and stay away when we could. We spent most weekends camped in with June, reading books and watching movies and having picnics at Treegap. It was their idea to start the Rydal Devil rumor—bet that's no surprise. Kept folks away, mostly. Nobody wanted to wander in the woods far enough to find us.

"And then, one night, I snuck him into my room. School was nearly over, and this cloud was looming over us—June was already at university, I was going to follow, and August was going to stay behind. He thought if he stayed and worked for his father, he'd have enough money after a year to come with us. But a year seemed so long—too long—and all I wanted was one night together.

"It was my mother who caught us. She flew into such a rage, and eventually woke the whole house. My brother practically marched August out of the house. I knew they didn't get along, but right then I saw something ugly in Charlie I'd never seen before—such hate, hidden beneath righteousness. He said he was protecting me, never once stopping to think I didn't *want* to be protected at all.

"August got sent away to live with an aunt for the rest of summer. My parents must have paid off his dad, though they never admitted to it. God, that summer seemed endless. Then I went to the lake one day, alone, sneaking out in a bikini my mother had forbidden, and I looked down at my stomach and thought, *Oh*.

"I was so nervous to tell him. I thought it would ruin us, this child that I already loved, that I wanted to keep, but I knew it wasn't what August had planned—his life was already hard, and it was about to be so much harder. I told him I wouldn't tell anyone it was his, certainly never my parents, and we'd be okay, the two of us: the baby and me. I watched him fall to his knees and thought it was all over, but then he reached out and placed the tiniest, gentlest kiss on my stomach. August had so much love to give, and in that moment it all spilled out, and this little baby, who had no name and who had been quietly growing all this time, became the most loved person in the whole world.

"The life I'd already outgrown became suffocating at that point. I wrote to June, and she told me to go. August had been planning too. We didn't have enough time to save the money we needed—but he was good with his hands, always making little trinkets, and he came up with the idea to switch the Adder Stone for a fake. It sounded outlandish, back then, but we needed to go, and we needed to go quickly.

"The night before we were supposed to leave, Charlie found my bags, and he flew into this . . . rage. I'd never seen anything like it. I thought—honestly, I thought he'd kill him. He found August in his loft. Dragged him down beaten and bloody and must have knocked the gasoline over by accident. I suppose the hay and the candles were always destined to be a disaster. The whole thing was up in flames in a few minutes. And Charlie was standing over August, saying he'd tell anyone who'd listen that August had forced himself on me, burned the loft down on purpose, anything he could think of.

"We were lucky the whole place didn't burn to the ground—it was only the rain that saved it, in the end. In the confusion, after, August and I slipped away. We had nothing except the clothes we were wearing.

"We waited the night in Treegap, alone, and in the morning the town was blockaded by police cars. Charlie had gotten his way after all.

"So we took one of the tourist rowboats, and we left on the lake. Warwick was such a small thing in the distance we could hardly see it anymore. And we hadn't a clue what we'd do once we landed on shore, but none of it mattered. I was—gosh, I was so happy. And August . . .

"It was such a stupid thing. The lake had always seemed so safe. All those summers we'd spent, swimming from shore to shore. But the storm had stirred up trees and branches and—

"August went in, and he never came back. I screamed for him, jumped in when I realized it had been too long. But he was gone.

348

They think—they think a tree, maybe, he must have . . . been trapped. I couldn't find him. I never found him. Nobody did.

"The worst part was getting that stupid boat back to shore. Trying to find help. It was all useless, in the end. None of it mattered.

"There was nothing worth saving after that. I could never go home again.

"So I left. I took the money I'd been saving, a bit taken here and there from my parents, and I did all the things we had planned together. Got myself an apartment in a faraway town, and made a life there: took you, Elliot, on picnics and rowboats, taught you to ride horses and swim in the ocean—showed you that the world was a big place and was right there waiting for you.

"June came to live with us for a while, in the beginning— sleeping on the couch and bouncing Elliot on her lap while she studied. We traveled when we could, with the little money we had left. Sometimes we'd just drive, until we crossed deserts and cities and arrived at what seemed like the edge of the world. We never needed much, and we were happy. Then June met your father at a concert one night, and soon she was pregnant too. I told her to stay, but she knew there wasn't enough room for two babies. And I think, honestly, she was tired of being wild. Losing August changed her—she wasn't invincible anymore, and she wanted to be with Delia when you were born. I met Dale a while after that, and he was charming and kind and didn't seem to mind that I didn't like to talk much about the life we'd left behind. For a while, it seemed like we both finally had the lives we'd always wanted.

"And then June got sick. So I packed it all up, that little apartment we'd filled with love and made our home, and we came back. It was never a question, she never asked, but she needed me, and I came. Found a house down the road, and then the rest . . .

"The rest you know."

17

Elliot stands up. Sits down again. And then his face crumples, and he begins to sob in earnest. I wrap my arms around him, while Quinn kneels on the floor. Levi looks helpless, and I realize this story has affected each of us, left a gaping hole and patched it over again.

"I was going to tell you when you were old enough to understand," Quinn says. "You were such a sweet baby, and I couldn't bear to tarnish that. And then the years passed, and I kept reminding myself that I had already decided, that waiting was the right thing to do. And one day I realized: You were going to be older than he ever got to be. And how do I explain that? How did I look at you and explain August: not the father you'd always pictured, not even a man yet; he was just a kid." Her eyes fill with tears and her voice breaks. "We were just kids."

Elliot sinks into her, and in that moment, it doesn't matter that his six-foot frame should dwarf her; he looks impossibly small, clinging to her, his shoulders shaking. "You should have told me," he whispers. "I wanted to know."

Quinn kisses his head and squeezes her eyes shut. "I know, I'm sorry. I'm so sorry. I'll tell you all about him, anything you want to know. I've been waiting so long to share him with you."

Levi leans back in his chair, covering his face. Quietly, I go and sit beside him, tugging an arm away. "You okay?" I whisper.

He swallows before he can answer, head bobbing. "Yeah, I guess. I mean, I have an aunt now. But Dad . . . it was all his fault."

"He didn't know what would happen. It was an accident." But I don't believe that, and I know Levi doesn't either. Hadn't I thought the same thing all along? Surprised on the few occasions his dad showed any sort of decency? I suppose this explains the effort he went to in order to remove Dale from their lives: penance for his failures. Maybe that's why he keeps August's poster in the station too.

Elliot stands up suddenly. "I can't. I can't be here right now. I need . . . time."

"Wait," I beg. "We'll go with you."

He shakes his head. "I just . . . I want to be alone."

He strides toward the door, with Levi and I thundering down the stairs after him. "Are you okay? Where are you going?"

He whirls on us, and I stop dead.

"I don't know! I just found out my dad is dead and the uncle I didn't know about hated him and my best friend is actually my cousin? I just—I'm going for a walk, okay? Don't, Brodie, don't follow, I know you're thinking about it. I'll be back. I just—I can't right now, okay?"

I nod reluctantly, and Levi wraps his arm around my shoulders as we watch him go, partly for comfort and partly to keep me there.

I watch until he disappears over the hill, and I sink to the ground, suddenly cold to my bones, and all I can think of is Mum and Quinn and August, three of them here, the three of us now.

"I thought we'd find August," I whisper. "I thought he was out there, somewhere."

"I know. Me too."

"It's not fair."

"I know." Levi kisses my cheeks. "I know," he says again. "Let's go inside. He'll be back soon."

I let him guide me back upstairs, creeping past Quinn's room. She's sitting on the floor, having finally given in to her own tears, rocking back and forth. I start for the door, but Levi gently grabs my hand, leading me away. "Give her some space," he murmurs. "There's time for questions later."

I nod, but my gaze drifts up the stairs, to the green light on the third floor. "I need a minute," I say, and his eyes follow mine.

"I'll wait," he says.

I used to sleep up here, when I had nightmares. The house was so big, and it felt so empty without Mum. The midnight creak of the floorboards would send me bolting upright, curling into the old reading chair beside Nan's bed. She'd leave the television on for hours, the gray-white light just bright enough to banish the shadows that kept me awake. I didn't stop until I went to Rowley.

The door to her room is open, the television on but muted, the screen all but a grainy blur now—the antenna has fallen to one side, and nobody bothered to fix it.

Nan is sitting on the edge of her bed, holding the old photo of Mum that usually sits on her bedside table. It was the first day Mum moved us back here; before patches of her hair were shaved away for more procedures. Before the lines around her eyes were from exhaustion instead of laughter. Nan brushes a thumb over Mum's smile, grinning at the camera.

"She asked me not to tell you," Nan says. "It wasn't her secret to tell, she said. And then it didn't seem like mine."

I ease beside her on the bed. The crocheted blankets are the same as when I left, faded in one corner where the sun hits them in the morning.

"Maybe I should have said something," she continues. "But there was so much loss already. August was such a sweet boy. Just about broke them both when he—when we lost him." She doesn't say *died*. She never does.

"Quinn was just starting to get her life back together when we lost your mum too. The two of them, back here. God, they were something to see, dancing around that kitchen at all hours. Drove your dad half mad. And the three of you kids, well, you reminded me so much of them. Then you started asking about the letters, and I thought maybe it was time. But Quinn wasn't ready. And I thought, *Look, they're here again, they're right here, there's life in this house again.* And I didn't want to ruin that, for you all."

Nan turns to me then, and her eyes are red. "No parent should have to bury their baby, love. And they're always your baby, even when they're grown." I realize she's wiping away my own tears, the soft pad of her wrinkled hands pressing into my cheeks. I wonder how she's weathered it all: losing August, losing Mum. Watching Quinn leave.

354

"The letters were Mum's?"

Nan nods. "Quinn wouldn't take them. And she didn't want anyone else to have them. I like to think she knew you'd find them, when she was gone." Did I? Find them after? It's been so long; the letters are tangled together with everything else. It seems like they've been here forever. I don't remember the first day—I remember the letters, being absorbed in them for hours, rushing to tell Levi the next day at school. But I don't remember what I was doing that morning. *Yes, you do,* something whispers.

I was wearing my funeral dress, still.

There was grave dirt on my shoes.

Mum left me an escape, I realize. A way to be with her, and remember her, even if I didn't know it yet.

"I didn't want to lose you too," Nan whispers. "I thought, after all this time, you'd be so mad. . . ."

And I can't keep it together anymore, so I throw my hands around her shoulders, holding tight. "I promised I'd always come home, didn't I?"

Nan hugs me back, and for a moment, I feel like a small child again, sheltering in her invincible arms. She always seemed so strong, not scared of the dark, or monsters under stairs, or the Rydal Devil. Now I think she was just better at hiding it.

"I have questions, about Mum. And the letters."

Nan pulls away, nodding. "Of course."

Mabel curls between us, heaving a sigh. Nan gives her a weary pat, eyes drifting closed for a long moment.

"Maybe we can talk tomorrow," I offer. "Do you want a cup of tea?"

Nan shakes her head. "That's about enough excitement for me today, poppet. Perhaps I'll just rest my eyes for a few minutes." She manages to lift her feet onto the bed without disturbing Mabel, and her breathing is heavy and even by the time I close the door behind me.

I tread lightly downstairs, careful not to wake her, and crawl on top of my bed beside Levi. "You waited," I whisper. I slump against him, tired of crying and tired of grieving.

"I said I would," he answers, fingers curling around my hair.

We sit in silence, until the room grows dark. Somehow, in spite of everything, my stomach growls, loud enough to echo in the small space between us. "Sorry," I mumble. "I think I'm hungry."

"Want to go down for dinner?"

I shake my head. "I know it's not Quinn's fault, not really, but I don't really know how to talk to her right now."

"Okay. How about . . . fries?"

"Fries are always a good idea," I say, and then I burst into tears again. When I've finally calmed down, and Levi has brushed away my tears with the sleeve of his sweater, we tiptoe down the hallway and slip over the balcony. I leave a note on the window so Nan doesn't worry, and then we climb into Levi's car and head to the Archie Arcade. He orders us fries and milkshakes, which make me feel sick but somehow also comforted. He brings me a game token, and I stare at it, thinking about the Adder Stone and how many nights Mum and Quinn and August had sat right here. Planning the futures they wouldn't get to have, none of them except Quinn, who hardly even dared to imagine a life away from this town.

"What are your grandparents like?" I blurt.

Levi shrugs. "Pretty much what Quinn said. They were always super, ah, conservative, I guess? Wasn't allowed to wear jeans when they came over, and Dad would make a big deal about saying grace for dinner even though we hardly ever do it when they're not around. Granddad's a bit, you know, not quite there anymore. But I can see how . . . yeah. I can believe they would have been that way."

He scruffs the back of his head, blowing out a sigh. "The irony is Dad probably got my mum knocked up only a couple months later. What a bunch of hypocrites."

We sit silently with that thought for a while, until I ponder aloud: "I wonder if he tried to find Quinn. After she left."

Levi shrugs. "I don't know. I never got the sense that there was *a whole missing sibling* in the family. But maybe in secret? Who knows?"

"Yeah," I say with a sigh. "Who knows."

"How are you feeling?" he says gently.

I shrug. "Fine. Mostly. I mean, it's nothing I didn't already know, right? And at least I got to *know* my parents, so I don't really have any right to be upset. But I wished I'd asked her more questions before . . ." I clear my throat. "You know how when you're little you don't really think of your parents as people, who had their own lives? By the time I realized, it was already too late. I wish she'd told me about them. About her. I wish . . . I just . . ." I finish suddenly and unintelligently, shrugging again. "I don't know. It's all a mess. Do you think Elliot's going to be okay?"

Levi sinks into the booth seat. He looks impossibly tired. I wonder if I look the same. "I hope so. To be honest, when we started looking, he kinda seemed to know the chances weren't exactly good. He didn't say it in so many words, but he sort of hinted that maybe the person we were looking for wasn't around anymore."

There's a rumble outside, then a distant crash, and the roof echoes with the faint drumming of rain. Levi frowns. "I didn't think it was meant to storm today."

I grab my bag, tucking it under one arm, and hold out my spare hand. "Come on. We should go. Elliot's probably back by now."

It's dark and miserable by the time we arrive home, and the weather vane groans on the parapet. Levi shrugs out of his jacket and tries to hold it over our heads as we run for the door, which is a valiant effort though mostly in vain. We tumble through the doors of the post office soaking wet and dripping water over the carpet. Quinn is standing at the counter, mechanically sorting through stock under the soft glow of a dying lamp bulb. She jolts when we enter, and sighs. "Thank god, you're back. Is Eli . . ." but she watches as the door slams closed behind us.

"He's not back?" I ask.

She shakes her head. "Maybe you could try calling him? He's not answering. I don't want him out in this weather."

I nod, pulling out my cell and dialing his number. It rings and rings with no answer. I turn to Levi, giving a curt shake of my head. Without needing to be asked, he tries from his phone. It rings out, and Levi presses another contact.

"Hey, Isaac. Have you seen Elliot today? Yeah? Okay. Sure. Thanks man." Levi hangs up and the tension drops out of his shoulders. "He's been at Isaac's place. He's probably on his way back now."

358

Quinn takes a deep breath, placing her hands flat on the counter. "Thanks, Levi. You—you're a good kid, you know? Just because things between me and your dad aren't good, doesn't mean I don't love you. Sorry, if that's odd to say. You don't have to say anything back. I've just—I'm very proud of you. I thought you should know."

Levi gives her a tiny smile. "I always wanted a big family," he says.

"Me too," she answers.

He takes my hand, backing toward the dead letter room. "We'll wait in here, if that's cool?"

"Of course," she says, and turns back to the sheafs of paper.

I hesitate on the threshold of the room. It always felt like an escape, a portal to another world, a peek into the lives of these strange and distant people, like watching a movie unfold over a lifetime. But now, knowing those letters belong to us . . .

I walk, stiff, haltingly, to the dead letters. Item 107. *Unclaimed.* Let my fingers trail over the envelopes, softened now from stiff paper to silken edges, from being opened and read so much.

"It's weird to think these were Mum's, all along."

Levi comes to stand behind me, wrapping his arms around my waist, chin atop my head.

"She always said we weren't done having adventures," I add. "Maybe she knew . . ."

"—that you were the most stubborn child to have ever walked the earth?"

I laugh. "Probably. Maybe she wanted us all to find each other. Like they did."

"Can I just say," Levi adds, "that it's very lucky it didn't end up being the other way around. What if *we'd* been cousins?"

I crinkle my nose, feeling the heavy weight in my chest lift. "Thank you, for somehow buoying my spirits with the thought of accidental incest."

"You're welcome," he says, nuzzling my hair. "Anytime."

I wriggle free and grab a stack of letters, taking them to the green chair to pore over again, even though I've read the words a million times.

Dear Winnie, did you know it is nigh upon impossible to lose your virginity in the back seat of a car? And not for lack of trying, either, but the space is seriously—

Okay. Not that one. Thanks, Mum.

Dear August, you heathen creature, you have bewitched my best friend and now she is horribly in love with you. It's revolting, the pining, the glassy doe-eyed, butterfly-in-stomach kind of love. It's terribly inconvenient to me, so you will simply have to love her back. Tomorrow is Valentine's Day. I'll pick you up at three; we're going card shopping.

And below that:

Dear June, it's quite rude to go around accusing people of black magic. Did you know that only 20 people were actually accused of being witches in the Salem Witch Trials?

Dear August, I did not. Fascinating. You are evading the subject.

Dear June, I already love her back, idiot.

Dear August, Good.
   Now tell me more about these witches.

I read, and Levi perches on the edge on the armchair, following over my shoulder. Suddenly, these letters make more sense. I flick through more, until I find the letter from August that mentions his dad.

"Oh," I breathe. "We never thought to ask Quinn who August's family is. He must live in town."

Levi cringes. "Actually, I'm pretty sure it's Dwight."

"*Dwight?* Drunk Dwight? Nearly-had-us-arrested Dwight?"

"Detained," he corrects.

"*Dwight?!*"

"Remember Quinn said they nearly burned down a building? That loft we were in, it was burned on the inside."

I think back, remembering the charcoal on my palms. The summer we'd played detective, we'd asked everyone in town if August worked there. And everyone said no, except Dwight. He'd cursed us out and told us to never step foot on his property again. At the time, I thought it was just because he was a cranky old jerk. But . . .

"Hey, I have to call my mum, okay? I don't really feel like going home tonight. That's assuming . . ."

"You can stay here," I say. "Everyone stays here, why not? Pick a room."

"Your room?"

I toss a cushion at him, which he catches and returns. He kisses me, again, which I've noticed he does a lot now. Little kisses, peppered across my head and cheeks and nose. I guess we're all sick of pretending that time like this doesn't matter. I catch his hand before he pulls away and kiss him back.

"I'm gonna stay down here a while, okay?"

"Sure," he says. "I'll go check on Quinn."

I read the letters until my eyes get heavy, and the storm rages on, and the windows rattle a tune in their awnings. I read until I can't tell if these words are real or dreams, and finally give in to the dark. I sleep through the storm, and wish I was still dreaming when someone shakes me awake, and I jolt from the sudden flicker of lamplight.

"Brodie, wake up, Elliot's missing."

Time is both too fast and too slow. The minutes it takes Detective Sawyer to arrive seem like an hour; the hour it takes for him to command a search party seems like seconds. I am told to sit, to be patient, but my legs jitter and I feel like I'm going to be sick, so I walk up and down the stairs, to and from the bathroom, gagging up nothing into the toilet bowl only to return and repeat the whole parade ten minutes later.

Quinn is wringing her hands, Nan is making tea, and Levi's dad is trying to convince everyone that Elliot is probably fine, and then Quinn yells at him to shut up because the last Maddon boy who went missing died. It gets quiet for a while after that: seconds, minutes, hours. I don't know anymore.

Isaac comes and leaves again. He couldn't take the sitting, either. He said he would go to all the spots they liked: the cinema, the bleachers, the café in Lancaster.

It's midday and Elliot is still missing. Levi comes downstairs and looks like a mess, but he tries to smile.

"You kids sure you don't know anything?" says another police officer.

"Yes, actually, I know exactly where he is and I'm maintaining this ruse because I think it's *funny*."

"Brodie!" Nan snaps. "Don't be rude. They're trying to help."

I steel myself, count to ten like that one therapist told me to. "No," I grit out. "I really, really don't know where he is. Cross my heart and hope . . ." The words trail away. The officer cringes.

Levi has a tick in his jaw, and I'm sure he's ground his teeth down to nothing by now. The adults cast a final gaze at us and file upstairs.

I rocket out of my chair the moment the last foot disappears from the landing. "Come on," I hiss. "Let's go."

"Go where?" Levi asks, eyes pleading. "I don't know where else to look, Brodie."

"Treegap," I say, exasperated.

"They're looking in the woods already—"

"—but they don't know it like we do, they don't know how to find the house. Where else would he *go*? Where else would he be that he can't answer—" My voice catches and a deranged hiccup strangles my throat. Elliot's phone no longer rings. It goes straight to voice mail. I tried it, over and over, until my own phone went dead in my hands.

Levi waits. Voices upstairs get louder, closer. "Fine," he says, deciding at the last moment. *"Run."*

I'm sorry, Nan, I think, as I hurl myself into Levi's car and slam the door shut behind me. "Wait!"

I throw the door open again and grab my bike from where it leans against the front door and throw it in his trunk. "Okay! Go, go, go!"

We peel out, and I twist in my seat in time to watch his dad sprint down the street, flailing his arms, calling out for us to wait.

"I'm sorry," I say. "I couldn't sit there. I couldn't—"

His hand finds mine. "I know. Me too."

We drive in silence to the woods: seconds, minutes, hours. We take my bike and ride to the edge of the trail, quicker than running on foot. We hurry down the stream, but it's flooded and the ground is muddy and every step feels like sinking. I'm crying by the time we finally make it to the clearing, while Levi has gone pale and completely silent.

"He's not here. He's not here." I can't breathe, the air in my chest is stuck, suffocating. Levi just turns toward Treegap, breaking into a sprint that I can't keep up with, but *I don't care, I don't care.*

I make it to Treegap to find Levi sitting on the porch with his head in his hands. "He was here," he croaks, holding out August's Adder Stone. "Why would he take this? Leave it here?"

364

I take the ring, threading it over my finger. Inside the cabin there's a few food wrappers that weren't here before, and the Polaroid of August. I don't know when Elliot took it back, but he's placed it on top of a book, the title worn and illegible. I pick it up and read the inscription. *For my son: May you make your own stories.* I flick to the title page and laugh. *The Devil's Storybook.*

"Did you know he had this?" I ask Levi, holding up the book.

He shakes his head, touches the book but doesn't hold it.

Be my devil, August, and I'll be yours. I shake my head. I can't think, can't tell what's myth and what's real, what are the letters and what's *us.*

The Rydal Devil takes children in the night, leaves gifts in the woods, grants wishes at crossroads.

"It's not real," I whisper, squeezing my eyes shut. "It was never real. Elliot is fine. It wasn't real." *They made it up. None of it was ever true,* I remind myself, *no kids ever went missing, except—*

"Oh god," I gasp. "The lake. I think—I think he went to the lake."

The last place his dad ever went. Beginnings and endings and beginnings, again.

I drop the book and we run, run as fast as the ruined ground will let us, slipping in the flooded creek, goose bumps racing across bare skin as the gale returns. The lake finally appears, the surface dark and churning, no longer a peaceful flat mirror. I search, desperate for any sign of him, for a speck on the surface, but there's nothing, no one, and then Levi points silently to a bike tossed in the shrubs. "He's out there," he says, broken. "Somewhere."

Levi has gone wooden. I have to shove him toward the harbor, where the dinghies are lined up and a jaunty, too-bright sign is strung up that says COME BACK SOON!

Yes, Elliot, I think. *Come back, come back to us.*

I'm about to jump into one of the boats when Levi calls out suddenly, "There! He's there!"

My head snaps up, and I stare out at the lake, and there's nothing, nothing, just an empty boat, abandoned halfway out. And then something, someone, surfaces. Climbs onto the boat, swaying so wildly I think it will collapse.

"Elliot!" I scream. "Elliot, stop!"

He jumps out of the boat, disappearing below the surface. Too long, too long. I pull at the knots tying the dinghy to the pier, but it's useless; my fingernails bend back and break, but it's stuck. I look out and Elliot has surfaced again, climbed into his boat. Jumps again.

I toss down the rope and start running. Too late, Levi realizes what I intend to do.

"Brodie, stop! It's not—"

The water hits me like cement—freezing cold, a current that tugs at my feet and drags me in the wrong direction. I kick off my shoes, shuck off my jacket, bobbing under the surface for a few seconds as I free my arms, and I hear Levi call out my name, and then I'm free and I'm swimming toward Elliot.

I can feel the silt on my feet, stirred up from below, branches that snag my jeans. *Oh god, this was a mistake, this is terrible, this is—*

The water rocks me, and I look up. Elliot has jumped again. It's all he's doing: climbing into the boat and jumping out. "Stop!" I cry, water flooding into my mouth, and I choke, thrown off balance. I go under again, kicking hard to push my head up and gasp for air. I swim toward him, nearly there, fingers numb and aching when I finally grip the edge of his boat. Elliot stares down at me, eyes unseeing. His skin is white, his lips are blue. "Stop," I gasp. "Stop it, Elliot."

He jumps.

I try to snatch at his clothes as he sinks, and the boat slams against my shoulder. My hand slips, and in the few seconds it takes me to focus, it's already drifted. How long has he been doing this? How far does it drift while he's under? I kick toward the boat again, hearing Elliot surface behind me. I don't dare glance back; I grab for the edge and pull myself in, gasping at the shock of cool air as wind rips across the lake. Elliot starts to grab for the boat again. "What are you doing?" I beg. "Elliot, this is *insane*; let's go home."

He turns away. He's going to disappear again, and if he keeps going, he won't come back up again. I don't know what else to do. So I grab him, throwing my arms around his waist, and I fall, letting all my weight drop back until we slam into the dinghy, wooden slats ramming into my shoulders, my head smacking against the edge so hard that the world turns white for a few seconds. Elliot tries to scramble away, but he's cold and weak and I cling to him with every ounce of energy I have left. "Stop it," I sob. "Stop it, Elliot, please. What are you doing? You'll kill yourself, *stop.*"

He scrambles but it's useless: I manage to maneuver myself on top of him, pressing my whole body down.

"Stop it!" I scream. "Just stop! I love you, I love so much, and *you are not leaving me.*"

He stops fighting for a second. I wrap my arms around his shoulders, my legs around his legs. His skin feels like ice. I don't know what else to do but lie here, pinning him to the boat. "Just stay here," I sob into his collar. "Just stay. Or you're taking me with you. That's it. Those are your choices."

His too-still chest moves underneath mine. "He's down there," he whispers, words so soft I hardly hear them. "They never found him. He's—he's down there. My dad. He's in the lake, he's always been in the lake. I have to find him, have to—"

He struggles against me, but I hang on. We're both crying. I don't know which sob belongs to who.

"Elliot, I'm sorry, I'm so sorry. But August isn't down there anymore—he's gone, he's—he's not here, there's nothing for you to find. But he didn't want to leave you, okay? He wouldn't want you to do this. Remember what Quinn said? He wanted you, he loved you."

"But he's not *here.* He's down there somewhere, *alone*, and it's— it's cold," he whispers. "I don't want him to be cold."

Then he doesn't say anything else because his arms are wrapped around mine and he's crushing me to him, and I'm telling him it will be okay, but I don't know if anything will ever be okay again.

The boat rocks, and Levi crawls in beside us, throwing silver space blankets over us that he must have grabbed from shore, and I shudder, not realizing how much my body ached for warmth. He cracks something small and square and shoves it against Elliot's chest, and the sudden flare of heat is almost painful. Then he grabs both of us, huddling us together, anchorless, drifting. The row boat he used to reach us has already begun to slip away, caught on the tide.

"You two are idiots," he says, voice breaking. "Don't you ever do that again. I thought—I thought I'd lost you both."

"S-sorry," I manage, teeth chattering. Elliot just leans into him, and the boat rocks in the current.

"I l-lost the oars," Elliot says.

"That's okay," Levi says. "We'll figure it out. It's okay."

"I'm s-sorry. You shouldn't have c-come."

"Shut up, Elliot," I say, squeezing his hand. "Just let us love you."

He doesn't say anything. Not for a while. Then he nods, once. "Okay. That would be okay."

And we find a way to be okay, after all.

18

The house is quiet and warm; Nan has built a fire in the study, even though she usually hates to leave it burning. But Elliot was still shaking when we brought him home, covered in extra blankets from the Coast Guard and lips still blue. We told them it was just a prank gone wrong, that we'd decided to take out a couple of the dinghies and the water got too rough. The captain gave us a good talking to, but at least he didn't report us to anyone—just made us promise to at least wear life jackets if we ever did something that stupid again.

We watched as Nan built up the kindling and Quinn tucked Elliot in like a little kid, even though it was hardly midday, quilt tucked up under his chin, patting his wet hair down. Levi and I loitered in the doorway until Nan finally shooed us away.

"Let a mother talk to her son," she'd said. "They need time."

I nodded, but my feet remained planted to the floorboards and my fingers wrapped around the doorway, still clinging on tight, just in case, scared he'd disappear if I let go again. Levi tugged the sleeve of my shirt until I relented, letting him drag me to the bathroom.

Now I sit on the edge of the tub, shivering, shirt slick and clinging to damp skin, numb with cold. I'd been given a blanket but had shrugged it off and added it to Elliot's pile—who knows how long he'd been out there by the time we found him. I hadn't even noticed the cold until now, but suddenly it was all I could think about. The kind of cold that runs down your bones. I stare at the pattern of the bathroom tiles, blinking; they look like snowflakes. They've never looked that way before. Ice creeps through the soles of my shoes and I shudder again, wrapping my arms around my waist and doubling over, trying to remember what warm feels like.

The shower faucet groans and sputters to life. "Wh-what are you doing?" I chatter, watching Levi stick his hand under the stream, waiting until steam clouds the glass screen.

"You're freezing," he says, crossing the room to help me up. "Let's get these off."

I stand without meaning to, surprised to find myself relenting as Levi gently peels my sodden sweater over my head. He kneels and unthreads my shoelaces, pulls off my soaked socks that had gone into the lake with me. I fumble with the buttons of my shirt, but my fingers are trembling and I can't make them catch.

"Here," he says quietly. "Can I?"

I nod, movements jerky. I'm wearing a tank underneath, but I still shiver when the material slips over my shoulders. His hands are warm and singe a line down my skin; I feel goose bumps follow the trail he leaves. Levi looks down at me for a long moment, and swallows heavily. Then he steps forward, kisses my shoulder, and

371

wraps his arms around me. He is warm and solid and I cling to him. His chin rests atop my head, and he's running his hands up and down my spine. I shiver and can't tell if it's him or the slowly ebbing cold.

"I know you think you're invincible," he says, voice hoarse. "But please never do that again."

"N-not planning on it," I say, pressing into his warmth. His shirt is a little damp where I'd leaned on him during the boat ride back, but otherwise he managed to stay pretty dry. "The lake is g-gross."

He laughs softly, and his arms drop away. I want to tell him to stay, but Nan is outside, and Elliot is down the hall with Quinn. And I don't know what *stay* would mean, or if we're ready for that.

I wrap my fingers in his, holding on for a few more seconds, then let our hands drop. He seems to understand, and slips away, closing the door quietly behind him.

I groan as I step under the hot water and find the warmth is almost painful on my icy skin. I stay there until my arms and stomach are glowing red and then wrap myself in fluffy towels.

Levi's not in my room when I return to shove myself into my warmest, ugliest pajamas, so I assume he's either gone home or to Elliot's room. I pad into the kitchen, finding Nan has left a cup of coffee on the bench for me, which I drink gratefully and feel my bones defrosting. The house is so silent, almost reverent; the floorboards don't creak, the windows don't rattle, the wind doesn't whistle between loose bricks, as though the house has decided *Shh, let them rest.*

In the unusual quiet, I hear footsteps behind me, and turn, expecting Nan or Levi, but it's Quinn. She looks drawn and tired, and her eyes are red like she's been crying. She glances up in a daze, surprised to see me.

"Oh, Brodie, I'm sorry, I—" She looks around, perhaps wondering if she should leave.

"It's okay," I say. "Do you want some coffee?"

"Sure. That would be nice."

I find the coffeepot still half-full and pour her a cup. "The boys are together?"

She nods. "I'm glad. You kids are so good to each other. I hope you always . . ." Her voice breaks, and she takes a sip of her drink before she continues. "I hope you always have that," she finishes.

We sit in silence for a few minutes until a quiet, huffing sound breaks the hush. I look over, expecting tears, but she's laughing instead.

"I guess you're not really kids anymore, are you? No more than we were."

"I'm so sorry," I whisper. "I wish he was still here."

"Me too. I miss them both. So much. God, you have no idea how lonely . . . not to hear her laughing, or him calling my name. I can't stand the quiet, sometimes." She scrubs a hand against her cheek and sniffles. "I'm sorry we kept it from you. That part of your mum, especially."

"It's okay," I answer. I don't really know if it is, but I know it will be, eventually. And I know what losing someone feels like: I won't be the person who makes it worse for Quinn. Not today.

"Elliot says you pulled him out," she whispers.

I look up, surprised. She gives me a small smile. "He came home soaking wet and wearing a survival blanket," she says ruefully. "There were only so many answers."

"I didn't pull him out. I don't think . . ." I duck my head low, eyes on my coffee cup. "I don't think you could have pulled him out, Quinn. Once he went under, I couldn't see him at all. You couldn't have saved August."

She nods once, primly, then covers her face with both hands and sobs. I stand up, closing the small gap between us, and hold on tight.

"Sorry. I'm sorry." She squeezes my hand, and I squeeze back. "I always wondered."

I shudder to think of that day. Looking into the water, wondering how long was too long, hoping for just a few seconds more . . .

"His poster is still up. In the police station. That's how I recognized him. I think they kept looking, even after . . ."

Her eyes are glassy, fixed on the counter and years in the past all at once. "I asked them to. I thought maybe the current . . . and he was a good swimmer. Maybe he was waiting, somewhere. But they were just being kind. They knew he was gone."

"I'm sorry. For all of it. I wish you'd found him." What if Elliot had gone under? Would I have ever stopped looking? I know the answer is never. I would look into that water every day and hope for *maybe*.

"Do you have it?" Quinn says, discreetly wiping her nose on the corner of her sleeve. "The key to my locker?"

It takes me a second to realize what she means. But the key to locker 604 is still looped through a hair tie in my pocket. I pull it out and place it gently on the counter.

"Was it you who left the ring?"

"I did," she says, picking up the key, holding it gently, like it was made of glass instead of metal. "It's a fake, did you know?"

I tilt my chin *yes*, and she smiles. "Clever girl. I found it in Elliot's drawer when we were packing to come here. There were police all over the house—I didn't know what to do, so I just took it with me. This was the only place I could think to keep it safe, until the dust had settled." She sets the key back on the counter, leaving it between us. "I've had this key for twenty years. Your mum gave it to me. It's how we'd leave each other letters. August had one too, but . . ."

The silence stretches out, full of all the things we can't say. Not yet.

"I think Elliot knew, for a while," I say. "He just didn't want to believe it. He saw a photo of you and August. I think that's why he took the ring; he just wanted a piece . . ." *of his dad.*

More things we can't say. The air is thick with them. "June took that photo. She was back for the holidays—it was only a few weeks, before . . ." Quinn clears her throat, a master of deflection. "I guess this means you don't get to solve your mystery."

"What do you mean?"

"The Adder Stone," she says. "The real one. I never did find out what August did with it."

"I thought—I thought you said he was going to sell it?"

She gives a delicate shrug of her shoulder. "He was, but there was no time to take anything after the fire. We left right away—I only had the bit of money in my bag that I'd been saving."

Goose bumps creep down my spine. "He didn't have it on the lake?"

She shakes her head. "Nothing, really, but the clothes on his back."

It's still out there. The real Adder Stone is still out there somewhere.

I look up the stairs, and Nan is loitering at the top. There's still a chance. A very small chance: a very small ring hidden in a very big place. But it's there, somewhere.

Nan clears her throat. "Right," she says. "Who wants their fortunes told? The attic ghost says it's time for a change."

Levi and Elliot are sitting on the living room floor the next day, wearing random articles of clothing they were able to find around the house: Levi in a pink, oversized cardigan and gray track pants that barely reach his ankles, while Elliot seems to mostly be wearing his own clothes but is also sporting a particularly fetching pom-pom beanie.

"You two look dashing this morning."

"I think this is my color," Levi says. "It brings out my eyes."

I squint at him. "Annoyingly, that is true."

Elliot leans into me when I fold down beside him, like he can't be bothered to hold his own weight up. "Cold," he says. "So cold."

"Still?" He'd slept through the rest of the afternoon and all night; I'd walked past his door a few times, just to hear him breathing.

He nods, pulling the sleeves of his sweater down over his hands.

"You know what fixes cold?" I say.

"What?"

"Pancakes."

Mabel sticks her head out from under his sweater and mews in agreement.

I frown at him. "Are you carrying my cat around under your sweater like a pregnant woman?"

Elliot shrugs. "I told you, she's my cat now."

Mabel retreats, proving his point. Only her tail peeks out of one corner, swishing happily.

"There's something wrong with that cat," Levi says. "She doesn't like me very much."

"Oh, darling, no one likes you very much," I coo.

Elliot snorts, and then shudders. "I can still taste lake. It's disgusting." He nudges me again. "Thanks for coming. And I'm sorry . . . for everything."

"We'll always find you. Always."

"It's true," Levi says. "I installed a bunch of tracking apps on your phone last night. Some of them shouldn't even be legal—huge invasion of privacy."

"*Hey*," Elliot objects.

Levi winks at him. "Kidding. Mostly."

"So," I say, drawing out the syllables. "How are you feeling today?"

Elliot drops his head back, looking up at the ceiling. His lashes flutter on his cheeks, and eventually he blows out a long sigh.

"I feel . . . tired. Angry. Sad. I miss my dad. And then I think that's dumb because I never even knew him. And then I get sad again." His throat bobs up and down. "Can we not talk about it today? Maybe not for a while? I just . . . need to . . ." He shrugs, and the sentence hangs.

"How about," I say, "we don't have to talk about it, unless you feel like maybe you'll jump in the lake again. And even then, you don't have to talk to us. We can have a code word. It can be . . ."

"Butternut squash," Levi supplies helpfully.

"The code word is not going to be *butternut squash*," I say, narrowing my eyes at him.

"Why not? It can't be a word you use all the time. How often do you use the word *butternut squash*?"

"When I say, 'Hey, I feel like some butternut-squash soup,'" Elliot says.

"Fine," Levi replies. "Widdershins, then."

"Widdershins?"

"Yeah. Counterclockwise, out of whack. Also, fun fact, my nana says Satanists walk widdershins to summon the devil."

I screw up my nose. "My nan says Satanists are misunderstood hippies with compassion toward all creatures."

"You and I have very different grandmothers."

Elliot snorts. "Fine," he relents. "In moments of great emotional turmoil, I will call 'Widdershins.' I make no promise as to whether or not demonic forces are involved."

Nan sticks her head through the doorway. "If you're going to summon something, don't do it on the rug in here." She steps into the room and claps her hands. "Now, I know this isn't original, but here's what I'm thinking: pancakes."

We agree in unison, and I wonder how long she's been loitering in the doorway. She looks tired today; she's abandoned her blue mascara and powdered cheeks for a bare face, framed by flat hair instead of her usual coif. I wonder how long she sat up last night, thinking about the three kids who came home and the two that didn't.

The cat-shaped lump moves under Elliot's sweater, and he pulls the collar away to coo something nonsensical at her.

Nan smiles, starts to say something, and covers her mouth. Then she sighs. "Your dad brought that cat home, you know. He and June found her in the junkyard—some bastard had locked her in the trunk of a car. August couldn't keep her, so . . ." *Cat June,* I realize. Another piece of Mum. "She's an old girl," Nan continues. "I think she spent her ninth life waiting for you."

Elliot looks down at his sweater again, one dimple forming on his cheek. "That true, Mabel?"

She mews.

His eyes get a little glassy, and we all find somewhere else to look until he blinks away fresh tears. "Thanks," he says to Nan. "It's nice . . . to hear those stories. Good ones."

Nan nods. "I'd like to tell you more, when you're ready to hear them. Both of you," she says, giving me an unusually soft smile. "I'll get breakfast started," she adds. "You kids come down in twenty, okay?"

The next two days are hazy and slow, like a sepia-tinted

slideshow that jumps and jolts between moments. We wake up, we eat. Sometimes we talk, sometimes we don't. Sometimes we sit in companionable silence.

Sometimes Quinn comes down and talks about August.

Sometimes Elliot asks questions. Sometimes he doesn't.

Levi goes home, but only long enough to pack a bag. When he comes back, the lines around his mouth are tight and he's quiet for a long time. "I don't know how to forgive him for everything," he says. "For the lie. For the fire. Everything might have been different." Elliot doesn't reply, and the silence between us feels like an agreement. Levi doesn't talk much about his dad, after that, but his phone often rings and is rarely answered.

Nan brings me up to the attic and unlocks a chest full of Mum's things: bright clothes and cheap plastic jewelry, a broken camera with film still trapped in the compartment, and a diary that Nan says she's never read but thinks it would be okay if I wanted to.

I stay up there for a while, balanced against Granddad's old chesterfield and legs propped up on a leather trunk. I think that Mum's diary will be from when she was young but am surprised to find myself in it: a baby, born in this house because Mum thought she just needed to use the toilet and it was all over so quickly no one even had time to call for an ambulance.

I close my eyes against the afternoon sun, thinking it's not fair that the house we've lived in, and loved in, and died in, isn't really ours. That some other family might move in and paint over the little numbers in the pantry and run carpet over the creaky floorboards. Might sleep in the room where Mum used to sing me to sleep. Might fix up the balcony so it can't be climbed, might rip off the weather vane that never spins when you think it will. I wonder how long we have left, in this house that is ours but not.

The stairs groan, and a shadow flickers by the landing.

"Want some company?"

I nod, and Levi slides down beside me. He knocks his knee against mine, solid and reassuring. "What's that?"

I close the diary, showing him the front cover. "It was Mum's. Nan had a few things she'd been saving. Mum mentions Elliot and Quinn, and August sometimes. You're in it too." I smile.

"You sure you want me to stay? If you need some time . . . ?"

I shake my head and wriggle down so I can lean my cheek on his shoulder. "No, stay. It gets lonely up here."

"What about the attic ghost?" he says ruefully, jostling my shoulder.

I frown, looking around the room. "Actually, I haven't heard from him for a while." I still don't believe in ghosts, officially. But it never hurts to be polite, just in case. How embarrassing to get to the other side and have your ghostly neighbors admit to having witnessed a lifetime of covert nose-picking.

Elliot thuds up the stairs ungracefully, blanket wrapped around his shoulders. "Isaac says hello," he says, collapsing onto a dust-covered couch and coughing when a plume of gray explodes.

I glance up. "Nice hickey."

He slaps a hand on the side of his neck so fast the sound echoes. "Kidding." I smile.

He clears his throat. "Anyway. What are you two doing? Oh wait, was this romantic? Am I making it weird? I'm making it weird." He starts to stand again but I wave a hand.

"You're not making it weird," I say. "But you've put your feet on the bone trunk, just so you know."

He spasms in an effort to get away from the chest and tips off the couch.

Levi just laughs and looks around the room. "Remember last time we were up here?"

"Looking for clues," I say.

Elliot has righted himself, perched on the edge of the couch again, feet safely planted on the floor. He reaches under his shirt, reaching for the Adder Stone—the fake one. He took it out of the locker last night and has taken to wearing it on a chain around his neck.

"I'm sorry you never found the real one," he says. "I know you . . ." *Needed it.* "I know you really wanted to," he finishes.

Levi flops his hair low over his eyes, and his hand finds mine. "We'll figure something out, okay? A bake sale, or a raffle, or I'll just start selling those hideous statues Mum keeps buying from that Tibetan recluse."

"The naked goat-people?" Elliot asks.

Levi shudders. "The very ones. People will pay for anything they think is *art*."

"Oh, I've seen those!" I say. "With gold, um, private parts?"

"They're golden goat nads, yes."

I snort. "Your mum is into that?"

"She says they're symbols of health, but your nan got the dream journal out and reckons they actually symbolize *lust and vitality*," he says, pulling a face. "I didn't need to know that about my parents."

The mention of his parents sort of kills the mood, and we all go silent. Levi leans a bit more into my side, and I wonder how deep this rift between him and his father runs. Irreparable canyons of betrayal? Or a hairline fracture, hardly a bruise, barely noticeable after a while?

I look back at Elliot and he winks, a reassurance that nothing is so broken it can't be repaired. My eyes catch on the golden glint of the ring, and I think about what Quinn said—that the real one wasn't lost to the lake after all—and wonder if I should say something. But it seems selfish now to chase some pirate's treasure when so much else is happening. *It's just money*, I try to tell myself. But it's hard to ignore that gnawing pit in my stomach that says it's not just money, it's a home and security and Nan. People who say money can't buy happiness have never had to stuff their undies into a single backpack with all their worldly possessions because they can't afford checked luggage *and* a cross-country train ticket.

Elliot's looking at me in a strange way: an intense scrutiny, narrowed eyes. "What's going on?" he says suspiciously.

I frown, confused, looking at the diary in one hand and Levi's hand in the other. Neither of these is strange, though, and I don't understand his question. "What do you mean?"

"That," Elliot says, with a tiny smirk. "That face."

"*What* face?"

"That's your secret face."

"I don't *have* a secret face."

"Yes, you do."

My frown deepens. "Why has no one ever told me this?"

"Because how else are we meant to know when you're scheming?" Levi says, tapping my screwed-up nose.

"I'm not scheming," I say defensively. I wasn't really. I mean, sure, I had wondered if I could slip away at night and search for the real Adder Stone. And if I did find it, I could go to the station one day when I knew Barb was at the front desk. Claim the reward anonymously—she'd keep my secret, I know she would. And then catch up on the missed repayments, make sure the bank didn't take the house back. I could tell Nan that I won a scholarship or something. She wouldn't *believe* me, but would it matter?

"Spit it out," Elliot says.

I hesitate, not knowing how to answer. "I don't think I should," I say cautiously. "It's not a secret; I just don't want to upset you, that's all. We can talk about it later."

"Red, there are very limited ways you could upset me more than I already am after the last few days," Elliot says, tugging the blanket tighter around his shoulders for emphasis. "Come on, what's bugging that tiny brain of yours?"

Levi squints down at me.

"Come on," he says. "What's going on?"

I take a deep breath, exhaling in a quick huff, wondering how much to say. "The Adder Stone—the real one—might not be . . . gone."

Elliot frowns, the blanket now forgotten and slipping off his shoulders as he leans forward. "What do you mean?"

"Your mum said that August didn't have it with him when he—" *Died.* "Left town."

I hold the journal up for them to see. "And Mum wrote something in here—at first I didn't think anything of it, but then I was thinking about Treegap and the codes they used to use, and why would you need to lie in your own journal, you know?" I shake my hands out, knowing I'm blabbering, and try to get back on track. "She wrote that she knew Quinn would never go back for the stone, and she wondered if she should do it for her, but it felt wrong to intrude without him. And then I guess after a while, she either forgot or she got too sick, I guess."

Levi is nodding slowly, looking at a spot on the ceiling, processing my strange ramble. "What does that mean, *intrude*? Without him?"

I take another deep breath, looking to Elliot. He looks confused but not upset, so I continue. "So, here's the thing. It's not Treegap, right? Otherwise we would have found it with his things. And Quinn said there was no time when the fire happened to 'take anything.' And if you were going to steal an ancient artifact worth thousands of dollars, wouldn't you want it somewhere you could keep an eye on it? So it probably wasn't in his school locker, which means . . ."

Elliot leans back, letting out a low sound of surprise. "It's still at the junkyard."

"I think so."

"And?" Elliot says.

I frown. "And what?"

385

He raises his eyebrows, like the answer is obvious. "And how exactly, Brodie McKellon, town felon, are you planning on stealing it back?"

My mouth drops open in surprise.

Levi flashes his teeth in a quick grin. "Come on, don't disappoint us now. Hang glide over the gates?"

"Burrow under the fence?" Elliot suggests.

"Lure the dogs with raw steaks?"

"Short the electric grid to kill the lights?"

"*Guys*," I object, about to plead my innocence. But they're both looking at me, waiting. And I know they'd follow where I went, not just for me, but for *this*: for the letters, and the house, and the history in its walls. For our parents. For *us*. Finishing what we started all those years ago, a happily ever after at the end of this strange and sad fairy-tale town.

"That's way too high-tech," I finally say. "I figured we'd just walk through the front door."

"Why me?" Emiko hisses.

"Because," I explain, for the fourth time. "You are a perfectly respectable member of society—"

"I swear you just called me boring."

"*And*," I continue, "Dwight doesn't know you. And Elliot can't drive."

She raises her eyebrows in the rearview mirror. "How many times have you broken in, exactly?" She cranes her neck to peer over from the driver's seat, looking at us all sprawled across her back seat, a tangle of limbs barely hidden under a picnic blanket. "Just the once?"

I pull a face, slumping lower in the seat, Levi's knees in my back and Elliot's elbow digging into my ribs. "Couple times," I grumble.

Levi makes a sound that I take to mean *more than a couple times.*

"That doesn't sound so bad," Emi says, considering.

"She stole his car," Elliot offers.

"That doesn't count!" I object. "Levi ended up buying it."

"Huh," Emi says. "I always wondered why you drove that piece of junk."

Levi nearly sits bolt upright in his seat, and I have to grab his sleeve to yank him back down again. "Do not," he says, "insult the Jeep."

Emiko snickers, and then gasps. "Okay, everyone down! We're here; he's out in front."

We listen as her tires crunch over loose gravel, small stones kicking up and pinging against the undercarriage. Her window buzzes down, and she chirps too loudly, "Hi! I'm looking for a car!"

Dwight's slow drawl comes in response. "Seems like you got a car already." There's a *thunk* to one side; he's kicked her wheel for emphasis.

"Oh! Ha! No, this is my parents' car. I need to get my own— going to university next year, out of state, you know how it is. . . ."

She trails off, and the answering silence makes it clear that Dwight does not, in fact, know how it is.

"Well," he says, hacking up a spit wad and presumably blowing it off to one side. "What's your budget?"

"Oh. Um. Like, five?"

"Hundred?"

"Thousand," she corrects.

"Huh."

"Oh, is that not enough? Maybe seven? I don't really know much about cars. . . ."

I imagine the greasy grin on his face as his tone suddenly changes. "Well, ma'am, why don't you pull on over there. We got some great cars for you, good solid gear," he says. Her answering reply is too low for me to hear, but his booming voice comes through clear as he continues. "You can pull on up here—yup, that's the way."

The car comes to a stop a short distance later, the engine turning off as her keys jingle. "Do you have dogs?" she says with a dramatic sniffle, slamming the door behind her. I cringe as she fakes a sneeze—Claire is definitely the better actor. "Sorry, I have *such* bad allergies."

"Huh. Dogs ain't out today."

"Oh."

He grunts, and a sound like the heavy patting of clothes drifts through the still-open window. "Might be the fur," he grumbles. "Damn things got fleas. They're inside, anyhow."

Emiko gives another fake laugh, charming as always. "That looks like a good one! Let's start over there."

Their footsteps crunch into the distance, and we wait until the junkyard falls silent before easing the side door open and creeping out, one by one. The plan is for Emiko to lead Dwight on an aimless stroll all over the junkyard for as long as possible, giving us time to make our way to the loft and search for the Adder Stone.

"How do you know it will still be there?" Levi had asked last night, when I'd explained the plan.

I shrugged in response. "Does Dwight seem like someone who suddenly came into twenty thousand dollars?"

"Point taken."

"Plus . . . I don't know. The loft seemed kind of abandoned when we were up there. I don't think anyone's been up there since the fire." I recalled the clothes and books, blackened and discarded. If the Adder Stone was ever there, then maybe it still was. Unless he hid it somewhere else, in which case we were screwed.

But I'm not thinking about that right now.

I ease the side door closed as quietly as possible and peer around the side of the car, watching Emiko point and stride confidently down a row of rusted-out junk.

We crouch low, dashing across the open space to the barn. In the daylight, the scored wood stands out in stark contrast, running halfway up one timber wall and fanning out in ominous swirls before bleeding out.

Elliot stops dead at the doors, looking at the dark. He swallows, and his throat bobs. I grab his hand, squeezing tight. "You okay? We don't have to do this; we can turn back."

His eyes travel up to the peaked roof and back to the doors. "Is it—is it safe?"

"Safe as anything else we've ever done."

He laughs, a strangled sound that catches and cuts off abruptly. "Okay. Okay," he says.

Levi goes first, twisting sideways through the barely open gap in the slats—it's been padlocked with a loose chain since the last time we were here, but Dwight did a pretty lazy job of it, and it's easy enough for me to slip through next.

Elliot comes last, taking in the small, dim space. I look up at the loft, seeing it with new eyes. Cramped and dirty, exposed on one side, cobwebs in the other. No cupboards or drawers to store anything—there's still a dirty red backpack in one corner, half hidden by shadow and hay sticks. The ladder to the loft is completely black, splintering on the lowest rung. The edge of August's camping cot is still visible, miserably thin and molding in one corner. *It's so cold*, I think. Was it always this cold? I remember the sleeping bag we found at Treegap, the very first time. Was it warmer there? Four walls and a small enough space to heat?

"He lived in here?" Elliot whispers.

Levi places a steady hand on his shoulder, and they stay like that for a minute, braced against each other. "It's not so bad," Levi whispers. "Would have been pretty nice, back then. All this space, some privacy." The lie sounds sweet on his lips.

Elliot just nods silently, tipping his head back to look up at the loft, aimlessly wandering. He touches the side of the Chevy. Picks up an arcade coin, puts it down again. Kicks at the hay scattered across the floor. Levi catches my gaze and I bob my head, signaling that we need to *move*. We split up, wordlessly beginning our search. I gingerly place one foot on the ladder, testing my weight.

As the smallest of the three of us, I have the best chance of not busting it completely. But it's brittle and thin, and charcoal flakes off the first rung. I test the second one, which seems more stable, and slowly make my way up, avoiding the step we'd accidentally broken last time. The loft looks the same, which is to say there's not exactly much to see. I shove the cot to one side, unearthing a few bugs and more mold. I pull a plastic pair of gloves over my hands, and run my fingers over the mattress, searching for any odd lumps and hiding spots. Nothing. I kick the hay to one side, and carefully pick through it all. I search the beams, sticking my hands into blind holes and praying they don't come out attached to a spider.

I peer over the ledge, watching a frustrated Levi making quick work of the few items left behind: double-checking a kerosene lamp, tipping the backpack upside down and tugging at the zips. Elliot sits hunched in one corner, hands over his ears. He mutely shakes his head when Levi offers him the backpack, which seems to have a few pieces of clothing in there. I wonder how much was lost in the fire: photos and letters and books.

The loft is a bust, so I begin to scurry back down the ladder. Levi shrugs when I make it back to the floor and points in one corner. "There's nothing else here. Just a bunch of rubbish."

"It must have been cleared out," Elliot says at last. "Right? This isn't all there was?"

I look around the sparse loft, hoping he's right. "Must have been," I agree. "There's no socks, or a toothbrush, or homework left over." No signs that a life was lived here at all. But then, August

391

has always been a ghost, and we've been chasing his shadow for years now.

Levi's gaze cuts to mine. "Where would you put it?"

"What? A sock drawer? I guess over in that corner so it's not—"

"No, the ring. If you knew it was valuable and you didn't want someone to stumble on it. Where would *you* put it?"

I look around the loft, considering. "*I* wouldn't put it here at all. Not out in the open at least. But then again, I keep my diary under a loose plank in my . . . oh." They both look up at me. "Start stomping. *Quietly,*" I add, as Levi overenthusiastically stamps on a section of floor.

We fan out, dropping to our knees to tap the ground, waiting for an echo. But there's nothing, *nothing*.

And then.

The sound of a chain clinking, a lock springing apart.

"Hide!"

But there's nowhere to go: The loft is too far, and the barn is otherwise just an empty square. The only thing inside is . . .

"Get in, get in," I whisper, hoping the clang of heavy chains and the groan of the barn doors conceals the soft opening of the door and the sound of us piling into the Chevy. I end up on the floor of the back seat, annoyed that we'll end the day exactly as we started it: hiding in the back of a car with absolutely no plan.

"Now, this one needs a bit of fixing, and I never thought I would sell it, but for the right price . . ."

"Oh no," Emiko says loudly. "I'm not sure about classic cars. The airbags make me nervous; probably not great in a crash."

Dwight laughs, and his heavy footsteps approach. I try to curl into an even smaller ball, and somehow end up with my nose shoved halfway under the passenger seat staring at a slightly rusted metal tin of Corn Flakes.

"Trust me," Dwight says. "Once you drive a classic, you're gonna make sure you don't crash."

Emiko's pleas come rapid-fire, but it's useless. The door gets thrown open and Dwight's voice gets closer—too close.

"Now, up on blocks of course, so you can't drive it today. But just sit in there, get a feel for it."

I squeeze my eyes shut.

"What in the *damn hell*? That the McKellon kid in there?" There's a wordless roar of rage, and the back door opens. "Get out, right now. Don't even think about moving; I'm calling the police."

The boys awkwardly ease out first, standing protectively over the open door. I frown at the cereal box, then snatch it before I stumble out.

"Afternoon, Dwight," I say with a two-finger salute.

"You nosy little—"

"So, I know it might look like we're trespassing, but I actually came in to buy something."

Dwight spits to one side, sending Emiko scuttling back. Levi subtly waves her out—no need for us all to be implicated.

"The locked door weren't a clue?" Dwight says. "It's always you two. I should've—" His eyes, until now, have been boring down on me, briefly sweeping over Levi. But now he's seen Elliot, and suddenly he balks, hand paused midair.

"Not seen you before," Dwight says gruffly.

"No, sir," Elliot answers, his jaw set and teeth grinding so hard I think they'll crack.

"'No, sir,'" Dwight repeats, nodding. "Awful polite. What's your name, kid?"

"Elliot, sir."

The hand that Dwight has half raised in outrage, shiny silver key dangling from a chain, starts to drop. His jaw rolls on one side, a pale look of surprise slowly washing over his features.

"You're him, then," Dwight says, and it's not a question. They look so alike, Eli and August. I pulled out that tiny Polaroid, the day after the lake, and I stared at it until I could see the outline of Elliot in its frame: the messy hair and elegant cheekbones. Quinn's nose, perhaps, but his eyes.

Elliot nods. If he'd ever imagined meeting his grandfather, I'm sure this isn't what he wanted. But still, he doesn't wilt like I expect. He stands there, tall, back straight. Eyes full of misery and hurt and confusion but refusing to be ashamed. He's gone so still, like he does when his mind is far away. One day, maybe, he'll have more to say. Questions to ask. Answers to demand. But Elliot doesn't waste words, especially on people who don't deserve them, and so Dwight is looking at the ghost of his dead son, and Elliot is staring back.

Dwight's still nodding, eyes glassy from drink or something else. He juts his chin in my direction, the metal cereal box still clutched in my hands. "Whaddaya want with that? It's a piece of junk."

"And this is a junkyard," I reply.

His lips pull back in a sneer, and I swear he contemplates calling the police all over again. Finally, he relents, and picks a number just to annoy me. "Fine. Twenty bucks. Bet that's some vintage thing. Worth something."

"Sure," I agree, feeling at my empty pockets. "Twenty bucks. Levi?" I turn to face him, holding out an open hand.

"Really?" he grumbles, though he pulls out his wallet and hands Dwight the cash. "You know, if you want me to buy you something pretty, I can take you someplace nicer than a *literal junkyard*."

"This is all I want," I whisper, handing the cash to Dwight. He seems to contemplate, just for a moment, the possibility of spontaneously growing a soul and refusing to take the cash. Letting us go for nothing.

But that's not Dwight.

"Get the hell out, then," he mutters.

I take a breath, leading us out from the dusty, dim loft and into the sun. The heavy crunch of Levi's boots follows. My heart hammers in my chest, senses begging me to run, to get out, go far away from this place and never come back. I think we've made it, think Elliot is free, until I hear Dwight's parting words.

"Be seeing you, kid."

Elliot doesn't answer. We walk, and then we run. Slam the car doors closed and tell Emiko to *go*. I clutch the box until my fingers turn white, ignoring Levi's curious sideways stare. But I don't open it, not until we're sitting in Treegap, just the three of us. The place where it all started.

Elliot shudders, even though his shoulders sit under the open sunny window. I fold down beside him, and Levi on the other, hands shaking as I prize open the lid with a hollow *thunk*.

Where would I hide something? I'd asked myself in the back seat of August's car, hoping for a few more seconds before we'd been caught.

Under the floorboards is a great hiding spot—but it's not a getaway plan, I'd realized, as my nose squished into the earthy-scented carpet. Too much time wasted prying it up with frayed fingernails and wrestling bloated wood.

When you need to *go*, when every nerve is telling you to get the hell out, to pack your things and bolt for freedom the first chance you get—you don't wait to pack. You have everything ready, your get-out-of-life-free card. Just knowing that you're ready makes staying more bearable. The whole time at RAGs, I had my bag packed and ready to go. Every day I repacked it: after I brushed my teeth, combed my hair, folded my favorite sweatshirt. A few snacks, for the road.

And my few, singular, precious things were wrapped inside a tampon box to protect from prying eyes and wandering hands.

Guess that wasn't an option for August, though, so . . .

Levi frowns. "I'm pretty sure we have cereal that was made this side of the century, if you're hungry."

I shake my head. "You know the good thing about metal?" I ask, slowly tipping the container upside down. Something small and heavy slides out, a dull echo as it hits the floor. "Fireproof," I whisper.

The Adder Stone looks exactly the same: unremarkable, rough brown edges. Golden center. But for the inscription inside, it really is identical to one we found in the letter box. But this one, the real one, is worth . . .

"Twenty thousand dollars," Levi says with a low whistle. None of us pick it up. We just stare at it, dumbly. After all these years, it's right here. It was here all along. How many times had Levi and I sat in that car? Crawled through the open windows and kicked our feet up on the dash?

After a few moments, I reach down with shaking hands. "I can't take this," I whisper, and the realization makes me feel sick. *Of course* I can't take this. As much as I want to save the house, this is all that's left of August, and he did all of this for the son he never met. We'll just have to find another way—sell everything we own, or I'll drop out of school and get a full-time job. It just can't be this.

I hold it out to Elliot. "You should have it," I say. "It should be yours to decide."

He smiles. He looks tired. Older. But not sad, not right now. "Keep it," he says, folding my fingers around the cold metal. "You found your treasure. I found my dad. It's what we both wanted."

I set the metal container down, but a flash of something white catches my eye. I reach a hand in—perhaps it's a letter, something private he wanted to keep from the others.

But it's a Polaroid—a twin to the one we found under the floorboards. The same day, the same shirt. August, grinning at the camera. And Quinn beside him with her round belly, his hand pressed to one side. *My son* is scribbled on the bottom. I hand it to Elliot, and he cradles it like it's worth more than any treasure.

He smiles at me, and I smile back. At him. At Levi. At this small space in this big house. At the ring in my hand, and the paths that led us here. And for the first time, I dare to hope that I'll get to keep it all.

"Come on," I say, hauling them to their feet. "Let's go home."

Three months later

Tommy is standing in the post office, holding a letter. He hands it to me with a small fist-bump. "Sorry, dude, I'm in the turtle business now."

"That's probably for the best," I say gently, patting his arm. "Thanks for everything, though."

"No worries. Kinda gonna miss this place. Weird shit happens here."

"Yeah," I say, taking his letter and placing it on top of the pile. "No kidding."

Nan looks up from her tarot cards. "Tommy, I foresee great things in your future. None of them involve math."

"Sick," he says, then hitches up his messenger bag and closes the register one last time. The accounts are all wrong, again, but I don't have the heart to tell him.

The bells jingle as he leaves, and I sigh. "It's just so hard to find good help, you know?"

"Hey!" Elliot calls from behind the counter. "I heard that."

I grin at him, handing him a stack of parcels that just came in. Elliot is weirdly efficient: His mind likes logic and patterns and solutions, and it turns out the post office is full of those. Nan pays him double what she should, but he's saving up for our trip next year and only occasionally objects when she hands him an envelope full of cash every Friday. Quinn moved out at the end of summer—she'd found an apartment in the city. We're going to visit her on our road trip. After that, neither of us really has any plans. Levi is hideously jealous, but I said it's not fair they get to be blood related and have all the fun, so the road trip is just ours. Besides, Levi has to be in the city for university soon. He's going to live in a unit near campus—he got a football scholarship, obviously. I keep telling him to enjoy the first year as a pretty, free-spirited jock, because after that Elliot and I are moving in too. Well, probably. We played our game again last night: where will you be in five weeks, five months, five years.

I don't really know the answer to any of those questions, but I'm excited to find out. Plus, it helps that Barbara happily handed over the twenty-thousand-dollar reward in exchange for the Adder Stone. I tried to split the money with the boys, but they refused. Said that we all needed a home to come back to, just in case. Nan tried to refuse the money too—the bank sure didn't, though. I ended up depositing it anonymously against the mortgage, and that night Nan came down, opened a bottle of gin, and poured us each a glass. She didn't say anything, but when she finally declared herself ready for bed, she turned back halfway up the staircase, watching us half-tipsy and giggling under the lamplight, and winked.

I saved the rest for Elliot. He doesn't know it yet, but we're going to buy back August's car. One day. It might take us a while, to save the rest, but he deserves to have this piece of his dad. Or he can buy a brand-new one. Either way, it's his.

Levi thunders downstairs, boots echoing on the staircase. His room is upstairs now too; he and his parents haven't been talking much lately. "Come on, we're gonna be late!"

On cue, Isaac raps on the door and sticks his head through the gap. "Hey, did you know a guy just tried to sell me a turtle in your parking lot?"

"Don't do it," Levi yells. "Little bastards pee out of their mouths."

I roll my eyes. "You really need to get over that."

He huffs and picks me up and throws me over his shoulder. I squeal, kicking, but he drags me out to his Jeep. "Just get in the car, Brodie."

I grin, jumping into the front seat, waiting for Isaac and Elliot to climb into the back. We watch them in the rearview mirror, fingers threaded together. Elliot meets our gaze in the mirror, gives a single nod.

"Ready," he says.

We haven't been back to the lake since that day. But it's warm today, bright and clear and the water glimmers. Emiko and Claire are already there, Jenn too. The entire football team huddles together, looking solemn. A few other students are there, some I don't know and some I do. Isaac's mum stands at the back of the gathering, with Barb and a few of the adults who decided to come. Dad's here, for once. He waves, and I wave back. That's enough for now. I start to walk toward the shore, when I notice someone loitering at the very back of the group, so far away he's half in shadow, barely off the trail. "Eli, look," I whisper, pointing to the man.

Elliot looks up, surprise rushing across his face for a moment before he manages to school it back to calm. It's Dwight, nursing a beer and staring out at the crowd. He sees Elliot, and gives a single, halting nod.

Elliot turns away. Some wounds might never heal, and that's okay. We've figured out how to be okay.

I kick off my shoes, wading into the shallows with Levi and Isaac. I take a deep breath, handing Elliot the parcel in my arms.

"You sure about this?" I say. All along, I thought this was my story. But it's Elliot's too—perhaps even more than mine. He takes the letters, every single one that begins with *Dear August*. He places them into the raft, watching it bob at his feet for a few seconds.

"Yeah. Yeah, I think so. He'd like this. Having a piece of Mum, with him."

I look up at the clear blue sky and blink. There's been a lot of tears, a lot of grief and confusion. But no more today. Today is a celebration.

Elliot turns and faces the crowd, cheeks turning pink. "I never really got to know my dad, but I wanted to do this today. Thanks for coming. So, uh. Here goes."

He turns and lights a sky lantern, waits while everyone does the same, and then gives the raft a little shove. It floats out on the current, carried out on the lake until it slips away, out of sight.

We hold hands, in a line, watching the surface ripple, watching the lanterns soar above while the letters sink below. Endings and beginnings.

The start of our own story.

Levi grins at me. Elliot leans on my shoulder. I smile at them both and turn to face the water. I think I see something on the surface, maybe the raft, but when I look again there's nothing there. I take a breath and whisper a final goodbye. *I'm sorry you didn't have more time, August.*

Elliot throws an arm around me. "Come on," he says. "Let's show everyone Treegap."

We walk back together, and I think that even though it's not forever, it's enough.

Right now, this is enough.

Acknowledgments

I started writing this book when the world was a very strange and lonely place. It has been such a joy to find that publishing it has been a different experience entirely, supported by the wisdom, guidance, and love of so many.

A writer is lucky to have one publisher on their side; I find myself blessed with *two* of the very best. Thank you to the incredible Erica Sussman in the US and to the wonderful Claire Craig in Australia. Working with you as a team has been the most enjoyable, enriching process—thank you both for your kind words, the love you had for this story and this world, and for embarking on multiple rounds of edits across two continents with such ease I began to be suspicious that there *must* be some sort of catch. There wasn't. You have instead wielded your editorial prowess with such ease that it seems nothing short of magic. Thank you for shaping this book into its final form—it could not exist without you.

Thank you to my superstar agent, Annabel Barker, who took my wildest dreams and brought them to fruition. I am constantly in awe of your work, and that you do it all with such grace—there is no one I trust more with this book. Thank you for every word of encouragement, every frantic text message, and for taking all my "what ifs" and making them happen. There are simply not enough adjectives to describe the gratitude I have.

A book is crafted by many hands, and this one has been guided by so many behind the scenes. Thank you to Sara Schonfeld, editor extraordinaire, who stepped in to guide this manuscript toward the finish line.

Thank you to the rest of the local HarperTeen team: Jon Howard, Gweneth Morton, Allison Brown, Catherine Lee, Alison Donalty, and Lisa Calcasola. There are so many people who work with such passion and dedication, many of whom are never seen by readers—their work is invaluable, and none of our books would exist without them. Thank you for everything you do to help books find their way onto shelves and into readers' hands.

Thank you also to Beatriz Naranjalidad, cover artist of my dreams. I adore your artwork and was thrilled to see Brodie come to life—you've captured their little corner of the world so beautifully.

Now to the home team.

Thank you to my sister, who immediately loved this book and saw the world I was trying to weave. It's so rare for someone to love your work the way you love it too, and I will treasure that instant connection forever. Thank you for being Brodie's cheerleader and Elliot's #1 fan, and for every text you ever sent theorizing about what happens before and after they leave us on the page. Thank you for the Pinterest boards, the fan casting, the messages that simply read "!!!!" and for keeping the excitement alive throughout multiple rounds of edits. Love you to the moon and to Saturn.

For my mum, who loves me no matter what I write or if I don't. Thank you for the cups of tea, the Sunday dinners, for the endless FaceTime calls, and for believing in me, no matter the dream.

Thank you to my wonderful writers group: Kate, Sue, and Tina. You've been there every step of the way, and *Return to Sender* would not exist in this form without you. Thank you for your guidance, your support, and, as always, for the potatoes. (I will never stop being smug about my plot spreadsheet. Never to be repeated, though, so don't get your hopes up.)

To my friends, who bought multiple copies of my first book, told *their* friends about it, sent flowers, wrote me beautiful messages— I cherish these moments more than you will ever know.

Thank you for loving me through all the Saturdays I've spent inside, chained to a keyboard.

For Rob: Thank you for everything. We'll always have Paris.

A very special thank-you to Taylor Alison Swift, who wrote the *folklore* album and accidentally created the soundtrack to the story in my head. I'd had this idea floating around for a while, and I could see the bones of this book so clearly: three friends in the past, three friends in the future. A town that's not magic but feels like it. A girl running away from lost love and coming home again. But in the midst of lockdown, I couldn't find the energy to actually write. The world was hard, and I was lonely, and I couldn't seem to will myself to sit at a computer long enough to try to get these people out of my head and onto the page. Music brought me back to writing again. The easter eggs are in her honor.

Thank you to every single librarian, bookseller, blogger, teacher, and parent who rallied around *The Museum of Broken Things* and made this book possible. Your work is so vital, and I'm grateful the next generation of readers is in your hands.

Speaking of: Thank YOU, dear reader. Thanks for being here and stumbling through this story together. I hope you had fun chasing memories and lost boys, running through the woods and escaping the real world just for a little while. Please know that sometimes I think of this book, sitting on shelves and dog-eared on bedroom floors, and am completely overwhelmed with gratitude. Thank you for spending your time, money, and attention on this book. None of it is possible without you. Stay wild, dream big. The world is waiting.